Mary Elizabeth Braddon

Joshua Haggard's Daughter

A Novel

Mary Elizabeth Braddon

Joshua Haggard's Daughter
A Novel

ISBN/EAN: 9783337031817

Printed in Europe, USA, Canada, Australia, Japan

Cover: Foto ©Andreas Hilbeck / pixelio.de

More available books at **www.hansebooks.com**

OSWALD AND NAOMI BECOME ACQUAINTED. [page 25.

JOSHUA HAGGARD'S DAUGHTER.

A Novel.

By MISS M. E. BRADDON,

AUTHOR OF

"AURORA FLOYD," "JOHN MARCHMONT'S LEGACY," "A STRANGE WORLD," "BIRDS
OF PREY," "FENTON'S QUEST," "DEAD MEN'S SHOES," &c.

Miss M. E. Braddon's Novels.

AN OPEN VERDICT. 8vo, Paper, 35 cents.

A STRANGE WORLD. 8vo, Paper, 40 cents.

AURORA FLOYD. 8vo, Paper, 40 cents.

BIRDS OF PREY. Illustrated. 8vo, Paper, 50 cents.

BOUND TO JOHN COMPANY. Illustrated. 8vo, Paper, 50 cents.

CHARLOTTE'S INHERITANCE. Sequel to "Birds of Prey." 8vo, Paper, 35 cents.

DEAD MEN'S SHOES. 8vo, Paper, 40 cents.

DEAD-SEA FRUIT. Illustrated. 8vo, Paper, 50 cents.

ELEANOR'S VICTORY. 8vo, Paper, 60 cents.

FENTON'S QUEST. Illustrated. 8vo, Paper, 50 cents.

HOSTAGES TO FORTUNE. Illustrated. 8vo, Paper, 50 cents.

JOHN MARCHMONT'S LEGACY. 8vo, Paper, 50 cents.

JOSHUA HAGGARD'S DAUGHTER. Illustrated. 8vo, Paper, 50 cents.

LOST FOR LOVE. Illustrated. 8vo, Paper, 50 cents.

PUBLICANS AND SINNERS. 8vo, Paper, 50 cents.

STRANGERS AND PILGRIMS. Illustrated. 8vo, Paper, 50 cents.

TAKEN AT THE FLOOD. 8vo, Paper, 50 cents.

THE LOVELS OF ARDEN. Illustrated. 8vo, Paper, 50 cents.

TO THE BITTER END. Illustrated. 8vo, Paper, 50 cents.

WEAVERS AND WEFT. 8vo, Paper, 50 cents.

Published by HARPER & BROTHERS, New York.

☞ Harper & Brothers *will send either of the above works by mail, postage prepaid, to any part of the United States, on receipt of the price.*

JOSHUA HAGGARD'S DAUGHTER.

CHAPTER I.

THE CRUEL CRAWLING FOAM.

THERE was darkness over the land, almost as awful as that we read of on the awfulest day this earth has ever seen—darkness that might be felt. In the midst of the ripe warm harvest-time, when all things were at their fairest, and the farmers about Combhollow were congratulating each other on the glorious weather, the storm came: a strange bluish blackness overspread the sky—metallic, tempest-charged, not one cloud or many clouds, but a darkening of the face of heaven. It was like a sudden twilight at noon.

"It mun be a 'clipse, I think," said old Jabez Long, the fisherman, contemplative of that awful horizon yonder, where one streak of copper-colored light made a narrow rent between sea and sky.

"'Clipse, man!" cried his neighbor; "how can it be a 'clipse, when there ain't none in the almanick? It's more like a judgment than a 'clipse, to my mind—a judgment agen the farmers for making bread so dear last Chris-selmas. Sarve 'em right if their corn's drownded afore they can get it under cover."

There was no rain yet; but when the rain came by-and-by, it would be a flood, thought that little group of awe-stricken fishermen gathered in front of The Ring of Bells public-house, at the fishermen's end of Combhollow.

"Look at the sea!" exclaimed Jabez, pointing seaward.

It had a curious look, the ocean — that sea which in summer-time was wont to seem a lake of emerald green, clear as the gem its color rivaled, with shadows of richest purple. To-day the water was a dull red, darkened to indigo here and there. There was a strong ground-swell, and the sea heaved like a passionate bosom stirred with deepest anger. White surf came creeping up the sand, and with every receding wave there rose a roar like distant thunder.

"An angry sea," cried Jabez. "I hope the young squire won't try to come in from Clovelly upon such a tide as this."

"Has he gone to Clovelly?" asked Mike Durran, the younger of the two men. Both were old and gray and rugged, and had a look of having aged rather from hard weather than from the flight of years. Time had crawled for these villagers, winters and summers creeping slowly on their sluggish course; much labor, little pleasure. They must have felt a century old, at least.

"Yes, he sailed yesterday morning, and was to be back to-day. Him and Jack and the lad Peter; not enough of 'em to manage that clumsy old tub of his, to my mind. He'll get into trouble some day, I'm afeard."

"Money's scarce with him, I'm thinking," said Mike.

"Money 'll never be any thing but scarce while the old squire's alive," answered Jabez. "There's money enough and to spare hid away somewheres; but nobody 'll ever see the color of it while he's alive."

"Not they," groaned Mike Durran; and there was a general groan from the little group of idlers, by way of tribute to the squire.

"Hard upon every body," said Jabez.

"Hardest of all upon his own flesh and blood," said another man. "His cruelty drove his second son to sea."

"Arnold!" said Jabez. "Ah, a fine lad that! I remember 'im; a fine out-spoken lad, with a kind word for every one."

"Ah, he were the right sort, he were," said Mike; "not like Mr. Oswald. He hasn't a word to throw at a dog, wrapped up in hisself, and proud as Lucifus; and as for the color of his money—well, I never see it."

This implies the deepest depth of unpopularity —a man unable or unwilling to give.

At this juncture there came a silence in the little assembly, and all eyes were turned in the same direction to look at a man who came round the sharply jutting cliff which cut off this straggling bit of Combhollow by the sea-shore from the bay, and the tidy little town that lay inland in a cleft of the fertile Devonian hills. On this side of the promontory there was the original fishing village, a row of ancient thatched cabins built against the cliff, and that popular house of entertainment, The Ring of Bells, a low-roofed, odd-fashioned dwelling, with steep gables and curious abutments, and ceilings which scarcely cleared the heads of its tallest customers.

The person whose approach commanded the general attention was a man of somewhat striking appearance. Tall, broad-shouldered, with a head nobly mounted on the throat of a gladiator, penetrating black eyes, boldly cut features, a swarthy complexion, a square lower jaw, and a capacious, strongly marked brow—he was a man to attract attention anywhere. Intellect and power had set their seal upon his face, and his bearing was that of one accustomed to command. A man of superior mind, stranded for life in such a place as Combhollow, might naturally think himself a king.

The new-comer's costume was that of the yeoman class. He wore knee-breeches, coarse, gray knitted stockings, and stout, buckled shoes. His only distinguishing characteristic was a white cravat, but this was a symbol which marked his power and authority over that little group of rough fishermen; and Mrs. Jakes, the landlady, who stood at her door listening to the discourse of her customers, dropped a low courtesy at sight of the man in the white neckcloth.

Joshua Haggard was a strong influence in the little town of Combhollow, being chief custodian of the souls of its inhabitants, from Miss Tremaine, the rich maiden lady at Tremaine Place, to the grubby kitchen-wench at The Ring of Bells, who cleaned herself once a week, and, with face smarting from the vigorous application of mottled soap and coarsest huckaback, went to Little Bethel to hear Mr. Haggard preach. It was over the womankind of Combhollow, doubtless, that Joshua was most potent; but the men, if they went to any place of worship, did it, for the most part, to please their womankind; and thus was Little Bethel crowded to overflowing on warm summer evenings; while the white-haired vicar of Combhollow preached his drowsy orthodox sermon to the school-children, the pew-opener and beadle, and the half-dozen stanch followers of the Established Church who had not overeaten themselves at dinner, or drunk too much after that ponderous and hearty meal.

Fifty years ago the Established Church was nowhere in Combhollow, as compared with Joshua Haggard and Little Bethel. The great Anglican revival has doubtless awakened that slumberous old parish church into new life and vigor, and left Little Bethel in the rear; but in those days Bethel was dominant, and to sit under Joshua was to be in the right way to salvation, in the opinion of Combhollow; always excepting certain old families of landed estate, and the more substantial of the tenant-farmers, who clung to the Established Church like barnacles to a ship's bottom, and with little more ability to reason upon their faith than the barnacles. They stuck to the Church of England chiefly because their fathers had done so, and they looked down upon Joshua as a ranter, and follower of that low person, John Wesley.

Mr. Haggard had his temporal vocation and business in life, as well as his spiritual profession; and a man of less energy and intellect would have hardly fared so well as he did with both. Haggard's was one of the best shops in Combhollow. Ostensibly devoted to groceries, it gave a counter to linen-drapery, supplied its customers with stationery, and was generally willing to procure any article that might be wanted in Combhollow from the larger resources of Barnstaple or the illimitable store-houses of Exeter. Enthusiast as Joshua really was in religion, he never neglected his trade; order and attention marked the conduct of his business; a scrupulous honesty recommended him even to careful housekeepers. No adulterated coffee, no sanded sugar came from his stores; to say that any article came from Haggard's was tantamount to saying it was the best that money could buy. Haggard's eight-shilling mixed tea was a specific for nervous headache, and for plasters in urgent cases no one thought of using any mustard but Haggard's.

Joshua being a widower of some years' standing, the feminine element in the business was supplied by his maiden sister Judith, a woman of commercial mind, frugal, housewifely habits, and energy as inexhaustible as her brother's. She was of Joshua's temperament as regarded mundane things, but lacked his loftier aspirations and spiritual views. Piety with her was of rather a mechanical order, dependent upon the number of her attendances at church. She took an ascetic view of life, especially as regarded the lives of other people, and was continually cutting off some small enjoyment or gratification of mind or senses as "a snare." She was the sole and despotic ruler of Joshua's household and family, the family consisting of one son and one daughter, the household of a sturdy maid of all work, a shopman, and a boy who carried out goods in barrow or basket, and occasionally came to grief by upsetting a box of eggs or breaking a vinegar-bottle.

Joshua Haggard's house and garden were always the pink of neatness, his shop was a model of cleanliness and precision; and his life altogether was so wisely ordered, so temperate, regular, and honorable, that he himself seemed the highest example of that sober Christian life he preached to others. When he read the first Psalm, in that rich sonorous voice of his, his congregation thought of him as the man whose " delight is in the law of the Lord, and in His law doth he meditate day and night.

"And he shall be like a tree planted by the rivers of water, that bringeth forth his fruit in his season; his leaf also shall not wither; and whatsoever he doeth shall prosper.

"The ungodly are not so—"

Ah, with what pious unction, with what a triumphant sense of superiority, with what confidence and security against the possibility of temptation assailing him, used Joshua Haggard to roll out the denunciatory verses that follow!

The minister, as Joshua was called in Combhollow, did not come to The Ring of Bells to drink or make merry. He was the most sober of men, without being an absolute abstainer, and, except a mug of small beer with his dinner and supper, rarely tasted any thing stronger than water. He came to the water-side tavern to reprove and exhort. Mrs. Jakes had absented herself from chapel for the last two Sabbaths, and this backsliding was a fact to be inquired into by a shepherd solicitous for the welfare of his flock.

"The Saturday nights have been so trying, Mr. Haggard," replied Mrs. Jakes to her pastor's grave remonstrance. "The fishermen will sit so late and get so quarrelsome. It's enough to make one feel tired and addled like, next morning."

"If you were more careful of the good of your soul than of filthy lucre, Mrs. Jakes, you wouldn't let the men stay late enough to tire you, or drink enough to get quarrelsome."

"Ah," sighed the landlady, with a doleful shake of her head; "it's lucky for they as was brought up to a virtuous business. I was brought up to mine by they as went before me, and I'm obliged to abide by it."

"Put it away, if you find it a snare, Mrs. Jakes. Put it away, if you see that it leads oth-

OUTSIDE "THE RING OF BELLS."

ers to evil ways. Selling drink to the intemperate is like going into partnership with Satan. Dissolve the firm, my dear woman, and put your trust in God."

"I might do that, Mr. Haggard; but how should I face the tax-gatherer, or the brewer's man, or the old squire's bailiff when he calls for my rent?"

"Have you forgotten how the sparrows are cared for, Mrs. Jakes?"

"Ah, sir, it's well for the sparrows; yet I've seen a many o' them tumble out of their nests, poor things! Sparrows is made without much sense, and there'd need be somebody to look after 'em. But I fancy Providence meant us to do for ourselves, and do the best we can in the business we're brought up to."

"You remind me of the young man in the Gospel, Mrs. Jakes, who went away sorrowful because he clung to his great riches."

"It isn't riches as I cling to, Mr. Haggard. It's bread-and-cheese. The leopard might as easy change his spots as I go out of the public line; and if I could take to another business, maybe my neighbors wouldn't like it. You wouldn't care to see me open a grocer's shop, now, would 'ee, sir?"

Joshua Haggard smiled, a comfortable, self-assured smile. He knew that his business was established upon a basis not easily assailable. Plenty of capital, shrewd judgment, long experience, unflinching industry. Who should prevail against these?

"Look!" cried Jabez Long, taking his pipe out of his mouth, and pointing to the livid horizon-line. "Look, lads, there she be—the Dolfing!"

A patch of white sail—ghastly white against the leaden sky—glimmered on the edge of the sea. All eyes turned to it in anxious, affrighted, scrutiny. Poor struggling sail, how it wavered and dipped—now vanishing, now re-appearing! It was like a human soul battling with the troubled waters of sorrow and sin.

The wind had risen while Joshua Haggard had been standing just inside the stone-paved kitchen discoursing the words of wisdom to Mrs. Jakes—a mighty wind that blew from the land, sweeping over those fertile hills, shrieking in the deep-wooded gorges, and rushing seaward, seaward, seaward, as if it longed to blend its fury with the angry waves heaving sullenly under the dark sky.

"He ought to ha' staid at Clovelly," said Mike Durran; "none but a madman would think o' making this here harbor in yon cockle-shell, with such a wind off the shore. That there boat 'll be smashed like a nut-shell agen they rocks, if he don't take care."

"He's a good sailor, isn't he?" asked Joshua Haggard.

"Good sailor! ay, to be sure. There isn't a better in these parts. He and his brother allus hankered after the sea. But if he don't get too much of it this time, I'm a Dutchman."

There was a coolness in the speech that astonished Mr. Haggard; but life is cheap on these rocky shores, and a man drowned, more or less, makes no great sensation. The young squire was no favorite with these fishermen. He was reserved, and they gave him credit for pride. He felt the restraint and injustice of his position as the son of a miserly father. He had nothing to give his fellow-men, and was thought mean.

"What!" exclaimed Joshua, "do you think that boat is in danger?"

"Looks like it," answered Jabez. "If the wind catches her side, she'll capsize like a walnut-shell."

"And you stand here quietly, smoking and drinking, while a fellow-creature's life is in jeopardy—you—seamen!"

The wind was gathering fury with every fresh blast, as if Nature had reserved her forces through days and nights of calm, to be lavished madly in one dreadful hour.

The fishermen looked at each other, and then at Joshua Haggard, doubtfully. They were none of them young men—declined into the vale of years rather, and much weather-beaten.

"We've wives and families to think about," said Durran. "They're o' more account to us than the young squire."

"A deal we should get by it if we risked our lives to bring the Dolfing safe ashore," added Jabez.

"And you would see a fellow-creature perish!" cried Haggard, horrified at this inhumanity. These were of his flock; it was to these he preached the Gospel—self-abnegation, love of one's neighbor—sometimes of a Sunday evening.

"No talk of perishing yet a while," said one.

"He ought to ha' staid at Clovelly," said another.

Joshua Haggard arched his hands above his eyes and looked out seaward. There was no actual signal of distress—what signal could they make on board that frail bark? But even to one who knew but little of the sea, the signs of trouble were plain. Huge waves, foam-fringed, swept over the boat, which was evidently beaten farther from her haven by that fierce wind. She was trying to make the bay on the other side of the rocky promontory, but her efforts against sea and wind seemed like the puny struggling of a mouse between two rival cats. If the sea did not get the better of her, the wind would.

"I can handle a pair of sculls with any man in Combhollow," said Joshua, after watching that contest for some time with grave anxiety. "Lend me your dinghy and a coil of rope, Jabez."

"What! ye're not going out in the teeth o' such a wind, Master Haggard?" cried Long. "You'd be blown across to Wales."

"I'm going to save human lives, if I can," answered Haggard. "He who walked the waters and stilled the tempest will be with me!"

"Nay, master, but we'll go instead of 'ee," cried Jabez.

"Ay, to be sure we will," said Durran; and there was an assenting murmur from the rest of the group, and a move toward the beach, where the boats lay bottom upward, trembling and groaning as the wind shook their battered old timbers.

"No," cried Joshua, decisively; "you have wives and families unprovided for. Mine will be well supplied with temporal blessings, if the waters should swallow me; and if they were penniless, I could trust them to Him who rules on sea and land."

"There's no call for any one going," grumbled one of the men. "The young squire's as good a sailor as any on us, and can swim like a fish;

and if he was wise he would run across to Swansea, with the wind at his back."

"But he isn't wise, you see," said Joshua, pointing to the laboring boat. "Look there!"

The signal of distress had come. A handkerchief waved wildly in the wind, a speck of white, just visible against a dark background of cloud and sea.

Joshua ran to the dinghy and pushed it down to the water, amidst the remonstrances of the fisherman, now all eager to rush to the rescue.

"Not one of you shall go with me," he cried, with that fiery enthusiasm which gave him his strongest influence on his flock. "The Lord has given these lives into my hand. I am going alone. Give me the rope and the sculls."

They obeyed him submissively; but a larger boat was pushed down to the water at the same time, and four men took their places in it. There was no question now of wives and families to be left to the tender mercies of the parish.

Joshua had not boasted when he called himself a good oarsman. He was a man skilled in many things—a man who must needs have been dominant in any station. Fate had made him a Dissenting parson; but if fate had chosen to make him a general, he would not have been out of place.

He handled his sculls cleverly, but the wind blew him out to sea faster than his sculls could carry him. The light tub-shaped boat skimmed the crests of the waves, and Joshua was half-way toward the yacht while the other men were fighting with the surf along shore. Presently the little group, watching him from The Ring of Bells, gave a cry of horror. The dinghy was bottom upward, and Joshua riding atop of her keel, like Arion on his dolphin.

They were gazing at him, breathless and full of fear, when the *Dolphin* gave her last headlong plunge, and the rag of sail vanished forever. The men in the big boat were across the surf by this time, rowing gallantly toward Joshua. Those on shore could scarcely see how it happened; but in the next moment there were two men on the keel of the dinghy, and then somehow one of them managed to right the boat, and they were both inside of her, one of them paddling with a single scull. The other scull had been lost when she capsized.

The fisherman's boat made for them, lashed the dinghy to her stern, and lay to on her oars, while a man, who had been swimming desperately, clambered aboard her. After that she lay off and on for a little, as if waiting to pick up some one else, and after that rowed for the shore. "There's two saved and one drowned," said one of the watchers. "There was three aboard."

Now came the struggle. The boats were carried ever so far before they could make the shore; but at last, by dint of hard rowing, and the wind abating some little of its violence, the fisherman contrived to beach the big boat just under the shadow of that jutting point of cliff which ran out into the sea like a bastion.

The lookers-on rushed eagerly down to welcome the saved from the wreck, curious to know whether the squire, whose single existence seemed to these Tory villagers to weigh against half a dozen common lives, had been one of the two saved.

Yes, there was Oswald Pentreath in the dinghy,

lying across Joshua's knees, the picture of death rather than life at this moment.

"Is the b'y gone?" asked one of the men.

"Yes, the poor b'y's drownded. Rose two or three times after the yacht went down, and then went to the bottom like a stone."

Joshua came on shore, carrying his burden with him. He made nothing of the squire's young figure, though Oswald Pentreath was no feather-weight.

"Tell Mrs. Jakes to get a blazing fire," cried Joshua, as he went slowly toward The Ring of Bells; "or, on second thoughts, I'll take him to my own house. There's more comfort there, a good bed, and my sister Judith, who's the next best thing to a doctor. Lend a hand one of you, and we'll get him up-street in no time."

Mr. Haggard's house was at the beginning of the High Street, the one single street of Combhollow, and was not more than five minutes' walk from The Ring of Bells. Half a dozen men ran forward to help the minister with his burden, but he bid the youngest of the group take Mr. Pentreath's feet, while he held him by his shoulders, and the two carried him thus easily round the point, across the little sandy bay, and into the street, at the corner of which, with one side to the sea, stood Joshua Haggard's house—a square stone cottage, with a shop built out at one side, and a couple of extra rooms on the other, making it altogether a building of some importance. There was a good garden of the old-fashioned utilitarian type, and behind the garden an orchard, on the steep slope of one of those hills which sheltered Combhollow from wind and weather. There was a stable adjacent to the house, in which the minister kept his gray cob, a useful animal, which carried Joshua or the groceries with perfect equanimity.

Architecturally, Mr. Haggard's dwelling-place had no claim to be admired. Not easy were it to imagine a building more commonplace, or one in which the useful so utterly predominated over the ornamental. But in this fertile Devonian land there is a wealth of color everywhere, which renders the meanest things lovely, and on a sunny day Joshua's house and garden would have made a study for a Turner or a Millais. There is, happily too, for the lowly-minded, a beauty in neatness and perfect order which comes home to every mind, and in this kind of beauty Joshua's home was rich. The pure floors, the spotless walls, the shining old furniture, transparent window-panes, bean-pots of sweet-scented flowers, polished brass fenders and fire-irons, the freshness and sweetness that pervaded all things might have charmed the inhabitant of a palace. The kitchen, with its rows of copper saucepans and brazen pipkins, scrubbed industriously every week, but kept more for show than use; the parlor, with its brass-handled bureaus, wide-backed chairs with broad horse-hair seats, fluted legs, and an unknown coat of arms painted on their polished panels, recalled the rich umber shadows and mellow lights of an old Dutch picture. The broad sanded passage, with low ceiling, paneled walls, and a glimpse of garden through the open door at the end, made a delicious bit of perspective. The best parlor was a temple of coolness and repose, odorous with dried rose-leaves, spices, and lavender—a room in which to slumber luxuriously on warm Sunday afternoons, the world forgetting, and most assuredly forgotten by the world.

The wind had dropped a little by this time, and the rain came down in sudden torrents, a straight downpour. It was as much as Joshua and his assistant could do to get under cover without a second drenching from fresh water. Judith Haggard flew to the door as the little crowd entered at the green wooden gate which divided the narrow strip of front-garden from the street.

"Why, what's happened, Joshua?" she cried, affrighted at that lifeless burden.

She was briefly told the state of the case.

"There's a good fire in the kitchen," she cried; "carry him in. Naomi, run and help Sally down with the mattress off the spare bed, and a blanket or two, and a pillow to lay under him. Why, Joshua, you've been in the water too!"

"Yes, Judith, by God's grace I was privileged to save him."

"Humph," muttered his sister, doubtfully, "I wish you'd ha' saved a better man than any of old Pentreath's breed."

The old squire kept himself close within his own domain, never went to church, and gave nothing to the poor; and Combhollow held him in awe as a limb of Satan, who could hardly require Christian burial with bell and book, but would be assuredly carried away bodily by his master when the predestined hour came.

It was a dim tradition in Combhollow that the squire in his early manhood had been a republican and a Wilkite, had rioted and blasphemed with the wild monks of Medmenham, and that the griping and pinching of his old age were intended to balance the waste and profusion of his youth. He had squandered his substance upon dissipations which the Combhollow people hinted at darkly, as something not to be openly expressed, like the vices of Commodus or Elagabalus—horrors to be shrouded in one of the dead languages, or communicated dumbly by nods and shrugs and significant pursings-up of the lips. He had raised money on mortgage, and wasted it on midnight orgies, in drink, in play; and the slow, laborious money-scraping of his later years had been in some wise necessary. Twenty years ago he must have been a poor man, said Combhollow, with the certainty which springs from a close acquaintance with our neighbors' business; but the mortgages were paid off about that time, and the intervening twenty years must have made the squire rich. A man who owns over seven hundred acres of cultivated land, and who neither spends nor gives, must needs become the Crœsus of his narrow sphere. Combhollow could imagine no wealthier miser than its squire, and they resented his miserly temper as a public wrong.

But although Miss Judith Haggard looked somewhat contemptuously upon the lifeless figure lying face-downward on one of her best mattresses, she set to work none the less vigorously to expedite Oswald Pentreath's return to life. She rubbed him, she shook him, she punched him in the back, and made returning animation such a severe ordeal that the struggling soul, feeling its envelope of clay so roughly handled, might naturally entreat to be allowed to stay in Hades.

Judith, however, without having the printed instructions of the Humane Society to guide her, evidently knew her business, and did it so well that, when she had made her patient disgorge all the sea-water he had swallowed, and had dragged him into a half-sitting position with his head upon her knee, her labors were crowned with success. The heavy eyelids slowly raised themselves; the dark-gray eyes looked round the circle of eager faces with a gaze of vague inquiry; a shuddering sigh broke from the parted lips.

"The Lord be praised!" exclaimed Joshua, solemnly.

"It's taken twenty minutes by grandmother's clock," said Judith, glancing at that authority—an ancient eight-day time-piece in a shining mahogany case, crowned with three brass knobs—a clock that was taller than Joshua, and the chief ornament of the kitchen.

There had been silence, save for furtive whisperings in the background, until now; but the opening of Oswald Pentreath's eyes seemed a signal for the loosening of every one else's tongue.

"Well, I'm glad he's come to," said Jabez Long, confidentially, to his next neighbor and favorite chum, Michael Durran; "but I'd liefer the minister saved him nor me."

"Why's that, mate?"

"Doan' 'ee know?"

"No."

"Why, I thought you was too good a seaman not to know _that_."

"What, lad?"

"Why, as no good never come o' riskying a drownding man. You fetches him out of the water at the risk of your own life, don't 'ee? Yes, and that there man's bound to do 'ee a hinjury. He can't help it. The deepest wrong as the minister ever had done agen him will be done by that young man. Them as lives to see it may remember my words."

He had raised his voice in his excitement, and his speech had been audible to Joshua standing in front of him.

"I knew you were an ignorant man, Long," said Joshua, turning sharply upon the guileless fisherman, "but I didn't think you were a fool into the bargain."

"It's trew as the tides and the mune, Muster Haggard. You beware o' that young 'un. He's bound to be your foe."

"Because I have done him the greatest service one man can do another? Nonsense, man. I'm ashamed of such folly."

"Them as knows the sea knows it for truth," said Long, doggedly.

"Come, my friends," said Joshua, too contemptuous of such foolishness to argue further. "Mr. Pentreath is all right, you see; so you may as well clear out of this, and let us make him as comfortable as we can. The more air we give him, the better."

"And you've got your own clothes to change yet, Joshua," said Judith. "If you're not in for the rheumatics after this, I shall be surprised. A man had need be careful when he has seen the last of his five-and-fortieth birthday."

The fishermen slowly withdrew, and the young squire was left with Judith and her brother. Naomi Haggard and Sally, the servant-girl, had been banished from the kitchen during the process of resuscitation, and were waiting outside in the passage, breathless with expectation, Naomi trembling a little, and holding Sally's stalwart arm.

"Let go, please, miss; you're a-pinching of

me," remonstrated Sally at last, as the grip tightened.

"I beg your pardon, Sally ; I'm so anxious."

"No call to be anxious, miss. He's drownded and dead, poor young man ; and missus is wasting her trouble. Did you see how blue his lips was? purplish, like my Sunday frock."

"Oh, Sally, I hope he is not dead?"

"Lor', miss, it ain't much odds. Them was never no good, they Pentreaths."

The fisherman had gone out by a door that opened from kitchen to garden, so Naomi and the maid-servant remained in ignorance of the patient's progress under Aunt Judith's ministrations. Ruth had been much too well brought up to think of opening the kitchen door, were it ever so narrow a chink, after she had been told to keep her distance. There was love, doubtless, in Mr. Haggard's household ; but the love was in some wise a latent element, and the more ostensible ruler was fear. From their babyhood upward Naomi and James Haggard had regarded their father as the one awful power in this world. They were fond of him and proud of him, but with a far-off affection and a reverential pride which admitted of no familiarity. They had never clambered on his knees, or rifled his coat-pockets. The nearest approach to making him a playfellow had been to stand by his chair on a Sunday afternoon, between dinner-time and chapel, and hear him relate the story of Joseph and his brethren, or of those never-to-be-forgotten children who made a mock of the prophet's bald head, in his deep, full voice, which gave additional solemnity to the Scriptural phrases.

While Naomi and Sarah were straining their ears to catch any sound that might penetrate the stout oaken door—a vain effort—the door suddenly opened, and Joshua appeared, supporting a curiously muffled figure in his arms. It was Oswald Pentreath wrapped in a couple of blankets.

"Light a fire in the spare room, Sally," cried Judith, as the girl ran off to the wood-house, while Joshua half-carried half-led the young squire up to that well-ordered chamber. Not often was Mr. Haggard's spare room occupied by a visitor, and he might as well have used that extra chamber for his own comfort, as a study or book-room. But in Judith's opinion it was the right thing in a respectable house to have a spare bedroom, and it was her pride to maintain that apartment in perfect order, and in a certain kind of splendor, even at some sacrifice of the inhabited rooms. Thus, while Joshua's four-poster was of painted deal, with washed-out chintz curtains and a coarse knotted coverlet, the spare bed had curly posts and an elaborate cornice, with a good deal of white fringe and dimity festooning, watch-pockets of silken patchwork, and a counterpane of the same industrious work, a little faded, but gorgeous still, with memorials of dead-and-gone brocades and satins, choice morsels which Miss Patterson, the Barnstaple dress-maker, had bestowed upon Mrs. Martha Haggard, her first cousin. The dressing-table in the spare room was an elaborate piece of furniture, with numerous drawers, an oval looking-glass, and faint traces of departed gilding on its pale-green paint — a dressing table which had evidently adorned a grander room in its time. The bedside carpets were Brussels instead of Dutch, bordered and fringed by Judith's own hands ; the pierced brass fender and brass-handled fire-irons were objects of admiration with all Judith's female acquaintance who came to the spare room to take off their bonnets at ceremonious tea-drinkings or social stepping-in for the afternoon. There were Swansea china tea-cups and saucers, the relics of an old set, on the narrow mantel piece, and oval gems of art in tent-stitch on the wall—Abraham and Isaac, and the infant Samuel.

In this chamber Mr. Pentreath was made to lie down, wrapped to suffocation in blankets, made still warmer by the administration of hot brandy-and-water, and bidden to sleep. His clothes should be dried and brought to him, he was told, before dark that evening, and a messenger should be sent to his father announcing the fact of his safety ; to which the young squire replied drowsily that they need take no such trouble—his father would not be uneasy about him.

"I'm sorry for the *Dolphin*," he said ; "and I think I might as well have gone down in her while I was about it ;" for which speech Mr. Haggard reproved him gravely.

"I hope you wouldn't say such a thing if you had quite come to your right senses, Mr. Pentreath," he said.

"Why, what have I to live for, do you think, that I should be overfond of life?" returned the young squire, carelessly.

"We can all make our lives good to ourselves and to others, if we set about it the right way, and seek the right direction," answered Joshua.

"Ah, you mean by preaching and praying. That's out of my line."

"I'll come and talk to you when you have slept," said Joshua, shocked at this reprobate speech ; "and I'll say a short prayer before I leave you."

The minister knelt beside the bed, and lifted up his voice in one of those supplications which he knew so well how to make impressive. His address to the Deity was rich in grandest epithets, to which his noble voice gave fullest force. Oswald opened his heavy eyelids and watched the uplifted face on a level with his own, shining with the faith of an enthusiast. He thought more of the man, perhaps, than of the prayer for "this sinner wandering darkly," but he was impressed. He had thought of Joshua Haggard hitherto as a smooth-tongued, canting rascal, who improved his business prospects by a pretense of sanctity. Brought for the first time in his life face to face with the man, he was moved to wonder at and even to respect him.

Having said his prayer, Joshua went to change his clothes, which had dried upon him ; and when this was done it was tea-time, and the little family assembled, according to their custom from year's end to year's end, at the parlor-table, where Aunt Judith, in her afternoon cap and gown, sat before the big wooden tea-board, and poured out the tea from a flowered china tea-pot, squat and square, which dispensed a mild and unexciting liquor of uniform strength and color. It is not to be supposed that Mr. Haggard's household lacked that evidence of respectability, a silver tea-pot. Aunt Judith had a whole boxful of good old silver, wrapped in baize, and safely bestowed under her bed, from which retreat the family treasures only emerged on solemn and festive occasions.

That afternoon gathering in Joshua Haggard's parlor was apt to be rather a dull business. Judith had gone through life with a fixed idea that cheerfulness and laughter, and all youthful trifling and unmeaning gayety, were so many snares and pitfalls set by the indefatigable enemy of mankind. She was happily exempt herself from these weaknesses; rarely smiled, save with the set smile she kept for after-chapel greetings and formal tea-parties; and suspected some evil in every unconsidered outbreak of gayety in the young people of her acquaintance. Judicious training and seasonable reproof—seasonable in this case meaning at all times and seasons—had made Naomi almost as serious as her aunt; but the boy James was his sister's junior by four years, and not so easily tamed. Naomi saw very little in life to move her to smiles or gladness; James had his joke with every truant and scamp in Combhollow. James was often late for tea, and brought discredit upon poor hard-working Sally by his dirty boots, which left their track along the sanded passage and across the red-brick floor of the kitchen.

"Hearth-stoning and cleanliness are thrown away where James is," Aunt Judith used to remark, vindictively.

They had taken their seats at the tea-table this afternoon, when Joshua came down in his good black clothes and fresh cambric neckcloth, looking like a bishop, Judith thought, as she eyed him admiringly. Her brother was the one object of Judith's reverence and love. She was not demonstrative, and rarely gratified or plagued him by any expression of her affection: but from her childhood upward she had worshiped him, toiled for him, and believed in him, with a single-minded devotion which is given to few brothers. This affection, like most intense feeling in this world, was not without its alloy of jealousy. Judith liked, nay, expected, to be first in her brother's regard, to receive his warmest praises, and to stand nearest him at all times. She would have been wounded if she had thought his own children could be as dear to him as she was.

It may be that Joshua's departed wife, laid at rest under the daisies in the parish church-yard ten years ago, had languished somewhat in the shadow of the domestic hearth, obscured by the more important figure of her sister-in-law. But if it were so, it is certain that Mrs. Haggard had never complained. She had honored and loved her husband, had praised his virtues, and been full of gratitude for the grave tenderness which sheltered and fenced in her innocent, uneventful life. She had come into his house meekly and quietly, and she faded out of his life as calmly as she had entered it; and no outbreak of jealousy, no desire to be paramount, had ever kindled the fatal spark of domestic warfare.

"She was a poor, harmless creature," said Judith, in bland approval, "and she did her duty by my brother. I won't deny that I always wondered what Joshua could see to admire in her; but the more mind a man has, the easier his fancy is satisfied; and one doll's face seems to do as well as another, if it's only pink and white enough."

The pinkness and whiteness which in Judith's opinion had constituted Mrs. Haggard's chief attraction in the eye of her husband had not been transmitted to Mrs. Haggard's daughter. Naomi had her father's olive skin, black hair, strongly marked brows, and dark eyes. She was a girl about whom opinion varied. Some people in Combhollow called her plain, for lack of that pinkness and whiteness which were essential to the Combhollow notion of beauty; but drape that tall, slim figure in Cleopatra's flowing robe, put a fillet of gold round that smooth, raven hair and low, broad brow, and you would have as noble an image of the daughter of the Ptolemies as ever shone on the painter's canvas or glorified the poet's page. But Combhollow had not awakened to the Cleopatra type of beauty, and was wont to speak of Naomi Haggard with a patronizing pity, as a young woman who ought to have been much more personable, having had such a pretty mother.

"Father," began Naomi, gravely, when Joshua had taken his seat, and his cup and saucer had been handed to him, "was not your life in danger while you were saving Mr. Pentreath?"

"My life was in the keeping of my Master, Naomi, just as much then as it is now."

"What, when you were holding on to a dinghy keel upward?" asked James, who had a matter-of-fact mind, and who had just come back from a business journey to a distant farm-house in time to hear of his father's heroism.

"I was as safe as Daniel in the lions' den, or as Shadrach, Meshach, and Abed-nego in the fiery furnace," answered Joshua.

"I don't know about that," said James, argumentatively. James would have argued with an archbishop. "I wouldn't trust myself among hungry lions on the strength of Daniel's coming off so easy, if I was you. Look at the early Christians in the Roman amphitheatre; they weren't Danieled; they were eaten up clean."

"How often must I tell you, James, that such talk as that is irreverent?" asked the father, reprovingly.

Naomi took up her father's strong broad hand and kissed it.

"How good you are, father! how brave, how unselfish!" she said, with a little gush of feeling. "All those fishermen standing by, and only you, a landsman, ready to help that drowning man."

"My dear, I had but to set the example, and those poor men were as ready as I. They were sluggish-minded rather than cowardly; slow to perceive the call of duty, but not unwilling to encounter peril. As for being a landsman, I was almost as much on sea as on land when I was a boy."

"You were nearly as bad as James for idling about in any bit of a boat when you ought to have been minding your business ashore," said Aunt Judith; "and that's saying a good deal."

"I love the sea," cried Naomi. "The first thing I can remember is the water rolling up over my bare feet, and the smell of the sea-weed, and the slippery green rocks, and the loud roar of the tide. I'm very fond of the country, with its woods and hills and deep green hollows, where the ground is like a carpet of primroses in April, and Springcomb Common all ablaze with furze; but, lovely as it all is, the sea's best. It seems somehow as if the sea's alive, and the land dumb and dead."

"I suppose you'd have been just as fond of

the sea if it had swallowed up your father to-day," remarked Judith, sharply. Perhaps she resented that little burst of affection with which Naomi had rewarded her father's prowess. The girl was not often so demonstrative.

"Oh, aunt," cried Naomi, reproachfully, "do you think I could have ever looked at the sea without agony if it had killed my father?"

"I don't know, I'm sure," replied her aunt. "When young women are as fanciful as you are, there's no reckoning upon 'em."

Joshua's dark eyes contemplated his daughter with grave disapproval.

"Fanciful," he repeated. "I hope no one is fanciful in my family. My children have been brought up to be sober-minded, and steadfast to the right."

"I wish we had been brought up to have more variety at meals," said Jim, taking the model of a fine set of teeth on his fourth slice of bread-and-butter. "Green meat is very well in its way, but bread-and-butter and green stuff every afternoon is rather too much of a good thing. I feel as if I was making a Nebuchadnezzar of my-self before the summer is over."

"Lettuces are good for your blood, boy," said Judith.

"As wholesome for your body as the sensual desire for dainty food is hurtful to your soul," added his father.

"Are shrimps sinful, father?" inquired the un-daunted Jim, "because they're only four-pence a quart this afternoon, and there's a good deal of sinfulness of that kind going on up street."

"If you hadn't grumbled I might have given you shrimps for tea to-morrow," said Judith; "but, after your wicked murmurings, I shall do nothing of the kind."

James made a wry face behind his bread-and-butter. He had not much faith in these frus-trated good intentions of his aunt Judith's.

"She's always meaning and unmeaning," he used to say. "If she really meant to give us any thing nice, she'd do it, once in a way, instead of telling us how she was going to do it if we hadn't offended her."

When the tea-cups were empty, and Jim had reduced the stack of substantial bread-and-butter to nothingness, Joshua improved the occasion by a prayer, or rather homily, in which he held up to his son the picture of his young infirmities as in a mirror. He took for his text the wise man's saying that "a contented mind is a perpet-ual feast." He set forth the sin of gluttony, the love of savory meats, which lost Esau his portion forever, and his father's blessing; he dwelt with lofty rhapsodizing on the duty of thankfulness, the free-will offering of praise and thanksgiving to an all-beneficent Creator.

There was real eloquence in his discourse, but it fell on somewhat stony ground with James, for whom such exhortations may have lost some of their power to move, from frequency of appli-cation.

"All this fuss about a plate of shrimps!" thought Jim; and he wished that his lines had been cast in another place than beneath the roof-tree of a disciple of Whitefield and Wesley.

CHAPTER II.

THE FAMILY CIRCLE.

OSWALD PENTREATH slept the deep and heavy sleep of exhaustion in the stillness of the spare chamber. Judith had lowered the blind and drawn the dimity curtains, and there was ob-scurity as of summer twilight in the lavender-scented room. But when Oswald opened his eyes, it was twilight without as well as within, and he had hardly light enough for the process of dressing in the garments that had been placed ready for him — Joshua's clothes, for the most part, his own not being dry enough to put on just yet.

He plunged his face and head into a basin of spring-water, and made himself as decent a fig-ure as he could in the minister's clothes, which were much too wide for his slender frame. He was dizzy still, from the buffeting the winds and waves had given him, a little dazed and uncer-tain as to the details of his misfortune; but con-scious that Joshua Haggard had saved him from drowning, and that the *Dolphin* was lost.

"Poor little boat," he said to himself, sorrow-fully. "It will be a long day before I get an-other. Poor little leaky *Dolphin*, my happiest days have been spent aboard her."

The house was very quiet when he went down-stairs presently, shyly, as in a strange place where he was not quite sure of being welcome. Even the man who had saved his life might consider him something of an intruder, now the peril was past. He went softly down the dark staircase, and in the passage paused and looked about him, uncertain which room to enter. There was a door on each side of the passage; that on the left stood a little way ajar; so he pushed it gen-tly open and looked in, expecting to find the minister and his family assembled there in the gloaming.

It was the hour for the closing of the shop, and Joshua and his sister were both engaged. People in Combhollow had a trick of running in for some indispensable article just before the shutters were put up, and this was sometimes the busiest time of the day—a period which demand-ed the united energies of Mr. Haggard, his shop-man, and his sister. For some reason of his own, Joshua had kept his daughter out of the business—an indulgence which had been some-thing of a stumbling-block to Judith.

"I dare say she'd be more worry than help for the first year or so," remarked Judith, "and I should have my work cut out to teach her the business; but I don't hold with bringing a young woman up in idleness."

"God forbid she should be idle," replied Josh-ua; "but you can find her plenty of work to do in the house, I should think, without bringing her behind the counter for every young man in Combhollow to scrape acquaintance with her, on pretense of buying half a quire of letter-paper or a stick of sealing-wax."

"Bless me!" cried Judith, "I didn't know we had such a beauty in the family to bring the young men after her."

"I said nothing about beauty, Judith," an-swered Joshua, in his grave, reproving tones.

"*I* was in the shop when I was sixteen," said Judith; "but I'm thankful to say I knew how to keep the men at a distance as soon as I knew how to weigh an ounce of tea. However, if you've your fancies about Naomi, I should be the last to interfere."

"I have no fancies," replied the imperturbable Joshua; "but I don't mean Naomi to be in the business."

"And when I'm in my grave, the shop may go to ruin, I suppose," said Judith.

"I see no occasion for that. Jim will inherit the business, and I hope he may have a clever, industrious wife to help him—as you have helped me, Judith," added the minister, in a propitiatory tone.

"Her cleverness and industry put together won't be much use to Jim, unless she's been brought up in the grocery line, and knows the substance of calico and printed goods," answered Judith, derisively.

"Then let us hope that Providence will give Jim a general-dealer's daughter for his wife," replied Joshua.

There the discussion terminated; but it left a lurking resentment in Judith's mind at the idea that her brother was making a lady of his daughter. These holy women of the last generation were apt to look with a jealous eye upon any aspiring tendencies in their nieces. What was good enough for them, they argued with a show of reason, ought to be good enough for those that came after them. There was a strong Conservative element in the Combhollow mind fifty years ago, and Conservatism at Combhollow meant stagnation.

Oswald Pentreath looked into the twilighted parlor, and beheld nothing to increase his shyness. A girl, tall and slim, dark-haired and dark-browed, stood by the open window looking listlessly out at the village street, across a row of stocks and mignonnette which adorned the window-sill. A boy of fifteen or so sat astride his chair, and lolled over a slate, with his elbows on the table.

"Nine into seventy-four will go—come, it must go six times anyhow—that can't be a tight fit—" muttered this youthful student; "perhaps it might go seven times—nine into seventy. There's seven tens in seventy, by-the-bye, and one off each of 'em brings seven nines—down to sixty-three—and put on another nine brings it up to seventy-two—why, that's eight nines, and two over. I hope the man who invented arithmetic came to a bad end; don't you, Naomi?"

"Why, Jim?" asked Naomi, absently.

"Just think of the misery he brought upon mankind. If there was no arithmetic, there'd be no ledgers and day-books; and if there were no tradesmen's books, nobody could get into debt. That's number one. Then, if there was no arithmetic, there'd be no usury, for the money-lenders couldn't reckon up their interest. In my opinion, the man who invented figures did as much mischief as Eve when she eat the apple. Why, it was numbering the people that got David into trouble, if you remember. The Bible's dead against figures."

"May I come in, please?" asked Oswald, gently.

Young men brought up in remote villages fifty years ago were prone to shyness. They were not gifted with that placid assurance of their own acceptability, and that calm contempt for every body else, which distinguish the species nowadays.

"Oh!" cried Naomi, with a little start, "it's Mr. Pentreath. Come in, if you please, sir. Father will be so glad you're better."

"Except for a headache, I feel as well as ever I felt in my life, Miss Haggard. But for your father I might be lying at the bottom of the sea. I want to thank him for his goodness."

"I don't think father would like to be thanked," said Naomi. "He looks upon all that happened as the work of Providence; but if you wish to speak to him," she went on, hesitating a little, "he'll be coming in to prayers and supper presently, and I've no doubt he'll be pleased to see you."

Oswald went over to the window and looked at the stocks, and at the prospect, which afforded a peep at the bay, beyond the angle of a garden on the hill-side. Opposite the minister's house there was some open ground, with a running stream between two roads which made a fork at the entrance to the town. At the angle of the fork stood the chief inn of Combhollow, The First and Last, where the coaches stopped, and where any sojourner of distinction—a black swan, which appeared about once in five years—was wont to take up his abode. This hostelry was supposed to be the first house the traveler beheld on arriving at Combhollow, the last on which his longing eye lingered when departing.

Oswald looked at the glimpse of sea yonder, dim in the evening gray—the air was curiously calm and balmy after the tempest—and then his eyes wandered to the face on the other side of the window. It was not quite unfamiliar to him. He had met Naomi Haggard walking with her father and her brother many a time on summer Sunday evenings after chapel, and had admired the darkly handsome face in which Combhollow saw so little beauty. For Mr. Pentreath, Naomi's face had a greater interest than the fresh-complexioned, buxom prettiness which prevailed among the daughters of the soil. This girl had a foreign look, he fancied, like a wanderer from a warmer, brighter land; and he was not surprised to learn by-and-by that Joshua had Spanish blood in his veins, and that if destiny had not made him a disciple of Wesley, and a Quietist of the William Law pattern, he might have been a follower of Loyola in the land of his forefathers.

Sally came in presently, with a pair of mould-candles in tall, brass candlesticks, and a snuffer-tray; and having set these on the side-board, began to lay the cloth. Supper was a formal meal in the minister's household, though it consisted generally of bread-and-cheese, or at most a cold joint. A fragment of fruit-pie or pasty was a thing for Jim to rejoice about, so rarely was his sensual appetite so much indulged. In Joshua's creed, temperance and sobriety meant a complete renunciation of the pleasures of the table. He eat just enough to maintain him in health and vigor, and his food was of the plainest. To murmur because a joint was overcooked or under-cooked, tough or tasteless — to sigh for savory sauces or appetizing condiments—to eat for the mere gratification of the senses after absolute hunger was satisfied—would have been, in Joshua's eyes, an indulgence of the fleshly lusts, and a sinful unthankfulness for the blessing of plenty. All such weakness of the flesh came under the head of Esau's shameful barter. The big, strong man, prosperous, secure of income, sat down to as plainly-furnished a table as if he had been a convict on jail allowance or a pauper in a work-house. Judith fell easily into her brother's way of thinking. He gratified his self denial, she her economy, which was a virtue she carried to the verge of vice; and every one except Jim was sat-isfied. There was plenty of this plain fare—no one need go hungry; and the hirelings of the household, seeing that they came no worse off than that good man, their master, were never known to murmur.

Naomi and Mr. Pentreath contemplated the storks and mignonnette in silence while Sally set the big home-baked loaf and liberal wedge of cheese on the table. They were silent simply because they had nothing to say to each other. They could not burst into lively conversation about the Royal Academy, or the evening pa-rades at the Botanical, the School of Cookery, or the last new skating-rink, like a young man and woman of the present day. They could not talk about hunting, for Naomi had never been on horseback in her life; or of theatres, for she hardly knew the meaning of the word; or of books, for their reading, limited in each case, lay so far apart.

James, who was not given to shyness, came to their relief just as the silence was growing op-pressive. He had finished his sum to his own satisfaction; though whether the results he had arrived at would satisfy his father was an open question.

"I'm sorry you've lost the *Dolphin*," he began, swaggering across to the window with his hands in his trousers-pockets; "she was a stunning lit-tle craft. I've often wished myself aboard her."

"She was the best I could get," answered Os-wald.

"Ah, but now you'll be getting a better one, I'll warrant."

"Not much chance of that. I had hard work to get that one."

"What a shame! and the squire so rich. He is rich, isn't he?"

"Jim!" cried Naomi, reproachfully.

"I have never asked him the question," re-plied Oswald. "It suits his humor to call him-self poor; and whether the poverty is real or im-aginary, I have to bear the brunt of it. It drove Arnold off to sea; but I suppose I haven't as much spirit as my brother. I dawdle about here, and contrive to rub on somehow."

This was quite a burst of confidence for Os-wald Pentreath, who rarely opened his mind to any one in Combhollow. He lived like some small medieval lord among his vassals, and only conversed with them upon the indispensable ques-tions of daily life.

Naomi looked up at him earnestly, full of sym-pathy and wonder. "Wouldn't you like to be a soldier or a sailor?" she asked.

"I have never felt myself tempted that way."

"I think I should, if I were a man. I should be so tired of Combhollow."

"It isn't the liveliest place in the world, cer-tainly—out of the hunting season."

"And I should so long to go far away into strange countries—to India, for instance."

"To die among cobras and blackamoors," said Oswald.

"Father has read to us about the missionaries in India. I should like to be a female mission-ary."

"And to be strangled by a Thug, or eaten by some back-sliding cannibal, or to be sacrificed to the god of the Khonds," said Oswald. "What a destiny for a young woman to sigh for!"

"I might do these poor heathens some good; and I should see the palm-trees, and the mount-ains that touch the sky, and the temples, and el-ephants, and jungles, and palanquins."

"And tigers, and rattlesnakes, and mosquitoes, and upas-trees," added Jim. "What a mixt-ure! I should have thought you had enough preaching at home, Naomi, without wanting to go and preach to the blackamoors."

Naomi sighed. She was a young woman of en-ergetic temperament, and her energies were be-ginning to feel cramped by the narrow bounds of Combhollow. The events of to-day had per-haps unduly excited her, and she was inclined to speak of half formed dreams and hopes that she would have shrunk from telling in a calmer mood.

"There can never be too much of what is real-ly good," she said, with a reproving look at Jim.

Joshua and his sister came in at this moment, their evening's labor finished. Oswald went straight up to his preserver and shook him by the hand.

"I feel how much I owe you, Mr. Haggard," he said. "I only wish you had saved a better life, or that I had better opportunities for proving my gratitude."

"I desire no gratitude, Mr. Pentreath, for I did no more than my bounden duty; but if you'll try to prove that I saved a good life, and not a bad one, I shall be doubly rewarded."

"Ah!" sighed Oswald, "I'm afraid your idea of a good life and mine would never match. I don't think I've any particular leaning to wicked-ness, but I don't feel any strong pull the other way."

"Without that strong pull, as you call it, Mr. Pentreath, there is not much chance for a man."

"I'm not going to intrude upon you any long-er, Mr. Haggard. If you'll allow me to take my borrowed clothes home with me, I'll see they're sent back to-morrow morning."

"You are heartily welcome."

"And they're a suit he's left off wearing," said Judith, "so you needn't make yourself unhappy about them. But I always mend 'em and put 'em away tidy. What's worth keeping at all is worth keeping decently. That's my idea."

"Good-night, Mr. Haggard," said Oswald, holding out his hand again.

"Nay, you'll not leave us till you've eaten a bit of supper," remonstrated Judith, who, despite her dislike to the name of Pentreath, objected to see this young man depart hungry. "Our table's about the plainest in Combhollow, I dare say; but what we have is good; and if it's not what you are accustomed to at home—"

"We are no epicures at the Grange, Miss Haggard," replied Oswald, "and I shall be glad to take a crust of bread-and-cheese with you be-fore I go."

Oswald did not know that by this acceptance of hospitality he had involved himself in the minister's evening prayer, and was a little sur-prised to see the shop-man, the errand-boy and the maid of all work come in and take their seats against the parlor wall, with solemn countenances and newly washed hands, while Joshua stood up, with his pocket Bible open in his hand, looking through the pages thoughtfully, as if seeking an appropriate chapter for the evening's meditation.

He began with the thirtieth Psalm : "I will extol thee, O Lord, for thou hast lifted me up, and hast not made my foes to rejoice over me" —a cry of a grateful sinner, trustful, and even glad, yet with deepest sense of his feebleness. And then he went on to the thirty-third : "Rejoice in the Lord, O ye righteous, for praise is comely for the upright." And when he had read these he preached a short sermon, taking gratitude for his text ; and, without being absolutely personal, reminded Oswald how deep a debt he owed his Creator and Preserver for the work of this day.

Oswald was impressed by the simple pathos, the unaffected power, of the speaker. Not actively irreligious at any time, but inclined to ridicule the fervid piety of Dissenters, the young squire was to-night more open than usual to good impressions. He was really grateful to Joshua, and in a secondary manner, as to a remoter and less tangible benefactor, grateful to Providence for his rescue ; and to-night he saw nothing absurd in these long prayers, this Scripture-reading and commentary. It lasted for nearly an hour, and the clock was striking ten when the family and their guest sat down to supper—the shop-man at his master's table, the servant-girl and errand-boy at a smaller table by the door—a curiously primitive arrangement, at which the young squire smiled, and of which Naomi felt ashamed this evening for the first time.

Mr. Pentreath, who had eaten nothing since he breakfasted at Clovelly, did ample justice to the simple fare, praised the home-baked bread and the home-brewed ale, much to the satisfaction of Judith Haggard, who was chief agent in the manufacture of both. Joshua was always cheerful and pleasant at supper-time. It was the one hour in which he unbent the bow. The duties of the day, spiritual and temporal, were done ; he could afford to enjoy life's innocent pleasures. The society of his children, a little chat with Judith about the day's takings and the steady improvement of the business, how fast that last chest of tea was going off, and what a run there had been on Dutch cheeses and Manchester printed goods lately.

To-night Joshua avoided all business talk ; he and Mr. Pentreath discussed the prospects of Combhollow, which was supposed to be making rapid strides in the march of improvement.

"If any body would work our mines, we might get on faster than we do," said Joshua : "but while there's no trade in the place but fishing, and a little boat-building, we can't expect much expansion. I sometimes wonder that the squire does not set one of those old tin mines on his estate going."

"He believes the lode exhausted, and he doesn't care about risk," answered Oswald. "If a company would take to the mines, I dare say he'd be very glad."

"But if the mines are exhausted, a company would only lose money. It would be as bad for the share-holders as for your father."

"So it would, I dare say," replied Oswald ;

"but I don't suppose my father sees it in that light."

Supper was over by this time, and the young man took his leave with reiterated thanks, and a shyly expressed hope that his acquaintance with Mr. Haggard and his family might not end here.

"I'm afraid there would be neither profit nor pleasure to any of us in its continuance, Mr. Pentreath," answered Joshua. "It's civil in you to wish it ; but you see we are only tradespeople, in a humble way of life, and you are a gentleman's son, with large expectations. What can there be in common between us ?"

"Friendship," said Oswald, boldly. "I don't think that is measured by social standing. If I can respect a man, he is more than my equal, for I should hardly do that unless I thought him better than myself ; and I do most assuredly respect you, Mr Haggard."

"You are free and welcome to come here whenever you please," answered Joshua. "I am not going to shut my door in your face. But I'm afraid if you were known to come often, Combhollow would begin to talk about it, and say you were forgetting yourself."

"A fig for Combhollow and its petty distinctions ! I have not so many friends in this Godforsaken place that I can afford to sacrifice a good one."

"God-forsaken !" repeated Joshua, horrified. "Do you think for a moment that we are farther from his care because we live off life's busier highways ?"

"Oh, of course not. It's only a way of speaking. Once more good-night. I shall tell my father how much I owe you ; and I shall drop in sometimes of an evening, Mr. Haggard, since you've promised not to shut your door upon me."

"A very civil-spoken young man," said Aunt Judith, approvingly, directly Oswald was gone. "I shouldn't have expected a Pentreath to be so mannerly, considering the way they've been brought up. What do you think of him, Joshua ?"

"A good-natured youth, but a weak one. An ash sapling, to be bent by any wind ; not an oak, to stand firm against the storm."

CHAPTER III.

FATHER AND SON.

It was not a bright or cheerful home to which Oswald Pentreath returned that August evening, after eating his supper at Mr. Haggard's. Nay, it is possible that if he had not supped with the minister he might have gone supperless to bed, for it was no easy thing to get a meal at the Grange after nine o'clock.

The house stood midway between the hilly high-road from Rockmouth and the edge of the cliff, in grounds that were rather wilderness than park, save immediately in front of the house, so little being done to keep them in order. Beautiful exceedingly were those gardens and woods, nevertheless—lovely in their wildness and neglect ; the blue sea shining through every break in the foliage ; ferns and wild flowers flourishing abundantly in the mild Western climate ; and a flush and glow of color on all things.

The house was large and gloomy, and had

been lapsing to decay during the last forty years, in which period there had been scarcely forty pounds expended upon repairs or renovation. Happily the old oak paneling could be kept bright with labor, and that, to the extent of his opportunities, the squire never spared. The spacely furnished rooms were neatly kept. The scanty draperies were free from accumulated dust or flue. The house was as clean as it was comfortless, save in that one sacred chamber, the squire's study—a little room next the hall-door, a closet of espial, from which the squire saw every one who entered or quit the house. Here reigned dust and disorder; here the spider spun his web, and the moth deposited her eggs; here the half-starved beetle fled for refuge, and the famished mouse nibbled the wainscot. Only at long intervals, and after deliberate preparation, did the squire permit this study to be cleaned. As a preliminary measure, he cleared away and locked up every morsel of paper, every parchment, account, or memorandum-book. At other times he simply locked the door of the chamber on leaving it, and carried the key in his pocket.

Miserly as the arrangements of the household were, it was kept up with a faint simulation of a gentleman's establishment. There was an old man who was called the butler, who had an underfed boy, an orphan nephew of his own—no one else would have staid—for his underling. There was a cook and housekeeper, who sent up fairly eatable dinners—the squire rather leaning to a good dinner, on condition that he got it cheap. There was a middle-aged house-maid of severe aspect, who spent her days in cleaning the great desolate-looking rooms and little-trodden staircases, and who seemed, from long habit, to have grown fond of cleaning for its own sake, as men are fond of athletics. Out-of-doors there was a handy man, who looked after the horses, the poultry, and did a little gardening in that cultivated portion of the grounds immediately surrounding the house, with the occasional assistance of a boy or a day-laborer. Out of this minimum household the squire got the maximum of work, and perhaps there was no house within fifty miles better kept than the Grange, and no neater garden than the Dutch flower-beds, narrow paths, and quincunxes in front of the squire's study. Was not the master's eye upon the gardener, or the gardener's help, while he worked—an eye that threatened summary vengeance upon idlers?

The squire looked out of his study as Nicholas, the butler, admitted Oswald at the hall-door. There was no gush of affection on the side of father or son, though the life of one of the two had been in mortal peril since they parted. Mr. Pentreath scrutinized his son through his spectacles, perhaps to make sure that he was sober.

"So you've lost your boat?" he remarked, after the scrutiny.

"Yes, father."

"Unlucky—for you. You don't expect to get another, I suppose?"

"I never expect any thing."

"So much the better for you," granted the squire. "So it was the Methodist parson pulled you out of the water? Canting hound! I dare say he expected to get something by it."

"I don't think he did," answered the young man, coolly. "He knew I belonged to you."

The father contemplated his son doubtfully for a few moments, but made no reply. He held one of the tall silver candlesticks in his hand as he stood on the threshold of his den. There was no other light in the hall. The oil lamp which hung from the ceiling had been extinguished at ten o'clock.

"You've had your supper, I suppose?" he inquired, with paternal hospitality.

"Yes, father."

"That's lucky for you. Nicholas cleared the table an hour ago. You'd better get to bed and take a good night's rest."

"Good-night, father."

"Good-night. And don't stay out so late again, keeping Nicholas up, and wasting candle."

"All right, father; it sha'n't occur again. A man is not on the point of drowning every day in the year."

Oswald took a chamber candle from the side-table in the hall and lighted it from the candle in his father's hand. Very dissimilar were the faces of the two men as they confronted each other across the flame. The younger face delicately chiseled, with complexion inclining to pallor, dark-gray eyes, wavy auburn hair—a face with something of womanly softness in its beauty, with a touch of melancholy too, as if it belonged to one who had but little hopefulness. The squire's was your true miser's face, pinched and hard. The eyes small, and set too near each other; the nose hooked and birdy; the thin lips inclining downward at the corners. Exposure to all kinds of weather had dried his skin like a russet-apple shriveled by long keeping. The air which had given softness and delicacy to the son's complexion had tanned the father's to the semblance of leather. His lean jaws had a knack of working with a curious muscular motion, as if he were munching something or talking to himself, at odd times. They worked to-night as Oswald lighted his candle. It was a sign of displeasure on the squire's part.

"I think I gave you fifty pounds toward that boat," he said, presently.

"We're neither of us likely to forget the circumstance, for it was the only fifty pounds you ever gave me in your life," answered Oswald.

"Don't be insolent, sir. Fifty pounds—fifty pounds gone to the bottom of the sea, through your folly and bad seaman-ship."

"You needn't make yourself unhappy about that. The loss is mine."

"No, sir, it is not," answered the old man, fiercely. "The loss is mine. The money was mine—the fruit of my care and economy. The loss is mine. Fifty pounds—one quarter's rent of Withycomb Farm—gone forever. Fifty pounds at compound interest—do you know what that would have been fifty years hence?"

"Haven't the least idea. As I never have had any principal, I can't be expected to know much about interest."

"You're a fool!" exclaimed the squire, turning on his heel. "Go to bed, before I lose my temper."

Oswald went upstairs without another word, glad to escape any further reproof. He had a bed-chamber that was spacious, and to his mind sufficiently comfortable, though it would have seemed bare as a dungeon to the sybarite. The deep-set windows looked seaward; there was a four-post bedstead wide enough for four, with chintz curtains, faded and attenuated by much washing; there was an old book-case which contained Oswald's meagre collection—Shakspeare, Milton, Byron, Shelley, an old volume of Wordsworth, a few of the classics, "Robinson Crusoe," "Tom Jones," "Roderick Random," "The Adventures of a Guinea," and three or four volumes of the British drama. A carved oak table at which he wrote, a dozen high-backed chairs, more or less rotten, and a clumsy walnut-wood wardrobe, made up the catalogue of furniture. Over the high chimney-piece hung the single picture of the room—a half-length portrait of Oswald Pentreath's mother, dead thirteen years ago. The portrait had been painted before Mrs. Pentreath's marriage—an innocent, girlish face, curiously like Oswald's in feature and expression; a girlish figure in a scanty white gown, with a lapful of flowers—one of those old-fashioned pictures which feebly recall the style of Reynolds and Gainsborough.

Oswald was tired, but in no humor for sleep. He had slept off his drowsiness in the minister's tranquil chamber, so he walked up and down the room thinking of the day's work, and wondering whether his escape from the mighty jaws of the sea was a thing to rejoice about.

"I suppose life is better than death," he said to himself; and then involuntarily repeated those words which depicture all humanity's abhorrence of death:

"To lie in cold obstruction, and to rot;
This sensible warm motion to become
A kneaded clod."

"Yes, I suppose, in the abstract, life is better. If I only knew what to do with mine! Yet some people would tell me I am a man to be envied, having a father who scrapes and pinches and toils, to enrich and extend an estate which in the course of nature must fall to me. Yes; but the course of nature is very slow in some cases. Heaven forbid that I should desire to see the old man's life shortened by so much as an hour! But it's a long vista to look at."

The young man was up betimes next morning and in the stable. Having lost his yacht, he had now only his horse to care about—a bony, long-legged, long-backed hunter, with an ugly head, but a good jumper, and with plenty of go in him. The brute was not spoiled by overfeeding, but was gratified with a greater variety of food than usually falls to the lot of his species, the squire expecting his stable to fatten upon the waste of his garden. In the apple season, Herne the Hunter ate so many windfalls that he converted himself into a kind of animated cider-press. He was an affectionate beast—licked his young master's face when they interchanged greetings, and would have followed him about like a dog, if allowed. Next to a sail in the *Dolphin*, Oswald loved a scamper across country on Herne the Hunter; up hill and down dale, reckless of the ground he went over, possessed with a conviction that Herne's experience and pluck would pull him through. There was no clear idea of the animal's age at the Grange. He had got beyond mark of mouth when the squire bought him out of a stage-coach, whose proprietor disposed of him cheaply on account of a propensity to bolting, which had exercised a demoralizing influence

on the rest of the team. Oswald had ridden any thing he could get to ride, ever since he exchanged petticoats for trousers—from a Flemish plow-horse to a thorough-bred colt; and to Oswald, Herne the Hunter was a most delightful acquisition. He had every vice that a horse can have, linked with one virtue—he was a rusher across country. Oswald hunted him four days a week in winter, and rode or drove him every other day in summer, and the two were devoted to each other.

An ancient white pony, which the squire drove himself in a shandrydan of the chaise tribe, completed the Pentreath stud; and these two beasts inhabited stables designed for the accommodation of sixteen hunters and four carriage-horses. Mr. Pentreath had put pigs and oxen into several of the loose boxes, and had converted one of the fine old coach-houses into a barn. The stable-yard was a stony wilderness, in which the poultry roamed in savage freedom. One small boy took care of the two horses, under the ubiquitous handy man, and presented a curious picture of man's dominion over the brute creation when he was seen lugging that huge beast Herne out of the stable by a bridle, which the brat could hardly reach on tiptoe.

"Good old Herne," said Oswald, as the long-legged animal stalked out into the yard, with his well-worn saddle; "you'll have to carry me a little oftener, my steed, now I've lost the *Dolphin*."

He swung himself lightly into the saddle, and rode out of the yard into the shrubbery on one side of the house—a jungle of laurel, arbutus, and bay, lying beyond that narrow region of Dutch garden, bowling-green, and *pleasaunce* which the squire required to be kept in order. A bridle-way through the shrubbery led into the park, which was more like a wood than a park; and a dilapidated fence, with occasional yawning gaps in it, divided the park from the actual woodland, which sheltered the Grange from north-east winds and wintry gales blowing across channel.

There are plenty of pleasant rides round about Combhollow, which small town lies in a deep cleft between hills as picturesque as the Trossachs, though on a smaller scale than those Scottish mountains. Not having any particular purpose in this before breakfast ride, Oswald let his horse go his own way, or fancied he did, and Herne's way was through the hilly High Street, where, at half-past seven o'clock, the business of life was already in full swing.

The first house of any importance on the left hand of the street was Joshua Haggard's. How bright and fresh the plain square dwelling seemed to Oswald's eye, after the ruined majesty of the Grange stables! Every window was opened wide to the sweet morning air, spotless muslin curtains fluttered within; and between those snowy draperies Oswald caught a glimpse of a girl's dark head bending over a row of flower-pots. Breakfast was over at Mr. Haggard's, and that spiritual light, Joshua himself, was to be seen in the orderly shop ministering to the temporal wants of his flock by packing a large parcel of groceries in stout brown paper, and seemingly as careful to make his package secure and compact as if he had been one of those pious Jews who, for pure love of the holy work, strove to re-erect Solomon's Temple. Aunt Judith was busy in her own special department—the drapery business—sorting packets of hooks and pink papers of pins in various little wooden boxes and drawers, her forehead puckered into the frown of absorbed attention.

Oswald drew rein before the shop door, much to the annoyance of Herne, who was apt to be cross-grained at starting, eager for the refreshment of a stretching gallop.

"Good-morning, Mr. Haggard," cried the young man. "None the worse for your wetting yesterday, I trust?"

"No, sir, thank you. I'm glad to see you abroad so early. You caught no cold, I hope?"

"Thanks to Miss Haggard's good nursing, none whatever. Oh, by-the-way, I have to thank you for sending round my clothes the first thing this morning. I told our boy to carry back the suit you so kindly lent me; but service at the Grange is rather slow."

"There's no hurry, sir."

There was a marked difference in manner between the minister of last night, anxious to exhort and even reprove, and the grocer of this morning. Joshua in his shop was the tradesman, deferential to the son of his patron and customer, squire Pentreath. Not that the squire was by any means a good customer. There were farmers' households among the hills and valleys between Combhollow and Rockmouth that consumed three times as much as Mr. Pentreath's shrunken establishment.

Oswald patted Herne's long neck, smoothed his disordered mane, and trifled with curb and snaffle for a few minutes, as if inclined to linger, yet hardly knowing what more to say. A nice-looking young fellow on horseback, even Judith was compelled to own; and Judith, dwelling among a Conservative people, was at heart an unconscious Radical. She derived her Radicalism from Jeremiah and Isaiah—by much dwelling upon those denunciatory passages in which the prophets scourge as with a whip of scorpions the sins and follies of earth's mighty ones—instead of taking the poison from Wilkes or Horne Tooke; but it was rank Radicalism all the same. She regarded the good old families, the patrician order of her neighbourhood, with a grudging mind and a jaundiced eye. She had that mistaken and distorted pride which reckons superiority of education or position as an injury, or even an insult, to the more humbly placed. Yet, looking askance at Oswald Pentreath this morning while pretending to be deep in consideration of the little paper packets, Judith confessed to herself that he was of a different breed from the young tradesmen and farmers' sons of the district. He was not handsomer or better built, healthier or stronger; he had only the superiority of grace and refinement, other looks, other tones and inflections of voice—another way of holding himself. The difference was indelible, but it was an all-pervading difference in form and expression.

The dark-gray eyes with their auburn lashes, fair skin inclining to pallor, long nose slightly aquiline, thin lips close shaven, auburn whiskers, auburn hair, tall slight figure, might have recalled a portrait of that Golden Age for wit and beauty—and no other virtue under the sun—the reign of Charles the Second. There was all the grace and all the weakness which characterized the gilded youth of that era in Oswald Pentreath's appearance. Judith did not look deep enough for this, but she perceived a certain effeminacy which offended her, and she was not slow to express her opinion when Oswald had obliged Herne by proceeding up the street—a progress to which Herne imparted a good deal of unnecessary clattering of hoofs, and a rocking-horse movement across the road highly alarming to the small children playing in the gutter.

"I hate a fop!" said Judith, decisively, her approval of last night modified by her morning temper, which always inclined to acidity.

"I don't think young Pentreath deserves your dislike on that score," answered Joshua, calmly pursuing his vocation behind the opposite counter; "he doesn't wear fine clothes, and he has no expensive habits that ever I heard of."

"For a good reason—he hasn't the money for either. But, take my word for it, he'll dress himself out like a peacock, and spend his money like a lord, as soon as ever the old squire is in his grave. I could see it all in the droop of his eyelids."

"You must be a shrewder reader of character than I, Judith, to see so much in so little," returned Joshua, with his quiet smile—a smile that had a certain loftiness of expression, as if he surveyed Judith's womanly weaknesses from an altitude, as one looks down on the petty life of a village from the mighty solitude of a mountain-top; "for my part, I rather take to the young man."

"I don't," protested Judith, shutting one of the little drawers with a slam. "He's too pretty for my money. I never could abide a pretty man. I might have been married when I was seven-and-twenty, if I'd cared for prettiness. There was young Chandler, the miller's son, with a complexion like a girl, and always on the simper, asked me times and often; but I used to come over as if I'd been eating too much treacle at the mere sight of him. His good looks made me bilious. What a life I should have led him, to be sure, if I had gone against my inside so far as to say yes—a poor pink-and-white thing like that lolloping about the place, and making believe to be a man."

"Yet it was a strong-minded woman married him, for all that, Judith."

"Very lucky for him. If he'd married a weak-minded one, they'd have lost themselves and gone to sleep in the woods one day, and the robin-redbreasts would have covered 'em up with leaves and made an end of 'em."

<hr />

CHAPTER IV.

WOOD AND WILDERNESS.

THE loss of the *Dolphin* weighed heavily upon Oswald Pentreath's spirits. His days seemed so much longer, his life altogether lost brightness and color, now that he was without his yacht. Love of the sea was innate in him, and his happiest hours had been spent in cruising round the romantic coast of his native county, making a summer voyage to the wilder Cornish cliffs, where Tintagel's ruined tower breasts the angry winds, or going as far afield as the Lizard or the Land's End.

The yacht being gone, he felt his occupation

gone with her, and for the first time in his life realized the fact that he was an idler. He had no profession, no hope of a career; he was absolutely without ambition. His future was marked out for him. In the fullness of time his father would drop into the grave, decaying as gradually as the old elms in the park, which shed their rotten old limbs one by one till the hollow trunks stood up leafless and shorn, breasting the wintry blast, sylvan images of the tenacity with which crippled age holds on to life. The squire would die, and Pentreath would belong to Oswald—a goodly estate, improved by half a century of economy and good management. That was Oswald's future. There was not much love between father and son, and the young man's calculations were not troubled by any sentimental considerations. He was too good-natured to desire his father's death; he only told himself that it was an event which must happen in due course, and that it would change the color of its own existence. By the time he was about forty he would most likely inherit the land, and then Arnold could cease those wanderings of his from sea to sea, and come back to his boyhood's home. They had been loving brothers in the days before Arnold, stung to the quick by his father's brutal punishment of some boyish offense, ran away to London, and got himself a berth on a merchant-ship bound for Bombay. Arnold's name had never crossed the squire's lips since the day of his flight, but the brothers had corresponded faithfully; and once in three or four months a letter from some foreign port informed Oswald of Arnold's wanderings. The boy had prospered, and at three-and-twenty the squire's second son was first mate on board an East Indian clipper-ship —a hard life, he told Oswald, but it suited him, and the owners would make him captain before he was six-and-twenty. He had saved one of their ships by his good seamanship when her captain had been knocked on the head by a falling spar and lay powerless in his berth, and he stood high in the favor of the firm. "It's a better life than that you lead at the Grange, my dear boy," wrote the sailor; "but as you are to be commander there by-and-by, it's best you should stick to the ship. I see the world, men, and manners; while you might as well be one of the Seven Sleepers, for all you see of the changes and chances of this life. However, I fancy that sleepy kind of existence suits you. You always took things easier than I."

Severance had done little to lessen affection, and Oswald's pleasantest fancy about the days when he should be master was the thought of Arnold's return.

"I'll have the finest yacht between this and the Solent," said Oswald, "and Arnold shall be skipper. I'll give him a thousand a year; and when he marries he shall have the prettiest homestead on the estate, and fifty acres of pleasure-farm rent-free. There have been hoarding and pinching enough for one century in this family; Arnold and I will enjoy life."

It was a pity so pleasant a day-dream could not be realized now, in the bloom and freshness of life's morning. A man's ideas of happiness alter as the day wears on. They become more complex, take a wider range, yet centre more narrowly in self.

Deprived of his yacht, and at a loss what to

do with himself when he was not riding Herne the Hunter, Oswald took to wandering about the woods and hills in a dreamy way, with a volume of poems in one pocket and a sketch-book and pencil in the other. He had some talent as a draughtsman—a facile, delicate touch, and an innate love of the beautiful—which made it sweet to him to sit for a couple of hours before a group of ferns growing in the clefts of a stone wall, reproducing every curve and feathery undulation with his pencil. His love of poetry was also innate: and just as he tried to reproduce the ferns and trees, and flowers and crags, and glimpses of the sea caught through some opening in the woods, so he tried, in a dimmer and less artistic manner, to echo the great singer of his time, whose harp's last notes yet hung in the air, and whose recent death was felt like a heart-wound by the young hearts that had yielded him homage that was akin to worship. In secret and at odd times of his idle life, Oswald's sense of something wanting in existence forced itself into rhyme —verses to be kept in his pocket-book and repeated occasionally with a blush. A man moderately gifted might have been made a poet by the rich loveliness of nature round and about Combhollow, and by a life of dreamy idleness like Oswald's; but it must be confessed that the squire's son never rose above the rhymster of "Pocket Magazines," "Caskets," and "Wreaths," who addresses his plaintive verses to Celia on her marriage with a happier rival, or indites a monody on the death of the Princess Charlotte.

Pleasant, though, even for one who had but poetic tastes without poetic power, to lie at ease among the ferns in Pentreath Wood and read "Manfred" or "The Corsair."

So was Oswald lying one August afternoon, a week after his rescue from drowning, when he heard a boy's shrill voice ringing clear through the wood, and then the rustle of a woman's dress, and anon a sweeter voice than the lad's treble, exclaiming at the beauty of the ferns:

"We have none like these in our wilderness, Jim. You must get me some of these," said the voice.

Oswald was on his feet in a moment. He had recognized the tones of the minister's daughter. She had a lovely speaking voice, round and full, like her father's voice softened to match her womanhood.

"Are you fern-hunting, Miss Haggard?" he asked, after they had shaken hands.

"We are very fond of ferns, Jim and I," she answered, standing before him shyly, as if she hardly knew whether to stop or pass on after that first greeting. Jim stuck his stick into the ground, and flung all his weight upon it, as if he were going to throw himself upon his sword like a noble Roman, or were meditating how that kind of suicide was done.

"Speak for yourself, Naomi," he said, jerking himself upright again; "I don't care for 'em, and they're precious hard to dig up. I have all the work, and you have all the glory. She teased father to give her a bit of waste ground on the other side of our orchard, you know," he went on explanatorily to Oswald, "and she's planted it with ferns and primroses, and Saint John's wort and periwinkle, and a lot of trumpery, and calls it a wilderness; and a nice life she leads me, hunting for weeds and such-like. I should plant something good to eat, if I had a bit of ground. Aunt Judith may well call it folly. Naomi's Folly, I call the place."

"Don't be unkind, Jim. You've spent many a pleasant hour there reading."

"Yes, when I could catch hold of a stunning good story like 'Rob Roy,' or 'Caleb Williams,' or 'The Mysteries of Udolpho.' It's a nice place to get out of Aunt Judith's way, I grant. It's too far off the shop and the till, for her to come bothering."

"It must be a delightful place, I should think," said Oswald, admiring the girl's glowing face, framed in a cottage bonnet of coarsest straw. "Won't you sit down and rest a little after your walk, Miss Haggard?"

"I will," cried James, throwing himself at full length on the grass; "we were pretty well baked on the road before we got in here. It's a jolly place, this wood of yours."

Naomi seated herself on a low bank beside the turf on which her brother sprawled, his corduroy legs extended at an acute angle. Jim's communicativeness had set her at her ease by this time. She looked wonderingly at Mr. Pentreath's book, which lay face downward on the mossy bank—a book in boards, covered with coarse blue paper: our ancestors were content to accept their choicest literature thus rudely clothed.

"Is that a tale?" inquired Jim, pointing to the volume.

"No; it's a play, by Lord Byron."

Naomi gave a little sigh—half surprise, half horror—as if she had found herself suddenly in evil company.

"Do you read Lord Byron?" she asked.

"Till I know every line by heart," answered Oswald, with a gush of enthusiasm. "There never was such a poet; there never will be. All other poetry—except Shakspeare's—is prose, in comparison. It is dull, dead, colorless—a thing of rule and grammar, a concatenation of carefully chosen words. Or, I should rather say, all other poets have written from the head, he alone from the heart. And to think of Byron admiring Pope! It is like Mont Blanc admiring Holborn Hill."

"Do you mean Alexander Pope?" inquired Naomi, as if there had been a clan of poets with that surname.

"Of course."

"I have some pieces of his in a book father gave me, and I like them very much. 'Vital Spark,' and 'The Universal Prayer,' and an elegy on a poor young lady who committed suicide. Do you know those?"

"Yes; they are good enough in their way, and the 'Essay on Man' is better. I don't deny the cleverness. Pope is full of wit and force and meaning. But I don't call that kind of passionless stuff poetry, you know, any more than I call Holborn Hill a mountain. Compare that with 'Manfred,' for instance," opening his book.

"But is not Lord Byron's poetry very, very wicked?" inquired Naomi.

"There is a good deal of it that I would not recommend to a young lady: but take all that away, and there is enough left to make the greatest lyrical genius of all time," answered Oswald, warmly. "Let me read you a page from 'Manfred.'"

"Oh no, please; my father has forbidden us to read Byron. I have read some extracts in 'The Pocket Magazine.' They seemed very beautiful—one of them, from 'The Bride of Abydos,' made me cry. I should dearly like to read more, but I am not likely to do that. Father has forbidden it, and he never changes his mind."

"Something like my father when he refuses me money," said Oswald. "He always stands to his guns."

"Are there any robbers in this here 'Manfred'?" asked Jim, who did not always remember that he had been carefully educated.

"No."

"Then I shouldn't care about it. I like such a man as Rob Roy. There's a fellow called Mazeppa in one of Lord Byron's stories. They tied him on the backs of wild horses, and let them scramble for him. That's the kind of person I like to read about."

"You like the 'Waverley Novels,' I suppose, Miss Haggard?" asked Oswald, feeling that literature was advancing his acquaintance with this dark-haired girl.

Naomi shook her head despondently.

"I have not read one of them," she said. "Father disapproves of novels. Jim had no right to read 'Rob Roy.'"

"That's nonsense," exclaimed Jim, sticking his hands deep in his corduroy pockets; "a man may read any thing. 'Mustn't' is a word invented for girls."

"I'm afraid your father disapproves of every thing pleasant," said Oswald.

"Oh no; he is very good, very kind; but he likes us to read serious books, and the Bible before all books. He says there is so much in the Bible, that we could never come to the end of it if we were reading it all our lives. We should always find something new—something to wonder at."

"Ah, I have felt that—about Shakspeare."

Naomi looked unutterably shocked. To compare a profane playwright with the Bible thus lightly!

"It's a pity," pursued Oswald; "the 'Waverley Novels' are so good. Some people say they are by Walter Scott, but I shouldn't think it likely that a man who writes poetry so well could suddenly burst out into splendid prose. And, then, the novels are better than Scott's poems."

Naomi sighed. She felt that he was talking of a world from which she was shut out—may, must always be excluded. It would be an act of rebellion, of actual sin, to cross the threshold of that wonder-world which her father taught her to consider a region of evil and temptation.

"I hope your father has been none the worse for his goodness to me the other day," said Oswald, perceiving that literary topics were exhausted. "He did not take cold, I trust."

"Oh no: father is very strong. I never remember his being ill."

"A wonderful man, powerful in mind and body."

Naomi's dark cheek glowed with pleasure.

"He is good," she said, "and he influences people for good. Many years ago, before he was married, he used to wander about the country preaching in the open air. He has told us how the miners used to come to hear him, and how the tears used to run down their blackened faces, making white streaks."

"I sometimes wish I hadn't been the son of such a saint," remarked Jim, yawning and looking straight up at the cloudless blue. "It's trying, rather, at times. There's too much holiness at home, and too little pudding."

"Ah, Jim, I hope God will give you a new heart some day," remonstrated Naomi, "and make you see things differently."

"I should like to see more upon the table at supper-time. If Aunt Judith had a new heart, we might find an improvement in the housekeeping. It's all very well to talk of carnal affections and sensual appetites; but what do apples grow for, if it isn't to be put into pasties? I wish Providence had set my lines in a farmhouse where there was plenty of squab-pie and junket. We never have a junket unless there's some of the saintly ones coming to tea, and they spoil the pleasure of good victuals by their psalm-singing."

Oswald laughed outright, and, laughter being infectious, the serious Naomi laughed too, in spite of her regret that James should so disgrace his father's teaching.

"Aunt Judith is much stricter about little things than father," she said; "and she and Jim don't get on very well."

"Aunt Judith mixes her religion up with every thing," said Jim; "she can't boil a potato without quoting Scripture. Father has more sense."

After this they talked about the ferns, and Oswald told Naomi the names of the different kinds —long Latin names, at which her dark eyes grew large with wonder. They rose presently, and he showed them where certain varieties grew best, and the stone or the soil they most affected. The rabbits scuddled away, flourishing their silver-gray tails, as the footfalls stirred the bracken. The spreading branches of elm and beech cast their afternoon shadows on the sunlit sward. There was a warm yellow light in the wood, and a perfume of unseen pine-trees.

Oswald showed them his favorite spots — little bits of woodland landscape, unsurpassable in their way. It was all familiar to Naomi, for this wood was her chosen ramble on summer afternoons; the scene of many a blackberrying and nutting in autumn; a paradise of primroses and violets in April, a thicket of hawthorn in May. Yet though she had known these scenes from her earliest childhood, they seemed to reveal new beauties when thus illustrated by an artistic mind.

"How happy you must be to think that this lovely place is your father's—that you belong to this wood, and it to you!" she said, presently.

"Yes, I am very fond of it. Our race has sent its roots deep into the soil. Pentreaths have lived on this land from the days of King Stephen. We have our pedigree cut and dried — Pentreaths of Pentreath — from sire to son. We have been rather fond of marrying cousins too, and keeping ourselves to ourselves, and our land together. Perhaps that's why we have dwindled into an enfeebled family of an old man and two boys. There are plenty of Pentreaths knocking about the world, I dare say; but of our particular branch Devonshire boasts only my father and his two sons. I am happy to say, however, that my father did not marry a kinswoman."

That soft, golden light of the westering sun reminded Naomi that it was nearly tea-time. She had no longing for tea and bread-and-butter—nay, would gladly have lingered among the ferns, in the flickering shadows of beechen branches, until the crescent moon floating yonder high above the tree-tops changed from pale to silver, and from silver to gold; but unpunctuality at meals was a crying sin in Aunt Judith's creed, and Joshua himself was displeased when his children absented themselves from the family board. So Naomi dropped a stately courtesy, and said:

"Good-afternoon, sir; we must be going now, I think. Come, Jim."

Jim, deeply absorbed in looking upward for a squirrel that had just shot out of sight among lofty boughs, abandoned the quest unwillingly.

"All right, Naomi. Yes, I suppose it's tea-time, and we should catch it if we staid any longer."

"Come to-morrow afternoon," said Oswald. "You can come into the park, if you like—not that it's any better kept than the wood; but we've some fine old timber."

"Any squirrels?" asked Jim.

"Plenty of vermin."

"Then we'll come. Now, Naomi, look sharp. Here are your ferns."

Jim thrust a bundle of green stuff into her arms, leaving himself free to flourish his newly peeled hazel, as he swaggered along by her side.

"Let me carry the ferns," said Oswald.

"Oh no, indeed. I couldn't think of taking you out of your way," remonstrated Naomi.

"It isn't out of my way: my way leads nowhere. It will be something for me to do; and your father said I might come and see him sometimes."

This was said with so decisive an air that Naomi submitted meekly, and abandoned the fern-roots to Mr. Pentreath's care. They all walked out of the wood together, and down the hill to the little bay or inlet—it was almost too narrow for a bay—at the mouth of that insignificant river which flowed behind the High Street of Combhollow, and dwindled into a brook yonder among the wood-crowned hills. What a sleepy old place Combhollow looked this slumberous summer afternoon! The vagrant cat, prowling stealthily along those moss-grown tiles upon an opposite roof, seemed an important personage in the quiet of the scene. The little group of children at play in front of The Ring of Bells, the lazy horse contemplating emptiness over a hedge, the fat old landlord of The First and Last smoking his pipe in the sunny porch, were all of life that the village held.

Naomi opened the little green garden-gate, which admitted her and her companions into a paradise of stocks, clove-carnations, and sweet peas, about ten feet wide by the length of the house. The shop had its frontage of barren gravel; but this little garden or forecourt gave a gentility and exclusiveness to the dwelling-house which was not unappreciated by Judith Haggard, despite her radical propensities. Indeed, it must be confessed that Miss Haggard's radicalism chiefly affected other people.

The parlor, with its high painted dado and flowered paper, looked cool and shadowy this afternoon. The dark tea-board and old-fashioned Staffordshire tea-service, sprawling blue flowers on a buff ground; the shining walnut-wood table and broad-seated chairs; the dimity window-curtains, with their knotted fringes and tassels; the flowers that made a bank of green and red and purple in the open window—all had some touch of pleasantness to Oswald's fancy. It was a commonplace interior enough, doubtless, but it was assuredly more like a home than the stately decay of the Grange.

Judith was sitting bolt upright before the tea-board, a picture of prim spinsterhood, in her gray stuff gown, broad muslin collar, coral ear-rings, and square mosaic brooch. Joshua was sitting in his big horse-hair-covered arm-chair near the open window, looking weary and exhausted. He had just returned from a long pastoral round among distant homesteads and cottages, where it was his custom to read and expound the Scriptures, to pray with the devout, or to pray for the unawakened. Much of the work, which in a better state of things would have been done by the parish priest, was left for Joshua. His flock were better cared for, more earnestly watched, than the sheep of the established and endowed shepherd; and it is scarcely to be wondered at, perhaps, that, while the duly qualified pastor saw his sheep dwindle, Joshua's flock grew larger year by year, until they threatened to become too numerous for the square barn-like Little Bethel at the top of the hilly High Street.

"We met Mr. Pentreath in the wood, father," said Naomi; "and he has come to see you."

"Yes; and I hope you've spent time enough in idleness," snapped Aunt Judith. "And those tea-cloths not hemmed yet, I'll warrant."

"I finished the last of the dozen before dinner, aunt," replied Naomi, with her grave meekness, which had nothing of timidity or foolishness, only a tranquil submission to supreme authority.

"They ought to have been top-sewed," said Judith; "hemming won't stand the wear and tear they'll get from such a girl as Sally."

"I sewed them, aunt; and you know Sally seldom washes the tea-things."

"Never, I should hope!" cried Judith. "There wouldn't be many of 'em left if she did; and it's a pattern you can't match nowadays, if you was to give its weight in gold."

"What a good thing that ugliness should go out of fashion!" retorted Jim, not thinking of the day when the commonest of those Staffordshire cups and saucers might take their places among the chosen specimens in a collector's cabinet.

"Ah!" sighed Judith, "they were your grandmother's; but that makes little difference to you. You've no reverence for those that came before you."

This conversation had been carried on in under-tones at the tea-table, while Joshua had given Mr. Pentreath friendly welcome. They all drew round the tea-board after this. Aunt Judith filled the cups with precision, and the conversation became more general and more ceremonious. There was not much to talk about—not much local chitchat—in Combhollow; but they did manage somehow to find something to say. Joshua talked of the people he had visited in his day's duty—tenants of the squire's most of them—their grievances; their ailments—scald from tea-kettles, wounds from scythes or reaping-hooks; their sick cattle. Mr. Haggard confined his talk to worldly subjects, being wiser in this respect than some of his fellow-laborers.

Oswald felt himself quite at home in the calm family circle, being happily ignorant of Aunt Judith's low opinion of him. He sipped his tea and eat his bread-and-butter, and looked at the flowers in the window and the colored busts of John Whitefield and John Wesley in Bow china on the mantel-piece, and familiarized himself with the aspect of the place. There was a mahogany book-case with glass doors on one side of the fire-place, and behind the glass rows of books, neatly arranged and neatly bound—books that looked as if they were treasured by their owner—not like Oswald's ragged regiment of volumes, always out of their proper places.

"You are fond of reading, Mr. Haggard," said the young man, looking at the book-case.

"Very fond. I give all my spare hours to my books, but my spare hours do not make many days in the year. I carry a volume in my pocket when I have to walk far, and read as I go. That is my best chance of enjoying a book."

"And who are your favorite authors?"

"Bunyan, Baxter, and Law."

These were strangers to Oswald Pentreath, save for a dim remembrance of "The Pilgrim's Progress," devoured and wondered over in early boyhood.

The conversation came to a dead stop at this point, but there was no embarrassment. A pause in the flow of talk is not such an awful thing in a Devonshire village as it is at a London dinner-table, where the fountain of wit is supposed to be inexhaustible, and a silence reflects discredit on the assemblage.

"Let us go into the garden," said Joshua, when every body's second cup was empty.

Jim had turned his bottom-upward and balanced his tea-spoon across it, thereby scandalizing Aunt Judith, whose reproving frown had no influence upon him.

"Yes, and I'll show you Naomi's wilderness," said the boy to Oswald, in a confidential undertone.

It was one of Joshua's leisure evenings. There was no service at Little Bethel, and until closing-time there was nothing for him to do in the shop. He could afford to lounge in his garden and refresh himself with a little repose after a toilsome day.

Aunt Judith went to the shop, where there was generally a run upon tape, needles, and such small gear in the leisure hours of evening; good housewives, who had been too busy to touch their needle-work in the day, discovering their wants after tea and running down to Haggard's to supply the same, and perhaps to spend five minutes or so inquiring after the health of that excellent man, the minister.

The rest repaired to the garden—a square piece of ground of about an acre, running off at the end into another acre of irregular shape, which had been an orchard for the last hundred years.

There was nothing picturesque about Mr. Haggard's garden. It was neatly laid out upon utilitarian principles, with just so much regard to ornament as is implied in narrow borders of old-fashioned cottage flowers in front of homely vegetables, and a row of espaliers screening beds of onions and turnips. It was a garden running over with fertility, from the young pear-trees, around whose lowermost branches the scarlet-runners had entwined themselves lovingly, to the golden pumpkins sprawling in the setting sunlight, and the deformed old quince-trees that hung over a pond in the corner by the wall. The narrow paths were neatly kept, and there were very few weeds among vegetables or flowers, Jim being held answerable for the condition of things, and laboring here himself daily, with some little assistance from the shop-boy and a good deal of help from Naomi, who was passionately fond of flowers.

Mr. Haggard walked to the end of the garden with the young people, and then, feeling tired after his long round by hill and dale, seated himself on a bench by the quince-trees, which, with an ancient walnut, made this the shady spot of the garden. There was a square grass-plot here upon which stood a rude table—a specimen of Jim's carpentry; and on very warm afternoons Aunt Judith was sometimes persuaded into an out-of-door tea-drinking here—a concession on her part only to be obtained by much diplomacy.

Joshua was fond of his garden in a passive way, and it was here that he communed with himself on Saturday afternoons, meditating his subject for the next day's sermons. It was here he read the Non-conformist divines, or indulged in that introspective study, that searching-out of his own heart, which formed a prominent part of his system. There was not much to search for in the minister's heart—no lurking evil to be thrust out of it. In singleness of purpose, in directness of aim, in simplicity of life, he came as near perfection as it is given to erring man to come.

The young people strolled on along the narrow path to the orchard, leaving Joshua to his meditations. If Judith had been there, she would have taken pains to prevent this unrestricted communion between the young squire and Naomi; but her brother, in his contemplation of far-off things, was apt to overlook trifles lying near at hand, and he saw no danger in the temporary association of these young minds.

"Come and see our wilderness," cried Jim, opening the orchard-gate.

The orchard was a queerly shaped inclosure, a strip of land running into a sharp point; and this triangular end had been allowed to be waste ground until Naomi's fifteenth birthday, on which privileged occasion she begged the bit of waste from her father by way of birthday gift; and from that time forward it had been her constant delight and Jim's occasional caprice to adorn the spot with all manner of nature's wildlings of forest, heath, and dell. It was a wonderful soil, that wilderness—every thing grew there. Plants that affected sand, and plants that hungered for loam; flowers that loved the sun, and ferns enamored of shade. They all grew together in harmony, like the happy family of birds and beasts, to oblige Naomi. Such primroses, yellow and purple; such bluebells and fox-gloves, and dragon's-mouths and marsh-mallows, and amethyst-hued heaths, and gold and silver broom, and ferns of every denomination.

"I think we could grow sea-weed if we tried," said Jim.

The old, old orchard was like a hospital of cripples, so lame, and twisted, and warped, and crooked were the ancient trees, with more gum-

my exudation upon some of them than fruit; such gray old bark, such yawning wounds in their trunks. The turf was deep and soft, all hillocks and hollows; and in one sunny corner there was a row of bee-hives, the produce whereof was usually sold by Aunt Judith, as a favor and at a good price, to some of the superior customers.

"Other people get the honey, and we run the risk of getting stung," complained James, who felt injured by this arrangement. "That's what comes of being brought up by an aunt. If mother had lived we should have had cakes and junkets sometimes, I'll warrant."

Jim had but a cloudy memory of his dead mother, and was apt to associate her loss with the idea of indulgences which would have flowed naturally from the maternal bounty.

They loitered a little in the orchard, talking in a lazy summer-evening way about nothing particular. It was long past the squire's dinner-time, and Oswald knew that he had forfeited his dinner by absence. There was no such thing as a meal served out of due season at the Grange. Mrs. Nichols, the housekeeper, knew her duty too well for such foolish concessions. But Oswald was reconciled to the loss of his dinner. Female society was almost a novelty to him. The squire lived like a recluse, and enjoyed the privilege of being eminently unpopular—a privilege which, in his own opinion, saved him five hundred a year.

"Your popular man is every body's friend except his own," remarked the squire, in his philosophic mood. "People are always asking favors of him. Nobody ever asks me for any thing."

Oswald therefore, as the son of a miserly hermit, stinted of pocket-money, and of a nature too generous to live easily under a weight of obligation, visited hardly any one of those pleasant country-houses which lay far apart among the fertile hills and valleys of his native place. He lived as lonely a life as ever a young man had to endure, and was in a better position to cultivate the Byronic temperament than most of the great poet's disciples. Happily nature had given him a disposition to take life easily, rather than the misanthropic mind; and solitary and secluded as his existence was, he tried to make the best of it, amused himself after his own simple fashion, and complained to nobody. There was a touch of bitterness occasionally in his intercourse with his father, the old man's meanness and suspicion being almost too much for endurance; but this was the only bitter in his life. To this young man, therefore, reduced of necessity to the society of peasants and boatmen, it was a new thing to find himself in the company of a handsome young woman, who spoke with a certain refinement and expressed herself fairly, although her range of ideas was limited. Those vague yearnings of Naomi's for something wider and brighter than the narrow life of Combhollow answered to the sense of loss in his own mind. There was sympathy between them already, though this was but the second time of their meeting.

"I suppose you would hardly stay at Combhollow if you were a man, Miss Haggard?" said Oswald, after they had discussed the place and its dullness.

"Oh no. If I were a man, I should be a minister, and I would go and preach to the Cornish miners, as father did when he was a young man; or else I would be a missionary, and go to India."

"Ah, you talked about that the other night."

"Yes; I should like to teach those poor creatures—to turn them from their hideous gods, their human sacrifices, their cruelties. Why do we let them go on with such dreadful creeds?"

"I fancy the work of conversion would be rather beyond us. A missionary may labor in a corner, set up his little school-room, and baptize a handful or so of dusky Christians, who will go back to Siva and the rest of them as soon as his back is turned; but to turn all India from her false idols is a project beyond man's dreams of the impossible. When Burke addressed the House of Commons on the evils of our government in India, the territory of the East India Company was larger than Russia and Turkey. We have extended our conquests since his day, and we are but a sprinkling among that vast population. I think you must put India out of your head, Miss Haggard. The Thugs would strangle you; or the Koords would bury you up to your neck and sacrifice you to their gods; or the tigers would eat you."

"Of course," cried Jim. "How few people ever go to India that don't get eaten by tigers, in the long run! I never took up a magazine yet without seeing a picture of tiger-eating."

They had arrived at the wilderness by this time—a corner of fern-tangle and sweet-smelling flowers, with masses of rough stone here and there among the greenery; which stone-work had cost Jim much labor. There were some elder-trees leaning over from an adjoining orchard, and the spreading branches of a mulberry, which shaded one side of the small inclosure. There was a stone bench, which Jim had picked up from among the ruins of an old manor-house; and in the middle of the wilderness, its rugged base choked with fern and primrose roots, there stood an old stone sun-dial, spoil from the same ruined mansion. That sun-dial and the monkish-looking bench gave an air of antiquity to the place. It was quite out of the world of Combhollow, as lonely as if it had been an oasis in a desert. One might have lived all one's life in the High Street, and never suspected the existence of Naomi's wilderness. A mild-faced sheep sometimes peeped at it through an opening in the blackberry-hedge, perhaps wondering whether those ferns and flowers were edible: but except the sheep, there was rarely any sign of life in the adjoining orchard.

Oswald praised the spot, as in duty bound. It could not appear particularly beautiful to him after the picturesque wildness of Pentreath park and wood: but it had a quaint prettiness that was not without its charm. He sat down by Naomi on the broad old stone bench, and watched her thoughtfully and in silence for a little. She had taken her knitting out of her pocket, and the needles were flashing swiftly under her slender fingers. The hands were brown, but slim and well shaped.

She was very handsome, Oswald thought—much handsomer than the Devonshire beauties, with their complexions of roses and cream. Her face had a noble look: the features boldly carved; the eyes deep and dark, with heavy lids such as he remembered seeing oftener in sculpture than in flesh: the mouth was full and firm; the chin a thought too square for feminine loveliness. If the face erred at all, it was that the girl was too like her father: manly firmness rather than womanly softness prevailed. But Oswald could not see any blemish in this noble countenance. He was drawn to its owner with strongest sympathy. It was not love at first sight, but friendship, confidence, companionship, which drew him; and he had no thought of peril in this new influence. What peril could there be, indeed, for him, even if he fancy had been of a warmer tendency? He had no money to spend, but he was the master of his own heart. He might dispose of that as he pleased.

"Marry a dairy-maid, if you like," the squire had once said to him, in his brutal fashion; "but I shall expect you to keep her until I'm under the sod. An impoverished estate can't afford to recognize early marriages, unless they bring land or money along with them."

They had been in the wilderness about half an hour; Jim exhibiting his chosen specimens, in pursuit of which he had, by his showing, more or less imperiled his life, hanging on to precipices like the samphire-gatherer, scaling inaccessible hills, and losing himself in pathless woods inhabited by the reptile tribe. The sun had gone down behind the old tiled roofs and thatched gables of the High Street, and Joshua had left his quiet garden for the bustle and business of the shop.

"We'd better be going indoors, Jim," said Naomi, rolling up her stocking. "You've your sum to do for to-morrow."

Oswald felt that he had no excuse for prolonging his visit. He walked back to the house with Naomi and her brother, but did not go indoors with them. There was a side gate opening into the street, and here he stopped to wish them good-evening.

"You might as well stop to supper," said Jim. "It would be livelier if you staid."

"I think I have intruded too long already," answered Oswald, ceremoniously; and as Naomi did not second her brother's invitation, he shook hands with them both and went away.

Aunt Judith was standing at the house-door when they went in—a surprise for both, as it was her custom to be in the shop at this hour.

"I hope you've wasted enough time with your fine gentleman," she said, with extra acidity.

"I wasn't wasting time, aunt; I had my knitting with me," replied Naomi: "and there was nothing for me to do indoors."

"A pity there wasn't. Idling about the garden with a gentleman above you in station! What would your father say to that, I wonder?"

"Father was with us part of the time," said Naomi.

"Was he really? and what about the rest of the time when he wasn't with you? Fine carryings-on, indeed, for a grocer's daughter! No good ever came of that kind of thing, Miss Naomi, I can tell you."

"No harm will ever come of it while I'm here," cried Jim, his face crimson with anger. "I'd knock down any man that said an uncivil word to my sister. As for the young squire, he's a gentleman, and as soft-spoken as a girl."

"I never trust your soft-spoken people," answered Judith; and at this juncture a shrill cry of "Miss Haggard! wanted, please," from the open door at the back of the shop diverted the spinster's attention, and she ran off to measure calico or printed goods for an impatient matron.

Supper-time, prayers, and Scripture-reading seemed a little duller than usual to Naomi that evening. The quiet monotony of life hung upon her heavily, like an actual burden. She had begun to ask herself of late whether existence was to go on always in the same measured round—eventless, unvarying; whether the portion which appeared satisfying and all-sufficient for Aunt Judith was also to content her; whether those vague aspirings of the soul for something loftier and wider, which stirred in her breast like the wings of imprisoned birds, were to wear themselves out by their own restlessness, and know no fruition. To-night the question seemed to press itself upon her more closely than usual. Oh, how much better to be a female missionary—a teacher of little tawny heathens in some clearing of the jungle; or to visit fever-poisoned prisons, like Mrs. Fry! How much fairer any life in which there was peril, and with peril the reward of brave deeds, the hope of glory!

"What use am I in this world?" she thought, on her knees in that solemn silence which ensued after Joshua's extemporaneous prayer—a pause which he bid his household devote to self-examination and pious meditation. "If I were to die to-morrow, no one would be the worse for my loss. Father would be sorry, perhaps, because he is good, not because I am of any use to him, or make his life happier by living. There is no duty I do that Aunt Judith would not do better than I if I were gone; and the tasks I do listlessly she would perform briskly, putting all her heart and mind into them. But if I were to go abroad and teach heathen children, I feel that I could work honestly and earnestly—yes, like those good women I have read of."

These were Naomi's musings on her knees to-night. No fairer scheme of life offered itself to her girlish fancy than the missionary idea. She resolved to work for that end, to read more, to be more attentive to her father's teaching, to raise herself to that higher level from which she might shed enlightenment on ignorant pagan souls. And behold, in the midst of these high resolves, her thoughts flew off at a tangent. "If I were Mr. Pentreath I would be a soldier," she thought. "I wonder if he is tired of Combhollow? But he has his horse, and, until the other day, he had his yacht. It is different for him. Yet, if I were free like him, with a good old name, I would try to be something more than an idle country gentleman. People respect his brother for running away to sea. I know that, by the way they talk of the two in Combhollow."

"You'd better take your candle and go to bed, child," Miss Haggard said to Naomi directly after supper. "I want to have a few words with Joshua."

Of all things most displeasing to the minister's human weakness was a few words with his sister Judith. That preface of hers as surely foreboded evil as the warning of the screech-owl or the minor howl of the dog. Nothing pleasant ever came of a few words with Judith.

"Well, Judith, what is it now?" asked her brother, as soon as they were alone, anxious to come to the worst without beating about the bush.

"Only that I think it's a pity you don't keep your eyes a little wider open to see what's under your nose. It's all very well to be looking toward the New Jerusalem, and I'd be the last to lose my habitation in that blessed city; but while a man lives among the Philistines he should have an eye to his own household."

"What's the matter, my dear? The new cask of Irish butter is not rancid, I hope? I gave a half-penny a pound more for it than the last."

"No, Joshua, the butter is as sweet as it new cobnut. But I don't like your daughter's goings-on with Mr. Pentreath."

"What do you mean, Judith?" cried the minister, with a flash of natural indignation.

"Bringing him home to tea as if he was her equal. A pretty thing to set tongues wagging in Combhollow!"

"I see no need for people to talk about us because the squire's son takes a cup of tea in my house. He is better born than my daughter, I grant you, but not better bred. Naomi is a lady in mind and nature, and, as such, no man's inferior. And she is something less than my daughter if she does not respect herself so much as to make every man respect her."

"That's all very fine," retorted Judith; "but you'd better look out that no mischief comes of it. You heard what Jabez Long said while I was working like a slave to bring the life back to that young man's body. It's unlucky to save a man from drowning. Take care the bad luck doesn't come our way. I don't like to see Mr. Pentreath hanging about the place."

"Why, Judith, you can't be weak enough or wicked enough to give heed to such a vulgar superstition?"

"I don't know about that. There's a grain of good sense sometimes in vulgar superstitions."

"Sometimes, perhaps; but in that particular superstition not an iota. Our fishermen get the fancy from the North. It is a common belief in Shetland."

"Have it your own way," said Judith, with an offended air; "but I'm afraid you've too much book-learning to be wise about the affairs of this life."

CHAPTER V.

THE MINISTER GOES ON A JOURNEY.

VERY tranquil was the progress of life at Combhollow. None of those bubbles called events rippled the calm surface of that Devonian mill-pond. Every day and every week brought the same duties—a beaten round of petty cares and unexciting pleasures—pleasures so small as to have been positively invisible to any observer surveying this quiet rustic life from the outside. Even the changes of the seasons brought but little change to the dwellers in the High Street. The farming folks had their harvest-homes, and apple-storing time, and cider-brewing, and all the variety of rustic life; but in the village—by courtesy, town—the dull, unalterable round went on from January to December. Save for the fire-glow upon cottage-windows, and the cheery look of the forge in the early dusk, you would hardly have known winter from summer. Frosts rarely visited this favored clime. There was a good deal of mist and rain, and sometimes fierce winds came tearing across the sea as savagely as if they meant to root up Combhollow altogether, but the traditional winter of the North—icicle-crowned and snow-mantled — was a stranger here.

Naomi, just nineteen years of age in this misty November, schooled her soul to bear the quiet of her life, and performed her daily duties with a sweet tranquillity which might have seemed the essence of patience to any one who could have looked into her heart and seen its eager yearnings for a busier existence. She had talked to her father of her desire for missionary work, and he had answered her in the words of St. Paul, "Let your women keep silence in the churches: for it is not permitted unto them to speak."

Very hard words they sounded to Naomi.

"But I don't want to preach, father," she pleaded; "I only want to teach the little children."

"There are children enough for you to teach here, Naomi. I am not satisfied yet with our Sunday-school. The boys are backward; and the girls, though a little better, are wofully unenlightened."

Naomi sighed and submitted. This was an unanswerable answer. If she could not do good work with these little English Christians, born and bred to belief in the Scriptures, how could she hope to make converts of little heathens, speaking a strange language? Mr. Pentreath had given her a Hindoostanee grammar that had belonged to his uncle, Captain Tremaine, and she had worked in secret at the language—learning a little bit at a time during the extra quarter of an hour she could venture to keep her candle burning before going to bed. Anything beyond a quarter of an hour might have drawn upon her the displeasure of Aunt Judith, who had a sharp eye to the consumption of bedroom candles, and would have suspected the unholy practice of novel-reading or a sinful lingering over the braiding of hair, had she perceived an undue diminution of the tallow. So Naomi, being convinced that she was not good enough or clever enough for a missionary, began to despair of ever releasing herself from the prison-chamber of life in a village. She had no yearning for fine dresses, or pleasures, or any of the objects that might have presented themselves to the mind of a girl brought up in a boarding-school, but she sighed for something more than Combhollow could give her; or else perhaps she needed some stronger anchor to hold her in those quiet waters than any which her household ties offered.

Her father loved her—of that fact she had no doubt; but his affection was so undemonstrative as to seem near akin to coldness. He was formal in his intercourse with his children — more given to reprove than to praise, to counsel than to caress. As a child—finding herself motherless in childhood—she had given him her father an almost romantic love, following him about with faithful solicitude, fearing, if he were out of her sight for a little longer than usual, that he would go away and she should never see him more, shedding childhood's passionate tears at the thought that he would die as her mother had died, and leave her lonely. The father had responded to this affection with an almost equal warmth, holding the little girl on his knees through many an hour of pious meditation, taking her with him on many a journey, carrying her when she was tired, watching by her little bed through childhood's fevers and illnesses, and,

in some wise, filling the dead mother's place, much to Judith's displeasure, who argued that a woman must know more about the treatment of a sick child than a man, were he twenty times a father.

Little by little, as Naomi grew from childhood to girlhood, this sympathy between father and daughter had dwindled—on the father's side, not on the daughter's. Naomi was still as fond, but more reserved in the expression of fondness. She was too old to sit on her father's knee. She must give up those pleasant wanderings by her father's side. She had her lessons to learn; her daily tasks, scholastic and domestic. Aunt Judith taught her household economy; Joshua trained her mind. The father was transformed into the school-master; and Judith took care to impress upon her brother that if he were too indulgent, Naomi would respect him too little to profit by his instructions.

"When we were boy and girl, we used to call father and mother sir and madam," said Judith, "You must remember that, Joshua."

"Yes, Judith. But I don't know that we loved them any more on that account. Father's a beautiful word. I should be sorry to hear Naomi change it for sir."

In pure conscientiousness, and with a view to the culture of his daughter's mind, Joshua abandoned those loving ways which had been so dear to his daughter's heart. The change was so gradual that she was hardly aware of its progress. It was only when she looked back to those happy childish days that she knew how much she had lost of life's sweetness. Yet she had no thought of complaint, nor was her father's goodness lessened in her estimation. He was still the one most perfect man her little world held; perfect as the best of those good men she had read about in her narrow range of literature.

Mr. Pentreath availed himself of Joshua's permission to call occasionally, and dropped in now and then of an evening, or came at dusk and drank tea out of the blue-and-buff Staffordshire tea-cups. Sometimes he staid for prayers and supper, and listened attentively to the minister's exposition of psalm or chapter. Perhaps he obtained more real knowledge of the Scriptures from these evenings than from all those Sunday services which he had attended, absent-minded and sleepy, in the old parish church, where the family pew of the Pentreaths was as large as a small room, and screened from the vulgar gaze by old oak paneling and faded green curtains on brazen rods—a fine place for slumber.

Joshua took the young man's visits as a matter of course; but Judith expended her spleen in various shrugs and elevations of thin eyebrows and depressions of thin lips.

"How fond the young squire is of us all!" she said; "we ought to be uncommonly proud. I'm sure. Is it you or me, I wonder, he comes for?"

Whereupon Joshua's frown warned her that she had better push her insinuations no farther.

It was summer-time again—early summer; the sweet fresh season of newly opened roses and new-mown hay. The young ferns were unfolding their tender green fronds under every hedge, on every stony bank; the hart's-tongues uncurling their pointed tips; fields purple with clover, or silver-white with blossoming beans; a time of sweetest, subtlest odors; the sea yonder, deep translucent green, shining through every opening in the undulating land, through ragged breaks in upland hawthorn hedges, above the beans and the clover, like another world, fairer even than this beauteous earth.

In such sweet summer weather Joshua Haggard had Combhollow on a journey that was to last a week. He wore his Sunday suit, stout buckled shoes, and carried a change of linen and the simple necessaries of his toilet in a small leather knapsack. His journey was to be performed for the most part in lumbering old stage-coaches, but the last twenty miles were to be done upon foot. Mr. Haggard was going to assist at the opening of a humble little chapel in the wild Cornish country, between the Lizard and Penzance. The minister of the new chapel was one of his pupils and disciples; a dark-browed young shoe-maker of five-and-twenty, who had come in of an evening with leather-stained hands to read and study under Joshua Haggard's direction, and had nursed a tender passion for Naomi which he had never ventured to reveal. Perhaps it was his consciousness that this affection was vain which decided Nicholas Wild upon turning his back on the quiet comfort of Combhollow about two years ago, and taking up his staff as a wandering preacher. He had kept his own body and soul together by mending the shoes of his hearers; and he had ministered to the souls of his shifting flocks without fee or reward, content if in field or on common he could see listening faces crowding round him, and hear the untaught voices pealing up to the open sky in the hymns he dictated to his congregation line by line. After an itinerant career of two years, Nicholas had become so popular in one particular district as to find it advisable to settle there altogether; and his congregation had contrived among them to build him a chapel—such a curious little tabernacle, in an angle of a field, as lonely as if it had dropped from the sky. The walls of cob; the roof covered with large thick slabs of roughly cut slate, like flag-stones; a small door at one end, a big window at each side, and about as much architectural design or beauty in the building as there is in a toy Noah's ark. But the Temple of Solomon was never lovelier in the eyes of its founder than was this rude barn to Nicholas Wild. He wrote to his beloved pastor and teacher, telling him of his good fortune; how the Word had prospered in these far western villages by his humble efforts, and entreating Joshua as a favor beyond all measure of gratitude to come and preach the opening sermon in this new-built chapel.

"Your voice would call down a blessing upon my work," he wrote, "and move the hearts of my faithful flock as I can never hope to stir them, though Providence has blessed my teaching. I want the opening of this lowly temple to be a golden page in their memories so long as they live. I want them to feel that this tabernacle among the hills has been sanctified and glorified by an inspired voice, by a chosen messenger of the Gospel, gifted above all other servants of God."

To an appeal such as this Joshua Haggard would have esteemed it sinful to turn a deaf ear. Nicholas Wild's intelligence and piety had made the youth very dear to him. He was proud of his pupil's success, as in a considerable measure his own work; and his heart warmed at the thought of that little chapel among the wild hills by that rock-bound shore, over whose craggy pinnacles the dark-winged cormorants and the silver-white gulls skim and wheel and scream and chatter.

To Joshua this Cornish coast was at once familiar and dear. He too had wandered there in his hardy youth. He had taught and preached from Camelford to Penzance, and his teaching had prospered. His name was a word of power in the West, and he seldom let a summer go by without making some such journey as he was making now—to preach, to inspect village schools, to spend a day here and there among old friends, and perform other duties of his office.

The little chapel was opened to the eager flock one bright June morning—men, women, and children in their smartest clothes, as if for a flower-feast; a congregation gathered from twenty miles round, so eager were these Independents to hear Joshua Haggard. The fervid extemporaneous prayers were poured forth above the heads of that assembly, all standing to pray after their manner; the enthusiastic hymns had been sung—hymns which compared this cob-walled barn to the gorgeous temple in the sacred city; and then Joshua ascended to the deal pulpit, and opened his Bible on the green-baize cushion and preached a two hours' sermon upon one of his favorite texts, "I was glad when they said unto me, Let us go into the house of the Lord."

No one felt that two hours' discourse a sentence too long, unless it were, perhaps, the children—some of whom yawned piteously; some shuffled on their seats, and were shaken or otherwise admonished by offended elders; while others of still more tender years sunk into placid slumber, and enjoyed the warmth of the atmosphere and the sonorous lullaby of Joshua's deep, melodious voice.

Nicholas Wild was in a glow of gratitude as he walked home to the adjacent village with his friend.

"They will never forget your words to-day, nor shall I," he said. "They have sunk into my heart. You have told us what the minister of such a flock should be. It shall be the business of my life to come as near as I can to that sublime type. It ought to be easy for me, having known you. I have but to imitate my master upon earth in order to approach nearer to the example of my Master in heaven."

"Gently, Nicholas, gently; you offend me by such words as those. Providence has been very good to me. My lines have fallen in pleasant places; life has been made easy to me. I have not been tried as some are tried, or tempted as some are tempted. I have known little sorrow. My faith has not been shaken by adversity. I have known neither hunger nor thirst, disease nor loss of fortune. My wife was a good woman, my children are affectionate and dutiful, my business is prosperous. I am like Job, before Satan asked to try him. What am I, then, that I should boast, or suffer others to boast of me?"

To which Nicholas replied with fervid eulogy:

"All that I am I owe to you," he said, "as Saul owed all to Samuel. And your lovely daughter, Mr. Haggard—to have known her, to have lived in her company for a little while, is to have held fellowship with angels."

"Nicholas, you must not talk like that. My daughter is a good girl, but—"

"She has more than common goodness. My sisters are good women, but they are not like Naomi. She is strong and noble, like the women of old; a woman to sacrifice herself for others, to suffer in silence; to do great deeds like the women of old time, like Jael or Judith."

"I would rather she should resemble Ruth or Esther," replied Joshua, smiling at an enthusiasm which betrayed the speaker's secret. "I would rather she should live her simple life, meek, obedient, faithful, domestic, happy herself, and the source of happiness to others."

"We have often talked together of spiritual things, Mr. Haggard, and perhaps Naomi has poured forth her heart more freely to me than she would venture to do to you. Her heart burns within her to do some good and great thing. She would like to go on a foreign mission; to teach the children of the heathen, to carry light into dark places."

"Nonsense!" exclaimed Joshua, contemptuously. "Let her stay at home and mind her own business. That is a woman's mission. Remember what St. Paul says about women."

"St. Paul had not the privilege of knowing Naomi Haggard," said the rapturous Nicholas. "But I will not presume to argue with you, sir; only tell me that she is well and happy."

"She is well, I am thankful to say; and I suppose she is happy. She has no cause for unhappiness."

"The female mind is a delicate thing, Mr. Haggard, and common blessings do not always suffice for its contentment. Has Naomi any thought of settling?"

"You mean, getting married?" said Joshua. "No, I think not. We have heard nothing about that yet a while."

"None but a superior person would suit Naomi."

"I think not; and her only admirer—not an avowed admirer as yet—is a person so far her superior in birth and fortune that I am doubtful whether I do right in encouraging their acquaintance."

Nicholas Wild's cheek paled at this. He had long ago despaired of winning Naomi for himself, but it was not the less a pang to hear that she was likely to be won by another, and that other a man of higher rank than himself. This gave a keener point to the knife that stabbed him, for Nicholas, though a good fellow, was not large-minded, and was inclined to believe that to be a gentleman by birth and fortune was to belong to the children of Belial.

"It would be hard to find any body worthy of Naomi," he said, "least of all a pampered idler, with nothing but fine clothes and a fine name to recommend him."

"The young man I speak of has not been very kindly treated by fortune, though birth has made him a gentleman, and he will have a fair estate by-and-by. You remember young Pentreath, the squire's son?"

"Remember him? yes; a pale-faced slip of a youth. He comes of a bad race, if all is true that folks say about the old squire."

"All that folks say of their neighbors rarely is true," replied Joshua. "I dare say the squire led a wild life in his youth, and I know that he is a hard, uncharitable man in his age; but there is no reason his son should resemble him in character any more than he does in looks, and there have seldom been father and son less alike."

Joshua told his disciple about the wreck of the *Dolphin*, and the friendship that had since arisen between Oswald and the minister's family.

"I have very little reason to suppose that his feeling for Naomi is any thing warmer than the friendship he has for the rest of us," concluded Joshua; "but they have been a good deal together, and they seem to have many ideas in common."

"He could not know her and not love her," replied Nicholas, warmly. "How does the old squire take it?"

"You mean, does he approve his son's intimacy with me and mine?" said Joshua. "So far as I can discover, he neither approves nor disapproves. He lets his son take his own course in all things, except spending money. His poor sordid soul seems to be so absorbed in the task of scraping together every sixpence he can screw out of the land, that he gives no care or heed to his son's existence. The youth who ran away to sea is not more remote from his father than the son who lives in the same house with him."

Here the conversation ended. They had arrived at the village where Nicholas lived. He had a comfortable lodging of two clean little rooms in a stone cottage, set in a square plot of land chiefly devoted to the growth of potatoes, but beautified by a few rose-bushes and a row of tiger-lilies on each side of the narrow path leading from the little wooden gate to the cottage door. His landlady had prepared quite a banquet in honor of the minister—a potato pasty and a boiled leg of pork, with cabbage enough for a large family.

Here Joshua lodged for the night. He set out at seven o'clock next morning, after a comfortable breakfast, on the first stage of his homeward journey. He might have taken the coach at Helston, only nine miles off, but he had made up his mind to walk at least as far as Truro, not always taking the straightest road thither, but taking a peep at various spots that had been dear and familiar to him in those wandering days of his youth, when he had carried the glad tidings from hamlet to hamlet and homestead to homestead, dropping unawares upon sequestered households far from the voices of this world, as if he had been in very truth a heaven-sent messenger.

"I'm afraid you'll find the journey tiring," said Nicholas, at parting; "the sun is so hot, and the roads are dusty."

"I love a hot sun, and I must put up with the dust," answered Joshua, cheerily. "It will do my heart good to see the old places and the old faces, and to find that I have not been forgotten."

He shouldered his knapsack, wrung Nicholas's hand for the last time, gave him a hearty blessing, and walked away upon the white high-road with that swinging stride of his which showed how easy such exercise was to him.

It was a glorious summer day—the blue bright sky without a cloud, the warm earth breathing perfume. This village among the hills—two straggling rows of cottages bordering a broad high-road—seemed to be set upon the apex of this Western world. There lay the bright green sea, ever so far below yonder dip in the broad fields, that stretched away to the edge of the cliff. No indication of the rock-bound shore below—the craggy arches and peaks and ragged bowlders—was to be seen from here, only corn-fields and meadows sloping to the cliff, and in the distance a castellated mansion rising from the soil, gaunt and lonely, like the castle of Giant Blunderbore.

Never had Joshua Haggard been in a happier frame of mind than on this fair June morning. He loved the sunshine, the soft westerly breeze, which warmed him even more than the sun. It was some hereditary instinct, perhaps, from his Spanish forefathers, some innate love of sunburned sierras and a torrid sky, that made him so fond of the breathless midsummer weather and the fierce noontide sun. He walked on for a good many miles without a halt, and in this solitary walk fell into meditation upon his family and their prospects. That conversation yesterday afternoon with Nicholas Wild had set him thinking about his daughter and Oswald Pentreath.

He was not an ambitious man, either for himself or for his children. He was not a man who sought for earthly distinctions or set his affections on the things of this world. Yet it pleased him to think that his daughter might be raised in the social scale by marriage with a gentleman and a man who took his rank from the land. In the minds of these country people there is a natural love of the soil which makes landed estate seem to them above all other fortune. A manufacturer with a million would have been a very small man at Combhollow compared with Squire Pentreath, whose race had occupied the land from time immemorial.

"Why should he not choose her for his wife?" argued Joshua. "She is a lady in education and principle. She has the manners of a lady, and beauty that is given to few women, be their rank of the highest. As for fortune—well, I could give her enough to make the marriage no imprudent one for Oswald Pentreath. I must get to understand the state of that young man's feelings. Judith may be right, after all. We have been going on too easily, perhaps. I must ascertain the old squire's sentiments. I will not have my daughter trifled with or slighted."

Having come to this conclusion, Joshua Haggard dismissed the subject. He was too clear-brained and definite to go on revolving his ideas in a mill. There had never yet been confusion or perplexity in his mind upon any subject; no question had ever arisen that he had not been able to grapple with and answer satisfactorily. But then, as he himself said to Nicholas Wild, his life journey had been an easy one. Heretofore Fate had given him no hard riddles to solve. But every man in his time meets the Sphinx, and must answer or die. Joshua's time had not yet come.

Very beautiful was that far Cornish land in the summer noon—a large, wild beauty, but neither desolate nor gloomy. The undulating fields had a fertile, prosperous look, the patches of common were golden with furze, and all the water-pools shone like jewels under that bounteous glorifier of all things, the sun. Three miles short of Penmoyle, a village made dear to him by pleasant youthful memories, and where he had determined to take his rest, Joshua Haggard turned aside from the sandy road, little better than a lane on this steep hill-side, and strolled on to a bit of rugged common-land, all hillock and hollow, with water here and there in the deeper hollows, and furze ablaze upon all the hillocks. Here, he thought, was a pleasant place for half an hour's repose. He had walked seven or eight miles, and had three more to walk to Penmoyle, where he meant to dine with some of his old friends. The Penmoyle dinner-hour would be over by an hour or two when he arrived, but the land was full of plenty. There would be a slice of corned beef or Cornish ham, or a wedge of cold pasty, at his service, to say nothing of crisply baked cakes, fried potatoes, and bacon—luxuries which the minister's soul renounced as dangerous, savoring too much of Esau's fatal feast.

Nothing could be prettier in its own peculiar way than that little bit of common on the top of the sandy hill. Perhaps it was its peacefulness that made it so lovely, or the summer atmosphere, in itself so delicious that it would have beautified a desert. There was a silence, save of sweet, vague summer sounds: the humming of insects, the whispering of that soft west wind, and presently, bursting out with a shrill gush, the carol of the sky-lark aloft, a speck in the dazzling blue.

Joshua Haggard sighed the sigh of utter contentment as he stretched himself on the mossy turf (the soil here grew more moss than grass), and inhaled the almond perfume of the furze—a warm sweetness, as if those golden butterfly blossoms smelled of the sun that had given them their color and their bloom.

It seemed as if that sigh of his woke the sleeping nymph of the scene: for there came in answer to it a faint fluttering sound like the rustle of a woman's garment—no *frôlement* or *fron-frou* of rich silken tissue, but a little fluttering noise of softer, humbler drapery, such as poor folks wear.

Joshua Haggard turned his head a little way, and looked across the ragged clump of furze that topped the hillock on which he had thrown himself. There was a tiny pool of water in the hollow below, and on the other side of the hillock sat a girl, bareheaded under the summer sun, a little bundle lying on the turf beside her, her bare feet in the water. They shone silver white under that clear water, and Joshua's heart gave a curious thrill—half fear, half wonder—as if he had seen a fairy.

There came back to his memory stories that he had loved in his childhood, before he had grown to believe that there were no other stories save Bible stories that were good for a man to read or admire. Dimly there came back to him a legend of a summer noontide such as this, and a princess transformed by wicked arts into a beggar wench washing her toil-worn feet by the wayside.

He could not see the girl's face as he looked down the slope on which she sat, with her back to the hillock and to him; but he saw she had the princess's long fair hair, fair as flax and bright as the silk his children used to wind from the cocoons of their silk-worms in the autumn evenings a few years ago.

"I am not much like the prince who met the disguised princess," he thought, smiling at his fancy, "nor yet like the lucky adventurer I used to read of in those fairy books. Poor child! I dare say she is some miner's daughter, who has been over the hills yonder to carry her father his dinner. I wonder whether she has ever read her Bible. I used to teach many such fair-haired children when I was in this part of the country years ago."

The furze rustled as he bent over to look down at that sunlit head with its loose flaxen hair, and the girl started and looked up at him, and gave a little cry of fear on seeing that dark, intent face bent above her.

She took her feet hastily out of the water, snatched up her bundle, and sprung up as if about to fly; but Joshua stepped quickly down from the hillock and stood beside her.

"Why are you running away, child? Are you afraid of me?"

She looked up at him with great blue eyes—those rare eyes that are absolutely blue, the azure of the summer sky—looked up at him in evident terror.

"Let me go!" she cried, as his strong hand grasped her arm, gently but firmly.

"My child, I have no desire to detain you. But you mustn't run away from me as if I were some terrible monster. I will not do you any harm. I would do you good if I could, poor wandering lamb. Alas! I fear the world has not used you kindly, or the sight of a strange face would not scare you so."

"You won't take me back to them!" cried the girl, with a shudder.

"I will take you nowhere that you do not wish to go. But who are these people whom you fear so much?"

"The people I belong to."

"Your father and mother?"

"No. I never had a father or mother—not to know them."

"Who are these people, then?"

"The strollers. I was at Helston fair with them yesterday; and I ran away and slept under a hay-stack last night, and came on here this morning; and oh, please, please, please, good gentleman, don't take me back to them!" she cried, clasping her hands piteously.

"Strolling players—mountebanks, you mean?"

"Yes. They act and dance and tumble at fairs and places; and they have some horses, and sometimes they call themselves a circus; and they made me dance on the horses' backs and jump through hoops. I fell once, and was nearly killed: it was only the sawdust saved me, they said."

"Poor child! Have you been with them long?"

"All my life," answered the girl, opening those innocent blue eyes. "I belong to them; I never had any other home or any other friends."

"My poor lost lamb! And were they unkind?"

The girl's red under-lip—fuller than the upper, like Sophia's—pouted a little as she meditated this question.

"They never starved me," she said; "they did not beat me often."

"But they did sometimes strike you?" cried the minister, indignantly.

"Yes, when I was stupid and could not learn what they wanted. I was fond of the horses and the jumping through hoops, though it was dangerous; but they wanted me to learn tricks with cards, and conjuring. I was stupid at that: the numbers puzzled me. And then the Black Cap-

tain—he's the master of us all—used to get into a passion, and hit me, and swear at me—such dreadful words."

The very recollection was appalling, for she burst into tears and sobbed passionately for a minute or two. Joshua was accustomed to be the confidant and consoler of other people's troubles. He patted this wanderer gently on the shoulder, and comforted her with a few soothing words.

"You shall not go back to these people, child, if I can prevent it," he said: "and you shall learn to read your Bible. You have never learned that, I fear."

"Is that the book people read in the churches?" she asked.

"Yes, and in chapels, and in every Christian home."

"What's that?" asked the girl, wonderingly; "I don't know what it means."

Then Joshua tried in simplest, easiest phrases to tell her what Christianity meant, and what its Founder had done for men. She listened meekly, and understood some part of what he said; but even that much was dimly comprehended by her. The veil of ignorance which shrouded her young mind was too dense to be penetrated easily by the light of truth.

"Tell me how you came to belong to these strollers," said Joshua, presently.

"I don't know. I belonged to them always."

"You have no memory that goes back beyond that strolling life? Your mind can not pierce to something behind that—far away—half forgotten—a different life, a fixed home?"

"No. The first thing I can remember is a little close room upon wheels, a room that was always moving, the hedges and trees going by outside. I used to watch them move. I thought it was the road that moved, not us; and I remember the little dark corner where I slept, squeezed in by the wall, and how I used to be almost smothered sometimes. That was when my first mother was alive. She was kind to me, and I loved her dearly; but she used to get tipsy sometimes, poor thing. She danced on the tack-rope, and she was very clever. She had been a rope-dancer in London, they said; and one night at Truro she had been drinking, and lost her balance, and fell from the rope, and hurt her head against a post, and she was very bad, and soon after she died."

Tears came into the girl's eyes as she told of her protectress's fate.

"How do you know that this woman was not really your mother?" asked Joshua.

"Because they all told me I had no father or mother. I don't know how they came by me, but I belonged to them, and none of them belonged to me. Somebody once said they had bought me. When Susannah Beck was dead I had another mother, called Harriet Long, and she was cruel, and used to beat me if I didn't learn the steps or the songs she taught me quick enough. She was a dancer too, but on the ground, not on ropes; and she sang and acted, and tried to do every thing. She didn't drink like poor Susannah, but she was greedy for money, and used to make me go round with a tambourine among the crowd begging, when the Black Captain—he did the ground and lofty—wasn't looking, and then used to take the money from me; and one day the Captain heard of it, and he beat her and me too, and then she took a dislike to me, and used to be very cruel; and then I grew up, and she said I was too big for my business; and then I made up my mind to run away the first time I could get off; and I watched and waited, and last night, at Helston, Harriet was asleep in the van, and the others were almost all tipsy, and I crept out into the fields. It was warm and starlight; I felt quite happy. I ran for a long, long way, till I heard the sea washing against the rocks; and then I came to a farm, and crept in among some loose hay beside a hay-stack, and it smelled so sweet, and I forgot that I was hungry, and fell asleep, and when I woke, the sun was shining and a little field-mouse was looking at me with its bright eyes, and I was ever so much hungrier."

"Poor child! Have you had nothing to eat since then?"

"Yes; a woman in a village I came through gave me a great thick slice of bread-and-cheese."

"Good woman! And now tell me what you mean to do?"

"To work in the fields, if they will let me."

"Field-labor! You don't look much like that. Show me your hands."

She laid a thin little hand confidently in Joshua's broad brown palm. Quite a delicate hand, sunburned on the outside, but with a soft pink palm and filbert-shaped nails; a hand that had done no hard work, and which, according to a popular theory, might be taken as a sign of a good lineage.

"My child, you were never made for field-labor," said the minister, with kindly seriousness; "we must find some other work for you. It would be better for you to be a servant, if any one would be patient with you and teach you for a little while. I feel sure you are teachable."

"I learned all but the card tricks," exclaimed the girl, innocently; "I know the rabbit trick, and I learned the nosegay trick and the pocket-handkerchief trick very quickly; but the numbers were so puzzling."

"Are you clever at your needle?"

"Nobody ever taught me to work. I used to mend the dresses sometimes, and sew on gold lace and spangles; but I'm afraid the stitches weren't very neat — they used to be so big." And the damsel measured off a Brobdingnagian stitch on her slender forefinger.

"You might be taught to work. You might be taught almost any thing, I am sure," mused Joshua, looking intently at the fair sweet face, so delicately, purely chiseled, with the pearly tints of a Greuze and the azure eyes he so loved to paint—just that exquisite ideal of girlhood's innocence which approaches as nearly as earthly mold can come to the angelic, and which may mean much or little. So innocent, so artless, so unconscious, so divinely lovely may Gretchen have appeared to the student in that vision in the witch's kitchen. This girl was of the Gretchen type, that fair Saxon beauty which seems made for love, and to have lived its hour and fulfilled its end when it has won its first lover. It was not the Cleopatra beauty, created to subjugate and hold a triad of heroes, but the transient perfection of a rose in June, which blooms once and for one only.

"If you will trust me and come with me, I will get you more fitting work than field-labor," said Joshua. "I have plenty of friends in the next village, and I shall find some one who will give you food and shelter for my sake. You will have to work for your bread, of course, and to be obedient."

"I always did what Harriet told me," answered the girl. "I will do any thing to earn my bread."

"Any thing that is honest," replied the minister's grave voice. "I hope you know the difference between right and wrong."

"I know that it is wrong to tell lies or to steal, but most of our people did it."

"You did not, I hope?"

"No, I tried to tell a lie once, but the words wouldn't come. Something inside me seemed to rise against it. I felt as if I should choke; and I thought, after all, they could only beat me, and I told them the truth."

"That was brave and good of you. And when you have learned to read your Bible you will love truth still more, and you will know many things that you do not know now."

"I'm afraid that will be a long time," said the girl, despondently, "for I don't know any letters except those our clever pony knew. It was he that taught me to count."

"A pony taught you?"

"Well, perhaps I taught myself when I had to show the pony. 'Now, Mr. Maccaroni, show us number ten,' I used to say, and the pony used to put his hoof upon the card with the number; and he could tell the days of the week, and a lot more."

"You shall learn to read your Bible, my child, and to work with your needle, and to be industrious in proper useful duties; and you must forget all about the pony."

"Poor Maccaroni!" sighed the girl. "I was very fond of him. He used to put his kind old nose upon my shoulder, and against my cheek; and I used to fancy that he pitied me. He was so clever, you see. I think he knew I was unhappy."

"What is your name, my dear child?" inquired Joshua, thoughtfully. Even in Penmoyle some kind of introduction would be necessary, and it would be as well to make sure of his protégée's name before he presented her to his friends in that village.

"Oh, I've had ever so many names," answered the girl, frankly. "Sometimes they called me Mam-selle Fantini, and sometimes The Little Wonder."

"Oh, dear, those outlandish names would not do!" exclaimed Joshua. "Were you never baptized?"

"If that's any thing to do with church, I should think not," replied the girl. "But they used to call me Cynthia generally. Perhaps that was my name."

"Cynthia! It's not a common name; but it's pretty enough, and it will do."

They have rather a leaning to fine names in Cornwall; and Mr. Haggard was not appalled by this fanciful name of Cynthia, even for a servant-girl.

"Come," he said, looking at his big silver watch, a huge machine in a double case, "if you've rested enough, we had better be moving on."

"You are not going to take me back to them?" asked the girl again, with an affrighted look.

"My child, can you not understand that an honest man's yea or nay is as good as an oath? I have promised not to give you back to your people. I am going to take you where you may earn your living, and learn to be a Christian."

"Is that as hard as conjuring?" asked Cynthia, simply.

"Oh child, child, what sad darkness—here, in this land of light! What need to seek far away for the heathen, when we have them round us, near us, calling upon us mutely, like dumb creatures neglected and in pain?"

Cynthia had dried her bare feet on the sun-scorched grass — such pretty little feet, arched and slender. If such feet were put up at auction at Christie & Manson's, peeresses would be racing one another for them. She tied on a pair of dilapidated boots, the most miserable things, which hung round her feet like ragged sandals. Had she been Scotch or Irish, she would have gone barefoot and been comfortable; but being an English girl, these apologies for shoes seemed to her better than nothing.

She took up her little bundle again, and was ready to follow her new friend. They stood side by side under that cloudless blue, the lark singing loud and clear, bees humming, sweet wild flowers abloom under their feet, the distant sea gleaming yonder above the hills, like a strip of brightness against the sky. They seemed alone upon this lonely earth, alone under that azure heaven: of human voices there was no sound, only the glad chorus of Nature—bird and insect, waving trees and falling waters.

"Come," said Joshua again; and they walked down to the white road side by side and in silence.

CHAPTER VI.

CYNTHIA GOES INTO SERVICE.

"You are not too tired to walk three miles farther?" Joshua asked kindly, when Cynthia and he had gone a little way along the sunny road.

"Oh no; I have rested, and my feet don't burn as they did before I bathed them."

"You were very tired when you sat down to rest on that common."

"Very tired. I felt as if I should like to have lain down by the roadside, and never get up any more. I thought that perhaps I should go on walking all day, and at night, when I was quite worn out, I should find a hay-stack, like the one where I slept last night, and I should lie down among the sweet-smelling hay, and never wake any more. I would rather have slept forever than waked to go back to Harriet and the Black Captain."

"You shall never go back to them. If your father and mother are not among them, they can have no claim on you. Remember that always. I shall place you with some good, kind people; and if ever those strollers find you, and try to take you away, you must refuse to go with them. You are mistress of your own life; they have no right to take you."

"Ah, but you don't know how strong the Captain is," said the girl, despondingly.

Joshua saw that she was not yet capable of learning that lesson of self-reliance which he wished to teach. She was not much more than a child in years, and had but a child's knowledge of life.

"Have no fear of the Captain or any one else," he said, "so long as you learn to read your Bible, and do your duty by the light that will give you. This Black Captain is a gypsy, I suppose?"

"He is very dark, with a skin like tarnished copper, and black fierce eyes, and he wears gold rings in his ears."

"Forget that you ever saw him," said Joshua. "I doubt if he will ever trouble your life again."

He was thinking what a transformation domestic life would make in this wild flower he had found by the wayside. That flaxen hair, now falling in picturesque disorder over the girl's neck and shoulders, would be neatly bound up under a thick muslin mob-cap. A pity to hide any thing so pretty; but, then, "it is good for a woman's head to be covered;" and a flower in a well-kept garden can not bloom in nature's profuse beauty like the starry traveler's-joy in the hedges. A neat cotton gown, muslin neckerchief, and large white apron would replace those disorderly rags, which now hung loosely on the slender figure. Her old companions would hardly recognize the runaway in this decent attire, should chance bring them to Penmoyle, which lay off the beaten tracks, and was about the sleepiest place imaginable.

Joshua began the walk at his usual pace of four miles an hour, but soon discovered that his companion was flagging, and altered his step to suit her. They were an hour and a half walking those three miles, and the minister questioned Cynthia still more closely upon her past life—that comfortless, wandering childhood, which held no sunny memories of childish pleasures: that unprotected girlhood, among dark scenes and dark minds. He found her a poor benighted creature, ignorant of all those things which, in his mind, were most needful or most hallowed; but he found no evil in her. She had lived among sinners, yet seemed to have remained sinless. No unclean or degrading thought shaped itself upon those lovely lips. It seemed to Joshua that in her beauty and youth there was a spiritual purity, which, even in contact with unholy things, had escaped all contamination.

Their way lay along a parched high-road, sometimes up hill, sometimes down hill. They were within half a mile of Penmoyle, when they turned into a narrow lane, between tall ragged hedges full of dog-roses and honeysuckle.

"Is this the way to the place where I'm to stop?" asked Cynthia, very tired.

"Yes; we are very near the village now."

"Do you live there?"

"No. My home is in Devonshire, a long way off."

"I'm sorry for that. I would rather have been your servant than any one else's, because you are so good to me."

The soft blue eyes looked up at him full of trust; sweeter eyes, it seemed to him, than had ever been lifted to his face before.

Perhaps that Cornish village of Penmoyle was as sleepy a place as one could easily discover upon this varied earth. There was no reason for its existence save that the fields must be tilled, and flocks and herds tended, and that the human beasts of burden who perform those agricultural duties must live somewhere. Yet slumberous, sequestered as it was, Penmoyle had a completeness and beauty with which Providence has not endowed all Cornish villages. It was an ancient settlement, and had its old priory church and its patron saint, and there were yet traces of the priory that had first given the spot name and dignity. It was the centre of a fertile oasis amidst the wild hills, and the meadows round about were full of fatness. On one side of the village street was the post-office: on the other an old rambling inn, with a good deal of empty stabling. Opposite the inn stood a clump of horse-chestnuts—noble old trees which made a shadow and a darkness beneath them, where the tramp and wanderer lay down to rest in sultry August noontides, and forgot all weariness and care under those spreading boughs, and where the village children played at sundown. To the right of this chestnut-grove stood the village dame's school—not a free institution, but a self-supporting academy, which exacted fourpence a week from its scholars—a white wooden cottage with neat latticed casements and green palings: a lattice porch, myrtle-shaded; a green door and brass knocker, exactly like the door of a doll's-house; a wicker bird-cage in the right parlor window, and a brazen one in the window on the left; a row of geraniums and mignonnette in vermilion pots on every window-sill.

It was three o'clock, and a Saturday afternoon, when Joshua Haggard and his companion entered the village. School was over for the week, and the voices of the children pealed shrilly from beneath the chestnut leafage. Joshua went straight to that myrtle-shadowed porch and knocked with the shining brass knocker; the girl standing a little way behind him, wondering at his audacity in approaching such a splendid abode.

The door was opened by a spinster of middle age, tall and thin, with dark hair neatly arranged in little bunches of stiffly curling ringlets on each side of her small square forehead. She wore a flowered challis gown, which Cynthia considered absolutely beautiful; and her neat waist was zoned by a broad ribbon band, to match the challis, tightly clasped by a large gilt buckle. Her square muslin collar was trimmed with pillow-lace, and her brooch was a jewel to wonder at. Round her brow she wore a circlet of narrow black velvet, and the ends of her long gold earrings touched her shoulders. Her eyes were black and bright like jet beads; her nose sharp and of noticeable length: her complexion russet and ruddy, with a hard look like winter apples.

At sight of Joshua she gave a shrill scream, expressive at once of wonder and delight.

"My!" she exclaimed, "did I ever? Who would have thought it? Debbie dear, come here."

This summons to somebody unseen was shrieked in a still higher key; and from the little parlor to the right emerged a second figure in a challis gown, so like the first in person and in all outward adornments that Cynthia stared from one to the other, transfixed by astonishment.

They were not twin sisters, these middle-aged

maidens; but sisters who live together, and have their garments cut off the same piece, are apt to become the image of each other. The Miss Weblings had spent five-and-forty years of life in constant companionship. They thought alike; eat and drank the same things, and by the same measure; dressed alike, walked alike, spoke alike, and uttered the same ejaculations with the simultaneousness of a single machine.

Deborah threw up her hands and eyebrows on beholding Mr. Haggard exactly as Priscilla had done a minute earlier.

"My!" she cried. "To think, now! Did you ever?"

Then followed a perfect gush of rejoicing from both spinsters, who took the minister between them and drew him into the best parlor. Both parlors were the pink of neatness, and ornate after their manner, but the parlor in which the brazen canary cage hung was the best par excellence. It was the room for Sunday-afternoon occupation and stately tea-drinkings, the room in which to lay the dessert on Christmas-day.

"The cowslip wine, Priscilla," cried the elder sister.

"And the seed-cake, love," added the younger.

Cynthia stood in the porch all this time, mutely wondering.

"And what blessed Providence has brought you this way, dear sir?" asked Deborah, while Priscilla unlocked a closet in the wainscot which was half as large as the room, and produced therefrom a decanter of dark-brown wine, and a seed-cake in a green dessert-plate.

Mr. Haggard explained his mission in the West briefly, while Priscilla filled a glass of wine and cut a wedge of cake.

"And you came this way on foot on purpose to see old friends," said Deborah. "How good of you! You don't know how we have missed your blessed teaching, and thought and talked of you since you were last at Penmoyle. Do you find the place improved?" she asked, with an air of latent pride.

"It looks as pretty and as peaceful as ever," replied Joshua.

"Oh, but didn't you take notice? They've built a new house on the left-hand side as you come from the Truro road. It makes quite an addition to the place. And Mrs. Simmons at the shop has enlarged her window, and has painted herself up a bit outside; and the church vane has been gilded. We were quite busy last spring, I assure you."

"And your school? I hope that has been going on prosperously?"

"We've been very well off for pupils, but I'm afraid children get slower and duller every year. It seems harder work to teach 'em. If we hadn't the comfort of knowing that we've got a nice little bit of property laid by, it would be too wearying. But when one knows one's old age is provided for, one can bear a good deal. You've come to make a bit of a stay, I hope, Mr. Haggard?"

"No, indeed; I'm sorry to say I'm not free to do that. I must get across to Truro in time for the night coach, for I must be at Combinllow for service to-morrow. There's no one to minister to my flock when I'm away."

On this followed lamentations from both sisters. They had hoped that he would stay; that he would preach in their tabernacle, which was a little bit of a building with a sloping roof, next door to the shop—a building that had begun life as a stable.

"I want to see all old friends at Penmoyle," said Joshua, this village having been one of his favorite abiding-places in the days of his Cornish wanderings; "but I came to you first, Miss Webling, because I've a favor to ask of you. There's a girl outside—"

"Yes, I saw her," cried Priscilla, eagerly, "a tramp. And she's there still, I declare," looking sideways at the porch. "Was there ever such impudence?"

"I brought her," said Joshua.

"You! I thought she had been begging of you. She looks an awful character."

"I do not believe there is any harm in her," said the minister; "and, then, remember who said that He was sent to the lost sheep of Israel. It is the duty of His ministers to seek and to save those that are lost. I found that stray lamb by the wayside."

"Ah, dear Mr. Haggard, I'm afraid she has imposed upon your goodness."

"I don't think so. I have questioned her closely, and she seems to me innocent and good, little more than a child in years, and in sore need of help and protection. Now, it struck me, my kind friends, that you would be the very people to help her."

"We! Oh, Mr. Haggard, when you know that we never could abide a grain of dust about our place! A creature like that, with ragged yellow hair, and not a thing upon her that isn't in tatters! What could we do for her?"

"Take her in, and make her clean and clothe her comfortably, and teach her to read her Bible and earn her living honestly. That's what I want you to do, Miss Webling."

"But consider, Mr. Haggard, the children. A creature with hair like that! What an example for them!"

"Twist her hair up into a knob like your own, or cut it off if you like; only make a Christian of her. You used to feel an interest in missionary work, Miss Priscilla."

"Yes, dear Mr. Haggard, but I never held with mixing things that ought to be kept separate. Converting the heathen is a good and gracious work, but you don't want to mix up heathens with ready-made Christians. Of course there's very little Deborah and I wouldn't do to oblige you; still at the same time—"

"Put me out of the question, Miss Priscilla, and think of the higher motive. 'I was a stranger, and ye took me in.' That poor child is waiting all this time, and I know she is faint and tired. Take her in and do what you can for her, and I'll tell you her story afterward."

Priscilla looked at Deborah and Deborah at Priscilla, and then they both looked askance out of the window, descrying Cynthia's drooping figure through the lattice of the porch.

"She looks tired," said Deborah, "and she doesn't look as if there was much harm in her, as tramps go. She doesn't look violent."

"It would go against us to refuse you anything, Mr. Haggard," said Priscilla. "But when we have dressed her comfortably and given her a good meal, what are we to do with her?"

"We'll settle that afterward. Teach her to

be your servant, if you can. She looks bright and teachable. You have no servant, I think?"

"No. We've tried a girl more than once; but girls are more trouble than they're worth, and make more dirt than they clean. What would such a girl as that be. I should like to know?"

"Perhaps better than the common run of girls. She seems to me to have more than the common intelligence."

"Well," said Miss Webling, decisively, "to oblige you, dear Mr. Haggard, we'll call her in, and make her decent, and give her something to eat. That reminds me that I've a question to ask you," added the spinster, with solemnity. "Have you dined?"

"I did very well as I came along," replied Joshua, evasively; "but I am ready to admit that a slice of cold pasty would be acceptable."

"You shall have it hot in less than half an hour. There's a couple of pasties in the oven. We always bake on Saturday, so as to have something cold for Sunday. They'll be ready in about twenty minutes. You can lay the cloth in the other room, Priscilla, while I see to the young woman."

"If I hadn't known you were a good soul, I shouldn't have come here to-day, Miss Webling," said Joshua, with a grateful look.

Deborah went back to the neat little passage, and opened the door. The girl looked up at her with rather an alarmed expression. This image of feminine respectability had something of a Gorgon-like aspect to her, although she vastly admired the flowered challis gown and the brazen buckle.

"Come in and be washed, young woman," said Deborah, somewhat sternly; and the address was so alarming that Cynthia shrunk away a little, and would perhaps have refused the invitation, if Joshua had not put his head out of the adjacent parlor just at this moment.

"You will do whatever this kind lady tells you, my child," said the minister, with mild authority; and on this Cynthia obeyed as meekly as a lamb, and followed Miss Webling into the back premises at the end of the narrow passage. Here they came to a neat brick-floored kitchen, with a grate and oven-door that shone like a jeweler's shop; and beyond that there was a secondary kitchen or scullery, also brick-floored, with a stone sink and a pump in one corner, a copper in another, and a couple of washing tubs in a third. It was into this chamber of purification that Deborah conducted the wanderer.

She hoisted one of the washing tubs upon the sink, after turning up her scanty gown and pinning it round her waist by way of preparation, and pumped it nearly full of the pure spring water.

"There," she said, showing the girl a little wooden soap-bowl, "there are soap and water for you; and now, if you've any notion of cleanliness, take advantage of your opportunity."

"I shall be very glad to wash the dust off, thank you, ma'am," answered the girl, submissively.

Miss Webling cast a glance round her scullery, as if to ascertain that there was nothing convenient for surreptitious removal; and then left the stroller to her ablutions, after pointing out the round towel, a most uncompromising strip of huckaback.

Miss WEBLING TAKES IN THE STRANGER.

"When you've made yourself thoroughly clean you can come into my kitchen," said Miss Webling, "and I'll see what I can do for you in the shape of clothes."

"Thank you, ma'am. I should like a flowery gown like yours," replied the girl, innocently.

"Nonsense, child. This was my Sunday gown for the last three years. I've only just taken to it for workaday afternoons."

And Miss Webling departed, locking the scullery door upon her doubtful guest.

Priscilla was in the kitchen, putting some things upon a tray to lay the cloth, and Mr. Haggard had gone out to look up some of his old friends, pending the preparation of his meal.

"Come upstairs with me, Prissy, and let us see if we can find any thing for this girl," said Deborah; and the two maidens ascended a cork-screw staircase to their lavender-scented bed-chamber, and there knelt side by side before a large trunk, in which they kept their superannuated clothing. Every thing had been neatly folded and carefully put away, and there was a perfume of rose-leaves and spices among the folds of linen and woolen stuff. The sisters made their selection very carefully, pondering long over certain garments, and then putting them back into the box again, as too good to be given away.

"If we knew that a good use would be made of them, we should be more inclined to make a sacrifice," said Priscilla; "but a creature of that kind may sell them directly she has left us."

Finally, after much serious discussion, a choice was made: such curious antiquated under-garments, with a great deal of frilling, the fabric yellow with age; a gown of printed cotton, and of a pattern which the modern mind associates with bed-furniture, and which would be hard to find nowadays hanging in long wet strips from the lofty ceilings of Hoyle's Printing Works, or rotating upon endless webs, or being boiled into a pulpy state in giant coppers.

Miss Webling went back to the kitchen with the bundle of clothes, unlocked the door of the scullery, and told her prisoner to come forth. The spinster's love of the beautiful had not been developed by culture, yet even she was moved to admiration at the vision which appeared at her call.

The girl's fair face was glowing and rosy from the bath, her eyes shone clear and bright, her lips were the color of opening rose-buds, her sunny hair hung over her shoulders in rippling showers, her neck and arms were pure as ivory against the dark bodice of her ragged petticoat. She had not put on the tattered blue-and-white cotton gown which had served as her outer garment.

"Gracious!" exclaimed Miss Webling. "You look all the better for a little soap and water. Come here, Prissy, and let's make her as decent as we can."

Priscilla came, armed with a very hard brush and a bone comb. Deborah laid a newspaper upon the bright red bricks, and bid the girl sit down on a little three-legged stool with her feet on the paper, lest those dusty shoes of hers should sully the bricks, which had been reddened that morning. Then Priscilla came with her brush and operated upon the stroller's hair, taking up the soft flaxen tresses in a gingerly manner.

Finding that soft hair very clean, she began a vigorous brushing, and then twisted the long tresses in one compact rope, and wound them round in a hard ball at the back of the small head. This new arrangement curiously altered the character of the girl's face, and gave something of a puritan look to the fair oval countenance. All that was wild and picturesque in that girlish head had been scared away by Miss Priscilla's comb and brush.

"Now," said Deborah, approvingly, "you begin to look decent."

"It feels so strange to have a knob at the back of my head," said Cynthia, shaking the tight lump of hair.

"Ah, I'm afraid you've come from a place where most Christian-like things are strange," sighed Priscilla.

Then came the process of dressing. All the garments were too loose and too long for the slender figure, and had to be tied up and buttoned over and generally adapted as they were put on. When the gown came, that striped brown-and-yellow cotton, Cynthia gave a little shudder at its hideousness. But it was whole, and her own was in tatters. She was obliged to feel grateful for the exchange. The huge leg-of-mutton sleeves almost swallowed her up, and one of Miss Webling's frilled collars hung over her shoulders like a small cape.

"You look clean and respectable," said Deborah, derisively; "and that's a good deal to have done for you."

Mr. Haggard had returned by this time. The table was laid in the every-day parlor, and the pasties had been taken out of the oven. They had a savory smell, beef and potatoes and onions entering into their composition, and the crust was brown and crisp. Poor Cynthia looked at them with longing eyes, as Miss Webling reviewed them on the dresser, choosing the best-baked for the minister's regalement.

Joshua seemed somewhat disinclined to sit down at the neatly arranged table. He looked at his watch, made some calculation about the coach, walked to the window, looked absently out into the sunny street, and appeared unconscious that his meal was ready.

"The pasty will be cold, dear Mr. Haggard," said Deborah, perplexed by this absence of mind.

"I beg your pardon. Yes, the pasty looks excellent. By-the-way, that poor child; she has had nothing but a slice of bread since last night. She must be hungry. If she might have a bit of this excellent pasty, now."

Miss Webling inwardly rebelled at the suggestion. What, this potato-pasty, which she had made with her own hands, of the choicest materials, and had baked with greatest care for Sabbath consumption! She remembered exceedingly that Mr. Haggard had always been careless and unthinking about victuals.

"I think if Priscilla were to cut her a plate of bread-and-cheese—" she began.

"This seems ever so much nicer," said the minister. "Let her come in here and have some. I want her to tell you her story, poor child; for I think she will win your sympathy by her artlessness."

Miss Webling complied, inwardly reluctant. She opened the parlor door, and called,

"Girl, come here."

And then she cut a plateful of pasty, and set

it on a little table under the wicker bird-cage—a table apart. It was not to be permitted that a tramp should sit at table with the minister. The minister's Master may have sat at meat with curious people; but that was a long time ago, before manners had reached that apogee of enlightenment to which they had attained at Pennoyle.

Cynthia came shyly, feeling in her brown-and-yellow gown as if she had been transformed into somebody else.

"Good gracious!" cried Joshua, not altogether approvingly, "what have you done to her?"

"We have done our best to make her tidy," replied Deborah, with dignity; "but, of course, our things are not altogether befitting her station."

"That wouldn't matter so much if they fitted her," said Joshua; "however, they are clean and whole, and I dare say she feels comfortable in them. Now, Cynthia, sit down and eat your dinner; and then you must tell these kind ladies all you told me on the common where I found you."

Cynthia obeyed, and meekly took the place assigned by Miss Priscilla.

The pasty was very nice, and hunger made it absolutely delicious. The spinsters were shocked to see that Mr. Haggard's *protégée* put her fingers into the plate occasionally.

"She doesn't seem to know the use of a split-spune," said Deborah; forks being graphically described as split-spunes, or sometimes as prongs, at Pennoyle.

"She will learn every thing in time," answered Joshua, kindly. That grave, deep voice of his had never assumed a gentler tone, not even when he talked of his daughter.

Having eaten her dinner, Cynthia told the sisters her story—not quite so naïvely as she had told it to Joshua; but with a frankness which neither Deborah nor Priscilla—though inclined to look with the eye of suspicion upon a strolling young woman—could mistake. The history of this waif—fatherless, motherless, friendless, left outside the Christian fold—was touching enough to move some tender feeling in the village schoolmistresses.

"Now, I will tell you what I want you to do for her," said Joshua. "Take her as your servant and your pupil. Pay her no wages for her work, which will at first, perhaps, be worth very little. I will pay you for her schooling, and provide for her clothing. Let her learn to read her Bible, and to write a plain, straightforward letter, and add up a column of figures. I ask for no more than that. Teach her to be handy with her needle, and a good servant. She is young enough and active enough to learn quickly and to be useful. And really, Miss Welding," added the minister, making a final appeal to feminine pride, "ladies of such refinement as yourself and your sister ought not to be without a domestic servant."

"We've tried girls before now, Mr. Haggard, and found them nothing but worry. We've a woman come in twice a week to scrub, and red-brick, and hearth-stone, and black-lead, and the rest we manage ourselves. A lady needn't be the less a lady because she knows how to use her hands."

"Of course not," said the minister; "but with advancing years—"

Priscilla bridled and coughed dubiously.

"We don't pretend to be young women," she exclaimed; "but I don't think either Debby or I feel age coming upon us yet awhile."

Joshua perceived that he had made a mistake.

"However, to oblige you, Mr. Haggard," said Deborah, "I think we might go so far as to give the girl a trial. Of course, coming to us with out a character, there's a risk. But she seems biddable; and I'll allow that there's a good deal of cleaning-up after the children, what with dirty boots and such-like, that I shouldn't be sorry to have taken off my hands. As for payment for teaching her to read her Bible, I don't think either Priscilla or I would like to take money for that; though I dare say we shall have to begin from the very beginning, and every body knows that's uphill work. For the matter of clothes she may be beholden to you, Mr. Haggard; and you won't feel the expense of a dress-piece now and then, or a dozen yards of calico, and two or three pairs of worsted stockings for winter wear, as it's all in your line of business."

"Certainly not," said Joshua. "It'll come lightly enough upon me. I thank you with all my heart, Miss Welding, for your generous consent to oblige me. If Cynthia does not turn out well under your care, it will be her own fault, and I shall feel no further interest in her."

"I shall try very hard to please them, for your sake," said Cynthia, looking up at him gratefully. Oh, what a lovely look it was, and how sweet is gratitude from eyes of heaven's own azure!

"These ladies will teach you to be a Christian, Cynthia," said Joshua, "and when I come to Pennoyle again I shall expect to hear you read a chapter in the Gospel."

"When will you come again?" asked the girl, eagerly.

"Next year, perhaps. I am always glad to come westward to see old friends."

"A year? That's a long time."

"Not long to people who are well employed," answered Joshua. "You will have a great deal to learn in the year, Cynthia, so time will pass quickly with you. You must learn to work with your head and your hands; learn to love and honor God, and do your duty to your neighbor."

"I wish I was going with you," said Cynthia.

"That's a foolish wish. I am leaving you with ladies who will be very kind to you."

"She shall have the little room in the roof to sleep in," said Deborah. "The roof slopes a good bit, and she must take care not to hit her head against it; but it's high enough in the middle for her to stand upright, and the room's nice and warm under the thatch."

"I don't care where I sleep," said Cynthia. "Any thing would be better than the van, it was so close and stifling. I'll sleep under a haystack if you like, ma'am."

"You must call me miss," said Deborah. "I'm not a married lady. And now, Cynthia—what a queer name, to be sure!—see if you can clear the table nicely, and carry the dinner-things out without breaking any thing, and then you must take the cloth out to the yard and shake it for the chickens. We never waste so much as a crumb, Cynthia, though we keep a liberal table."

The girl obeyed, pleased to be occupied, and

removed the plates and dishes quickly and carefully. She had been a drudge in the tents of her wandering tribe, and had learned to be quick with her hands and feet. Deborah looked on quite approvingly.

"She's better than the girls we've had, I do declare," she said, when Cynthia had gone out to administer the fragments of the feast to the poultry, beginning to think that in doing a work of benevolence she was perhaps securing a positive advantage. This girl seemed handier than the miners' or agricultural labourers' daughters of the district, all of whom were exorbitant in their demands for wages, asking as much as a pound or even twenty-five shillings a quarter.

Joshua looked at his watch again. He had a twelve-mile walk between him and Truro, and the night coach left that town at ten. It was now five, and the village had that delicious look of repose which such places put on in the mellow light of afternoon.

"I think I must be moving," said the minister.

"Oh, Mr. Haggard, not till you've had a cup of tea!" cried Priscilla. "It's past our time already, and the kettle's on the boil. I'll have tea ready in five minutes, and perhaps you'd do us the favor to expound a chapter while the tea-pot draws. That's a privilege we don't often enjoy."

She ran out to the kitchen, where Cynthia was folding the cloth neatly, showing quite a natural gift that way. Priscilla taught her how to set the tea-things — blue willow-pattern cups and saucers, shallow cups with high handles, and very beautiful in the girl's eyes. There was a white-and-gold covered bowl for the sugar, oval, with colored landscapes on each side. Cynthia had never seen any thing so lovely; and from a place of concealment in her bed-chamber Deborah brought down a glittering silver tea-pot with a black handle—a tea-pot that had belonged to the grandparents of the Weldings, and was in itself an evidence of respectability, a silver tea-pot in families of this class taking the place of a pedigree. This ancestral treasure was drawn forth from its wash-leather retirement to do honor to the minister.

Cynthia carried the tea-tray into the parlor, Priscilla following with the silver pot, lest by any chance the stroller, being intrusted with it, should make a sudden rush to the front door and carry off that valuable.

"Sit down in that chair by the door, Cynthia," said Deborah when the tray had been placed, "and try to derive profit from Mr. Haggard's teaching."

Cynthia took the chair indicated, and sat with her great blue eyes fixed wonderingly on the minister, doubtful whether he was going to perform conjuring tricks with cards, or to manifest his knowledge of arithmetic and the days of the week, like the learned pony.

The sisters seated themselves primly by the tea-table, with folded hands and an expectant expression of countenance, as if ready to meet enlightenment half way with superior intelligence.

Joshua, seated easily, with one arm thrown across the back of his chair, opened his pocket Bible and began to read.

He chose that thrilling description of the last judgment which he had quoted to the sisters earlier in the afternoon. "And before him shall be gathered all nations: and he shall separate

them one from another, as a shepherd divideth his sheep from the goats."

When he had read to the end of the chapter, he preached his brief sermon on the text; a simple and touching commentary that drew tears from Deborah, who was the softer-hearted of the sisters, as Priscilla was the more learned and brilliant. Cynthia listened and wondered. She was too ignorant to be moved by the text; but when Joshua, after his own familiar personal fashion, set forth the duty of charity and compassion, his words came nearer to her heart, and a faint ray of light stole through the darkness of her mind. She clasped her hands, and looked gratefully from Joshua to the maiden sisters.

"And now you can go to the kitchen and sit there, Cynthia, till you are wanted to take away the tea-tray," said Miss Welding, with condescending graciousness. "I'll set you some needlework on Monday to employ your time of an afternoon;" on which Cynthia dropped a courtesy—she had learned to courtesy gracefully after her little dances in front of the booth—and retired.

"There's one thing I'm uneasy about," said Priscilla, when she was gone. "With a girl like that, who has dropped down from the skies, how can we ever feel secure about the silver?"

This family plate consisted of half a dozen attenuated tea-spoons, a pair of sugar-tongs like scissors, a mulincer, and the tea-pot.

"If I am any judge of character, that girl will not rob you," said the minister. "But you will soon be able to judge for yourselves. If she is honest in small things, depend upon it she will be honest in large. If she tells the truth, be sure she will not steal."

Mr. Haggard praised the tea, of which he drank three cups, to the sisters' infinite gratification. There are few points upon which housekeepers are more assailable to flattery than on this of tea-making; and tea and sugar in those days were more precious, costing much more than they do now, and the use of them implying gentility.

"And now I must really be going, my kind friends," said Joshua. "I shall not talk about my gratitude for your goodness to-day, though I do take it as a favor to myself; for you have done a Christian act, and will obtain your reward. I should like to say a few words to Cynthia before I go away."

"Shall I call her?"

"No: I'll go to the kitchen and see her there."

He went into the passage, and opened the door at the end of it. The kitchen faced the west, and was all of a glow with the afternoon sun. Roses and honeysuckle garlanded the low wide casement, and pots of yellow musk upon the sill perfumed the warm air. The red-floored kitchen, the dresser with its array of brightly colored crockery and shining tin and copper, made a Dutch picture; and in the mellow light of the casement stood Cynthia, looking dreamily out into the garden—a garden that sloped upward in a gentle incline to the tall hedge that divided it from the pasture land beyond. The hedges were white with elder-bushes in flower. There was a well in one corner, a pig-sty in another; and on a small square grass plot in front of the kitchen window a brood of soft yellow chicks were disporting themselves under the eye of a fussy Dorking hen.

" I have come to bid you good-bye, Cynthia," said Mr. Haggard, kindly. "You feel happy here, I hope?"

" Yes; it is so peaceful. I feel that no one will scold me or beat me. But I wish you were going to stay."

" Why, my dear child?" asked Joshua, touched by the look of affection that accompanied the words rather than the words themselves. " Of what good could I be to you? I could not teach you to sew and to be a clever domestic servant, as these kind ladies can."

" No; but I like you best," replied Cynthia, naively.

" I shall come to see you next summer, remember, my dear. It will please me very much if you have learned to read your Bible by that time."

" Then I'll learn," replied Cynthia, decisively.

" And to be useful and industrious. You must be obedient to your kind mistresses in all things, mind, for I am sure they will never bid you do any thing that is not right. And you will attend the chapel twice every Sunday, and on week-day evenings whenever there is a service."

" Yes; I will do all you tell me."

" God's blessing and mine be upon you, dear child," said Joshua, solemnly, laying his hand upon the girl's soft hair; " and may he receive you among his chosen children and servants! Good-bye."

" Good-bye, sir," said Cynthia, dropping a low courtesy.

And so they parted; and for many a day and many a month to come the minister carried the memory of that sunlit kitchen, with its rose-garlanded window, in his mind like a picture; and the lines of the picture grew not less vivid with the progress of time.

CHAPTER VII.

NAOMI'S HOLIDAY.

MIDSUMMER had come and gone, and it was sultry August weather again, just a year after the loss of the *Dolphin*; and life in the minister's house went smoothly on in its established course, every day the exact image of its defunct brother, yesterday. Joshua had been a little more watchful of Oswald and Naomi in consequence of that conversation with Nicholas Wild; and, perceiving nothing in the manner of either that passes the bounds of friendly feeling, had refrained so far from any overt interference. When the time came he would be ready to speak and to act; but it seemed to him that the time had not come. He was not going to offer his daughter to any man; and to attempt to interrogate Oswald as to his feelings or his intentions would be, in a manner, to make such an offer. He had a hearty liking for Oswald Pentreath, and he had confidence in the young man's honor and principle. The life of a man who lives in such a place as Combhollow is tolerably open to inspection, and no one had ever been able to charge Oswald with evil-doing. His pride, his supposed meanness, had been commented upon sharply enough by those who knew him least, and whose ideal squire was a rollicking young man with plenty of money to spend, and a leaning to getting tipsy in the company of his inferiors. But those who liked

him least had no more to say than that he was close-fisted and proud; and the few who knew him well praised him warmly, and looked forward to the day when he should rule in his father's place.

Joshua Haggard, after duly considering these things, held his peace.

" I will bide my time, Judith," he said, when his sister attacked him on the subject. " I have seen no love-making between my daughter and Mr. Pentreath."

" As if they'd let you see it!" exclaimed Judith. " There's plenty of time for sweethearting behind your back. In the Wilderness of an evening, when he brings her plants with crackjaw names — such rubbish! not a flower among 'em equal to a marigold or a nasturtium — and ferns (ferns was nobody's money when I was a girl) — do you suppose that isn't sweethearting? And she seldom goes for an afternoon walk but what she meets him."

" Combhollow isn't a large place," said Joshua.

" Of course not; and it's easy for young people to make their plans and not miss each other."

" Jim is always with his sister."

" Yes, and with his eyes on every bird and bush, and he running off to climb trees half his time. I know that by the state of his clothes."

" I can trust my daughter," replied Joshua, with a dignity that silenced his sister. " Naomi will keep no secret from her father."

One evening early in this golden harvest month the minister took his daughter aside, and questioned her about Oswald Pentreath.

" We have made a new friend within the last year, Naomi," he began — "a friend of whom you see rather more than I do. What do you think of him?"

The dark-fringed lids drooped over the thoughtful eyes, and a deep crimson glowed on the oval cheek.

" You mean Mr. Pentreath, father?"

" Whom else should I mean, my dear? We don't make many new friends. Tell me frankly how you like him."

" Very much, father."

" That's a straight answer, at any rate. Has he ever professed any thing more than friendship for you — such friendship as any well-bred man may naturally feel for a superior young woman?"

" Never!"

" And you think him good and true, Naomi?"

" Indeed I do. I should be very sorry if any one thought otherwise of him."

" Why, my love? He is so little to us, that, except for charity's sake, it could matter little what people think of him."

" I should be sorry if any one thought ill of him, because I know that he deserves people's good word. I know how good he is. I know how patient he is with his father — how glad he would be to make things better for the tenants; how dearly he loves his absent brother; how kind he is to all dumb things, and to Jim — and me."

" He has my good opinion, Naomi, and I am glad to hear you speak well of him. But if ever he should seek to be more than your friend — if ever he were to change from friend to lover — you would tell me, wouldn't you, my dear?"

" Yes, father. I would not think of keeping a secret from you. You are always first in my thoughts."

"There are some, doubtless, who would say I do wrong in allowing any friendship between you and Mr. Pentreath, on account of the disparity in your station. But, to my mind, a young woman of high principles and good education is not the less a lady because her father happens to keep a shop; and although I can not boast such a good old name as Pentreath, I think, by setting my good character against the squire's bad repute, we may fairly balance the account."

After this understanding with his daughter, Mr. Haggard felt quite easy in his mind about Oswald Pentreath. He knew that Naomi had the higher and nobler nature; that union with her would be moral elevation for Oswald; and he thought it a small thing that the conventionalities should be outraged a little by the marriage of the squire's son with a grocer's daughter. Again, he had enjoyed so much respect and even reverence from his fellow-men in Combhollow, that he may naturally have fancied himself as great a man as the squire. He knew that he was better liked and trusted, and that in any conflict between the two powers he could command a majority.

He had told his sister and his children that adventure of his on the way to Penmoyle. Naomi had listened with interest, warmly approving her father's conduct to the waif. Judith had taken a chilling view of the whole thing, and had opined that Joshua would live to repent his benevolence.

"I never knew any lasting good to come of mixing one's self up in other people's lives," she said, with conviction. "You set 'em going right for a little while, perhaps; but they're pretty sure to go wrong again as soon as your back's turned. It's all very well to teach 'em—of course that's our duty; and no harm ever came of teaching, if it doesn't always do good. But when a minister goes beyond his sphere, and tampers with the bodily wants of any idle vagabond he may meet on his way, he's pretty sure to do mischief—at least that's my opinion."

"Fortunately for the poor, it is not an opinion based upon the Gospel," replied Joshua.

"You don't find St. Paul going about the world getting situations for young women, and hampering himself with the expense of their clothing," retorted Judith. "He preached to them. That was his mission, and he stuck to it."

Joshua took no trouble to defend his line of conduct in this matter. He was so far lord of himself and of his own life as to do what he pleased on all occasions, without any explanation of his motives. But when he came to pack a parcel of materials for Cynthia's clothing, Miss Haggard, who had the drapery business under her thumb, made herself as disagreeable as she could by picking out the ugliest printed goods, the coarsest calico, and flannel very little superior to that which she dealt out to Sally for the washing of stone floors.

"If you must clothe paupers, clothe them suitably," she remarked, as she bounced a piece of hideous print upon the counter, the pattern an ace of clubs on a dingy yellow ground.

"I won't have yellow," said Joshua, decisively, recalling that brown-and-yellow striped gown in which the Miss Weblings had arrayed his protégée.

"Nothing better to wear and wash," replied Judith; "and she'll want stuff that'll stand wear. Servant-girls can't afford to choose things for prettiness. I sold a gown off that piece to the house-maid at the Grange."

"I'll choose for myself," said Joshua, inspecting the shelves.

He selected two inoffensive patterns in a cool, clean-looking lavender.

"That's one of the dearest pieces of goods we've got in stock," objected Judith.

"I want something that will stand wear," replied Joshua. "Measure a gown off each of those, while I look out something for Sundays."

"She can wear this on Sunday, and plenty good enough, while it's clean."

Joshua continued his examination of the shelves without noticing this remark, and presently pulled out a piece of printed stuff—quite a lady's pattern—white ground dotted with tiny pink rose-buds, fresh and innocent-looking.

"You're not going to cut that piece, surely, Joshua!" cried his sister, horrified. "I've been saving that for Miss Tremaine. She wanted something neat and pretty for frocks for her nieces."

"There'll be plenty left for Miss Tremaine's nieces after I've taken off a frock for Cynthia," replied Mr. Haggard; and without another word to his sister he measured off the regulation quantity, and then changed the flop-sack calico and the coarse flannel for materials of fair and decent quality. Then he looked into the drawers under the counter, and chose a bonnet ribbon, and packed all these things securely in stout brown paper, for the Truro coach.

"I can't think what's come to you, Joshua, meddling with such fiddle-faddle," said Judith, discontentedly.

"I should have left it for you to do, Judith, if you had been disposed to do it with good grace," answered Joshua, calmly.

He wrote the address upon the parcel, and carried it to the Truro coach in his own hands, and gave it into the guard's keeping, with special instructions for its conveyance to Penmoyle. He experienced a mild thrill of happiness after doing this, such as a loving mother feels when she has sent some gift to a child at school.

Shortly after that confidential talk between Naomi and her father, Joshua Haggard gave his children a summer-day's outing, such as they had been accustomed to enjoy once or twice in every summer from their earliest childhood. It was a simple and inexpensive treat enough, consisting of a drive in the general dealer's tax-cart to some distant town or village whither his duties, spiritual or temporal, or both combined, summoned the minister and shop-keeper. This August the holiday was to be a drive to Rockmouth, where there were one or two small shop-keepers who took their supplies from Joshua, and several families who derived their spiritual sustenance from his lips, and who looked upon his expounding of the Scriptures as one of the rarest privileges of their lives.

To Jim these outings were particularly delightful; for while his father transacted his earthly business, and then went from cottage to cottage reading and exhorting, he and Naomi were free to wander where they listed, provided they arrived at the inn at the time appointed for the return journey. Aunt Judith also was wont to relax her Spartan severity on these occasions, and to prepare a liberal basket of provisions; that cold potato-pasty which the boy loved, or perchance a parsley-pie—a pie in which tender young chickens nestled in a bed of parsley and cream, preferable, in the mind of a West-countryman, to all the bloated goose-livers of Strasburg in their cruckery pie-crust.

This trip to Rockmouth had been talked of for at least a fortnight before Joshua could find a leisure day; so it was scarcely wonderful that the intended journey should be a fact familiar to Oswald Pentreath as well as to numerous other members of Combhollow society—notably the stout landlord of The First and Last, who lived in his porch all summer-time, and could see people's intentions through their open windows, if he did not become possessed of them in conversation.

The day came at last—glowing harvest weather and a sky without a cloud—when Joshua felt himself free to order Gray Dobbin to be harnessed in the cart. Off sped Jim to assist in the operation of harnessing; which performance gave rise to as many "stand overs" and "come ups" in the little stable-yard as if a whole team of impatient thorough-breds had been getting on their leather. But when Gray Dobbin came out into the road, sleek and shining, with his dark mane symmetrically combed and glossy, his white hind feet pure as newly-fallen snow, ribbons at his ears, and an air of conscious pride in the carriage of his firm bull neck, James felt that his care had not been wasted, and the minister approved.

Naomi came tripping down the narrow staircase somewhat hurried and fluttered, for the trip had at last been decided upon hastily, but all aglow with beauty, in her cottage-bonnet—a kind of house or sentry-box, in which a woman sheltered herself in those days, and lived secluded from the world, even while she took her walks abroad—and lilac-muslin dress, starched and ironed by her own industrious hands. The cottage-bonnet, of coarse Dunstable straw, was trimmed with white ribbon and lined with pale pink—such a bonnet as Eugénie Grandet wore when she took that dismal morning walk with her father; her petticoat was short enough to show the neat narrow feet in white stockings and "low shoes;" her waist was short also; and a black-silk scarf crossed over her breast and tied behind completed her costume.

Her father contemplated her approvingly.

"You and Dobbin have put on your best looks this morning," he said.

"I always wear my best bonnet when I go out with you, father," answered Naomi, meekly, but blushing a little at the thought that she had cherished a vague idea of Oswald's appearance at the last moment, asking permission to accompany them on Herne the Hunter.

"He could not know that we were going this morning," she told herself.

Naomi mounted to her seat in the cart, the post of honor beside the driver. Jim and the basket of provisions occupied the back of the vehicle; and that youth received numerous injunctions not to jog this, or spill that, or let the cork out of the other, from Aunt Judith, who came to the gate in her morning head-gear of curl-papers to assist at the departure.

"Sit up straight, and don't crease your scarf,

Naomi," she cried. "There never was a better bit of silk; and you'll have to be careful of that muslin frock, if you mean to wear it next Sunday. Two starched frocks in a week would be more extravagance than I could reconcile my conscience to, even if you could; and you don't get any more starch out of me this side of Monday, remember."

With this injunction in her ears, Naomi left home behind her; but earth was too fair this day for any one's mind to be worried by the thought of a starched frock. What is there between the North and South Poles fairer than an English landscape—Devonshire lanes and commons, woods and vales, Devonshire's coast and sea, in the vivid August sunlight? Can any Alpine grandeur, can all the glory and color of the tropics, surpass this tender English beauty—beauty that creeps into one's soul and makes one glad; beauty that melts the ice of frozen hearts, that warms age into the exuberance of youth, that bids the wanderer lay down his bundle of cares, his knapsack of perplexities, and rejoice because the sunshine is so kind and earth so fair?

Naomi was in the humor for rejoicing this morning, but her joy was very quiet. She sat by her father's side in silence, and watched the landscape dreamily, thinking of her lover. Her lover? Yes, for she loved him. Yes, for she believed that he loved her.

Joshua too was silent and had his own thoughts this August morning. Gray Dobbin was quiet to drive, or, in other words, required no driving whatever, but took his way steadily over familiar roads, and plodded cautiously down hills of appalling steepness, and clambered up the same hills cheerfully, as an animal that knew he had been foaled in a hilly country and was contented with his lot. So Joshua sat with the reins loose in his left hand, and dreamed his dreams; and the commons were golden with furze, and the reapers were busy in the tawny corn-fields, and a covey of partridges went whirring upward every here and there from the shelter of some hedge, and the poppies gleamed scarlet amidst the wheat, and the bindweed's white bells hung on every hedge, and the traveler's-joy shed its aromatic perfume on the air, and the orchards on hill-side and in hollow were ruddy with ripening fruit, and all sweet things that blossom late in the summer were in perfection.

No sign of Herne the Hunter yet awhile, though they had traveled half their journey, and Dobbin had stopped to have his mouth washed out at the hamlet of Simondale, a handful of cottages and a battered old public-house at the feet of two steep hills—a village in a pit.

"He won't come to-day," thought Naomi, with a sigh; and the holiday seemed not quite so perfect as it might have been—not so perfect as it was last year, when there was no such person as Oswald Pentreath in her thoughts, and the glory and beauty of the earth had no double meaning.

Over another common and up and down more hills, and then from a narrow road descending a wooded steep, they see Rockmouth lying at their feet—not a tourist's resort in those days, but an obscure little fishing-village on a rocky shore.

There it lay—the lonely cluster of thatched cottages, the humble patches of garden, the wells, and pig-sties, and bee-hives, and hay-ricks, and straw-yards; the village forge; the church, standing aloof on a hill, looking down at the abodes of its congregation; the squire's house—red-brick and spacious, set on a slope of meadow-land or park—a little way off, with its front to the sea; and, as the curve of the bay widened, rose the rocky wall of the tall cliff, precipitous, dangerous, yet not too steep for sheep to browse upon its rugged breast.

"How lovely!" cried Naomi, surveying that rocky coast, with its wild variety of crag and pinnacle. "Wouldn't you think they were castles, father, over there—keeps and watch-towers? I can fancy men in armor firing their arrows down into the valley, or keeping guard upon those battlements against enemies from the sea."

"How jolly nice it must be for smugglers on such a coast as this!" remarked Jim. "Plenty of caves to hide their plunder in, and those rocks to climb when they want to survey their ground, and to hoist signals upon—tar-barrels and such-like. Where shall we have our dinner, father?"

"I shan't have much time to waste upon dinner, Jim," replied Mr. Haggard, indifferently. "You and Naomi had better take charge of the basket, and settle it all between you."

"Oh, come, father, you must have your share of the pasty. I saw Aunt Judith making it—she happened to be in a particularly good temper, or she wouldn't have let me—and I know it's prime. Such juicy steak, and lots of potato! Won't the gravy gush out when you put your knife into it, unless it's turned to jelly! My eye, ain't I hungry!"

"Don't be so vulgar, Jim," remonstrated Naomi, with a depressing conviction that such a young man as this would be no fitting brother-in-law for young Squire Pentreath. Since that serious conversation with her father, she had thought much of social differences and distinctions, and had told herself despondently that, good and great as her father might be, there was a wide gulf between her and Oswald Pentreath. But, then, Love has a knack of spanning such gulfs, and the good old story of King Cophetua and the beggar-maiden is always being acted over again after some fashion or other.

"I'll tell you a tiptop place for dinner, father," exclaimed Jim. "You see that rock yonder—the tallest one, the shape of a castle—there's a grassy hollow just under it, facing the sea, quite safe, for the cliff isn't half so steep there as it is in other places; and the ferns grow there lovely, and purple mosses, and red stone-crop just like coral, and all sorts of things that Naomi's fond of. Will you come there with us, father—it isn't above a mile from the inn where Dobbin stops—and dig into the pasty before you begin your business calls?"

Mr. Haggard looked at his watch meditatively. He did not much affect these picnickings and carousings, but he was glad to oblige his children on such a day as this, which was a kind of annual holiday, a rare occasion on which he went out of his way a little to give them pleasure. Dobbin had come at a good pace, so it was early yet, not much past noontide, and the days were still long.

"Very well, my dears," he said; "I'll come and have some dinner with you, and then I'll leave you to amuse yourselves among the rocks while I go my rounds."

Dobbin was safely installed in his stable at The Traveler's Rest, a comfortable little inn just at the bottom of the hill, and then Jim shouldered the basket as if it had been a trifle, and trudged sturdily on ahead, while Naomi and her father followed at a more sober pace.

The path they trod was a wild and romantic footway, a narrow ledge cut out of the cliff. Below them shelved the steep craggy slope, rich in the varied colors of wild flower and moss, with lonely sheep feeding here and there, or bounding, chamois-like, from peak to peak. Far away spread the summer sea, placid as an Italian lake, and as lovely in hue.

"Isn't it lovely, father?" cried Naomi. "I always feel grateful to God for having given us such a beautiful world when I come to Rockmouth."

"We ought to be grateful at all times and under all circumstances, Naomi, even if our lot had been cast at the bottom of a coal mine."

"Yes, I suppose so," sighed the girl; "but gratitude comes easier to people who dwell among lovely scenes. It must be hard work to be grateful for life that is all misery."

Joshua had no answer. These problems in man's existence were not easily to be solved.

"There is a better world, Naomi, where the balance is adjusted," he said, after a pause.

"I know, father. And if the unhappy people in wretched places can believe that, it must comfort them. But it must be difficult for people who have never known what it is to be happy on earth to believe in the blissfulness of heaven."

They came to the castle rock, a spot where there was a break in the steep wall of cliffs, as if some mammoth battering-train had made a breach in the island's battlements; and here a green cup-shaped valley opened in the craggy shore—a vale scattered with rocks and bowlders, moss grown and fern-embellished.

"How sweet!" cried Naomi.

"Isn't it prime?" inquired James, who had arrived some minutes in advance of his companions, and had already unpacked the basket, or "mannd," as he called it. "There's a pasty for you, and cheese-cakes, and a big stone jar of cider, and a couple of tumblers, and plates, and knives and prongs, and all complete. Sit down, father, that's your place; and here's a little mossy seat for Naomi, just as if it was made for us."

Then came half an hour of real domestic harmony. Joshua and his children being hungry, ample justice was done to the pasty and cheese-cakes, and much commendation bestowed upon Aunt Judith as the provider of the feast. It seemed such a curious thing to eat a meal without that pragmatic presence—without fear of being called to order for the too free use of God's creatures, in the shape of beefsteak and pie-crust. Even Mr. Haggard, though he would have been unwilling to own as much, enjoyed this dinner on the castle rock, with the green valley and the jasper sea spread out like a carpet at his feet, better than any meal he had ever eaten in his respectable parlor, where there was no wider prospect than a glimpse of The First and Last, and a background of wooded hill, seen across the tops of the geraniums and double stocks that somewhat bounded one's view of the outer world. To-day these picnickers seemed to have a universe all to themselves.

"I feel just as if we had gone out somewhere in a ship and landed on an unknown island," said Jim. "I wonder if we shall meet any of the natives by-and-by, and if they will scalp us?"

"I think there is nothing in life so nice as a picnic," exclaimed Naomi, "except having you all to ourselves, father. That is better than the party."

"I wish you would stay with us all the afternoon, father, and tell us stories about foreign countries," said Jim.

"That would not be doing my errand at Rockmouth, James," answered the minister, pulling out his big watch once more. "It's nearly two o'clock, and we must start for home at six. I must leave you, my dears. I trust Naomi to you, James, remember. Be sure you lead her into no dangerous places. You'd better not go any farther along the cliff, but take a stroll across the valley, and up the hill to those woods yonder. You'll find plenty of new ferns for your wilderness up there, I dare say, Naomi."

"Don't be uneasy, father," replied James, confidently: "I'll take care of her."

Joshua departed, thoughtful of all that he had to do, of his duties temporal and spiritual—the prices at which he could afford to sell tea and sugar and other colonial produce; the bedridden old men and women to whom he must administer counsel and consolation.

It was just the sleepiest, goldenest hour of the summer day. Naomi sat in her mossy hollow under the overhanging rock, with her head resting against the stone, and her eyes fixed dreamily on a silver-shining sail far away on the edge of the sea.

"I could watch the sea and sky for hours on such a day as this," she said, too deliciously idle to look in the direction of the individual to whom she addressed the remark.

"And I could be content to watch beside you, or to swim such a sea to come to you," answered a voice—not Jim's—close at her side.

The suddenness and the closeness startled her. She turned white and then red.

"I'm afraid I frightened you," said Oswald, apologetically.

He had come up from the valley, his footfall noiseless on the soft mossy turf.

"You did startle me a little," replied Naomi, breathlessly, with a hot blush still staining her cheek.

How should a country girl, unschooled in shams of any kind, know how to hide her emotions?

"But you must have known that I should come," said Oswald, looking up at Jim, who had climbed a loftier peak, and was taking a survey of earth and ocean from about the most unsafe footing he could find for himself.

"How could I know! I thought perhaps that you—" faltered Naomi, plucking little tufts of coral-tinted sea-moss from the crag at her side.

"Did you think that I could endure Combhollow for a day without you, having the power to follow you? I knew all about your picnic, but not when it was to be; and I made up my mind to join you. I should have been here earlier, only my father took it into his head to want me this morning; and I was closeted in his study, reading over leases to him, for a couple of hours. It was twelve o'clock when I went out for my ride. I called at the shop as I passed, and the man told me you had come here with your father: so I let Herne have his head and bring me over to Rockmouth as fast as he liked. I've left him at The Traveler's Rest."

"That's where Dobbin stays," said Naomi.

"Yes, I saw him munching hay in a dark old stall. And how long are you going to stay here, Naomi?"

"Oh, ever so long! Jim and I are free till six o'clock, and we are going fern-hunting."

"Never mind the ferns to-day. Let me take you for a ramble along the beach."

"Is it safe? Father told us not to go into any dangerous places."

"It is quite safe. Do you think I would lead you into danger? I know every bit of this coast. We'll hunt sea-anemones instead of ferns; they are much more interesting."

"Sea-anemones?" cried Naomi, opening her eyes.

She had some acquaintance with the tribe, but did not know them by name.

"Yes; those lovely pink and white and green and blue things, which uncurl their petals and expand, and close again like living blossoms—the roses and lilies in old Neptune's garden; animal flowers, the naturalists call them. Let me introduce you to them. We'll go down to the beach. You're not afraid to trust yourself to my care, are you, Naomi?"

The noble dark eyes met his with a look that was all truth and trustfulness. Faith, hope, and charity were the three virtues that looked out of Naomi's eyes—infinite faith in the goodness of others, infinite pity for the sorrows of others, infinite hope in all things pure and fair on earth and in heaven.

Naomi looked down at the beach, with shining patches of wet yellow sand here and there, and low rocks covered with many-colored sea-weed—slippery, perilous rocks, no doubt, but very beautiful in their brilliant coloring under that summer sky. It would be nice to explore that beach, Naomi thought: but at this moment her eye caught the basket, which Jim had deposited in a sly cleft of the rocks.

"You have had no luncheon, perhaps," she said. "Wouldn't you like to try Aunt Judith's pasty before we go to look for those sea-flowers?"

"Aunt Judith's pasty would be most apropos."

"I am so glad!" cried Naomi, delighted to minister to his wants.

She opened the basket and brought out the remains of the pasty, and spread a napkin on a ledge of the crag, and made things quite comfortable, in picnicking fashion. There was some cider left in the stone jar. She looked beyond measure happy as she sat by Oswald's side while he eat, and poured out the cider for him in a little old-fashioned tumbler with a foot. He enjoyed this rustic meal vastly, but would not waste much time upon eating.

"Come," he said, folding the napkin and putting it back into the basket, "let us go after the anemones."

"May Jim come with us?" asked Naomi.

"Of course he may."

On looking round over land and sea, however, there was no James to be seen. Naomi called, but there was no answer.

"What a tiresome boy! And father was so

anxious that he should not go into any dangerous places."

"He's safe, depend upon it; boys always are. Nothing serious ever happens to a boy, no more than it does to a cat. Boys tumble from places and tear their clothes, but nothing ever hurts them."

"That's rather true about Jim," replied Naomi. "He's always frightening us somehow or other; but he never comes to any harm."

"Of course not. I dare say we shall find him on the beach."

The beach seemed as likely as any other place for finding him; so Naomi assented, and they went down the narrow path—the slenderest footway—and Naomi stepped lightly from crag to crag with her hand in Oswald's. It was like going to heaven the reverse way. Her soul fluttered and soared, and rose higher and higher, as her mortal frame descended the cliff.

How lovely it was on the beach—those smooth shining sands, those treacherous rocks, slippery and cruel and deceitful as the heart of man! How lovely sea and sky, and the fertile earth sloping upward from the sands! How lovely to live in such a world, and to feel as Naomi felt, her hand still locked in Oswald's—perhaps unaware—as they walked slowly along the sands, pretending to look for sea-anemones in all those still water-pools in the hollows of the rocks—darkly shining water, like black diamonds!

"Naomi," said Oswald, in a low voice, "how sweet it is to be alone with you!"

Naomi crimsoned at the speech, commonplace as it was.

"We are often alone—in the wilderness," she said, shyly. "There's one, striped purple and white. How pretty!" pointing to a creature in a pool.

"I dote upon the wilderness," replied Oswald. "But we are not often alone there: Jim is generally good enough to keep us company. He is a dear fellow; but I would rather have you all to myself like this. Look round, Naomi: except for yonder white sail we might be in some unknown island of the Southern Sea. Are you glad that I found you to-day, Naomi?"

She looked at him thoughtfully, gravely, with those truthful eyes, and then answered, deliberately,

"Yes."

"The day is sweeter to you because we spend it together?"

"Yes. You are the only friend I have in Combhollow—the only friend who seems to understand all I think and feel and hope. I have other friends, of course—people I like; only they seem far off compared with you."

"Does that mean love, Naomi?"

"I do not know," she answered, with drooping eyelids.

"Tell me that it does, Naomi, and make me the happiest of men. I have waited for an hour like this—solitude calm as this—to tell you all I feel, to show you my heart. It has been yours for a long while, dear. You have made my life happy: you have given me hopes and dreams I never had before. You reprove me sometimes for my willingness to live what you call a purposeless life at Combhollow. My darling, I have no purpose in life but to live happily with you; no ambition except to win you for my wife."

4

"A very poor ambition," she answered, with a grave, sweet smile, "and perhaps a foolish one. I will not say that I am surprised, Oswald," lifting her eyes shyly to his earnest face—"I will not say that I did not think you—cared for me. I have thought it lately, and thought of it very seriously; but my mind is not clear. I am not sure that it is for your welfare or mine that I should let you speak to me of love; that I should ever be any nearer to you than I am now, as your faithful and true friend."

"My gentle sermonizer," exclaimed Oswald, contemplating her with admiring eyes, and stealing his arm round her waist, "and why these doubts?"

"We are not of the same rank in life; we are very far apart. What would be said in Combhollow if you should marry a grocer's daughter?"

"Why, I suppose the verdict of the majority would be that I had married the prettiest girl in the place," he answered, lightly.

"Oh, Oswald, please be serious! I know that people would say hard and bitter things. They would say you had lowered yourself by such a marriage; that father had set a trap for you. And you yourself would be sorry after a little while. How would you like to have Aunt Judith for your aunt, and to know that your father-in-law was standing behind a counter?"

"I will put up with the counter and Aunt Judith for your sake."

"Why should you make such a sacrifice when you might marry a lady?"

"I have seen no better lady than you, Naomi, and I will have no other lady for my wife. I respect your father as much as if he were a bishop, and shall never blush for my alliance with him. I suppose I am a republican at heart; for I have no idea that the fact of a man keeping a shop makes him my inferior. There is no huckster living that will haggle longer or make a closer bargain than my father when he has a farm to let. Is he less a trader because his stock in trade is the soil? He is so much the less to be honored for its possession that it came to him from his father, instead of being the fruit of his own industry."

"That is the way a great many people talk, and very few people think," answered Naomi, thoughtfully.

"I am one who think as I speak. Come, love, let us not argue social questions. I want an answer to a question that touches us nearer. I love you with all my heart, Naomi; I want you for my wife; I recognize no social difference between us. I shall be as proud to win you as if you were the daughter of a duke. I shall feel as triumphant on our wedding-day as if you were a princess of the land, and our marriage set all the church-bells in this island ringing. Answer me, dearest. I give you true and ardent love; have you nothing to give me in return?"

"I will not answer lightly," said Naomi, grave to sadness. "Think how awful a question you wish me to answer. All our lives to come depend upon our wisdom in this matter. We must not decide thoughtlessly, either you or I. And I am afraid you are thoughtless in most things, Oswald," she added, looking up at his smiling face.

"I do not think love and thought are very close allies, Naomi. I love you too well to analyze my feelings or argue about my love; and I think if you loved me ever so little you would be less disposed to make difficulties."

"Do you feel that you will love me all your life, Oswald? that this fancy of yours will not wear out? that, if I were to be your wife, the day would never come when you would regret your choice, when you would feel that you might have chosen more wisely?"

"That day would never come, Naomi; my heart answers for that. Come, love, have we not seen enough of each other to be very sure of our own feelings? I have known you a year, dearest. It is no sudden fancy which I miscall love. My affection for you began as friendship, grave and sweet and tranquil, and slowly ripened into love. Have I not the right to answer boldly for such a love as this? We have bared our hearts to each other, we have no secrets from each other, we have knelt side by side and prayed together, we have been as familiar as if we were of the same household. Can you fear change or decay in a love that has so ripened? Indeed, my dearest, there is no need for fear."

Naomi had made up her mind to be very serious—very firm—whenever this question came to be argued; to yield only on conviction, and to be very slow to be convinced. But she felt her reasoning powers beginning to fail her. Sincerity was written on Oswald's brow, truth shone in his eyes, and she loved him—loved him with all the trustfulness and hopefulness of first love. How should she argue in such a case?

"Answer me, Naomi; tell me that I have not fooled myself with baseless hopes—that you give me love for love?"

"I will answer nothing for myself," she replied, releasing herself from his arm; "my father shall decide for us. He shall choose."

"That's a cold answer to give a lover," said Oswald, offended.

"It is for life," she answered. "I will not answer lightly; I will not trust myself to decide."

"If you loved me, Naomi, you would not let any one else decide my fate."

"If you think that I do not love you, put me out of your thoughts," she answered, with a little touch of dignity. She was thinking more of his future happiness than her own. Would it not be ineffable bliss to be his, to belong to him as his servant, his bond-slave?—how much more as his equal companion and helpmeet!

"You are cold-hearted and cruel."

"No, Oswald, I am trying to be wise. I think my father will answer as you wish, but he will not answer rashly. If he did not think it for your welfare that we should be married, he would say no, although he might think it was for my happiness."

"It is hard to have to deal with such good people. Any other girl than you would have answered differently."

"How would she have answered?" asked Naomi.

"Silently, perhaps. She would have looked up in my face, and our lips would have met and sealed the bond between us. Our first kiss would have meant for ever and ever. She would not have preached me a sermon about social differences and my future welfare," said Oswald, angered by his sweetheart's measured replies.

He had made up his mind that he had but to speak the word, and she would put her hand in his, and accept her fate as submissively as Esther received the crown, or Ruth gave herself to Boaz. He was quite willing to sacrifice all social distinctions and descend to the level of Joshua Haggard's family, but he expected that sacrifice to be regarded in some wise as a favor.

They walked on slowly and in silence for a little while, and there was no more talk of the sea-anemones. Naomi looked at the shining pools among the rocks with eyes that saw not; Oswald gazed steadily seaward.

He got the better of his angry feelings after a little while, and was ashamed of his ill-temper.

"Forgive me, Naomi, for my ungraciousness," he said. "I know that you are one of the noblest of women; but there is a leaven of selfishness in man that makes him impatient of high principles when they oppose the tide of his passion. You are good and unselfish and true, and strong as a rock. You are not like Byron's women, Naomi. They are love incarnate; ready to sacrifice themselves or their lover at the shrine of love. They look neither backward nor forward; with them the present is infinite and eternal, and the present is love. They are gloriously happy for a little while; then come despair and ruin, and they die untimely, broken-hearted. They are not made

"'Through years or moons the inner weight to bear,
Which colder hearts endure till they are laid
By age in earth.'"

"Do you want me to be like that?" asked Naomi. "It seems a hard destiny."

"No, Naomi; but I wish you had less thoughtfulness and more feeling."

"You have not sounded the depths of my heart," she answered, with her grave smile.

"No, because you keep its treasures too closely guarded. Come, dearest, only tell me that you love me, and I will be satisfied."

"And you will abide by my father's decision?"

"Yes, for I can not believe he would be so cruel as to part us."

"Then I will tell you the truth. I love you with all my heart. You have changed all things in my life. I used to have great thoughts of doing some good work, far away, among heathen children in strange, benighted lands. They are all gone now. I have no thought—except love and duty to my father—that does not belong to you."

"Bless you, Naomi, for that sweet confession. I fear nothing now. Your father would have parted us long ago if he had meant to part us ever. I am content to abide his decision; but I wanted the assurance of love from your own dear lips."

Cheered by this assurance, Oswald was very happy for the rest of that summer afternoon, and the tranquil radiance in Naomi's eyes told of an equal, and perhaps a deeper, joy. They wandered on that bright shore, and made believe to be interested in the study of natural history; but their talk drifted away from jelly-fish and sea-weeds and rosy-shining shells to vague speculations about their own future—Oswald talking of what he would do for Combhollow by-and-by when the squire should sleep with his forefathers, and how his brother Arnold would come back and live with them, and how Naomi should build a new chapel for her father and a school for her own little flock, and the grocery business should be handed over to Jim and Aunt Judith, and Joshua should have more leisure for his duties as preacher and teacher.

"And you will never be ashamed of your Methodist wife and your Methodist father-in-law, Oswald?" asked Naomi, anxiously.

"Never, dearest. Shall I scorn the light because it shines from a lamp of a different fashion from that the State prescribes? Who knows that I shall not turn Methodist myself some day? I have learned more of the Gospel in your father's parlor than I ever learned before I came among you, and have been more moved by his sermons than by the sleepy doctrinal treatises our good vicar gives us—a weak dilation of Tillotson or Blair."

The westering sun warned them that it was time to look for James, and to think of getting back to The Traveler's Rest, where they were to meet Joshua after his labors. Oswald looked at a large white-faced watch that had belonged to his mother, and was not the most reliable of time-keepers. It was a quarter to five; so they walked slowly back to the point at which they had descended, and climbed the devious way to the castle rock, where they had the satisfaction of finding James seated at the base of the crag, with the basket between his knees, devouring the remains of the pasty.

"Where have you been hiding yourself all the afternoon, Jim?" asked Naomi.

"Ah, I dare say! a deal you've looked for me. Where have you been all the afternoon? down on the beach making a regular panorama of yourselves. You didn't know any body was looking, did you? You didn't know I was on the top of the cliff all the time enjoying the view. Never mind, Naomi, I forgive you."

"We've had a very happy afternoon, Jim, and Naomi has promised to be my wife—with her father's consent."

Jim clapped his hands, and performed a kind of war-dance on the little bit of sunburned sward at the foot of the crag.

"I'm so glad," he said. "Of course, I saw what was coming—at least, I saw that you and Naomi were getting very fond of each other, and thought you were the right sort, and wouldn't be ashamed to marry a grocer's daughter if you loved her dearly—like Caroline in the song, who married the sailor bold."

And Jim began, with strong Devonian twang, to sing the opening verse of a popular ballad—

"Caroline was a nobleman's daughter."

Oswald was too deep in love just now to be struck by the idea that this would be rather an inconvenient brother-in-law; and perhaps Jim was not much more vulgar than boyhood is in general.

They went back to the village of Rockmouth through the valley, instead of taking the narrow path on the cliff, and there was some loitering by the way to dig fern-roots from the interstices of a low stone wall. It was a pleasant sauntering walk; but they contrived to reach The Traveler's Rest just as the clock struck six. Dobbin was harnessed, and standing patiently before the door. Joshua Haggard sat in the porch talking to a little group of men.

He showed some surprise at seeing Oswald with his children, but greeted him with hearty friendliness. Jim stowed away the empty basket, Naomi took her seat in the chaise-seat without loss of time, Heine the Hunter was brought out of his stable, and the little party started on the return journey, Heine curveting beside the near wheel of the cart, while his master talked to Naomi and her father.

What a delightful homeward drive that was, by hill and dale, across those wide, rippling commons, where the yellow gorse looked pale in the twilight; past those deep and silent valleys, where a lonely homestead here and there made the solitude seem more intense; through hamlets that had a sleepy look already, as if half their little world had gone to bed! And by-and-by the full round harvest-moon rose yonder above the sea, and steeped all this fair world in glory.

Something in that moonlight splendor moved Oswald—as nature's deepest beauties are apt to move hearts that love—and he leaned over to Naomi and clasped her hand; and in that hand-clasp it seemed to both as if they locked their lives forever.

Oswald had an interview with Joshua Haggard next day, and pleaded his cause with warmth and generous feeling, to which Naomi's father responded with perfect frankness.

"I am not too proud to confess that I am proud of your choice," he said. "I know it is out of the beaten track for the son of a land-owner—a man of old family—to marry a trades-man's daughter. If I were a wholesale trader in the city of London, and had made a million of money, it would be a different thing. I know that hard things will be said of such a marriage, and that there are people who will slight your wife if you are not wise enough to keep her out of their way. I know all this, Mr. Pentreath; and yet, knowing also that here are two fresh, unsullied young hearts cleaving to each other naturally, like twin hazel-nuts in the same shell, I can not bring myself to study the world's opinion, and to withhold my consent to your marriage with my daughter."

"I knew you would not," cried Oswald, impetuously.

"All I ask—and that I insist upon—is that this marriage shall not be entered upon rashly; that you shall have ample time to know your own mind, to weigh the consequences of such an act, to make sure against the possibility of repentance. You are both young—Naomi only on the threshold of womanhood. Give me your promise that you will think no more of marriage for the next two years; that in all your communion with my daughter you will keep within the bounds of a sober friendship; that there shall be no foolish love-talk between you. And if at the end of those two years your heart still inclines to her, if you still believe that it will be for the happiness of both that you should marry, I will freely give my blessing on your union, and feel that I have wronged no man."

"Those are somewhat hard conditions, Mr. Haggard," said Oswald, reduced from rapture to disappointment. "You will surely allow me to be considered Naomi's affianced husband during these two years of probation?"

"Not so, Mr. Pentreath. You will be welcome here as the friend of the household; but I will sanction no engagement between you and my daughter till the end of the time I have named. I ask only for your promise that you will be Naomi's friend, and not her lover. I think I can trust you: I know that I can trust my daughter."

"I would submit to the hardest conditions rather than be parted from Naomi," replied Oswald, after a pause; "and I know that she will obey you, however hard your decree. It must be so, then, I suppose, Mr. Haggard. I will say no word to Naomi that a household friend might not say; I will forbear from all talk of our future; I will give her reverence and honor, and keep all sweeter thoughts and hopes locked in my heart."

"There is my hand upon it, Oswald," said Joshua, calling the squire's son by his Christian name for the first time. "You shall be like a son of the house henceforward. And now let me ask you a question: Has your father any idea of your attachment to Naomi?"

"He knows that I have spent many an evening in your house—I have never kept that a secret from him—and I think, from certain hints and innuendoes of his, that he has suspected the nature of the attraction that has drawn me here so often. I do not believe that he would entertain any strong objection to my marriage with Naomi; and if he did object, I should refuse to submit to his arbitration in this matter. He has not been so tender a father that I should sacrifice my inclination to his whims."

"He is your father," said Joshua, "and you are bound to obey him."

"Yes, in all right things. But I do not think that he will oppose any hinderance to my free choice of a wife, so long as I choose one who has been carefully brought up, and who will not squander the money he has scraped together."

CHAPTER VIII.

THE SQUIRE MAKES A BARGAIN.

ANOTHER year had gone in gentle tranquillity —a year marked by no shadow of trouble, doubt, or dissension in Joshua Haggard's household. Oswald had been true to his promise, and had held religiously to his prescribed position as a friend of the family. The simple, uneventful life had glided on in its allotted course: the tea-drinkings in the parlor; Aunt Judith's lectures on the economies and duties of existence; dawdling evenings in the wilderness, in which nothing progressed but the gray-worsted stocking on Naomi's shining needles, which, being only taken off to give place to another stocking of exactly the same shape and color, seemed to Oswald a fair type of eternity; the Scripture-reading and exhortation at even-tide; the homely suppers and friendly partings with Naomi and her father at the little wooden gate—placid, monotonous joys, which had not yet begun to pall upon Oswald Pentreath. If there had been any hollowness in Joshua's life, any shams to be discovered in his household, familiarity would have vulgarized this quiet home circle; but all here was good and true. Even Aunt Judith, though far from pleasant, was at this stage of her existence transparent as the

daylight. There were no skeletons in cupboards for the stranger to stumble upon unawares, no domestic dust-holes to reveal themselves to the disgusted explorer.

Very quiet and peaceful and passionless was this courtship which was no courtship, and yet meant as much to the two actors in the little comedy as if they had been lovers of the most romantic type, and had never opened their mouths save to pour forth a torrent of sentimentality. No cloistered nun was ever truer to her vow than Naomi to the promise she had made her father that there should be no talk of love or marriage between her and Oswald during this time of probation; and Oswald, although given to occasional little gusts of rebellion, was fain to submit and to accept his position with a good grace.

"I am like a shop boy in your father's employment," he said. "If I behave pretty well during my apprenticeship, and keep my fingers off the sugar and figs, and refrain from extracting odd sixpences out of the till, I am to be taken as a partner when I am out of my time. I am on trial: isn't that it, Naomi?"

"It is your future happiness that is on trial, Oswald. If you can be constant to friendship you will be constant to—"

"Hush!" cried the young man, putting his hand upon her lips. "The forbidden word was nearly out."

Naomi blushed and hastened the flight of her knitting-needles, while Oswald laughed heartily at his small joke.

They were innocently happy together in these fair summer days, like children in ignorance of all the world outside the narrow circle of their individual lives, with not one thought or desire hidden from each other, and finding it as natural to be together, to think together, to hope together, and to dream together, as if they had been a new Ferdinand and Miranda, and this quiet nook, Combhollow, an enchanted island.

With Jim for their companion, they wandered in the squire's wood and park, and Herne had easy dreamy days in his loose box, where he stood with his head hanging down as if he had done with the world, and had not strength left in him for another mile; while Oswald taught Naomi how to use her pencil in copying lop-sided old elms with yawning chasms in their trunks, or a little bit of ragged bank clothed with ferns and bright with fox-gloves. Her intense love of nature made art easy to her.

It is not to be supposed that the life of Mr. Haggard's daughter was given over altogether to a blissful idleness such as this—to dreamy afternoons in the wood, to the cultivation of Nature's wildlings in her wilderness, and to primitive efforts with a lead-pencil. She was up at five on these summer mornings, and helped Sally in the performance of her house-cleaning till breakfast-time. It was Naomi who arranged the parlors and polished the old mahogany tables and bureaus, and brightened all the brass-work, and kept every bit of old Chelsea or Battersea ware free from dust and stain. That tall, straight figure of hers was none the worse for assiduous table-rubbing, which widened her chest and gave lissomness to her limbs; and her clear, pale complexion was all the better for early hours and an active life. The flower-pots were in Naomi's care, and a withered leaf on fuchsia or geranium (fuchsias were new in those days, and esteemed highly by flori-culturists) would have been a kind of disgrace. She starched and ironed all the muslin curtains, and Aunt Judith's idea of gentility demanded a great deal of decorative drapery in starched muslin.

The house-linen was also in Naomi's charge, and many a modern housekeeper who gives thirty or forty guineas for a dinner-dress might blush on comparing her linen-closet with that roomy lavender-scented repository at the head of the staircase where Naomi kept her glistening table-cloths and Irish-linen sheets and pillow-cases, all neatly marked by her own hands and laid in orderly piles along the broad oak shelves. Naomi had the care of her father's and brother's wardrobes, and kept every thing in neat repair, taking as much pains with a difficult job of darning as a young lady of the present day would devote to an elaborate achievement in *point Turque* or *point de Venise*. Naomi made her own dresses, which were not uselessly numerous, and occasionally confectioned some decorative article for Aunt Judith, who required to be propitiated with an industrious effort of that kind now and then.

It will be seen, therefore, that when Mr. Haggard's daughter enjoyed the sweets of Arcadian leisure, she had fairly earned the privilege of idleness. No unhemmed duster cried out against her, no buttonless shirt, lurking in drawer or wardrobe, bore witness to her neglect. Life smiled at her with its serenest smile, and no accusing twinge of conscience reminded her of a forgotten duty.

Whether the squire had known of his son's attachment to the Dissenter's daughter from the time when Oswald's visits to the Haggards became frequent, or whether the fact revealed itself to him suddenly this summer through the gossip of Combhollow, would be difficult to decide. The squire was a gentleman who could be as blind as a mole when it pleased him, or as sharp-sighted as a ferret if sharp-sightedness suited his purpose. On this occasion he played the mole and pretended to know nothing, until one midsummer day, when he pounced upon his son at dinner-time with a sudden charge.

"So, sir, you have been deceiving me," he exclaimed. "You have taken advantage of the liberty I give you to form low acquaintance."

"What do you mean by low acquaintance?" asked Oswald, turning pale. "I associate with none who can be called by that name."

"What, sir! are you not hail-fellow-well-met with that grocer Haggard?"

"I thought you professed republican sentiments, sir, and despised the petty differences of social rank."

"So I do, when a duke undersells me by letting his land at so low a rate that mine will hardly bring me three per cent.; but I don't want my son and heir to keep company with counter-jumpers. Trade is an honorable calling. I'm republican enough to admit that; but this friend of yours is a Jack-of-all-trades, and deals in fire-and-brimstone on Sundays. I might forgive him for being a grocer, but I can't forgive him for being a canting, hypocritical knave."

"Why should you call him that? You don't know him; and you, you have no religion at all, can not be prejudiced against him because he is a Dissenter."

"I call him canter and hypocrite because he trades on his piety, and sells his tea and sugar and candles faster than any other tradesman on the strength of his Sunday ranting."

Oswald kept his temper with an effort. Abuse of Joshua Haggard was more than a man who loved Naomi could meekly bear.

"I happen to know Mr. Haggard thoroughly," he said, "and I know that he is honest as a trader and earnest as a preacher; that piety with him is no sham put on to serve a purpose; that in the old days, when persecution was the reward of faith, he would have testified to his belief at the stake. Yes, sir, this homely village shop-keeper is of the stuff that martyrs are made of."

"I wish there were any probability of this wear and tear of this stuff being roughly tested," retorted the squire. "These Dissenters are very fond of howling about fire-and-brimstone in a remote and shadowy future. I should like to see them brought face to face with a pile of blazing fagots in the present. However, this is wide of the purpose, young gentleman. I want to know what you mean by courting this Methodist's daughter."

"What court-ship generally means, sir—the prelude to marriage."

"What, you, Oswald Pentreath, seriously intend to marry a grocer's daughter?"

"Certainly, my dear father, if she will have me. I think you should be flattered that your son shows himself so apt a disciple of your gospel of liberty."

The squire, who had lived through that all-uprooting whirlwind in history, the French Revolution, had often preached second-hand Marat and Danton to his son, to say nothing of second-hand Wilkes. But he was not prepared to have his opinions cast back in his teeth after this practical fashion.

"Then you mean to marry this girl?" he said.

"I do, sir. I shall be sorry if my marriage offends you; but as it is a matter which involves the happiness of my life, you must not be angry if I choose for myself."

"A pretty choice for a gentleman's son!" exclaimed the squire.

"Supposing it were a bad choice, which I deny, what opportunities have I had for making a better? You have chosen to live your own life—you have shut yourself up in this house and isolated yourself from your fellow-men. You have kept me so complete a pauper, that I could not venture to make a friend in my own station lest I should be put to open shame some day on account of my empty pockets. I have accepted the life patiently enough. I have assumed a pride that I never felt, to save myself from humiliation. I have fenced myself round with a dogged reserve, to escape the degradation of being patronized by men who are my inferiors in all but purse."

"How much money can this person of yours give his daughter?" asked the squire, suddenly changing his note.

"That is a question I have never thought of asking."

"Humph!" muttered the aggravated father. "You ought to have been a prince in a fairy tale. You're about as much sense as that young man who picked up the glass slipper, and offered to marry the first woman who could get her foot into it. Now, hark ye, sir! If Joshua Haggard can give his daughter five thousand pounds on her wedding-day—no settlements or rubbish of that sort, mind you—you can marry her without let or hinderance from me, and you can bring her home here. One young woman won't make much difference in the housekeeping, I suppose, for the first year or so."

"I don't know about the five thousand pounds," replied Oswald, "but I thank you for the friendliness of your offer. I believe Mr. Haggard has saved money; but I should not like him to think I had any expectation of gain in proposing for his daughter."

He told his father of his promise to Joshua, and under what conditions he was received in the minister's household.

"I have another year to serve before my apprenticeship is finished," he said. "I shall give you proper notice of my marriage, you may be assured."

"That's dutiful; but be sure you don't marry without a dowry. A few thousand pounds spent on improvements, as the leases run out, would raise our rents five-and-twenty per cent. As far as my inclination goes, I'd as lief you married the grocer's daughter as the finest lady in the land, or liefer. I want no fine lady here to waste and squander, to find fault with the old-fashioned furniture, and quarrel with the old servants, and spend a fortune on new-fangled flowers with Latin names, as some do."

Oswald was deeply grateful for thus much favor; and father and son spent the rest of the evening in the friendliest manner, the old squire prosing about his estate, the rents he got as against the rents he ought to get, leases that were nearly run out, and leases that had a long time to run; but not by one word did he hint at money saved and invested.

"I sometimes wonder what becomes of your rental, father," said Oswald. "We seem to spend so little, and yet you never have any money."

"Ah," groaned the squire, "I was a fool in my time: I've had to pay for my folly. And you don't suppose that a house like this is kept up for nothing—servants to pay, two horses in the stable; and we all eat and drink, remember."

"I should have thought four hundred a year would pay for every thing."

"Should you?" cried the squire, ironically. "You know no more of figures than a baby. Wait till I am under the sod, and see how far four hundred a year will go in a barrack of a house like this."

"But the empty rooms don't eat and drink, father, if we do."

"I can't argue with a fool," cried the squire, testily.

Oswald was very glad to have got over the revelation of his engagement to Naomi so easily. That condition about a dowry was something of a stumbling-block; but he felt assured that Joshua did not mean his daughter to be portionless, and there was plenty of time for all business-like discussion. He felt happier in his wooing after that talk with his father—more at ease with Naomi, better satisfied with himself.

The squire was a practical man, and having made up his mind upon a subject, was not slow in putting his ideas into action. Three days after

having come to an understanding with his son, the old man presented himself at Joshua Haggard's front door in the drowsy afternoon. Sally, the maid of all work, started back as if she had seen a vision on opening the door to that formidable visitor. She had just sense enough to usher Mr. Pentreath into the best parlor, and just strength enough to totter to the opposite room, where Naomi sat at her plain sewing. There was a drizzling rain falling from the dull gray sky, and no possibility of Arcadian rambles on this particular afternoon. Jim was in the shop, being inducted into the mysteries of stock-taking.

"It's the squire," gasped Sally, "and he wants to see your father."

Naomi grew pale at the announcement. Oswald had told her nothing about that talk with his father, the squire's condition about the dowry being a hinderance to any such confidence. Naomi thought that the squire had come to remonstrate. This happy year that was nearly ended was to be the beginning and end of her delight. Some crushing stroke was about to fall, annihilating love and happiness. No one had a good word for the squire, and she could only think of him as a tyrant and an enemy.

She opened the door of communication with the shop.

"You are wanted, father. Mr. Pentreath has called to see you," she said, faintly.

"Tell him I shall come in to tea."

"It's not Oswald, father; it's old Mr. Pentreath."

"What, the squire! Then I must come at once. You'd better do no more till I come back, Jim; you'll only get things in a muddle."

And Jim, nothing loath to be released from his labors, shut the big account-book with a slam, jumped off his high stool, and came, whistling, out of the counting-house, a little railed in pen at the end of the shop.

"I'll wash my hands and come to the squire directly, Naomi," said Joshua; and then, seeing the girl's pale face, he stopped to pat her gently on the shoulder. "Don't be frightened, my dear; the squire can do us no harm. We have been honest and straightforward throughout."

"I feel as if he had come to end my dream, father."

"Life is something more than a dream, Naomi; and a good woman's happiness is not to be blown away by the breath of a bad man."

He went out to the back premises to wash his hands; and then, in no wise discomposed by his visitor's importance, made his appearance in the parlor, where the squire was peering at the flyleaf of the family Bible on which Joshua's marriage and the birth of his two children were recorded. Mr. Pentreath, who knew the names and histories of his neighbors for forty miles round Combhollow, was pleased to see that Naomi's mother had been a Penrose—a name which implied the probability of a dowry, the Penroses being wealthy farmers on the other side of Rockmouth.

He greeted the minister with unusual affability.

"I hope I didn't disturb you in your business occupations, Mr. Haggard," he began, graciously.

"I have wished to call upon you for ever so long; but I am a busy man myself, as I dare say you know—my own steward and bailiff; pay all my accounts with my own hands, and see to ev-

THE SQUIRE'S VISIT.

ery detail—the only way to make a moderate estate thrive. Pray be seated, my dear sir; I want a friendly talk with you," concluded the squire, ensconcing himself in the large chintz-covered arm-chair—chintz daintily clean, and smelling of lavender.

Joshua drew out one of the ponderous horse-hair-seated chairs from the wall, and seated himself opposite his guest.

"Now I suppose, Mr. Haggard, though you and I have never met on friendly terms before, we know as much about each other as if we had been living under the same roof for the last ten years. Nobody has any secrets in a place like Combhollow. You know that I was what is called wild in my youth; that I spent a good deal of money—very wild that—and mortgaged my estate in order to drink and gamble with a pack of ruffians whom I thought wits and fine gentlemen then, and whom I regard with ineffable contempt now. The only thing that has remained to me from those days is a certain liberality of opinion, which places me above the level of these country bumpkins you and I have the misfortune to live among."

"I count it no misfortune to live where I do, Mr. Pentreath. I have an honest liking for most of my neighbors, a warm affection for some of them."

"Ah, you are Christian-like by profession," sneered the squire. "I suppose the animal creation in Combhollow is as good as any other cattle of the same breed; but when one has lived with men who think for themselves, and interchange ideas of some sort—no matter how spurious or how shallow—when they talk, these sons of the soil are but poor company. However, as I was saying, my friends of ninety-five robbed me of my money, and gave me nothing but their freedom of thought in exchange. The school I graduated in held that a shop-keeper was as good as a land-owner any day."

"The school I belong to holds that all men are equal in the presence of their Creator," replied Joshua, quietly; "but we are not the less ready to respect distinctions of class upon earth, and to honor our superiors."

"Yet you allowed my son to come courting your daughter."

"Under such restrictions as would enable him and me to be very sure that he was in earnest before I suffered him to marry her."

"Upon my word, sir, you carry things with a high hand. And it never occurred to you to consult my feelings in respect to this alliance?"

"I considered your son old enough to make his own election."

"Perhaps you did not know that I could disinherit him if he offended me?"

"Yes, Mr. Pentreath. I knew your estate to be unentailed, and your power to dispose of your property unlimited; but as I value your son for what he is himself, rather than for any possibility of inheritance, this consideration had no influence upon me."

"You mean to tell me that you would marry your daughter to a penniless gentleman?"

"I mean to tell you that I would marry her to an honest man who honestly loved her, and trust to Providence for finding him an occupation and a livelihood."

"You would make him turn preacher, perhaps?"

"Not unless he had the gift and inclination for such a calling. I would rather tie a linen apron round his waist and teach him to sell tea and sugar."

"A Pentreath turned village grocer!" cried the squire; "that would be pushing freedom of opinion to its utmost. Well, Mr. Haggard, I admire your independence, and I am not going to interfere with my son's courtship of your daughter. He shall marry her if he likes and you like, and he shall have Pentreath Grange and all that belongs thereto in due time. There may be some of my neighbors who will call me a fool for this indulgence of a young man's fancy; but as my neighbors and I have never been on very friendly terms, I can afford to let them say hard things of me behind my back. Oswald may marry that handsome daughter of yours and bring her home to the Grange as soon as he pleases. And now, Mr. Haggard, having settled the main question, we can proceed to details. How much money—you're a warm man, I know, my good friend—how much, now, do you mean to give this only daughter?"

"That is a question I have never asked myself."

"Perhaps not; but it is a question you must have expected somebody else to ask you, sooner or later. My son has no more idea of life's realities than a bread-and-butter miss at boarding-school. He would never ask you such a question. It's my duty, as a man of the world, to think for him in this matter. You must have saved a good bit of money, Mr. Haggard. Your father had the business before you: and while you were roaming about the hills preaching to the miners and such-like, he was selling tea at twelve shillings a pound. He left you something comfortable, I know, and your wife brought you a tidy little bit of money—didn't she, now?"

"My wife did not come to me empty-handed."

"Of course not; a sensible man like you would not marry a pretty face with an empty pocket. Now, to be perfectly frank with you, I am anxious that my son should be in a position to improve his estate. There's a great deal might be done for a few thousands—building larger barns, draining the low-lying meadows, and so forth. The money would not be squandered, my good friend. Your grandchildren would profit by any sacrifice you might make."

"Good," said Joshua Haggard, thoughtfully. "I think that, upon those conditions, I might give Naomi three thousand pounds for her portion."

"Not half enough for those necessary improvements. If you could say six thousand, now—"

"Impossible. I have a son to think about."

"Your son will succeed to your business."

"For which he must have sufficient capital. We are wholesale dealers in a small way, remember, Mr. Pentreath, and supply a good many village shop-keepers."

"Of course. What a splendid business yours must be! You can give your daughter six thousand pounds without feeling it."

"I could not give her so much without injustice to my boy, and nothing could tempt me to that."

"Pshaw! your business will have doubled itself before your son inherits it. Do you want to make him a millionaire?"

"I want to act fairly between him and his sister. The utmost I could give Naomi, either on her marriage or at my death, would be four or five thousand pounds."

"Say five, and consider it settled," cried the squire, eagerly.

"And I should expect you to settle land of the same value on my daughter, the rent of the same to be paid to her separate use and maintenance during her life, and the property to descend to her children, with reversion to her husband if she dies childless."

The squire's countenance fell, and his small eyes sparkled angrily.

"Why, this is taking a mortgage on my land!" he exclaimed.

"No, Mr. Pentreath; it is only taking care of my daughter. She is incapable of spending such an income on herself, and her receipt of the money would be doubtless a mere form; but I want to feel that I have given my five thousand pounds to her positively, and not to her husband or her father-in-law. Should she be widowed early, the estate so settled would serve to keep her. Should you take it into your head to disinherit your son, the income from his wife's settlement would keep him out of the work-house."

"You are a man of business, Mr. Haggard," exclaimed the squire, divided between disappointment and admiration.

"I should be sorry to be in business if I were not. There is Mallowfield Farm, now; I have heard that valued at five thousand pounds. Settle Mallowfield on my daughter, and Oswald shall have the five thousand on his wedding day, which is as much as to say you shall have the money to spend on barns or drainage."

"Mallowfield!" gasped the squire, "the most compact bit of property on the estate!"

"I can keep my five thousand pounds and my daughter, Mr. Pentreath."

"There isn't better land in the county than those low-lying pastures. Well, I'll turn it over in my mind, friend Haggard. If you would say six thousand, now—"

"I never say more than I mean."

"Come now, I came here prepared to be liberal. Your daughter shall have Mallowfield. How canny of you to pitch upon the best of my farms! And look ye, Mr. Haggard, we'll have the settlements drawn up next week, and you and I will dance at our children's wedding before harvest-home."

"No, Mr. Pentreath. I told your son he must wait two years for my daughter. He has another year to wait before he calls her wife."

"Pshaw! you are as bad as that old gentleman in the Bible who served his son-in-law such a shabby trick. Why shouldn't these young people be married out of hand?"

"I don't believe in hasty marriages, sir. My wife and I had been promised to each other three years before we were married."

"But here, where there is no impediment—"

"There is difference of rank. I want to feel very sure that your son is in earnest—that there is no possibility of after-regrets. He has stood firm for a year, and I believe he loves my daughter. Let him be constant to that attachment for one year more, and I shall be content to trust him with her future. She is very precious to me. I can not let her go lightly."

"Egad, I dare say it's the five thousand he won't let go," thought the squire.

He ceded the point with a tolerable grace, eager as he had been to get the grocer's money into his clutches. After all, it might be well to have time to weigh the matter quietly—to see if there were no better match possible for Oswald, no more money to be made in the open market of matrimony. He was in bad odor among the county people, and had held himself aloof from them churlishly, not taking the trouble to assoilzie himself and get rid of that evil taint left by the past, as he might have done by a little deference to popular prejudices. His unpopularity had reflected itself upon Oswald, and the young man had grown up without a companion or a friend, and quite outside that charmed circle in which rich young spinsters revolve. Still it might not be too late.

"There are places where young fellows pick up heiresses," mused the squire: "Tunbridge Wells, or Bath, or Cheltenham, or Brighton—places where a good-looking man with a good old name and a patrimonial estate might marry a fortune for the asking. But my son has no brains. An adventurer without a sixpence would outmanoeuvre him anywhere."

And then the squire, composing his features into a satyr-like grin, which was meant for a smile, asked to be presented to his future daughter-in-law; whereupon Joshua opened the parlor-door and called Naomi, who came from the opposite room, pale and trembling a little, as if about to make the acquaintance of an ogre.

The shriveled old squire, with his large head and shrunken body, was not altogether unlike the popular idea of the ogre family. His gray hair straggled in sparse locks over his narrow brow, and he wore a pigtail on his high collar of bottle-green velvet—velvet which long and constant wear had made sleeker and more shiny than velvet ought to be. Indeed, the pigtail, for the most part in motion like a pendulum, made its impression upon the velvet.

At his waist the squire wore a large bunch of keys and seals, which he was wont to rattle as he talked. His large gold watch was known to be the exactest time-keeper in Combhollow; and often when the whole town had lapsed ignominiously to the rear of Greenwich time, Mr. Pentreath's bell might be heard ringing up his household in the bleak wintry morning with a rigid exactitude to the very moment marked on the dial at the National Observatory.

Very like an ogre looked the squire as he drew Naomi's head downward to his withered old lips, and honored her with the least agreeable kiss she had ever had in her life.

"Good bless your handsome face!" said the old man, graciously. "From this time forward you must think of me as your father."

"I never can have but one father, sir," answered Naomi, gravely: "but I shall always honor and love you, for your son's sake."

"And you'll come and live at the Grange very soon, my dear, I hope, and keep those idle servants of mine in order"—this at the hardest-working household in Combhollow—"and look to the dairy. I never have a morsel of butter worth eating. This obstinate father of yours talks about Oswald waiting another year, but I see no reason why you should not be married in a month."

"Father always knows best," said Naomi.

"What a demure pass it is! If your father were going to be married himself he'd be in a greater hurry, child. I'm an old man, and may not live to see next summer, and I should like to dance at my son's wedding. That is to say, I should like to see him comfortably married," said the squire, correcting himself; "for us to real ding dances, or any such tomfoolery, I never hold with them. Life's much too serious a matter for its most solemn changes to be ushered by squeaking fiddles and lively jigs."

Having settled a business matter to his satisfaction, and having, as he believed, made himself eminently agreeable, Squire Pentreath took his leave, escorted to the little green garden-gate by Joshua, and contemplated from the other side of the open street by the landlord of The First and Last.

"Every thing is settled, my dear," said Joshua, bending down to kiss his daughter. "My sweet girl will be a lady—mistress of Pentreath Grange, and with manifold opportunities of doing good in her generation. But I hope she will never forget that, before all and above all, she is a Christian, and that earthly blessings are but charges and responsibilities in the sight of God."

"I should be something less than your daughter if I forgot that, my dear father," answered Naomi, tenderly.

Never had she loved her father so dearly as in this moment, when the flood-tide of happiness rushed in upon her soul with overwhelming force.

"Your lover has been true to you for a year, Naomi, and constant under restrictions that some would think hard; let him but prove steadfast for one year more, and I can give you to him without a shadow of doubt."

"He will be steadfast, father," answered the girl, firmly, replying out of the fullness of her own faith, which she knew to be incapable of change or wavering.

CHAPTER IX.

"LOVE IN ONE HAND HIS BOW DID TAKE."

It was summer-time still, the tangled hedges fragrant with honeysuckle and the fields purple with clover, when Joshua Haggard entered the little village of Penmoyle again, after a year's absence, on foot and alone. He had been to the extremity of the peninsula to see Nicholas Wild, and to exult in the progress of that young man's ministrations and the growth of his influence; and now, upon his homeward way, he turned aside from the straight road to Truro, to take his rest in the fat pastures of Penmoyle.

He had arranged things better this time than on the last occasion, and had planned his holiday so as to spend a Sunday at Penmoyle and to preach to the little flock there. As on his former visit, it was a Saturday afternoon when he entered the village, and about the same hour. How peaceful, how unalterable every thing looked, a beautiful placidity pervading all the scene—a quiet profound as that almost awful stillness of smooth mountain lakes locked in a circle of silent hills! And yet death found out Penmoyle now and then; and people's joints were racked with rheumatism; and fever, like a furious Malay, ran amuck among the simple villagers; and bad sons grew up to be the torment of neglectful fathers; and village innocence went astray; and all the evils that rend society at large were repeated in little in this narrow world of Penmoyle. But, smiling under a cloudless sky at the close of June, one might think the place a little bit of heaven that had broken off and fallen upon earth. Round it far and wide lay the wild hills of earth, pierced here and there with the shafts of deserted mines: but this green oasis must be a fragment of paradise.

Joshua contemplated the place with a curious delight. It was not half so picturesque as Comb-hollow, but its inland beauty, its fertile frame of meadow and flowering hedge-row, moved him to deepest admiration.

"How pretty the village is!" he said to himself. "I never used to think it so beautiful."

There was the little chestnut-grove, where the street widened into a village green, just opposite the homely old inn. And there, at the corner of the green, stood the Miss Weblings' neat abode, the brazen knocker shining, the brazen bird-cage gleaming in the afternoon sun, all the windows shut—it being a principle with the spinsters to exclude dust at some sacrifice of fresh air—the muslin curtains drawn back in neat loops, the flower-pots as red as of old.

But there was something that distracted Joshua's eye from flower-pots and bird-cages, and that was a girlish figure standing by the gate, a girlish face looking dreamily down the empty village street.

It was Cynthia, indulging in a few minutes' idle contemplation of the external world after her day's work was done, and that afternoon toilet which was known throughout Penmoyle as cleaning one's self had been carefully performed. There was not much to look at, certainly, in the High Street of Penmoyle, not much excuse for dawdling or frivolous curiosity, but still Cynthia looked. There was a lumbering old wain, loaded high with fragrant hay, standing in front of the inn, while its custodian drank deep of a stinging cider in the bar; there were the inn-keeper's poultry picking up a free living in the highway; there was the landlady's pet jackdaw discoursing hoarsely to the empty air from his wicker cage in front of the parlor-window with its scarlet curtain, which looked so cheerful on dark winter nights: there were the children playing Tommy Tonelwood under the chestnuts, and making as much noise as if a second Herod had just issued his edict for the extermination of another fourteen thousand innocents. And here came the tall figure of Joshua, in his black coat and breeches, well-fitting gray stockings, and neat buckled shoes, walking slowly up the street.

Cynthia gave a start at sight of him, and flung the gate open and ran to meet him, blushing, impetuous, her blue eyes full of joy.

"I knew that you would come," she said.

Had she grown lovelier in the year that was gone, or had she always been thus supremely lovely? Joshua asked himself wonderingly. It seemed to him that he had never beheld any thing so beautiful as that innocent face lifted up to him in tenderest regard, those frank eyes, that rosy, smiling mouth, a complexion as of blush-roses—the old half forgotten blush-roses that grew in the gardens of long ago, ivory-white petals deepening to a soft carnation at the heart of the flower.

"I knew you would come," repeated Cynthia. "Miss Priscilla said you would write first to say that you were coming; but I thought you would come just like this, when no one expected you, walking quietly up the street some Saturday afternoon. I thought it would be on a Saturday; and I have watched for you every Saturday since the roses began to flower. You said you would come in the summer. Are you going back to Truro for the night coach?"

"No, Cynthia; I am going to stay till Monday, if my friends will have me."

"How glad I am!" she cried, clasping her hands. "And you will read to us again in the best parlor?"

"Yes, Cynthia. I hope you have been good."

"I have learned to read the Bible."

"That's good news. And have you been industrious and obedient?"

"I don't quite know; but I think the ladies are pleased with me. Miss Priscilla has given me her flowery gown, and Miss Webling has given me a buckle; and they let me sit with them of evenings when there's no company."

"Then I think you must have been good. Worthy people like the Miss Weblings would treat you according to your deserts."

"They have been very kind, and I am very happy."

"And you have never wished yourself back among those show-folks?"

"Never, never! I was fond of the pony; but he was the only person I really cared for. If I were quite sure nobody would ill-use him, I should never give a thought to my old life; but I do think about him sometimes, poor fellow."

"You have never heard or seen any thing of your people?"

"I have never seen them. Some of the school-children saw them last September on the Truro road — I know it was them by the pony — but they never came nearer than that. I have dreamed about them many a time, and woke crying, thinking I was with them again."

"You shall never be with them again, Cynthia. Why, if they were to come this way now they would hardly know you, you have grown so—sedate-looking."

She was neatly clad in one of those lavender prints he had selected. She wore a muslin handkerchief across her shoulders, a muslin cap on her fair soft hair, which was simply dressed after her own fashion, in which she had reproduced unawares the style of a Greek statue. Her round white arms were bare, the hands reddened a little with labor, but neither large nor ill-shaped.

"I shall hear what your mistresses have to say of you," said Joshua, as he moved toward the doll's-house door; "and if they give a good account of your conduct, I shall be better pleased than I can say."

He had little fear of their report. Such innocent gladness as made radiant Cynthia's face never went with evil-doing. The girl ushered him into the best parlor, and then ran up-stairs to rouse her mistresses, who were taking a gentle siesta on their comfortable tent-bed — a bedstead whose posts had been decapitated to accommodate them to the lowly ceiling of the Miss Weblings' chamber.

The spinsters reposed side by side upon the coverlet, the *County Chronicle* spread under their feet to guard the spotless counterpane, their hair repapered, lest the corkscrew curls should relax from their wiry stiffness in the temporary dissolution of slumber. On hearing of Mr. Haggard's arrival, the simultaneous movement of the sisters was to rush to the small square looking-glass, and take their hair out of papers; the next, to smooth out their ample muslin collars—assisted in this operation by Cynthia—and to adjust the velvet bands upon their foreheads. Then they washed their hands with sisterly familiarity in the same basin, not forgetting to expectorate genteelly in the water lest it should lead to unsisterly tills, and anon descended the corkscrew staircase.

In the parlor the greetings of last summer were gone through again with exact reproduction. The "seedy" cake and the cowslip wine were brought out of the paneled cupboard, and Mr. Haggard was asked solemnly if he had dined. This time he was able to reply conscientiously, that he had eaten a hearty dinner of pork-and-greens at a road-side inn; for people used to dine upon pork-and-greens in those days, and were not ashamed to own it.

"I am going to spend Sunday at Penmoyle," said Joshua. "There are friends I was not lucky enough to see last year; so I have given myself a holiday to-morrow."

"That's good news," cried Deborah; "and you'll stay here, of course? Our spare room is always kept aired, though we don't often have a visitor, unless it's when old Uncle Weston comes from Penzance."

Small as the cottage was, it boasted its spare bed-chamber over the best parlor—a room glorified by a good deal of fine art in the shape of various samplers executed in crewels by the Miss Weblings' prize pupils.

"I shall be very pleased to stay here," replied Joshua, "if you're sure I sha'n't be putting you out."

"Putting us out!" exclaimed the impulsive Priscilla; "dear Mr. Haggard, when we value your acquaintance as one of our most blessed privileges!"

"And as for linen," said the more practical Deborah, "we've the stock of house-linen our dear mother left us — every bit of the yarn her own spinning — the sheets and table-cloths we top-sewed when we were children."

"And now tell me how you have got on with Cynthia," said Joshua, trying to feel as if the question were not one that touched him nearly—trying to approach the subject with the same equable spirit in which he would have discussed the welfare of any member of his little flock at Combhollow. "Has she been docile and useful? Do you think you shall make her a good servant?"

"Mr. Haggard," said Deborah, so solemnly that Joshua thought something bad was coming—he felt himself breathing quicker, as in a moment of fear—"Mr. Haggard, that girl is a treasure."

"Thank God for that!" exclaimed Joshua, with infinite relief.

"It's not many people would pick up such a pearl by the wayside; but it's natural that angels should come unawares to such a good man as you."

"Never mind me," interjected Joshua, eagerly. "Tell me about Cynthia."

"I don't think there's a better girl in the West of England, or one that's quicker and neater with her hands. Of course, sister and I have taken pains with her. I'm not going to deny that, or that we took all the more pains with her out of regard for you. But she has been so quick to learn, with her hands especially. I don't pretend to say that she has a powerful mind—not like sister Priscilla's, for instance." (Priscilla screwed her lips together and tried not to look proud.) "Not a mind to grasp long division or the genealogies of the tribes of Israel, or the wars with the Philistines." (Priscilla shook her head gravely, as if it held as much Scriptural knowledge as Dr. Smith's "Dictionary of the Bible.") "But for handiness, and willingness, and neatness, and goodness of heart, there's no one to surpass her. She nursed me beautifully for three weeks, when I had a bad attack of my quinsy last winter; and if you'd seen how prettily she ornamented this parlor with holly and greenstuff at Christmastime, you'd have been quite struck."

"I am more pleased than I can tell you," said Joshua; and the unwonted glow upon his dark cheek told that the pleasure was very real.

"Of course you'd naturally be anxious. It was an awful risk. I'm sure I used to wake in the middle of the night often, when she was first with us, and tremble for the silver tea-pot. She might have cut both our throats and gone off with the plate, if she'd been badly inclined."

Both sisters shuddered at this appalling possibility.

"And she has learned to read, she tells me," said Joshua.

"Bee-autifully!" exclaimed Priscilla. "We never had a pupil, young or old, that learned so quick. She said she wanted to learn, to please her kind friend who took her out of bondage—meaning you, Mr. Haggard. Many an evening has that poor child sat puzzling over her book, when she first began—and even the letters were some of them strange to her—and wouldn't leave off when we told her."

"I am proud to think that I was not mistaken in her," said Joshua, "when I read truth and innocence in her countenance."

"And there's something so genteel about her," pursued Priscilla. "She never presumes upon one's kindness, or forgets her station. I'm sure the way we've let her sit with us of an evening and taken her for walks would have turned some girls' heads; but she has always kept her place and respected ours."

"It does my heart good to hear this account of her," said Joshua. "And now I'll go down the village and look in upon my old friends. Mr. Martin still lives next the chapel, I suppose?"

"Yes, dear old gentleman! and though he's getting feeble and is not the preacher he used to be, people come from six miles off to hear him, and the chapel's so crowded that on warm Sundays sister and I are obliged to take peppermint lozenges to keep off the faintness. There's many a heart will be stirred if you preach to-morrow, Mr. Haggard."

"Don't forget that we tea at five," said Deborah.

"No, I shall be back by five," replied Joshua, slowly.

He had very little inclination to leave that best parlor of the Miss Weblings, although he had come to Penmoyle to see all his old friends. It was not to be supposed that he would waste two days of his earnest working life—a life in which leisure was almost unknown—upon an inquiry about the progress of that waif and stray he had picked up by the wayside. A letter would have served to make that inquiry. No; he had come to Penmoyle to see those brother Christians to whom he had preached justification by faith, a Saviour's infinite atonement of all human sin, years ago; he had come to talk with those in whose hearts he had been the first to kindle religious fervor.

He left the Miss Weblings' parlor with some sense of effort, notwithstanding; a kind of apathy as to those old friends of his seemed to have stolen upon him since his arrival at Penmoyle. He desired nothing so much as to sit in that neatly ordered room and hear Cynthia read, or hear her mistresses praise her. But the call of duty was paramount, so he took up his hat and went.

Mr. Martin was a little old man with white hair, who remembered John Wesley, and had imbibed his enthusiasm from that fountain of simple and spiritual earnestness. He was a good old man, and much beloved by his humble followers; and though he preached in a somewhat cracked and quavering treble, and spun the same thin thread of doctrine through many sermons to attenuation, and generally chose his text from some obscure passage in the minor prophets, he was listened to with devout attention, and admired as an oracle. He was great at tea-meetings and love-feasts, and repeated his little elderly jokes and told the same anecdotes about the Wesleys year after year. He had some pretensions to the literary faculty, and had written an account of the last hours and death-bed conversations of an interesting member of his flock, a girl whose piety had been the delight of an admiring circle, and who had been cut off untimely by "a consumption." This little volume of fifty pages was more popular at Penmoyle than any of that pernicious literature which an unbelieving race accepted at the hands of such arch-offenders as Byron, Moore, Godwin, Monk Lewis, and Shelley—names which had been breathed as by some wandering blast from Pandemonium in the awe-struck ears of Penmoyle. An inhabitant of this remote settlement, on entering the literary circles of the metropolis, would have been astonished to find that Mr. Martin's biography of Miss Elizabeth Lucas was not considered a classic, nor as familiar to the reading public as "Rasselas" or "The Vicar of Wakefield."

On the female mind in Penmoyle the book had exercised as strong an influence as had the "Confessions of Rousseau" or the "Sorrows of Werter" on the world in general; and a young woman of Mr. Martin's flock would have considered that, next to marrying a rich farmer and driving one's own chaise-cart, the happiest destiny would be to die early and discourse wisely on one's death-bed, like Elizabeth Lucas.

Mr. Martin wore his literary laurels meekly, but, in his heart of hearts, was prouder of having written that little book than of all his long and blameless life and its good influence upon his fellow-men. He amused his leisure hours by mild coquetting with the Muses, and composed sacred verses of the feeblest strain, which he screwed out of his seething brain with infinite labor, and had some idea of publishing by subscription, could he but get the lines more of a length, and resolve his own doubts as to certain rhymes which necessity had constrained him to use, although his ear had not approved them.

This simple-minded pastor lived in a four-roomed cottage next his chapel—a cottage neatly furnished, and beautified not a little by various offerings from the Methodists of the district. An ancient widow, whose family and belongings were lost in the darkness of prehistoric Penmoyle, ministered to the good man's modest wants, and kept his habitation spotless, laboring at her mission with activity and industry which would have done credit to those younger servants who were known at Penmoyle as "bits of girls." This faithful house-keeper, neatly clad in a black gown, widow's cap, and muslin kerchief, opened the door to Joshua's knock. She had worn a widow's cap for the last forty years, and would have doubted her own identity had she seen herself in a glass with any other head-covering.

"Lor sakes!" she exclaimed, with a low courtesy, "if it ain't Mr. Haggard!"

As the cottage door opened straight into the parlor, Mr. Martin, writing with laborious slowness at his table, heard the ejaculation, and rose hastily to welcome his guest, with a formal cordiality full of a certain old-fashioned dignity, as of one who had been accustomed all his life to be respected and to confer a favor by his kindness.

"And what has brought my good friend this way?" he asked. "Glad am I to see him once more beside my hearth. Go, get a mutton-chop or a steak, Martha, and cook it nicely for Mr. Haggard. I have a cask of cider from the same orchard as that you used to drink twenty years ago."

"You needn't trouble about the chop, Mrs. Hope. I have dined, my dear sir; but I shall be pleased to drink your health in a glass of that excellent cider before I leave you. I am thankful to see you looking hale and hearty."

"Ay," replied the old man, with a tremulous cheeriness, "Providence has been very good to me. Except for a little stiffness in my joints in winter-time, and a slight uncertainty in my hearing, which I can hardly call deafness, I might easily forget that I am getting old. I can still enjoy the manifold beauties of God's earth, and my books," glancing with pride at his neatly arranged library, guarded by the glass doors of an old-fashioned book-case. "I can still employ my leisure hours in poetic musings, which, although perchance beneath the regard of finite man, are, I venture to hope, acceptable to an infinite God. Ah, my dearest friend, it is a strange and fearful blessing for the aged to be spared when Time's sickle mows down the youthful."

Here the pastor's eye glittered with a tear of regret for his beloved pupil, Elizabeth Lucas, and Joshua made haste to change the conversation. He had heard that story of Elizabeth Lucas's lingering illness and pious discourses a good many times from the gentle old pastor's lips, and rather dreaded a repetition thereof. The pious platitudes were milk for babes rather than meat for strong men; and although Joshua had a firm belief in the Christian graces of the departed Elizabeth, he was not quite clear as to her share in these holy dialogues; just as, in reading the "Phædo," some students may entertain a doubt as to which is Plato and which is Socrates.

Having fortunately escaped this conversational quicksand, in which he saw himself on the point of being ingulfed, Mr. Haggard and his elder friend talked pleasantly of each other's ministrations, and the welfare and progress of their particular sect, which, although taking its origin from the great evangelical movement begun by Wesley, was but a minor division of the dissenting Church. Mr. Martin talked of his crowded chapel; his night-school for farm-laborers; his afternoon class for young women in domestic service, which young persons of a superior social standing were invited to attend, could they so far subjugate their pride as to sit side by side with the hard-handed daughters of toil.

"That is a bright little creature over yonder," said Mr. Martin, with a nod in the direction of the Miss Weblings' domicile; "she has come to my class-meetings regularly, and has made wonderful progress. I never met with a clearer mind. I do not say that it is deep, or that she is a being of lofty aspirations, like my sainted Elizabeth—"

"I am delighted to hear you speak so kindly of her," exclaimed Joshua. "You have heard, I dare say—"

"How you rescued her from the children of Belial? Yes, my good friend; she has told me of your kindness with tears. She has a grateful and a tender heart; she has a pleasant voice, too, and sings our hymns sweetly. It was but last Sabbath that I was moved by hearing her sing the 'Land of Canaan.' There were tones which reminded me of that heavenly-minded girl, whose last hours—"

"And my poor little waif and stray has made spiritual progress?"

"Undoubtedly. I don't think you could ask her a question about the Israelites in the desert, or the building of Solomon's Temple, that she would fail to answer correctly. And now, my good friend, tell me how long you are going to stay among us, and if you will give us one of your powerful discourses to-morrow. We are collecting funds for a new chapel, our present humble building being sadly inadequate. A sermon from you would insure a good collection."

Joshua declared his willingness to assist so worthy a cause; and, after half an hour's cheerful conversation, left his old friend to resume his gentle flirtation with the Nine, and went on to visit other acquaintances of the past.

Five o'clock found Mr. Haggard at the little green door, where Cynthia stood watching for him on the threshold, just as she had watched by the gate that afternoon.

"The tea's mashed," she said, brightly, "and the ladies told me to watch for you."

She darted back to the kitchen before he had time to reply, having the baking of certain rock-cakes, seedy and curranty, esteemed a delicacy in Penmoyle, on her mind. Mr. Haggard looked after her curiously, wondering at the difference between this light and airy form, just vanishing from his sight at the end of the passage, and the rotund and robust Sally who ministered to his wants at home. Yet both were of the same clay, he reminded himself, and the one as precious in the sight of her Maker as the other.

The sisters Webling, glorified by additional embellishment in the way of ear-droppers and brooches and buckles—but not in their Sunday gowns; *those* Mr. Haggard would see to-morrow—received the minister amidst the stately elegance of the best parlor. There was the silver tea-pot he knew so well, with its horn handle and little perforated basket dangling at the spout: there were the willow-pattern cups and saucers, and crisp home-baked bread, and slices of ham garnished with parsley, and three new-laid eggs in glass egg-cups, and a plate of strawberries—quite a collation.

"I hope you have brought us a good appetite, dear Mr. Haggard," said Priscilla.

"Indeed, Miss Priscilla, I am not accustomed to such luxuries. Our tea at home is a very plain meal. I was brought up to live plainly, and have brought up my children in the same way. But I have no doubt I shall do justice to your plenteous table."

Cynthia came in with the rock-cakes, and retired as soon as she had set them on the table, dropping her modest courtesy as she went out at the door.

Somehow, in spite of the strong tea, the new-laid eggs, the excellent ham which the hospitable sisters pressed upon him—in spite of that exalted appreciation of his own merits which breathed in every sentence spoken by these spinsters—the tea-drinking, protracted for an hour or more, seemed rather a weary business to Joshua. He found his thoughts wandering backward to the little red-floored kitchen, luminous in the rosy sunset, and the gracious figure of girlhood by the open casement. He found himself reflecting what a blessed thing it was to have rescued this wild weed, neglected by the roadside, and to find her blossoming so fair a flower, instead of listening, as he ought in common courtesy to have listened, to Deborah's account of one of her old scholars who had gone to America, and was on the high-road to a fortune, and who had avouched in a letter to his mother—a letter written on the other side of the broad Atlantic—that he should never have come to any good if the Miss Weblings had not taught him his multiplication-table.

"He was a dull boy," said Deborah; "many's the time I've had to put the dunce's cap on him and stand him up on a form, though it went against me. And the trouble I had over his pot-hooks—there, it was really trying! But it's nice to think that he should remember and be grateful, so far away. It speaks well for human nature, you know," concluded Miss Webling, in a patronizing tone, as if she belonged to a different species.

After tea came the usual request for a chapter and Mr. Haggard's exposition thereof; and Cynthia, having removed the tea-things, took her seat below the salt, that is to say, on the chair nearest the door; while the spinsters, each seated in her particular chair, straightened their long backs, and folded their mittened hands, and assumed exactly the same expression of countenance.

This time Joshua took the story of the traveler coming down to Jerusalem who fell among thieves. Perhaps some faint resemblance between that sacred record and his own rescue of the girl yonder may have influenced his selection, but he hardly owned as much to himself. His simple yet eloquent commentary touched the girl deeply; every word of those Gospels was now familiar to her. She had read the New Testament with fervid interest. The sacred story, new to her girlish mind, had been verily a revelation, and she had accepted this new creed—the first ever offered to her understanding—with faith and affection that knew no limit. It seemed all intensely real to her ardent nature. Her imagination pictured every scene, filled up every detail: she could see the divine face shining upon her, the little children gathered round the gracious Teacher; the blind, the sick, the lame, the leper, the outcast, seeking comfort and healing from that inexhaustible fountain of mercy. She saw all these things in holy waking dreams—saw them as really as some hysterical nun in her ecstatic trance.

But for Joshua Haggard she would never have known this blessed history, never have belonged to those happy and elected souls chosen to share the Master's rest when earth's brief pilgrimage was over. But for him she would have lived her wretched life among the lost ones, doomed to perdition after death, shut out forever from the glorious light which shone upon that happy section of humanity selected for salvation. That without Joshua's mediation she might have come into the Christian fold, that some other friendly hand might have opened the door to her, was an idea that had never occurred to her mind, more inclined to enthusiasm than to logic. She accepted Joshua as her spiritual sponsor, the benefactor who had given her the heritage of salvation, and her gratitude was measureless as her value of the blessings she had so nearly lost.

There were tears in her eyes as he dwelt on the story of the Samaritan.

"You did much more than that for me," she said, softly, when he had finished. "It was not my body you saved, but my soul. When I stopped to rest on the common that day, I did not know that I had a soul, or that heaven was any more than the blue sky where the birds sing."

"It's wonderful to think of," exclaimed Priscilla, proud of her pupil: "and now she can say off the books of the Bible as quick as anything without missing one. Let the minister hear you, Cynthia."

The girl obeyed, and rattled over the titles of the holy books in a string, as she had been taught by Priscilla.

"Now let's have the counties of England and Wales, my dear."

Cynthia repeated an ancient rhymed list of the shires, which sounded like an incantation. Her preceptress listened approvingly, with her head on one side, in a critical attitude, proud of her work.

"I should like to hear you read a chapter in the Gospel, Cynthia," said Mr. Haggard.

Whereupon the girl turned over the leaves of her Testament thoughtfully, and then read the story of the raising of Lazarus. She read beautifully, with feeling and understanding in every tone. Tears of gladness filled Joshua's eyes as he listened. This was the richest reward he had ever reaped for his good works.

When she had read her chapter, Cynthia withdrew modestly to her more correct sphere in the kitchen, and resumed her plain sewing by the last rays of summer daylight, while the Miss Weblings entertained Joshua for the rest of the evening.

At half-past nine—quite a late hour for that feminine household—Joshua was invited to say an evening prayer; and Cynthia again appeared at the tinkling of a small hand-bell which Priscilla held outside the door; and after the prayer, which was long and fervent, like all Joshua's prayers, and personal also, glancing at his blessed work in this lowly handmaiden's conversion from the paths of darkness and error, Cynthia was ordered to sing a hymn.

She stood before them with hands meekly folded, and in a voice clear as a bird's, a bright and silvery soprano, sung one of the favorite hymns of that particular sect—simple, not unmelodious verses, telling of the happy land beyond death's awful river—verses set to a tune that had a lively lilt in it, and was hardly so suggestive of devotion as one of Mozart's sacred numbers.

After the hymn Joshua was pressed to refresh himself once more with cowslip wine and seedy cake; and on refusing those luxuries, he was escorted, with a newly set candle and as much ceremony as a cork-screw or belfry staircase will admit, to his lavender-scented chamber, where the dimity draperies were starched to such a degree that they stood alone.

The midsummer moon looked in at him through the diamond panes of his casement as he laid himself down, a little tired after a twenty-mile walk and the various emotions of the day. What was this strange feeling, too sweet for pain, too thrilling for happiness, which swelled his breast? What this unknown rapture which moved him to tears?

"Thank God!" he ejaculated involuntarily, yet scarcely knew what new blessing that was which moved him to such thankfulness. He dared not question his own thoughts. He was like one awakened out of a trance, who finds himself in a land where all things are strange. He sunk to sleep with that vague, mysterious happiness in mind and heart, fell asleep and dreamed that he had passed into that happier land on the farther side of the dark river, and that the first to give him greeting there was Cynthia, with a face like an angel's.

CHAPTER X.

"OH, LET MY JOYS HAVE SOME ABIDING!"

PLACID and happy, after its quiet fashion, was the Sabbath which followed. The scene of Joshua Haggard's life was so rarely shifted, that he may be pardoned by the hearth-goddess for feeling a certain satisfaction in finding himself away from home. The novelty of Sunday at Penmoyle was pleasing. It was a relief not to receive exactly the same greetings he had received last Sunday; not to hear precisely the same speeches, accompanied by the same tones, and looks, and becks, and nods, and even the same oratorical flourishes of a stout green-cotton umbrella or a neatly polished oak sapling; and a relief, perhaps, to the eye not to see those particular coal-scuttle bonnets or bottle-green spencers which adorned his own Bethel. The differences between Combhollow and Penmoyle were only differences of detail; but he felt that he was in a strange land, farther west, among people still

more simple than his own flock, and people who loved him no less.

His sermon was a success. Sixpences and shillings rattled into the metal platters which the smug-faced deacons, in their glossy Sunday coats, held at the doors of the chapel. The temple was crowded to its utmost capacity, and handkerchiefs were used freely for fanning ruddy faces or for mopping perspiring foreheads, while peppermint lozenges and smelling-salts were interchanged among friends.

In a corner of the Miss Weldings' narrow deal pew sat Cynthia, in a straw gypsy-hat, her head thrown back a little as she looked up at the preacher. He saw those spiritual blue eyes gazing upward—saw and was moved by that unknown passion of joy or pain which had thrilled him last night. He tried to forget that intent face—tried to thrust every earthly influence out of his thoughts as he pleaded for his Creator's glory, for due honor to be paid to the Lord of heaven and earth, as he urged with warmth the duty of sacrifice and unselfishness upon that open-mouthed hurdle flock—the duty of surrendering something of earth's enjoyments, some portion of their temporal blessings, to render homage to him who gives them all.

"If we had a friend who was always showering gifts upon us," he urged, in his familiar way, "should we begrudge him some small offering now and then in return? Should we take all and give nothing? Should we not be miserly and mean if we did? Should we not secretly despise our own meanness, even if we contrived to hide it from the eyes of men? And we have a Benefactor who is always giving. Our sleeping and our waking, our uprising and our downsitting, our health, our strength, our household joys, our homes, our fields, our gardens—all are gifts from Him. Shall we offer nothing for all these things, not even a house in which to worship the universal Giver of good? My brethren, the pagans, whose gods were foolishness, made their temples so beautiful that the beauty of the tabernacle has preserved the memory of the god. Yes; for two thousand years these childish fables have lived in the memory of men, because those who believed them spared neither gold nor silver to testify to their belief. The gods of the Greeks were as real to the Greeks as your God is to you, and the splendor of their temples has remained to posterity as a testimony to the reality of their faith. These were foolish heathens, the children of darkness. Shall we, the children of light, leave nothing behind us upon earth to show our descendants that we, too, were in earnest—that the God of truth has had as faithful followers as the god of liars?"

Verse by verse, he read them—commenting as he went along—the description of Solomon's Temple, his picturesque mind reveling in the gorgeousness of the record. He was asking for funds for a chapel which might be built for three or four hundred pounds; and as he enlarged in glowing language on the glories of that Jewish shrine—the carven cherubim and palm-trees and flowers overlaid with gold, the door-posts of olive-tree and the doors of fir, the floor overlaid with gold within and without, the pillars of brass and the chapiters of molten brass, the nets of checker-work and wreaths of chain-work, the lily-work and pomegranates, and that mighty sea of molten brass standing upon twelve sculptured oxen—his hearers thought within themselves that it behooved Penmoyle to do something; not to be behind the Jews of old, people with hook-noses, and, perhaps, old-clothes bags, and a plurality of hats, whom folks looked down upon nowadays. And Solomon, who at his best was only a Jew, had been able to build this sublime temple, nay, if tradition were to be credited, sent as far as Penzance for tin and copper ore wherewith to accomplish this great work. This moved them much more than any idea about the Greeks, whom they depictured to themselves vaguely and variously, according to their several imaginations.

To Cynthia, this sermon, which might have seemed trite and commonplace to that mordant modern intellect, which, like the Athenian mind, spends itself wholly in going after every new orator, from Monsignor Capel to Moody and Sankey—to Cynthia this sermon was full of color and meaning. Of romance she knew nothing; poetry was a dark language to her, save the mute poetry of stars or flowers, earth's loveliness or heaven's sublimity. She had never heard fine music or seen a stage-play, except the rude representations of showmen at a fair; eloquence, pictures painted in words, were new to her, and she listened spell-bound. She could have given you no definition of greatness, yet in her mind she was assured that Joshua was a great man. She thought of St. Paul holding a vast and adverse throng by the magic of his discourse, and it seemed to her no blasphemy to compare Joshua with that saint and apostle. Her youth, her ardor, had nothing on which to fasten except this ideal of a good and perfect man. She was grateful to her mistresses for their small kindnesses and indulgences; but she vaguely felt the element of ridiculousness in the little fidgety ways and petty particularities of these elderly damsels, and the flowers of her fancy did not entwine themselves around the images of Miss Deborah and Miss Priscilla. The garden of her young mind was a fertile soil, however, and the flowers that sprung there must have something about which to cling and blossom, so they wreathed their ductile tendrils round that sturdy oak Joshua.

The afternoon was occupied by a second service, in which the mild exhortations of Mr. Martin had a somewhat sleepy sound to those who had dined heavily. Spirits weighed down by roast meat and potatoes, and a regretful conviction that the Sunday joint had been a thought too greasy, joined languidly in prayers and hymns; and there was a sense of relief when the lengthy service came to a close, and the congregation poured out of the oven-like chapel into the sweet fresh air.

Several friends dropped in upon the Miss Weblings after service; some who had known Joshua of old, others who were eager to be presented to him; Mrs. Gibbs, the butcher's wife, in her green watered silk, and with a gold watch—one of the few gold watches known to be extant in Penmoyle—reposing on her portly side, almost the grandest lady in the village; Miss Toothy, from the general shop, who was somewhat eccentric in her attire, but reported wealthy; Mr. and Mrs. Pamble, tenant-farmers of some importance, occupying a square stone house on the

outskirts of Penmoyle—large people both, and given to pomposity, as conscious that they had never been a day behind with the half-year's rent, and could afford to trust in Providence when times were bad, having laid by a small fortune before the Peace.

These filled Miss Webling's parlor to overflowing, and taxed the resources of the household in the way of tea-pots. If Cynthia had been less handy, things could not have gone off so genteelly; and the sisters might have been lowered in the esteem of Mrs. Pamble, who really condescended somewhat in visiting them, by sloppy tea; but Cynthia contrived to have a fresh brew in the every-day crockery tea-pot ready to replenish that silver vessel which adorned the tray. She brought in the rock-cakes hot, and nestling in a clean napkin, and she was never behindhand with bread-and-butter of the genteelest thinness.

"That's a handy girl of yours, Miss Webling," said Mrs. Pamble, approvingly, when the chapel and the day's sermons and the possibilities of the building-fund had been amply discussed.

"And an uncommon good-looking one too," added the farmer, in his beefy voice. "You won't have her long, miss, I fancy; some of the young chaps will be wanting her to get married. These here pretty ones go off the hooks so soon."

The spinsters bridled, taking this in somewise a personal affront. They had been accounted personable in their time, they could have informed Mr. Pamble, though they had not gone off the hooks.

"If she's as sensible as I give her credit for being, she'll be in no hurry to get married," replied Deborah, bridling. "Single life is not without its advantages."

Miss Webling knew that Mrs. Pamble was one of those disagreeable women who are as proud of having secured a husband and added largely to the population as if those achievements were novel and remarkable facts in the history of womankind.

"Ah, but they're all glad to get a husband; even the sensiblest of them," chuckled the farmer. "They're all ready to say snip to the first as says snap. It's a feminine failing."

At which vulgar speech Mrs. Pamble and Mrs. Gibbs laughed until their silk gowns, or the rigorous corsets under the gowns, creaked ominously.

Miss Toothy looked daggers. She had never said snip to any one's snap, and she felt that the conversation was becoming odiously personal.

"Of course I'm not eluding to ladies like you," said the farmer, perchance perceiving that he was on dangerous ground, and accenting his speech by a slap on Priscilla's spare shoulder. "You've had your offers and throwed over your sweethearts—you and Miss Deborah and Miss Toothy yonder; but servant-gals and such-like ain't so partickler. A husband's a husband to their mind, so long as he's got a hat, and ain't blind or deaf. They wouldn't object to his being dumb, I dare say, for the sake of havin' all the talkin'."

This being an old-established joke, everybody except Joshua laughed heartily.

"She's got very uncommon-colored hair, that gal of yours, Miss Webling," said Mrs. Pamble. "I don't know as I call it pretty for a young woman, though it's very winning in a baby. My

Jimmy has hair just that color; and when he's naughty it goes more against me to slap him than it does the dark-haired ones—he's got such an innocent look with him. But I think flaxen hair's rather too simple-like for a young woman; it gives her a foolish look."

"What matter looks if she is not foolish?" said Joshua, almost sternly. "If you can bring up your daughters to be as sensible and as pious as that servant-girl, you will be a happy woman, Mrs. Pamble; and if God makes them as lovely, pray to him to give them hearts as pure and minds as innocent as hers."

From any one else such freedom of speech would have offended the farmer's wife; but she had come to see Joshua as a great preacher, and one must expect hard sayings from prophets and privileged persons of that kind. She only sniffed dubiously, and looked at her watch, a homely silver one, which compared disadvantageously with that shining golden time-keeper pendent from Mrs. Gibbs's waistband.

"I'm afraid we must be going," said Mrs. Pamble, as if loath to pronounce a sentence which must naturally afflict the company. "There's the dairy never gets properly looked after unless I'm standing behind that girl of mine."

"Ah," granted Mr. Pamble, "you women can do nothing without a lot o' cackle. Missuses and maids is pretty much alike. There's so much scolding goes on in the dairy I wonder it don't turn the milk. No need for rennet, I should think, where there's women's tongues."

"It isn't the women that sits arguing about nothing for three hours at a stretch in a public-house," observed Mrs. Pamble, as she drew her white Paisley shawl across her robust shoulders, and skewered it on her breast with a large mosaic brooch representing St. Peter's at Rome; and after this home-thrust, she rose to depart, the farmer meekly following.

These magnates of the land being gone, after leave-takings at once friendly and ceremonious, Miss Toothy discovered that she was wanted at home, having promised her girl an evening out; and Mrs. Gibbs pronounced herself pledged to her domestic in the like manner. So there was a clearance of the smart little parlor, and the Miss Weblings folded their hands and leaned back in their chairs, feeling as exhausted after this unwonted assembly as a lady of fashion when her reception of three or four hundred of the upper ten thousand is over, and life's green curtain falls on the social comedy.

"I hope I was polite to them all, Priscilla," said Deborah, somewhat anxiously; "but I felt a little confused in my head by their all dropping in together. I'm afraid Miss Toothy might feel herself passed over. She's rather hard to draw out; and the Pambles are so lively."

"Miss Toothy hasn't seen much company," replied Priscilla, excusingly. "You can't expect her to be very conversable. But she's a great reader, and knows more about politics and the royal family than anybody in Penmoyle. She has friends in London that send her a newspaper every week; and she's got some nice books too, Mr. Haggard. She lent me the 'Romance of the Forest' last winter, and I read it aloud to Debbie in the long evenings. I don't see any harm in a good novel once in a way, if you take your time over it, and don't loll by the fireside half the day,

poking your nose into a book and letting your house go to rack and ruin."

"I have forbidden my daughter to read novels," replied Joshua, finding himself thus directly appealed to, "lest the unrealities she would find in them should give her a false picture of life, and encourage her to form baseless hopes or foolish desires. But when she is married, and the mother of a family, she may seek amusement for an evening hour in some innocent fiction, and be none the worse for it. And, of course, at your discreet age, Miss Priscilla, an appeal to the imagination can do no harm."

"There never was a more particular man than my father," said Deborah. "He couldn't abide the sight of a book, when once his children had learned to read, except the Bible on Sundays and Dr. Watts's Hymns. He said books about a place were just an encouragement to idleness, and that as long as women had the use of their hands they ought never to waste time in reading. Yet, you see, Priscilla and me wouldn't be as independent as we are if Providence hadn't given us a taste for learning."

Joshua bowed assent. He had been somewhat wearied by the tea drinking, the fulsome compliments which Mrs. Gibbs and Mrs. Pamble had paid him, the stuffy atmosphere of the parlor smelling of toast and bread-and-butter. He was yearning for a breath of fresh air.

"I think I'll take a turn in that neat little garden of yours," he said, as if asking permission of the sisters, who both had a drowsy look, and regarded him blinkingly, like owls in a zoological collection.

"Do, dear Mr. Haggard; and try and get an appetite for your supper. You made a very poor dinner."

It was a minor duty of hospitality with the Miss Weblings to pretend to think that their guests had fared badly, just as it was the major duty to press their viands upon a visitor's consideration until he was so obliging as to overeat himself.

There was no way of reaching the garden save through the kitchen, so to the kitchen Joshua went. The door at the end of the narrow little passage stood open, and the westward-fronting casement was shining like a jewel at the end of the vista. The kitchen was newly swept and garnished; no sign of unwashed tea-things or broken victuals; the polished grate winking and twinkling in the red light from a neat little fire; the red-brick floor spotless as if it were a floor in a picture; every pot and pan arranged with the grace that belongs to perfect order; a dark-brown jug of roses and syringa on the window-sill; but the figure Joshua had expected to see by the casement was not there. Cynthia had gone for a walk, he thought; had gone to meet and mingle with those other handmaidens whose privilege it was to enjoy a Sabbath-evening ramble; perhaps to keep company—odious phrase—with some rural swain. The idea was repulsive to him. It seemed to him that there was pollution in such contact.

He went through the tiny scullery and out into the garden, which he had surveyed from the window that midsummer evening just a year ago when he bid Cynthia good-bye. There was not much to admire in the garden, perhaps, save for those eyes which are in the habit of looking at all rustic things as pictures, and which can see a

5

study in brown in an old well and an empty bucket, or a nocturne in purple and gold in a cottage thatch steeped in moonlight. To Joshua, whose only experience of landscape-painting had been derived from tea-trays, that sloping bit of garden seemed commonplace enough. Even for politeness' sake he would not have gone so far as to say that he thought it pretty, and yet it charmed him somehow; there was a beauty in this vulgar rusticity which he felt, although he could not recognize or understand it. The picture of grass-plot and flower-bed and crooked old apple-trees spreading their gray branches against the yellow sky; the sweet-pea hedge, the stocks, the sweet-williams, the blush-roses, the thymy pot-herbs; the little thatched shed for the pig yonder in an angle of the hawthorn hedge; the steep bank where the strawberries grew—the homely charm of this picture crept into his heart unawares. He walked slowly across the little grass-plot, where a self-sufficing bantam was pecking at imaginary worms in dignified solitude; he ascended the narrow path, which had been cut into steps where the slope was steepest; and on the higher ground by the hedge discovered Cynthia standing by the pig-sty, and actually exchanging endearments with the pig, whose black head lolled across the edge of his sty, and who expressed the gratification he derived from having his ears pulled in a series of confidential grunts.

"I thought you had gone for a walk, Cynthia," said Mr. Haggard.

"No, sir. I go across the fields sometimes, and as far as the copse"—pointing to a dark, waving line against the sunset—"and gather a bunch of wild flowers, when the ladies give me leave."

"You go with your friends, I suppose; some of the young women in service here?"

"No, sir. I have no friends except my mistresses."

"And no sweetheart, Cynthia?"

"No," she answered, with a curious little smile. What a relief it was to find that her girlish fancy had not idealized some boor!

"Ah, the time will come when you will begin to think of a sweetheart, I dare say; but I'm glad it hasn't come yet. I am going for a stroll across the fields, as far as that wood, perhaps. Will you come with me, and show me where your wild flowers grow?"

"Yes, sir."

"And are you quite happy here, Cynthia?" asked Joshua, when they had walked a little way. There were sheep in the meadow, and the sheep-bell was ringing with a pleasant sound in the twilight.

"Yes, sir; quite happy: most of all when you come here."

"That is not often, Cynthia," he answered, his dark eyes softening to tenderness as they looked at her. Why did she say these things in her thoughtless innocence, and why should words so simple, a mere childish expression of grateful affection, set his heart beating?

"No," answered Cynthia; "it isn't often you come, sir. But it is something to think of, and something to remember."

"I can not tell you what pleasure your progress has given me," said Joshua, gravely, but with a tenderness in his voice that was quite involuntary. "I have thought of you often in the year that has gone, and have supplicated for you in my prayers every day of my life. But I never hoped to reap so rich a harvest. I never thought God would reward me so bounteously—to find your intelligence so bright, your heart so pious, your conduct so exemplary. It is very sweet to me: sweeter than words can say."

There was a mist before his eyes as he looked away to the broken line of wind yonder, not trusting himself to look at his protégée.

"Could I do less than strive hard to learn what you wished me to learn, sir?" asked Cynthia. "Can I ever forget what you have done for me? I was a heathen, as bad as those poor creatures the missionary told us about last winter. I was left outside in the darkness. I must have gone to the habitation of the lost but for you. I pray for you night and day; but my prayers are so little, they can never repay you. I wish I could be your servant, that I might work my fingers to the bone to prove my gratitude. I pray for you, I think of you, I dream of you sometimes; and I see your face all shining, with a glory upon it, like Stephen's when the wicked Jews stoned him."

"Foolish dreams, my dear. I am neither saint nor hero: only a common man, with all our common infirmities; prone to sin when tempted, and chiefly blest in having led a life exempt from temptation to do wrong. Providence has been very good to me, Cynthia: my lines have been cast in pleasant places. I have never known hardships or ill-usage as you have, poor fragile child. No dark shadow has ever fallen across my path."

"It would be hard if you had sorrows to bear, sir; you who are so good," said Cynthia. "Miss Priscilla has told me about you: how you used to preach to the rough miners—men almost as wild as savages—and how their hearts were melted; how you used to walk many miles and suffer hardships, for the sake of doing good and teaching God's word, when you had a comfortable home, where you might have staid if you had chosen. She told me that you offended your father by field-preaching, and that you were likely to have lost all the money he had to leave you, yet you never gave way. Was not that being a hero?"

"No, my dear; it was only being steadfast. The man who is without steadfastness will neither do good to others nor to himself. I saw that there were waste lands to be made ready for harvest, and I put my hand to the plow. God gave me health and strength, and love of the work. It would have gone much harder with me to stay at home behind my father's counter than to bear the worst hardships that ever befell me in my wanderings."

"Yes, I can understand that," said the girl, looking up at him full of enthusiasm; "that is because you are good and great. It was sweeter to you to help others than to be happy yourself. Every soul snatched from darkness and death was a rich harvest. Some of those you have saved are in heaven now. How sweet it must be for you to think that they are pleading for you at the throne of God!"

"My dear child, you let your affection carry you too far. I have but done a humble share of a great work; I only tread in the foot-steps of greater men who have gone before. I am but one of many."

"The Bible does not say that," replied Cynthia. "'The harvest truly is plenteous, but the laborers are few.'"

"That was in the beginning, Cynthia, when God's light was but dawning on the darkness of this world. The prayer has been heard, and the laborers now are many. Let us pray that they may labor aright. You have a lively and ardent mind, my dear; God grant it may never be led astray. For a nature so fervent, so ready to admire and believe, an evil world is full of snares and springes; but so long as you are content to remain at Pennoyle with our kind friends, I feel assured you will be safe and happy. The life is somewhat monotonous, I dare say, but I hope you will not grow weary of it."

"I shall have your coming to look forward to," said Cynthia.

"And, perhaps, in time, if you advance steadily with your education, the Miss Weblings will let you teach in the school; and by-and-by, as they get into years, they may give you the entire management of their pupils; and you will be doing a holy and useful work, and occupying an important place in your little world. So you see, Cynthia, you have something better than domestic service to look forward to, if you go on improving yourself."

"I shall try to do that, to please you," replied Cynthia. "I never forget any thing you say to me. I think I could tell you every word you have said, from the time you first spoke to me on the common."

Joshua was silent. There are some emotions whose ineffable sweetness is akin to pain; there are thrilling moments in which the soul burns with a rapture that is almost agony. How was he to construe these innocent expressions of regard, these little gushes of grateful feeling? Could they, did they, mean something warmer than regard, something deeper than gratitude?

They had crossed a couple of meadows and come to the edge of the copse by this time. It was only a narrow strip of wood, pine trees for the most part, dividing one farm from another—a ragged edge of wilderness upon the skirts of cultivation and fertility; but to Joshua, that Sabbath evening, it was as solemn as that darksome dell Dante walked in—a forest full of mystery and mystic awe. He could scarcely see his companion's face under the pine-trees. It was pale as ivory, shadowy as the face of a spirit.

"It is too late to find any flowers," said Cynthia; "but it was a lovely place in the spring. There were violets and wild crocuses, and blue-bells and wind flowers. There are rabbits, too; look—do you see them flashing past that dark-red trunk yonder?"

Joshua was too preoccupied in spirit to look at rabbits. He walked with his head bent, his hands clasping his stout oak stick, his lips tightly drawn, as if he were trying to solve some problem. One might suppose that he had forgotten the existence of his companion.

He was putting curious questions to himself: "If I were so foolish—if I who have thought myself so strong, should be weak enough to lay down my life at this girl's feet, to set all my hopes on her, to give her the rest of my days—would there be any going backward in such an act? Is it sinful to love her for her youth and her beauty, her sweet tones and looks, and fond, winning ways? Is the attraction that draws me to her despite myself sensual or devilish, a snare of Satan set to catch me in my pride, or is the charm as innocent as it seems to me to-night? God enlighten me and give me grace to be wise; for, whether it be for good or ill, I love her."

Silver arrows of pale summer moonlight pierced the feathery pine-branches, evening's breath crept through the wood with a plaintive sound that was half whisper, half sigh. It was time that Joshua and his companion should go back to the white cottage yonder on the lower ground across the meadows.

"It is getting late, sir," said Cynthia; "the ladies will be wanting me."

"Yes, Cynthia; but I have a question to ask before we go. Soon after day-break to-morrow I shall be on my way home—for I mean to walk the best part of the way—and then, unless you wish, I shall not see you for a year—perhaps never again; for who can tell how your mind may change in a year?"

"It can never change so as to forget your goodness, sir."

"Child, you make too much of my goodness. What I did for you I would have done for the lowest, the ugliest, a leper standing outside the gate and crying, 'Unclean, unclean!' I would have gathered a weed by the wayside, my dear, and cared for it as truly as I cared for the flower. But God chose that I should gather the fairest flower that ever grew in his earthly garden, and keep and cherish it to adorn his heavenly paradise. And this sweet flower, unaware, has grown very dear to me. Cynthia, in your child-like gratitude you have said many words of which, perchance, you have not weighed the meaning. You have spoken lightly out of the innocence of your mind, but your words have gone deep into my heart. You have talked of being my servant, of working for me all the days of my life. Look up at me, love, with those sweet eyes; look at me, my cherished one, my darling, with the straight look that goes from soul to soul, and tell me if you could love me well enough to be my wife—love me well enough to live with me, and be a part of my life, the blessedest, brightest, fairest part of life, all that this earth holds for me of human happiness. I have given my daughter to her lover; henceforth I hold the second place in her heart. O Lord, let me have something that shall be all my own! I have tasted but little of temporal joys; I have given my hopes and desires for others. Before age creeps on, before my day is done, let me have something on which to pour forth my treasure of earthly love; let me be blessed like Abraham and thy chosen ones of old, in the sacred joys of home! Child, child, it is the cry of a strong man's heart that goes forth to thee. Answer, and answer faithfully. Do you love me well enough to be my wife?"

He held her in his arms, held her to his heart, looking down into her eyes. They had both grown accustomed to the half-light of the wood by this time, and saw each other's face very clearly; hers looking upward, pale, earnest, full of sweetness and a rapturous content, as of one in sight of her earthly heaven; his whitened with suppressed feeling, the mouth firmly set, the eyes grave and sombre.

"Answer, love, answer; and as God sees us

here in this wood, under this evening sky, answer truly."

"I love you well enough to be your slave," she said, in a low voice—"well enough to serve you barefoot and in chains, and to be made happy by one kindly look from your eyes. I could never be your equal—could never feel myself good enough to sit by your side, to be called by your name; but I love you with all my heart and strength and mind, as I have been taught to love God. Here, on my knees, savior, protector, friend, I give you my love, my life, myself."

She slipped from his breast to his feet before he was aware, and knelt there with clasped hands, looking up at him—a lovely image of devotion.

"Not at my feet, but next my heart, dearest," he cried, raising her from that humble posture. "You have made me happy beyond my measure of earthly blessedness. If I could have known, when the path seemed most difficult, that behind the curtain of long years God held this joy in store for me, it would have been like a star shining on me, and beckoning me on. How light all present labors, all present perplexities would have seemed, measured against this reward!"

The moon shone full on the face lying on his breast. Purity, innocence, truth, a humble, child-like love, were written there—love so blended with reverence that it had something devotional in its character. Why should the young heart ever change or fall away from affection so pure in its beginning, so holy in its growth? Why, indeed, save for the reason spoken of by the prophet: "The heart of man is deceitful above all things, and desperately wicked: who can know it?"

A moment never to be forgotten—a solemn crisis in life's history, to be remembered with awe in all the years to come—a moment in which earth and earthly things seem to fall away, and spirit speaks to spirit.

They went back through the dewy fields together, Cynthia's hand in Joshua's—the hand which was his own henceforward—a symbol of their life-long union. The sheep were running about the field, and the bell ringing. The church-clock struck nine with a sonorous knell, like the bell of time counting the measure of man's years. A little while, a little while, and the end shall come. While your heart beats so passionately, while your hopes build so boldly, while your fancy makes palaces and earthly paradises to dwell in, time is passing, and the end is at hand. Life is but a journey, and the home where you are happiest is only an inn, from which you must be gone to-morrow.

"Dear heart alive!" cried Deborah, waking from her gentle nap to find herself in darkness; "what's become of Cynthia, and why hasn't she brought candles and the supper-tray? We must have been asleep ever so long."

"The heat quite overcame me," said Priscilla; "and Mr. Pamble is so noisy; his coarse jokes and loud, vulgar laugh gave me the headache. I'm afraid Mr. Haggard must have been shocked with him."

"I could see it in his face," replied Deborah.

Cynthia came in with a pair of mold-candles in shining brass candlesticks and snuffer-tray to match. Joshua followed, grave of countenance, and paler than usual.

"How tired you look, dear Mr. Haggard!" cried Priscilla. "I'm afraid the sermon this morning and those noisy Pambles have wearied you. You must have a glass of cowslip wine this minute. It's very reviving."

Joshua consented, absently, to be revived, and sipped the home-made nectar with a dreamy look, while the sisters watched him curiously. He looked liked one whose spirit has detached itself temporarily from the flesh. The body was there, but the eyes saw not, the lips spoke not; it was a mere automatic body.

"I'm afraid he's ill," whispered Priscilla to Deborah; "and not a drop of brandy in the house!"

Joshua looked up presently, and saw two pairs of affrighted eyes gazing at him as at a spectre.

"I am ready to read and pray with you, dear friends, at the close of this peaceful day," he said.

"It has been a day that will be remembered in Penmoyle for many a year to come," exclaimed the ardent Priscilla.

In the placid monotony of her life the advent of such a man as Joshua made an event of mark. She was not likely to forget his rare appearances in that remote village. She had indeed cherished his image for these fifteen years past—ever since his widowhood made it a lawful thing to worship him with a more individual regard than that reverent affection which the flock gives its shepherd.

Joshua opened his pocket Bible, and read the second chapter of Ruth; Cynthia seated meekly in her accustomed place by the door. In his commentary on the text he spoke of that instinct of the heart which has been called love at first sight, but which is rather an inspiration, a divine prompting of the spirit, which leads man to his fittest help-mate. He touched tenderly on the favor which the gentle Moabitess found in the sight of the stranger; how his heart went forth to her at the very first, even before his servants had told him her pathetic story. He dwelt on the blessedness of such a union, and how God had crowned this marriage with richest honor, his chosen servant David being descended from this stem.

Priscilla wept copiously, her sentimental soul moved deeply by Joshua's discourse; and after he had said his evening prayer, she approached him with a little gush of rapture, and exclaimed:

"Dear Mr. Haggard, it has been my privilege often to hear you eloquent, but your words were never so melting as they have been to-night. The hardest heart must have shed tears," added Miss Priscilla, too enthusiastic to care for anatomical truth.

Joshua blushed. Yes, through the dark clear skin there glowed an actual blush, as he looked at the Miss Weddings almost sheepishly.

"I thought that tender story would win your sympathy," he said; "and I am glad, for I want you to look with added favor upon my Ruth."

He put his arm round Cynthia and drew her to his side. The fair-haired child nestled there, looking up at her mistresses, half shyly, half proudly.

"What!" cried Priscilla, with a shrill scream; "you don't mean—"

"I am like Boaz," he said. "I have no need to tarry any longer in doubtfulness of my own heart. This damsel has found grace in mine eyes, albeit she is a stranger. Heaven gave her to me that summer-day, on Springfield Common. Heaven has given me new thoughts and new hopes since I have known her. I am more blessed in having found her than if all the riches of all the mines in Cornwall had been poured into my lap. God give me grace to love and cherish her, and to make the life she has trusted to me happy!"

"You are going to marry that child!" cried Priscilla, plucking at the velvet circlet on her brow in the wild agitation of the moment. "You, a sober, serious man of forty and upward—a chit younger than your daughter!"

"If I am not too old to find a place in her heart, I care not how young she is. It will be all the sweeter duty to protect and cherish her."

Priscilla flung away her velvet head-band, reckless of the little mourning brooch, with her father's silver hairs behind a tiny square of crystal, which confined it on her intellectual brow. She looked wildly round the best parlor, gave a stifled shriek, a gurgle or two, flung herself on the chintz-covered sofa, grasping the hard bolster convulsively in her agony, and went into vehement hysterics.

She lay there gurgling and choking, with occasional bursts of shrill laughter, for the next ten minutes, while cold water was sprinkled over her head and face, to the detriment of her Sunday toilet and the sofa-cover.

"You shouldn't have told her quite so suddenly," said Deborah, somewhat ashamed of this emotional display. "She has such a mind. The shock has been too much for her. She hasn't had such a fit of hysterics since father died."

Priscilla recovered sufficiently to be led up the corkscrew staircase, and, before departing, cast a piteous look at the minister.

"I should be the last to fling a shadow on your happiness," she said; "but I thought you'd never marry again. I thought your mind was lifted above it; or that if you did, it would be some one of a suitable age, and with a mind fit to mate with yours. But the human heart is a mystery."

And with a strangled sob Priscilla drooped her disordered head upon her sister's shoulder, and suffered herself to be assisted up the corkscrew staircase, an operation which occasioned some bumping of heads and rasping of elbows at awkward turns in the stair.

This was the beginning of evils that came out of Joshua Haggard's second marriage; an event in the life of man to which his kindred in particular and his friends in general are especially apt to take objection; and yet the responsibility of the act is all his, and the good or ill thereof is a cup which his lips alone can drink. Whether he chains himself to a fury who shall make his days and nights miserable, or wins to his side an angel who shall shed upon his pathway the sunshine of domestic bliss, and make his progress to the grave pleasant as a noontide ramble through a rose-garden, it is he who shall pay the penalty of a foolish choice or reap the reward of a wise one.

CHAPTER XI.

"WE ARE IN LOVE'S LAND TO-DAY."

A SLEEPLESS night shed the sober light of reason upon those clouds of sentiment which had obscured Miss Priscilla Webling's mind. "When all is done," said Reason, "you know but too well that you had no hope of having Joshua for a husband, suitable as might have been such a union, blessed as you might have made his days by your cherishing and ministration. You know yourself a creature especially adapted to be an Independent minister's wife; but his eyes have been blinded to that fact; he could not pierce the modest veil in which maidenhood enfolded you and discern the image of the perfect wife behind it. His mind—too much given to spiritual things to be acute upon earthly matters—has been caught by the surface beauty of a foolish child. It is for you to pity rather than resent an error for which he will doubtless pay dearly when he lies down in damp sheets, or drinks tea made with half-boiled water, or eats potatoes as hard as stones, and suffers in various other ways from the mistakes of an inexperienced housekeeper; to say nothing of the likelihood that so young a wife may be dressy and flighty, and given to standing at her door of afternoons gossiping, to the neglect of the house-work."

Thus counseled by reason, Priscilla assisted at the seven-o'clock breakfast with a tranquil demeanor, and even smiled upon Joshua with an assumed cheerfulness, which had some element of the heroic.

"I hope you do not think my choice foolish or blameworthy," said Joshua, meekly, as Deborah helped him to fried potatoes and bacon.

"Indeed, dear Mr. Haggard, marriage is such a serious consideration—and a second marriage, where there are grown-up children, more particularly—that I don't feel qualified to form an opinion. Cynthia is a good girl, as girls go; that I should be sorry to deny, after the way she nursed me through my quinsy last winter. But there's a wide difference between a servant-girl and a minister's wife, and a great deal will be expected of her in that position."

"I am not afraid," said Joshua, "if I can but make her happy. In the innocence of her heart she has given me her love. God give me grace to keep and strengthen that affection in the days to come!"

"She has so much reason to be grateful to you," began Priscilla.

"I am not talking of gratitude," interrupted Joshua, almost angrily. "She has given me her love. I know not why I am so blessed, but I know that she loves me. It is the rich reward of all my days of care and toil. I have not felt my labor heavy. I have no foolish pride in my work; but the sum of it has perhaps been pleasing in the sight of Heaven, and this reward has been granted to me—love and renewed youth, a life that seems beginning again from the starting-point of twenty years. I feel as young as on the day I first preached in Pennoyle—before there was a chapel here—on the bit of green waste at the opening of the lane that leads to Mr. Pamble's farm."

"That was four-and-twenty years ago," said Deborah; "for it was the very year father died, and sister and I walked through the dusty lanes in our new mourning to hear you."

This, to Deborah's mind, was almost equal to self-sacrifice to walking over red-hot plowshares.

"It was before we opened the school," said Priscilla, "and when folks were recommending us to take situations as housekeepers, instead of profiting by our education."

"I feel as young as I felt that day—four-and-twenty years ago," exclaimed Joshua, triumphantly.

This was an intoxication of the mind which seemed to the Miss Weblings fraught with peril. It was a positive duty to say something depressing.

"Ah!" sighed Priscilla, "if poor Mrs. Haggard could have looked forward to this in her long illness, she would have felt it trying. It's a blessing that we're not permitted to see into the future."

"I am not going to act hastily," said Joshua, ignoring this dismal suggestion. "I thought it my duty to tell you my intentions without delay; but I shall tell no one else yet a while, not even my son and daughter. I shall leave Cynthia with you for some time longer. She shall have time for reflection—many peaceful days in which to consider the promise she has made me. If any change should come to her mind, if she should discover that she has been mistaken in her feelings toward me, I shall be ready to set her free. It will need but a word from her to loosen the bond between us. I shall tell her this before we part. If she hold steadfast to her promise of last night, I shall come back to fetch her before this year is ended. Meanwhile I know that you will be kind to her, and that she will be happy with you."

"We have always tried to do our duty by her," returned Deborah, rather stiffly.

She could not quite forgive Mr. Haggard for his absurd choice, when the superior mind of her sister had been lying open before him for these last twenty years like a wise and valuable book, and he had not had the sense to read it.

"I'm afraid she'll be puffed up by the change in her prospects," suggested Priscilla, "and not so obedient and dutiful as she has been. We can hardly expect it of her under the circumstances."

"I do not think you will find any difference," said Joshua. "She is sincerely grateful to you for your goodness to her."

"Yes; but in our case her gratitude does not turn into love," retorted Priscilla, sharply.

Cynthia brought in the tea-kettle to make the tea, and took it out again to be kept on the boil on the kitchen-hob, with a meekness which seemed to give the lie to her mistresses' doubts; and presently, when Joshua had finished his breakfast and went out to the kitchen to bid his newly-betrothed good-bye, he found her scrubbing the deal-table with vigorous industry, which had brought a vivid pink to the fair young face.

She put down the scrubbing-brush, and he took her in his arms and kissed her—with a kiss which was fatherly in its protecting gentleness, lover-like in its suppressed passion.

"Dearest love," he said, softly, holding her in his embrace all the while, and looking down at her with tender seriousness, "I am going to leave you for a few months. I am going away,

dear, so that you may look into your heart and be very sure the love you talked of last night is real, and not a childish fancy which may melt away like the memory of a dream when we awake. In our sleep we wander in a beautiful garden, and clasp the hand of a friend—loved and dead, perhaps, long ago; and in the morning we awake, and there is nothing left of our dream—hardly a memory. Your love for me might be like that, Cynthia."

"No, no," she answered, eagerly, looking up into his eyes—"no, it is real, like your goodness, like your wisdom."

"I am old enough to be your father, Cynthia. I have a daughter older than you."

"What has that to do with it? I did not think about your age when I began to love you."

"When did you begin to do that, sweet one?"

"When you went away from here I felt that there was something gone out of my life, and I knew that I liked you very much. But perhaps I might never have known that I loved you if—"

She stopped, blushing deeply, and trifling with the lapel of his coat.

"If what, dearest?"

"I don't like to tell you; it is so foolish."

"Please tell me, dear."

"Young Mr. Price, at The Rising Sun, wanted to be my sweetheart. He used to wait for me coming out of chapel of an evening, and follow me across the street, and stop me at the garden-gate talking to me. And when he talked about loving me and wanting to marry me, I hated him dreadfully; and then I knew that I loved you."

"And I hope you made Mr. Price quite understand that you didn't care for him?"

"Oh yes; I told him so very plainly, and he was rather offended, and Miss Priscilla said I was very foolish to refuse so good an offer. But you've no idea how I hated him when he talked about being fond of me."

"God bless you, darling; and good-bye till I come back to fetch my young wife, or till you write me one little line to say you have changed your mind."

"I shall never write that," replied Cynthia, with conviction.

And with these words, they kissed once more and parted, Joshua setting out on his homeward journey with the light heart of youth, weaving visions of his happy future as he walked in the brier-scented lanes, painting pictures of that familiar home which was soon to be beautified by Cynthia's sweet presence. It seemed to him that he had never known what beauty and grace in woman meant before he found that wanderer on the sunburned common—before he looked down on those loose locks of palest gold, and saw the white feet gleaming under dark water, the delicate figure half sitting, half reclining, on the grassy hillock with the listless grace of repose.

He speculated how he could make the old home a little brighter for its new mistress. That dingy carpet in the common parlor must be exchanged for a new one. He would buy a harpsichord or one of those new pianos people talked about, and Cynthia could learn to play hymntunes. He would buy a gig or a four-wheeled chaise to drive his wife in, instead of the taxcart. When Jim got steadier and married—

events which ought to happen within the next half-dozen years—Joshua told himself that he might retire from the grocery business altogether, and devote himself exclusively to the chapel. There was a cottage on the slope of the hill, at the upper end of Combhollow, which he fancied would be a charming home for himself and his young wife—a romantic cottage, with a garden in which some ambitious tenant had made a fountain. It seemed to the lover's fancy that this cottage, with its fountain and weeping-ash, was better adapted as a background to his picture of Cynthia than the substantial, commonplace old house opposite The First and Last. Yet it would go against him to leave the old house. His father and mother had lived and died there. It was his first idea of home. No; if Cynthia were satisfied, he would stay there. And that cottage with the fountain was probably damp. Picturesqueness and rheumatism often go together.

And Judith? How would that tight-waisted, tight-lipped damsel get on with a lovely young wife? Judith must be taught to bridle that sharp tongue of hers, to put the curb on her quick temper. There must be no biting blasts to wither his tender flower.

"I shall make Judith understand at once and forever that she must be kind and gentle to my wife," thought Joshua. "She has always respected and obeyed me—I am bound to remember that."

He was in no hurry to tell Judith, or even his faithful Naomi, of the change that had come upon his life—that startling and wondrous change which had made him a new man. It would be time enough when he took his young wife home. No one had any right to question his choice or to doubt his wisdom.

He felt somewhat embarrassed, notwithstanding these arguments, when Naomi questioned him, with a dutiful interest in all his doings, about the girl he had found on Springfield Common.

"Has she been well-behaved, father? Has she learned to read yet?"

"Yes, my dear. She has made wonderful progress."

"And is she as pretty as when you first saw her sitting with her feet in the water, and with her hair falling loose about her shoulders?"

Naomi's fancy had pictured the scene: her father's dark face looking down at the fair-haired wanderer; the thymy hillocks and gorse-bushes and wild broom under the blue warm sky.

"I think she is even prettier."

"What a sweet little thing she must be! I should so like to see her! If Sally were to get married now, we might have Cynthia for a servant, mightn't we, father?"

"There's not much chance of that, Naomi."

"Of Sally's marrying? I'm not sure of that," replied Naomi. "I know she has thoughts of it."

"You shall see Cynthia some day, Naomi, and I hope you will learn to love her; but it will not be as a servant. Nature has made her fit for something better than servitude. I do not mean to say that service is not worthy, or that all men and women are not equal in the eyes of their Maker. But Nature has set a mark upon us all, and we have each our appointed station. I do not think Cynthia was created to work like Sally, or to take pleasure in the things that please Sally."

"You might get her a better place, father—as lady's maid, for instance."

"To be some fine lady's drudge! That would be worse, rather than better. Don't concern yourself about her, my dear, till you come to know more of her. I have made up my mind as to her future life."

"How good you are, father, to take so much trouble for a poor nameless orphan!"

"There is more selfishness than goodness in the matter, Naomi. It has been a pleasure to me to do as much for her."

This was all that he said to his daughter about Cynthia; but he was pleased to think that Naomi had shown a friendly interest in the subject, and he fancied that Cynthia's beauty and Cynthia's sweetness would at once appeal to the girl's heart; that it would be natural for these two to love one another, and that they would cleave to each other like sisters. It never occurred to him that Cynthia, as the recipient of his charity, was quite a different person in the eyes of Naomi from the same Cynthia as his second wife; and that in proportion to his daughter's love for him would be her disinclination to divide his affection with a new-comer and interloper. In the fullness of his content, which inclined him to see all things on the sunnier side, he could foresee no domestic difficulty, unless it were a little extra snappishness on the part of Judith, an exhibition of temper which he meant to put down with a high hand.

He was very happy. It seemed as if his capacity for full and perfect happiness had never been called into play till now. His life had been prosperous, successful; but the rainbow hues of joy had not entered largely into the fabric of his existence. A gleam of vivid color here and there had flashed across the dull gray woof; but now warp and woof were all brightness and color. He saw all things under an altered aspect, apparelled in the beauty of a dream. Nature, which he had viewed hitherto with a mild regard, moved him now to loving worship. He thanked God for having set him in so fair a world, for having given him such a goodly heritage. In his daily walks he was continually repeating to himself those psalms which breathe joyfulness and thanksgiving, those canticles which tell of triumph and rapture for the Lord's chosen people. There was more eloquence in his sermons, more fervor in his prayers. His congregation even felt stirred by that strong flood-tide of joy which filled his own breast.

In this state of mind he was naturally disposed to look with an indulgent eye upon Oswald Pentreath's wooing. He remembered with a guilty sheepishness what the squire had said to him—that if he, Joshua, were going to be married he would not be for such long delay; and, moved by this recollection, he told Oswald one evening in the wilderness that, if he liked, the wedding might take place early in the year—say in March, when the spring flowers were coming in and the days getting bright.

"Now that your father has given his consent, there is less reason for me to hold you to the letter of your promise," said Joshua. "If you are quite sure of your affection for Naomi—quite sure she is the one woman you would choose for yourself out of all the world—it makes little difference whether you marry her in March or July."

"There is no fear of any change in my feelings," answered Oswald. "I love her better every day, and honor her more as I get to know her better. She is the noblest and best of women. I feel myself small and weak in comparison with her."

Oswald lost no time in telling Naomi that the length of his apprenticeship, as it pleased him to call it, had been lessened.

"We are to be married early in March, Naomi, when the woods are yellow with daffodils; and you are coming to brighten that dismal old house of ours. I shall be a respectable married man by mid-summer. I must get my father to buy me a gig, and put Herne into harness, so that I may drive you about. We shall be a regular Darby and Joan."

Naomi blushed at an imaginary picture of herself sitting beside Oswald in a high-wheeled gig, with that unreliable horse swaying the vehicle against banks and hedges, and making wild bolts round awkward corners. The idea of driving with her husband in a gig, like old married people, seemed to bring their marriage closer home to her than any gush of poetry on the lover's part could have done.

"And we must think of smartening the old rooms a little bit before you come to us," continued Oswald, cheerily. "I dare say a coat of whitewash for the ceilings will be about as much as the squire will care to afford; but I must see what Phœbe—that's our old house-maid, you know—can do with a few yards of chintz and muslin. She's a capital manager, poor old thing, and has made her elbow-bones twice their natural size with rubbing the paneling and furniture. There's no such polish in Devonshire, I should think, as poor Phœbe's elbow-grease. I see her at it sometimes at six o'clock in the morning when I'm going for an early ride; and I often wonder why she takes so much out of herself to embellish rooms that hardly any one sees. I fancy it must be a part of her religion. There are Jumpers, you know, and Shakers; perhaps there is a sect of Rubbers—an extra devout sect, like the Essenes."

Naomi looked disapprovingly here. As a Dissenter herself, she was not prepared to think lightly of even Shakers or Jumpers, who had doubtless some reason for the faith that was in them—an innate conviction of truth, perhaps, so strong as to counterbalance the ridiculousness of their outward manifestations.

"But when you come, the old oak panels will have their use," said Oswald, gayly. "They will serve as mirrors to reflect your imperial beauty. I always fancy you like the good Agrippinas and Julias, Naomi. There were one or two virtuous Julias, you know, though the majority turned their attention the other way; and there may have been a decent Agrippina, though there I'm doubtful. I always picture you as a Roman lady, with golden embroidery on your robes, and a golden diadem on that dark hair of yours."

Naomi had read neither Tacitus nor Gibbon. All she knew about Rome was that St. Paul had acquired the Roman franchise, and that the Romans had persecuted the early Christians. But she knew that Oswald meant to praise her beauty when he likened her to these imperial ladies of doubtful character.

These two also were very happy, but with a more quiet joy than Joshua's. The bloom of novelty had been worn off their love by this time. They had grown accustomed to look forward to a life spent together; to think of themselves as bound to each other. Oswald surveyed his future with a tranquil contentment. He liked Naomi better every day, leaned upon her more entirely, felt her superiority and his own weaker nature, and looked forward confidently to the part she was to play in his life. Naomi's feelings lay deeper, and but seldom found expression in words. She could not speak playfully of a love which was the most solemn element in her life. She thought of her happiness—of this most perfect boon Heaven had given her in Oswald's love—with a subdued sense of awe. If he had never loved her; if he were to be taken from her? She dared not picture to herself the hideous blank which life must have been in the first case, nor the gloomy ruin life must become in the second. Sometimes she recalled that dreadful day when the storm had swept over Combhollow and her father's strong arm had snatched Oswald from the greedy, devouring waves. If he had not been saved, and she had never known him! She was not metaphysician enough to contemplate life under such seemingly impossible conditions.

Aunt Judith's attitude of mind in relation to the lovers was one of equable disapprobation. She thought that Joshua was sacrificing to Baal by giving his daughter five thousand pounds in order that the misguided young woman might be raised from her proper position in life to a station for which Providence had never intended her. Five thousand pounds at five per cent. meant two hundred and fifty pounds a year, Judith reflected, or nearly five pounds a week, which division made the money seem a great deal more, as it was thus brought nearer the housewife's eye. Why, the entire housekeeping expenses of Mr. Haggard's establishment—after debiting all goods had out of the shop against the house—seldom came to more than five pounds a week. And Joshua was to surrender all that money to make his daughter a fine lady.

The idea of this monetary sacrifice weighed heavily upon Aunt Judith. She had begun a system of small economies as a kind of set-off against Naomi's dowry. Puddings now only graced the board thrice a week, and these were puddings of the homeliest and least expensive character; puddings of a substantial and filling character specially dear to prudent housekeepers, as they do not require eggs in their composition, and are, for the most part, independent of butter. The tea-table was furnished even more sparingly than of old, and, with a view to the economizing of butter, the careful manager pressed upon the maturer taste of her nephew and niece that thick and slab molasses which their childish fancies had affected. She doled out the week's allowance of soap more grudgingly than of old, and was a despot in the matter of soda.

"I don't know what's come to your aunt, Miss Naomi," the aggrieved Sally remarked, despondently. "It's as much as I can wash out a pair of white stockings for Sunday afternoon without her going on about my vanity and extravagance, and throwing Jezebel in my teeth, as if I was the wickedest young woman in Comb-hollow."

These infinitesimal savings, though they inflicted some annoyance on the household, could go about as far toward counterbalancing the loss of five thousand pounds as the laborious exertions of an industrious beaver in the construction of a dam designed to stem the waters of Niagara; yet these vain efforts afforded some mental solace to Aunt Judith's perturbed mind. She scraped the butter off her bread, and felt herself a domestic martyr.

"There'll be fine flaunting when she's a married woman and her own mistress," thought Judith, "with two hundred and fifty pounds a year for her own spending—silk gowns trimmed with thread-lace on workadays, I dare say. We sha'n't see her often at chapel, I should think. She'll be going to church for the sake of sitting in a big pew among the gentry. If I were Joshua, I'd as lief have my daughter dead and buried as married to a fine gentleman that would look down upon me."

Judith had never been able to get rid of the idea that in his secret soul Oswald Pentreath despised the Haggards and their surroundings. Her narrow mind could not conceive it possible that the son of a land-owner could believe in his equality with shop-keepers; that the odor of soap and candles was not hateful to the nostrils of a gentleman who sealed his letters with a coat of arms that looked almost royal, and bore a name which was engraved on the oldest brazen tablet in the chancel. She was unable to understand that easy-going temper of Oswald's, to which rank and wealth were of small moment compared with the blessings of personal well-being and the gratification of one's own inclination. She had a lurking conviction that Mr. Pentreath, be he ever so polite and respectful, was secretly laughing at her; that he did not admire her Sunday gown, and thought her pronunciation vulgar; and that he encouraged that impudent jackanapes Jim in the practice of grinning behind her shoulder as she poured out the tea or carved the cold joint at supper. This conviction, and a general sense of injury, chiefly referable to that marriage portion of five thousand pounds, made Aunt Judith unpleasant company to herself at this time, and not the most agreeable company for other people.

The young people were happy, after their tranquil fashion, untouched by the blighting influence of this aggrieved spinster. They had their afternoon rambles together, and Naomi made progress in the art of pencil landscape, sitting for many a happy hour copying the bold curved lines of the hart's-tongue and the delicate tracery of parsley and oak-leaf fern, or the larger outlines of elm or beach; while Oswald lay on the grass at her side reading "Marmion" or "Ivanhoe." Gentle, peaceful time—a cup filled to the brim with perfect joy—to be remembered in days to come, when the memory shall be life's crowning sorrow.

The lovers had been employed thus one afternoon in August. Oswald had just read that intense and dramatic scene of Sir Walter Scott's most romantic poem where Constance de Beverley defies her pitiless judges. There had been an ominous stillness in the air for the last half-hour, and the birds were uttering those subdued twitterings by which they seem to warn one another of approaching evil; but Naomi had been too much absorbed by the story to give any heed to these whisperings of a coming storm, when one big drop, falling on her penciled group of ferns, startled her out of her complacency. Oswald had been reading the stirring lines somewhat sleepily, the heavy air under those tall elms exercising a narcotic effect upon his senses, and he, too, had been heedless of a change in the heavens.

"Why, I declare it's raining!" he exclaimed, when one of those big drops had alighted upon his nose; "and what a black sky! I'm afraid we're in for a storm. And you in that thin dress, Naomi! Let us get to the house as fast as we can."

"To the Grange?" cried Naomi, with a look of alarm, as if he had proposed the most awful thing in the world.

"Why not, love? It is to be your home next spring. Is it too much to ask a little shelter from the old roof to-day?"

"The squire might not like—" faltered Naomi.

"He would be delighted. He has not asked you and your father formally to visit him, for then, you see, you would be visitors, and it is against his principles to squander his substance upon entertaining people; but if you were to drop in upon him unawares he would be enchanted. Come, dear; the rain-drops are falling faster—and there's the first thunder-clap."

It pealed among the trees, sounding so close to them that it seemed a local thunder-clap intended for them in particular.

"What a threatening sound it has, Oswald!" said Naomi, as they hurried toward the little gate which opened from the wood into the path.

"Yes; one can fancy the first murderer hearing such a peal as he fled. It sounds like the voice of Nemesis, doesn't it? There's a blinding flash! Run, Naomi!"

They were at the gate by this time, and only a broad stretch of turf lay between them and the house. The squire's oxen kept the turf closely cropped, and Oswald and his companion were able to run quickly over the short, crisp grass. Naomi arrived at the porch with her cambric dress only lightly sprinkled by the rain.

The hall door stood open, and Oswald led her in. He tried the handle of his father's den; but that sanctuary was locked. The squire was out, and had the key of his study in his pocket, no doubt, according to custom. Naomi stood in the grave old hall, looking about her wonderingly. It was the first time she had ever entered this house, in which she was to live and die. She felt as if it were a solemn moment in her life—a moment to be remembered as the beginning of an epoch. This house was henceforward to mean something more for her than a tradition or a feature in a familiar landscape: it was to embody her idea of home.

She looked round her doubtfully. The fine square hall; the brown-oak paneling, adorned with half a dozen family portraits browner and darker than the old oak; the wide, shallow staircase with its solid balustrade; the pavement of white-and-black marble, had doubtless a certain dignity and beauty of their own. She felt that she was beneath a roof which had sheltered many generations; but there were a bleakness and barrenness in the scene that chilled her. A house built for the accommodation of a large family and numerous servants must needs have a cheerless and empty look when it falls into the occupancy of a miser's shrunken household.

"Let me show you the rooms that are to be all your own," said Oswald, opening the door of a long drawing-room, an apartment so rarely used that it had assumed a ghost-like air, as of a chamber conscious of old family secrets, and made gloomy by the mysteries of the past. It was a narrow paneled room, painted white and salmon, and this very delicacy of tint, which would have made the apartment cheerful under favorable conditions, enhanced its chill, phantasmal aspect in the gray light of this thunderous afternoon.

All the furniture was at least a century old. Naomi had never imagined such spindle-legged tables, such narrow high-backed chairs, such a general straightness and spareness of outline; the bareness of all ornament, save the small oval mirrors and crystal candelabra, and the lack of color, struck even her inexperienced eye, which had been accustomed only to the plainest furniture. The brocaded window-curtains, once sea-green, had faded to a neutral tint; the seats and backs of chairs and sofas were covered with holland. There were no books, no pictures.

Oswald watched his betrothed, expectant of some expression of admiration. He fancied she would be delighted with rooms so much larger and more aristocratic than those in which she had lived all her life.

"It's a handsome room, isn't it?" he asked. "Forty feet by eighteen."

"It's very long," said Naomi, rather stupidly, her lover thought.

"Perhaps you'd like to see the dining-room?"

"Very much."

Any thing would be a relief after this ghastly saloon, with its white, cold walls and general emptiness.

They crossed the hall and entered the dining-room. Here brownness and gloom replaced the ghostly whiteness of the saloon. Here, too, the furniture was scanty; but there was more homeliness, a greater look of occupation, this being the room in which the squire and his son lived from January to December. There were newspapers, books, and writing-materials on a table in the bay-window; there were whips and walking-sticks in the corners; the large oaken sideboard was adorned with a pair of solid old silver tankards, and surmounted by a portrait of the present squire, painted in the bloom of youth, when waistcoats were worn long and "Wilkes and Liberty" was still a party cry.

The lightning flashed across Naomi's face as she looked out at the large bay-window, surveying that neatly kept garden in front of the house, which was separated by a close-cut holly hedge from the neglected domain beyond, the wide stretch of turf which had once been a lawn sacred from the feet of cattle, and on which the squire's store oxen now browsed at their ease. He could see no good in land which produced nothing—grass that was mown at much cost of labor only to be thrown on the manure-heap.

The day had grown darker, and the thunder-peals seemed to shake the old chimney, down whose wide throat there came gusts of wind and rain. It was an awful chimney for the wind to howl in; and the squire and his son, sitting silently by the hearth on a gloomy winter evening, had often felt as if evil spirits were howling wild threatenings at them from the house-top.

Naomi looked at the dark hearth with an affrighted glance, as if she had heard the family banshee shrieking at her.

"What an awful noise?" she said.

"It's only the wind, love. And now I must show you the family portraits, and my mother's sitting-room, which will be yours so soon. I think it is the most cheerful room in the house."

Naomi was glad to think she was going to see something cheerful. The gloom of the dining-room had been more depressing than the ghostly pallor of the drawing-room.

They went up the uncarpeted staircase to a gallery which occupied the whole length of the house, with a row of long narrow windows looking westward, and a deep oaken seat in each window. Here there were family portraits of the usual character; sea-pieces, battle-pieces, fruit-pieces, and a Dutch picture or two to give a touch of human interest to the collection. Here, too, there were some old delft jars, filled with dried rose-leaves—roses that had been gathered by fingers that were now clay, and which exhaled an odor of the past.

Oswald showed his betrothed the untenanted rooms, all neatly kept by the indefatigable house-maid. The room that had been his mother's was the prettiest Naomi had seen yet. The white walls, embellished with carved garlands of fruit and flowers; the old furniture, painted white; a narrow old-fashioned book-case on each side of the fire-place; cabinets of shells and sea-weeds between the windows, local shells and local weeds, which the squire's young wife had collected in her idle, uneventful days.

Naomi went eagerly to look at the books. They were many of them strange to her even in name. Old poets—Spenser, Cowley, Waller, Dryden, Prior, Pope—in white vellum, with gilded lettering. The essayists, in neat duodecimo volumes, with faded calf bindings; Richardson's voluminous novels, in thin octavos, bound in brown. Naomi read the titles with keenest interest. The great world of books was an unknown region to her, save for such feeble glimmer as was afforded by the *Pocket Magazine*, a folio Milton, with awful mezzotint pictures of Sin and Death, Satan and his Council, which she used to look at shudderingly in her childhood, and those books of a theological or devotional character which formed the staple of the minister's small collection. Joshua had never been a great reader, save of his Bible and those good old puritan divines whose teaching was after his own heart. His life had been too full and busy to admit of his acquiring the habits of a student. He read the Scriptures, or Baxter's "Saints' Rest," or Law's "Serious Call," by the wayside.

"What dear little books!" exclaimed Naomi, admiring the neat rows of thin volumes—literature spread over a wide surface.

"They all belonged to my grandfather, and came to my mother at his death. She was very fond of them, the poets especially."

"I did not know there were so many poets. I knew of Pope and Spenser, but all these other names are strange to me. Why have you never told me about them?"

"They are dead, my dear; gone to the limbo of forgotten genius. Byron sent the whole crew to Hades. They have a kind of fossil life in old-fashioned libraries, like flies in amber. Their music was sweet to mawkishness, their loves and sufferings were as unreal as their periwigs; they were the poets of a patch box-and-powder period."

He took out a volume of Waller and read the "Lines to Amoret," that elegant excuse for being in love with two women at once:

> "Amoret! as sweet and good
> As the most delicious food,
> Which, but tasted, does impart
> Life and gladness to the heart.
> Sacharissa's beauty's wine,
> Which to madness doth incline:
> Such a liquor as no brain
> That is mortal can sustain."

"Not a bad definition of the love that satisfies and the love that intoxicates, is it, Naomi?" asked Oswald, as he closed the book. "These periwigged poets red iced I've to a science. You are my Amoret, Naomi, and have given life and gladness to my heart."

"I hope you may never meet your Sacharissa," replied Naomi, gravely, "since it seems that poets can love two women at once."

"My dearest, that was written in the days of Charles II., when poets were fops and courtiers, and it was incumbent on a court poet to have a new mistress as often as he had a new coat. It was a scenic age, unreal as a stage play. And yet there were true lovers and broken hearts while Charles Stuart was king; but you'll find no trace of them among his poets."

"I'm afraid I'm not clever enough to like that kind of poetry."

"But you like my mother's room, Naomi?"

"It is lovely."

"I am so glad to hear you say that. It will be your own after next March."

"I have been trying to think of this house as my home, Oswald; but I have such a strange feeling about it. I can not imagine myself living here. I can not make a picture of our new life. It all seems far away and shadowy, like my idea of the life to come, which neither my own faith nor my father's teaching could ever make real or visible to me. I must have a very weak imagination."

"Perhaps you have too much common sense, Naomi. You will not give your fancies scope. You think of yourself as Naomi Haggard, living in your father's house in Combhollow, and you can't realize the fact that next year you will be Naomi Pentreath, and sole mistress of these desolate old rooms. Your coming will alter everything, dear. Even my father looks forward to it with pleasant anticipations."

"He is very good. If it were not foolish or even wicked to give heed to such fancies, I should think that this feeling of mine was a presentiment that God does not intend me ever to live the happy life you speak of. It is such a settled feeling in my mind to-day; it comes between me and my happiness, just as those stormy clouds come between us and the day."

"Naomi?"

"Oh, it is because I love you so dearly, Oswald! I can not believe that Heaven means me to be so perfectly happy all my life, to have no sorrows, no trials—I who have been taught that our journey on earth is to lead us through thorny places—your love given to me in all its fullness. It is too much to expect from Providence."

"My dearest, you have been taught a gloomy creed. Do you suppose Providence has never favored true lovers—never smiled on a happy union before our time? There are old men and women who loved each other fifty years ago just as faithfully as you and I love to-day, and who have climbed the hill of life and gone down into the valley hand-in-hand. Providence means us to be happy for the most part, I believe. Naomi Earth's most miserable men are those who have made their own sorrows. That is my creed."

The squire's harsh croak was heard in the hall below at this moment, and made an end of the conversation. Oswald took Naomi down to greet her future father-in-law, who had ridden home from one of his outlying farms in the rain, and was changing his coat and boots with the assistance of the old butler.

He stopped in the operation to kiss Naomi.

"We were caught in the storm, father, while we were sketching in the wood," said Oswald, "I brought Naomi in for shelter. I've been showing her my mother's sitting-room."

"Very proper. It will be hers when she's married. She'll keep her accounts there, and do her sewing; won't you, my dear? My shirts and cravats are in a wretched state. It'll be a blessing to have a clever young woman like you to look after them. What a dreadful storm! It will do no end of mischief to the corn where it isn't out—an excuse for tenants being backward with their Christmas rent."

"The rain has stopped, I think," said Naomi, timidly, looking out through the open door, "and I must go home to tea."

"Never mind your tea, my dear. Oswald shall get you a dish of tea before you go," said the squire, in a gush of hospitality.

But Naomi declared that her father would be alarmed at her absence; and, the storm being really over, Oswald and she set out for Combhollow.

CHAPTER XII.

"SHE IS FAST MY WIFE."

SEPTEMBER was nearly ended. Harvest-homes were over, and in Combhollow there was a general impression that winter was a season in the immediate future, and that linsey and merino would be soon the only wear. Household fires began to have a cheery look in the dusk, and ruddy light flickered on the walls and ceilings of cozy parlors at tea-time—in that dim hour when the busiest housewife might lay aside her daily task of making or mending, and fold her hands for a brief span, with a virtuous sense of having earned the luxury of repose, while she discussed the character or prospects of her neighbors, or talked of that last dreadful murder chronicled in the county papers, or the latest scandal about England's crownless queen.

Joshua had gone on another journey in this tranquil autumn weather. He had not told his family much about the object or design of this last excursion, but had contented himself with stating that it was a matter of business which called him away, and that he should be absent at most a week.

Judith was not a little offended at this reticence.

"I don't know what's come over your father, that he's taken to gadding," she said, to Naomi. "He's never been the same man since he went to open young Wild's chapel. One would think it had turned his head. And yet it was no great honor for him to be asked to do it—an out-of-the-way place like that, where the people are as ignorant as negro slaves, I dare say."

"I can see no change in father," replied Naomi. "He is as good as he has always been, and as thoughtful for others. If there is any change, it is that he seems kinder than ever."

"Ah!" exclaimed Judith, with vexation: "what's the use of talking to girls in love? It's throwing away good words. You've no eyes nor ears for any one but your lover. If you were in the business, you'd see the change in your father fast enough. Half his time his wits are wool-gathering."

"Perhaps he's thinking of his sermons, aunt."

"He never used to think of 'em when he was behind his counter."

Naomi had no further explanation to offer. It had indeed seemed to her of late that her father was kinder and more sympathetic than she had ever known him to be since the days of her childhood, when she had been his prattling companion in many a rustic walk. He had entered into her feelings about Oswald, he had talked to her of her future; and to Oswald himself he had been all kindness and indulgence. Never had her home been pleasanter to her, or her life happier, than during the last three months. Perhaps this is why she had found it so difficult to imagine herself transferred to any other home, the scene of her life shifted from the homely house in the High Street to the gloomy dignity of the Grange.

Joshua had been absent more than ten days, a breach of faith upon which Aunt Judith enlarged with some bitterness.

"A stranger in the pulpit, and our last butter-cask nearly empty! If that isn't a change in your father, I don't know the meaning of the word. But some people can twist words any way: one 'ud need a new dictionary to understand 'em," exclaimed the anxious housewife, as she and Naomi sat together at tea in the glow of an afternoon fire.

Jim had gone to Barnstaple to order goods. He was gradually emerging from the chrysalis of boyhood, and showing an aptitude for business which his aunt lauded as the crowning ornament of manhood. He was sharp and energetic, intensely matter-of-fact, and more eager for gain than his father cared to see him, but a good boy withal, soft-hearted and kindly.

"Perhaps father may be home to-night," said Naomi, soothingly.

"Ah, that's what you said last night, and the night before last. If he isn't home to-night or to-morrow, there'll be no service on Sunday, for Mr. Scrupel only promised for the one Sabbath. And there'd be a pass for things to come to! How could your father hold his head up in Combhollow after that?"

"I am sure my father won't neglect his duty."

"Won't he? How about our next cask of butter? Where's that to come from, I should like to know, before we've been out of Irish ever so long? It was more than I would take upon myself to write to Ireland for it."

"You might have ordered another cask, aunt."

"I wouldn't be so venturesome. A deal of thanks I should get for my pains if the butter turned out rancid. No, Naomi; if your father neglects his business, he must bear the brunt of his own conduct; and if there's no service on the Sabbath—"

"There will be service," cried Naomi, starting from her chair at the sound of a vehicle drawing up in front of the gate. "That's father!"

"Why, there's no coach to bring him in at this time, child. The Barnstaple mail won't be in for a good hour. Why, bless us and save us, if it isn't a post-chay, with a trunk on the roof, too!" exclaimed Aunt Judith, looking out of the window. "Your father took nothing with him but a bag, and unless he was gone clean out of his mind he wouldn't come home in a shay."

"He may be ill," cried Naomi, alarmed; for this apparition of a post-chaise was one of those startling appearances which must mean something out of the common—possibly evil.

"It must be a mistake," said Aunt Judith, following Naomi into the passage. "No; there's Joshua getting out, and no more the matter with him than there is with me," she added, in a tone of disgust.

Yes, there was Joshua confronting them in the twilight, with a curious look on his dark face, a kind of shy triumph, as of one half ashamed of a great happiness. He drew Naomi to him, and kissed her with more warmth of feeling than he had ever shown after so short a severance.

"How is my dear daughter?" he asked, gently.

"Very well, father, and very glad to have you back again."

"We're all but out of Irish butter," said Judith, accusingly, from the obscurity of the passage.

"Ah, Judith, is that you? Never mind the butter. We'll soon set things tight," replied the minister, going back to the chaise.

"You won't get another cask till the end of next week, with all your cleverness. I thought you'd broken a leg, at the least, or you'd never have come home in a shay," added Judith.

"I came in a chaise because I had some one to bring with me, my dear," replied Joshua, calmly.

He handed out a girl—a slim, girlish figure, a lily face under a gypsy bonnet tied with a broad white ribbon. Naomi saw tender blue eyes looking up at her beseechingly in the twilight, and rose-bud lips that were faintly tremulous. She had never before beheld such flower-like beauty, loveliness so delicate in form or coloring.

Joshua put the stranger's hand under his arm and led her into the house, and into the fire-lighted parlor—Judith falling back against the passage wall as they went by, as if she had made way for a spectre; Naomi, following her father, full of wonder.

"I have brought you a companion and friend, Naomi," said Joshua, when they were all in the parlor, Aunt Judith having followed automatically, like Hamlet after the ghost. "I have brought you some one whom you must love and cherish for my sake."

"If you've brought this young woman to help in the business, you may give her the drapery department altogether. I wash my hands of it from this moment!" exclaimed Judith, awful in her indignation.

"I have brought her to occupy the first place in my household, as she holds the first place in my heart," answered Joshua. "This is Cynthia Haggard, my wife."

Sister and daughter stared at the minister with wonder-stricken countenances, pallid with horror. This calm announcement of his went so far beyond their ideas of the possible — this fact of a second marriage was an event so wide of their wildest dreams — that both aunt and niece were dumb. To both it seemed that Joshua must have gone out of his mind; that he must be talking distractedly under the spell of demoniac possession, rather than that this thing could be true—this slender, flower-like girl the grave preacher's second wife.

Joshua Haggard looked at the two women, surprised at the consternation his words had caused. Having once made up his own mind that Cynthia was his fittest helpmate, created for him by his God, as Eve for Adam, it had not occurred to him that other people could have any occasion to wonder at his choice. Her youth, her beauty, were blessings which Heaven had bestowed upon him with the free gift of her love. She loved him, she had chosen him; gladly, willingly, she had nestled in his arms, and yielded him a love which was almost worship. She had spanned the gulf of years that yawned between them; she had flown to him as a bird to its nest. By her free choice she had justified his boldness in loving her. Had any one else the right to count his years, or see unfitness in this union of youth and maturity, if she had not done so?

He was angry at his daughter's blank look of surprise. From Judith he had expected rebellion, and he took no heed of her mute horror.

"You do not give my wife a very warm welcome, Naomi," he said, with suppressed indignation. "I had expected more from your sense of duty, if not from your affection."

"Forgive me, father," said Naomi, with a look of unspeakable pain. Those deliberate words of Joshua's had shown her that this thing was very real. "I was so surprised, I could not speak." And then, going up to Cynthia, she put out her hand, and said, gently, "I am very glad to see you."

Cynthia took the proffered hand, which was cold as ice, bent her graceful head, and kissed the cold fingers tearfully.

"I am sorry you should have been so surprised," she said. "I asked Mr. Haggard to tell you before we were married, but he thought it was better not."

"I fancied my marriage would have been a pleasant surprise for my daughter. I thought she might be glad to know that when she leaves me, I shall still have some one to care for me —"

Aunt Judith's overcharged breast relieved itself by a groan.

"Some one young and bright and pleasant for my companion."

Judith groaned rather louder than before.

"For the rest, I had no one's leave or license to ask for my marriage. And now, Judith, perhaps you'll be good enough to get us some tea, while I go out and settle with the post-boy. We've had a long drive from Barnstaple. Naomi, you can show Cynthia the way up-stairs, and help her to take off her cloak and bonnet. My room is ready, I suppose?"

"It's ready for you," replied Judith; "I don't know whether it's good enough for Mrs. Haggard" —throwing a spiteful intensity into the mere utterance of the name which showed great power of expression. "She may be used to something better; though I might have known what was likely to happen when you ordered new chintz for the bedstead and windows."

"What is good enough for me will be good enough for my wife," said Joshua, looking fondly after his bride as she left the room with Naomi. "And now bestir yourself, Judith, like a kind soul, and give us a comfortable tea — a dish of ham and eggs, or something substantial. Cynthia eat hardly any dinner."

"Cynthia!" ejaculated Judith, as if suddenly awakened from a state of semi-consciousness, "Why, that's the name of the young woman you found on the common!"

"It is."

"And you've married that young woman—a tramp, a servant girl!"

"I have married a lovely and innocent girl, whom Providence designed to be the blessing of my later years," replied Joshua. "God gave her to me for my own that day on the common. She has loved me from that day, and I am not sure that my love for her was not born in me then. My thoughts have followed her and cared for her all the time, though I only knew last mid-summer how dear she had become to me. You look at me as if I were talking a strange tongue, Judith."

"It might as well be Hebrew, for my understanding of it," answered Judith. "However, you've made your bed and you can lie upon it. You don't want my leave or license, as you say; no man wants leave or license to play the fool. That's an act of free-will with most folks."

"Come, Judith," cried the minister, sternly, "if you think that I am going to submit to insolence or insult in a matter that touches me so nearly as this, you are mistaken. A man's worst foes are those of his own household. I will have no enemy to share my daily bread and my daily prayer. If you and I are to live together, you must love my wife as you love me. She is a part of me—the brighter, better part. An insult to her is twice an insult to me, and I shall resent it twice as keenly. And now, Judith, shake hands upon this, and take it into your heart; or else find some other shelter than this roof before you lie down to-night. No one shall live in my house that is an enemy to my wife."

"That's short notice," said Judith, grimly. "Well, there's my hand. You've been a good brother to me, and I've not been a bad sister to you. We won't quarrel about a — pretty face. May you be happy!"

They shook hands — heartily upon Joshua's side, with a shade of reservation on Judith's. The minister felt that he had conquered; but these household victories sometimes leave behind them the seed of future warfare.

Judith bustled out to prepare a meal for the travelers; and soon there was a cheerful hiss-ing sound — an odor of fried ham from the kitch-

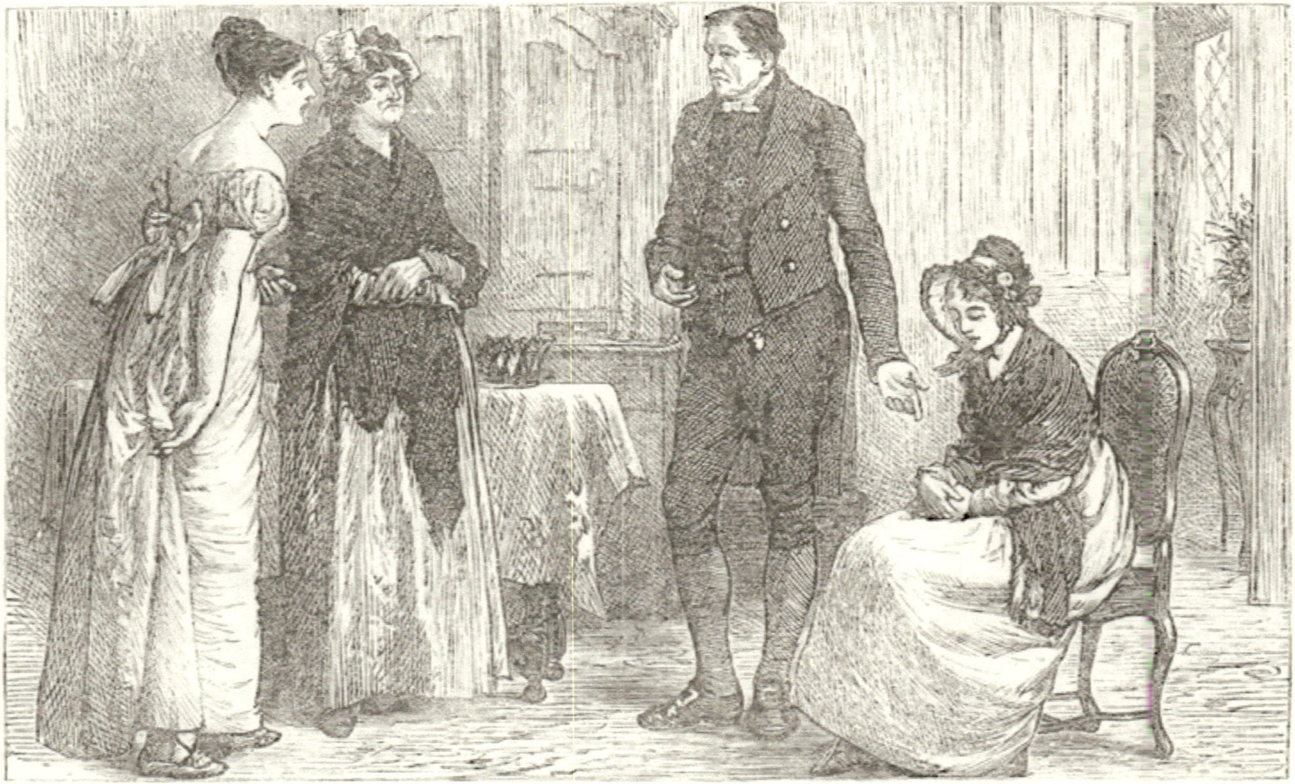

"THIS IS CYNTHIA HAGGARD, MY WIFE."

en, where Judith stood over the frying-pan with a moody brow, while Sally obeyed her orders in fear and wonder.

"Get out the best tea-things and the plated candlesticks, and get a pair of wax-candles from the shop," said Judith; at which command Sally stood, open mouthed and speechless. There had been no such preparations since the last tea-party.

"Your master has got married, Sally. We must show him how pleased we are."

"Married!" cried Sally. "Is it Mrs. Trimly?"

Mrs. Trimly was a corpulent widow, with a very respectable fortune that had been made in a tan-pit. She occupied a large, red-brick house—her own—at the upper end of Pennoyle; she wore silk gowns every afternoon, gold spectacles, and the smartest caps in the town, and was a devoted disciple of Joshua's, wheezing through the service every Sunday morning, and sometimes guilty of nasal breathings of an unmistakable character on a Sunday afternoon.

To Sally it seemed the most natural thing in the world that Joshua should espouse the tanner's widow, although she was fifteen years his senior, and a sufferer from high-feeling and chronic asthma. Sally had made up her mind ever so long ago, on the occasion of a state tea-drinking, that Mrs. Trimly looked with peculiar favor on the minister, and that the comfortably furnished brick house, with its twenty acres of orchard and meadow, as well as a fortune in the Funds, might be Joshua's for the asking.

"No," said Judith; "it isn't Mrs. Trimly. That would have been a sensible marriage, if you like. But when men of my brother's age marry, they don't think of pleasing sensible people. They marry to please their eye, Sally. Your new mistress has got flaxen hair and blue eyes, Sally. That's enough for my brother. I hope you'll like her, and that you'll take the same pains with polishing the furniture that you have taken in my time."

"You are not going away, are you, mum?" gasped Sally, with a vision of a paradisiacal life opening before her almost too dazzling for the mental eye.

"No, Sally, I am not going away; but I'm going to be a cipher," replied Judith, severely.

Sarah's spirits sank. She did not know the meaning of that substantive cipher, though she had a distant acquaintance with the same word as a verb. But she felt that so long as Miss Judith remained upon the scene her toil would know no relaxation.

Meanwhile the two girls—wife and daughter—were upstairs in Joshua's bedroom, stealing shy glances at each other by the dim light of a candle which Naomi held while Cynthia stood before the dressing-table taking off her bonnet.

There were tears in the young wife's eyes, and a sad look about the sweet, rosy mouth, as she smoothed her bright hair with Joshua's hard black brush, looking in the glass at a misty reflection of that half-sorrowful, half-frightened face. Inexperienced as she was in the varieties of humanity, instinct was keen enough to teach her that her husband's marriage was distasteful to his kindred, that there was no loving welcome for her in this strange home.

She looked at Naomi with unspeakable awe. Was this the affectionate daughter, the tender companion and friend. Joshua had promised her? That tall, erect figure, that nobly chiseled face, with its crown of raven hair bound in a thick coil round a high comb on the summit of the head, inspired admiration, but held love at a distance. Cynthia felt that she could never be familiar with this handsome step-daughter; and yet the face was like Joshua's, and for that reason must needs seem dear to her.

"I am so sorry your father did not tell you sooner," she began, falteringly. "I'm afraid his marrying me has made you unhappy—"

"It has surprised me very much," Naomi answered, gravely. "I have never thought of my father marrying—the idea never came into my head. If any one had suggested it, I should have been angry. And you are so young—so much fitter to be his daughter than his wife."

"No wife could love and honor him more than I do," said Cynthia, the tears streaming down her cheeks.

"No one could know him and not honor him," replied the daughter, proudly. "Don't cry; I am not blaming you. I have no right to blame him. I don't want to speak unkindly of you, still less to speak undutifully of my father; but his marriage is a great surprise."

Here Naomi broke down, and the two young women performed a sobbing duet. Naomi was the first to recover.

"I am very wicked," she said, remorsefully. "As if my dear father had not the right to be happy in his own way. I am jealous, unreasonable, abominable. Poor little thing"—drawing Cynthia to her with protecting tenderness—"don't cry. I am not so cruel or so ungrateful as I must have seemed just now. But I love my father so dearly, and I thought I should have him always all my own; and the idea that he could love any one else more than me was too bitter, just at first. I was selfish, cruel, undutiful. Dry your tears, dear. We must be fond of each other for my father's sake."

Cynthia's sobs ceased. She clung lovingly to the tall figure, hanging on it like ivy on an oak.

"Oh, if you will love me a little, I shall be so happy!" said the girl-wife. "He ought to have told you. I know I must seem an intruder. But if you could know how I love him: how from the first—when he took me under his care, a poor runaway creature, without a friend, used to hard usage and hard words—from the first I worshiped him! He was so true, so strong, a rock of defense. I feared no one when he had taken me under his care."

"Yes, he told me how he found you," said Naomi, thoughtfully. "Poor child!"

This was the waif of whom her father had spoken—the girl in whose story she had felt a tender, pitying interest, never dreaming that this nameless wanderer was to rob her of her father's heart.

"Did he tell you that I was a heathen then," asked Cynthia, solemnly, "knowing nothing, believing nothing, without one hope beyond my daily life—and that was altogether hopeless? I had known no father on earth, I knew of no Father in heaven. I thought death was the end of all things, and I sometimes longed to die."

"Poor child!" repeated Naomi, with grave pity.

"Poor then," said Cynthia, "the poorest of

the poor. But from that blessed day rich beyond measure. 'Henceforward there is laid up for me a crown of glory.'"

There was no touch of sanctimoniousness or cant in her utterance of these words, only a childlike and implicit faith.

"Yes," answered Naomi, with deepest gravity, "if you win the race."

Her more serious nature was not so easily assured. These triumphant party-cries and watchwords of evangelism sometimes awakened doubts and anxieties in her reflective mind. For St. Paul such a glad burst of triumph was but the natural expression of a victorious soul; but for these followers of St. Paul, who had endured nothing, accomplished nothing—who had fought no battle, won no victory—from them this bold assurance of felicity seemed arrogant to the verge of blasphemy.

"And you will try to love me a little?" said Cynthia, pleadingly.

"I shall love you very much, for my father's sake, if you make his life happy."

"I shall honor and obey him, and wait upon him like his servant, if he will let me," answered Cynthia. "And may I call you Naomi?"

"Yes, Cynthia."

And from that moment they spoke to each other as Cynthia and Naomi. There was no question of the word mother; but in Naomi's manner to her step-mother there was from the first a touch of motherliness, a protecting kindness, which was in a manner the reversal of their positions.

The wife's weaker nature, clinging, dependent, child-like in its exquisite womanliness, leaned on the firmer and more masculine character of the daughter.

"I thought you were never coming," said Joshua, when they went down to the parlor, where the tea-table had assumed a positively splendid appearance, lighted by wax-candles, such as were supplied at three-and-sixpence a pound to Mr. Haggard's most aristocratic customers.

Judith sat bolt-upright, with her hands folded, watching the candles burning, as a larger soul might have watched the blazing pyre which consumed the fortunes of an imperial house. There was a depth of desolation in this sacrifice of the wax-candles, a bitter irony in the setting-up of these waxen tapers to do honor to that wandering beggar-girl whom Joshua had chosen for his wife.

"What have you two girls been talking about all this time?" asked Joshua, with an attempt at cheeriness; "making friends, I hope?"

"Yes, father," Naomi answered, with a look that was full of duty and affection; "we have made friends. Cynthia and I are going to be sisters. It would sound foolish for me to call her mother, for she is two years younger than I am, and looks younger than she is."

"Very well, my dear. You shall be sisters, then. I care not what name you give the bond, so that you love each other. And now, Judith, the tea."

Miss Haggard had placed herself at a corner of the table remote from her accustomed seat in front of the tea-tray. There she sat, rigid, impenetrable. She did not frown; no sour expression of visage betrayed her discontent. She had composed her features to a sublime self-abnega-

tion—a resignation of all active share in the life passing around her. She looked what she had called herself in her late discourse with Sally—a cipher.

"Oh dear, no!" she exclaimed: "I couldn't think of such a thing! I have done with the tea-pot. Mrs. Haggard will pour out the tea, of course; it's her place."

"Oh, please don't make any difference on my account," cried Cynthia, with a timidly beseeching glance at that stony countenance. "I have never been accustomed to pour out the tea. I should feel quite awkward, unless Joshua wished it," with a little look at her husband, which plainly said, "His lightest wish is my law."

"I desire nothing that can cause discomfort or ill will in this household," answered Joshua. "All I wish is that we may live happily together, in perfect peace and union. Pour out the tea, Judith, and let there be no senseless fuss about trifles."

"I'm not one to make a fuss about nothing," replied Judith, with dignity. "But it's just as well to put things on a proper footing at once. It saves misunderstanding afterward."

And with this protest she assumed her accustomed position, which she never afterward offered to resign. Cynthia took the chair nearest her husband, nestling to his side, and looking up at him with bright glances of admiration and regard as he talked about home affairs with his daughter.

Jim came home by-and-by full of importance, and was presented to his father's wife. The surprise was startling for him as well as for the rest, but he received the blow much more coolly than his aunt and sister. His brain, sharpened by a course of wholesale-and-retail grocery, took in the material aspects of this change in his family circumstances, rather than that spiritual side of things which had troubled Naomi. He did not think regretfully of his father's second marriage as a foolish and undignified act in a grave career; but he began to wonder what effect this union might exercise upon his own prospects.

"As long as father gives me the business, I'm content," he told himself. "And my step-mother looks a pretty, foolish thing, that wouldn't be likely to make one's life unpleasant. I hope she'll take the reins out of Aunt Judith's hands, and let us have puddings every day."

It was not till after prayers that Naomi left off expecting Oswald, who rarely let an evening pass without coming in, were it but for half an hour. But on this particular evening the squire had taken it into his head to be prosy, and kept his son at home, talking politics by the wood fire in the dining-room, while the autumn wind sighed and moaned in the wide old chimney.

"I wonder what Oswald will think of father's marriage?" was Naomi's chief thought that evening.

———————

CHAPTER XIII.

"I LEAN UPON THEE, DEAR, WITHOUT ALARM."

NAOMI awoke with a strange feeling of trouble on the morning after her father's return with his young wife. She felt like one who, after some sudden bereavement, awakens to the old familiar world to find it desolate and empty.

"I have lost my father," came like a cry of despair from her troubled heart; and then came Reason, the calm and quiet teacher, and sat down by her bed, and argued the matter to its logical issue, and showed her that her father had done her no wrong. She blushed at the thought of her own selfishness—she to grudge her father this new happiness—she who had given so much of her heart to another—she who was so soon to abandon the home-nest.

"But my father has always been first, my father will always be first, in my heart," she said to herself, excusingly.

"Let her only make my father happy, and I shall be satisfied," she thought, as she stood before the little looking-glass, twisting the heavy coil of hair round her neat tortoise-shell comb. "I wish she were only a little older. She has such a childish look, I can not fancy her a companion for my father."

Naomi went down-stairs with a determination to be very kind to the poor little wife—to shield her, if need were, from Aunt Judith's acrimony; but on this first morning Aunt Judith was scrupulously civil; if she erred at all, it was on the side of overpoliteness. She was inclined to be righteous overmuch in her dealings with the new member of the household.

Jim greeted his step-mother with frank familiarity, and offered to take her for a nutting expedition in the woods after dinner.

"Of course you're fond of nuts?" he said.

"I'm very fond of the woods," answered Cynthia, whose heart overflowed with kindly feeling for these step-children, and who was grateful for the smallest token of regard on their part.

"I should like to know how the business is to go on, if you're out nutting every afternoon," said Judith, turning sharply on her nephew. She was not going to waste civility on him.

"Come, now, I've been sticking pretty close to the shop for the last six months. I don't often play truant, I'm sure, and there's not much doing in my line between dinner and tea."

"Of course, if Mrs. Haggard wishes you to go out walking—"

"Call me Cynthia, please," cried the girl, and then added, timidly, "unless you would like to call me sister."

"You're very kind, but I couldn't turn my tongue to it. I never had a sister, and I can't bring myself to make believe. As to calling you by your Christian name, I should feel myself wanting in respect to my brother's wife; and nobody shall ever have cause to lay that at my door."

"I shall call you Cynthia, though," said Jim. "It would never do for a great hobbledehoy like me to be calling a pretty little thing like you mother. Folks would split their sides with laughing. And you'll come nutting this afternoon? There's hazel and cobnuts, and no end, in Matcherly Wood. It's three miles from here; but you can walk that much, I dare say."

"I am a pretty good walker," answered Cynthia, delighted to be on such good terms with her step-son.

"Shall I wash the tea-things?" she asked, when breakfast was over and Joshua had gone out.

"I've washed 'em for the last four-and-twenty years, and I shouldn't like harm to come to them," answered Judith, politely; "you needn't trouble about it, Mrs. Haggard. All you've got to do is to amuse yourself; you're the mistress here, and it's your place to be waited on."

"But, indeed, Miss Haggard, I have never been accustomed—" protested Cynthia.

"What you may have been accustomed to has nothing to do with it," replied Judith. "You are my brother's wife, and you shall be treated as such. There's the best parlor, when you like to sit by yourself. We haven't need it on workdays; but, of course, that's no reason why you shouldn't."

"I had rather sit in the room you use," said Cynthia, oppressed by so much courtesy; "I should be very sorry to cause any trouble or alteration in your life."

Naomi was somewhat restless in her goings in and out, and up and down stairs, between breakfast and dinner, on this particular morning, having an idea that, as Oswald had not paid her his accustomed visit yesterday, he was likely to come early to-day; and she was anxious to be the first to tell him of the startling change that had taken place in the household, to soften the edge of his resentment should he be inclined to resent this act of her father's. She had not quite realized the fact that no one had any right to question Joshua's disposal of his own life.

There were the usual morning tasks: a batch of starched curtains to be ironed on the board in front of the kitchen window; the best parlor to be dusted and beeswaxed; flowers to be trimmed and watered. But throughout her performance of these duties Naomi was listening or watching for Oswald's coming. Dinner-time came, however, and no Oswald.

Joshua went out directly after dinner, and Judith retired to her stronghold behind the counter. Cynthia and Jim started for their walk to Matcherly Wood, and Naomi was standing at the parlor window, in her afternoon dress, in that quiet hour of the declining day when the sky takes a golden tinge above distant woods. She had been watching some time, when she saw her lover coming round the bend of the road, walking slowly till he caught sight of her, and then quickening his pace, and approaching her with a smile. She went out to the garden gate to meet him, and they went to the garden together, instead of going into the dull old house. They greeted each other with the tranquil affection of lovers whose future happiness is secure, whose present bliss is undisturbed by outward influences or inward doubts.

"Why didn't you come yesterday evening, Oswald?"

"Because my father took it into his head to be unusually conversational, and I did not like to leave him without a listener. I thought I could make amends for last night's self-denial by coming to tempt you out for a morning ramble in the woods; but this morning the squire discovered that he was not well enough to keep an appointment with his tenant at Chale, and sent me off to represent him; so, after a ten-mile ride upon Herne, I had to walk about a farm all the morning, hearing complaints and excuses, and inspecting improvements of whose nature or advantage I had only the vaguest idea, yet about which I knew I should have to stand a rasping cross-examination on my return."

6

" Poor Oswald !"

" I'm afraid I never was made to grow rich out of the soil, Naomi. And did you really miss me, dearest ? That would be a wonderful admission from you. You don't often gratify my self-esteem by letting me think myself necessary to your happiness."

" Oswald !" she said, with a tender reproachfulness in the serious eyes, which meant much more than words,

" You would have me believe that love's best language is silence," he answered, playfully ; " but I sometimes wish you were just a little more given to sweet words."

" There are some feelings that are too sacred to be spoken of lightly. If it should please Heaven to put my affection to the test, you would not find it wanting."

" I believe that, dear. I have a measureless faith in your truth and constancy, only I am exacting enough to sigh for a little more warmth as well. There are moments in which I have asked myself, Is this love, or only a sublimated friendship? We have schooled ourselves to such perfect tranquillity. We have so stifled all the agitations and emotions which poets depict as love's necessary adjuncts — nay, love's very atmosphere — that I have found myself asking, Is it really love? or is it some calmer, softer, holier feeling, such as the saints of old felt for each other — a sentiment which might be breathed through a convent grating, or communicated by martyr to martyr in a pitying sigh on the pathway to the stake ?"

" I don't know whether my love is like the love your poets write about. Oswald — that court poet, for instance, who was in love with Amoret and Sacharissa at the same time — but I know that, if my life were weighed against it, love would conquer life."

" My dearest," cried Oswald, tenderly drawing her to him, " I will never say these foolish things again. Yours is the true love. Yours are the depth and steadfastness, and I am a shallow wretch who can not properly understand any feeling that does not gush forth in a torrent of words. Darling, I will trust you, and believe implicitly in the love that is not loud."

They had come to the end of the garden, and to that green oasis of grass-plot, where there were a bench and table under the shade of trees whose leaves were now fast falling, or hanging limp and yellow on the dark-brown branches. It was one of those still autumnal afternoons on which the earth seems to rest in a dreamy silence, as if wearied by summer's long pageant. Her corn is garnered, her fruits are stored ; she has done her work, this faithful Mother Earth, and she folds her hands in the soft September atmosphere, and composes herself for winter's long sleep.

" My Naomi, how grave you are !" said Oswald, when they had strolled to the wilderness without a word on either side.

" I have something to tell you, Oswald," she answered, looking at him anxiously.

" Nothing bad, I hope. No postponement of our marriage ?"

" No. It is something about my father. Something that will surprise you very much — perhaps shock you—"

Oswald was puzzled. He had been taught to consider Joshua Haggard a rich man — a man who made money fast, and spent it slowly ; but Naomi's words and manner suggested trouble of some kind, and he could only imagine financial difficulty.

" You mean that your father's business is not so profitable as we believe," he said ; " he has some apprehension of failure ?"

" It is nothing about business. My father is married again, Oswald. He brought his wife home to us yesterday evening."

Oswald gave a long sigh of astonishment.

" That is a surprise ! But as long as it does not make you unhappy, darling, and I don't see why it should, as you'll soon be out of a step-mother's power, it can't make any difference to me. Who is the lady? Is she very grim and awful ?"

" She is very pretty, and younger than I."

" You don't mean it ?"

" I hope you won't despise my father, Oswald ?" said Naomi, deprecatingly.

" Despise him for marrying a pretty young woman instead of an ugly old one! No, my dear, I am not so inhuman. The fact is sudden enough to be startling, but it is not unnatural. And a pretty girl will hardly be a Gorgon as a step-mother. You are not very much afraid of her, are you, Naomi ?"

" Poor child ! I think she is more inclined to be afraid of me. It is such a relief to have told you, Oswald. You will not think any the worse of my father, will you, dear ?"

" Think worse of him for being human enough to fall in love. No, Naomi ; I am too deeply entangled in the meshes myself not to have a fellow-feeling for another prisoner in the net. And for a man of your father's age, love is a very serious business. Cupid has a stronger grip upon sober manhood than on shallow and frivolous youth. Tell me all about it, dear. Who is the lady? Young, you say, and pretty? Do I know her? Have I ever seen her? Is she one of your Bethelites ?"

" No, Oswald ; she's quite a stranger. She was never at Combhollow till yesterday evening."

" And do you know nothing about her ?"

Naomi was silent. Here was a divided duty, Oswald, as her future husband, had a right to possess her confidence ; yet loyalty to her father demanded that she should keep the secret of his wife's lowly origin ; and she had some sense of personal shame in the idea that her father's wife had been, one little year ago, a homeless wanderer upon the country side, without name or friends — a waif, whose only history was of starvation and ill-usage.

" Is she vulgar, or disagreeable in any way ?" asked Oswald, taking Naomi's silence as an evidence of embarrassment, and picturing to himself some miller's blowzy-cheeked daughter, or, worse perhaps, the vivacious bar-maid to some roadside inn.

" No ; she is gentle and quiet. I do not think you will dislike her. I only feared that you might think my father foolish for having chosen such a young wife."

The church-clock struck five, the inevitable tea-time ; and Naomi turned to leave the wilderness, where the patriarchal ferns were already brown and yellow, while younger varieties still retained their tender green.

HE LOOKED AT CYNTHIA SILENTLY, LOST IN WONDER.

They went back to the house by the long, straight pathway between the borders of rose-bushes and old fashioned autumn flowers, which bounded the neat expanse of vegetables, in carefully kept rows; the celery-bed, which already breathed forth its aromatic odor, the dark leaves of beet-root, and straggling winter kale. Oswald felt a mild curiosity about the preacher's new wife. He was slightly amused at this revelation of human weakness in the reserved and dignified Joshua, a man who had seemed to occupy a higher stage of life than that on which human weaknesses have sway. He followed Naomi into the house, and stood close behind her as she opened the parlor-door, and, looking over her shoulder, saw Joshua's wife.

Cynthia was kneeling by the newly lighted fire, with her straw bonnet hanging over her arm, just as she had come in from the nutting expedition; her loosened hair falling a little over her face, her cheeks flushed to a delicate carnation by air and exercise, her eyes looking dreamily at the bright flames leaping up from the newly kindled wood—a pretty picture, assuredly, concentrating all the light in the dusky room. The tea-things were laid, but the family had not yet assembled. Cynthia was alone.

She started up as Naomi entered with her lover, and stood before them shyly, too much abashed by a stranger's presence for speech.

"I hope you enjoyed your ramble?" said Naomi, kindly.

"The wood was lovely. It was very kind of your brother to take me there."

"I think it was kind of you to go with him. This is Mr. Pentreath; I—I have told him about my father's marriage."

Cynthia courtesied, and Oswald held out his hand, at which she gave him hers shyly, never having shaken hands with any one so different from the young men of Penmoyle, whose hands were always red and inclined to coarseness, and who breathed hard in society. She was not awed or impressed by Oswald's appearance as she had been by Joshua Haggard's dark and earnest face, but she considered him highly ornamental. Oswald was surprised by this delicate and flower-like beauty. He had expected to see a pretty young woman, buxom and good-tempered, with rosy cheeks adorned by large bunches of curls, not innocent of bergamot-scented pomatum, coral ear-rings, perhaps, and one of those velvet head-bands which he so heartily detested; the kind of young woman he had seen in a tobacconist's shop at Exeter.

He looked at Cynthia silently, lost in wonder. Where could Joshua Haggard have discovered this gracious creature? It was as if he had come unawares into that homely parlor and found Milton's Sabrina or Ovid's Daphne standing by the hearth.

Mr. Haggard came in presently, followed by his sister. He gave his wife a little look of greeting which was full of quiet tenderness, and then welcomed his future son-in-law with a hearty shake-hands.

"You see I have stolen a march upon you all, Oswald," he said. "At my age a man does not care to make a fuss about getting married, and I knew that Naomi and you would give my wife an affectionate welcome. I had no occasion to stipulate for that beforehand."

Cynthia had slipped away to carry her bonnet upstairs. She had been too well trained by the Miss Weblings not to know that a bonnet flung carelessly on a chair in the family sitting-room would be an offence to Aunt Judith. She came back breathless, with her hair neatly arranged, and took her seat by her husband's side, but not before Miss Haggard had exclaimed:

"When ever are we going to sit down to tea, I wonder? It's a quarter-past already. I don't know what's come to the house."

<hr />

"TROP BELLE POUR MOI, VOILÀ MON TRÉPAS."

THE actual machinery of life, the common details of domestic existence, underwent little change after Joshua Haggard's second marriage, and the introduction of a fair girl-wife into the sober household. The change was in the minds of the household, not in outward things. Aunt Judith abated no jot or tittle of her authority. Her assumption of her accustomed post at the tea-table upon the evening of Cynthia's arrival was symbolical of her maintenance of supreme authority in all domestic matters. She did not even offer to surrender the keys of those awful and impenetrable repositories in which she kept the jams and jellies, the pickles and home-made wines, and all those items which, in Jim's opinion, gave savor and relish to life—the ornamental margin of existence's daily needs, like the labyrinthine scroll-work and illumination which border the texts of a mediaval Bible. She retained supreme authority in the kitchen; and this young wife's coming did not benefit her step-son by so much as an extra pudding on week-days, or a currant cake, flavored with saffron and of that golden hue his soul loved, on Sundays.

Before Cynthia had been established in her new home for the space of a week, she had discovered that her domestic duties and rights were alike usurped by another; that in yielding the tea-pot she had given up her place in her husband's home. This was a disappointment; for in her happy dreams of life with Joshua she had seen herself ministering to him, providing for his comforts, working with those busy, clever hands of hers for his small needs and simple luxuries, lending new graces and pleasures to his daily life, were they but the smallest things, such as a bunch of fresh flowers on his breakfast-table, or a dish of light cakes at tea-time. She had a natural taste for and love of household work—a handiness in all womanly offices which had won her the approval of her mistresses at Penmoyle; and to be shut out of these offices was a hardship she felt keenly.

Not one word of complaint was ever spoken by her, or Joshua would have promptly transferred the domestic sceptre. She was by nature submissive, and the experience of her brief life had made obedience a habit. She bowed her neck to Judith's yoke, and resigned her simple household privileges without a murmur. Joshua thought it right, no doubt, or he would not look on approvingly. She did not know that Joshua —whose temporal and spiritual duties filled his time and thoughts to overflowing—had never thought about the matter at all. She remembered what he had said on that first evening — "Let there be peace in the household, and no foolish fuss about trifles;" and she accepted this speech as a command. Any opposition to Aunt Judith would be rebellion against her husband.

Cynthia's position in the family, therefore, seemed rather that of daughter than wife. She sat by her husband's side at meals; she spent her mornings in needle-work, and her afternoons in serious reading, or occasionally in a ramble on the sea-shore or in the woods with Jim. She would have been better pleased to accompany her husband on his pastoral visits to distant homesteads and cottages, but Joshua told her gently that her presence would be out of place on such occasions. She taught in Mr. Haggard's Sunday-school, held in a roomy loft at the top of the chapel. She often went to read to the sick and aged among her husband's flock, delighted to be of some use in this manner; but these occupations left a wide margin of her life to be filled somehow; and there were afternoon hours in which she sat with the Bible or Baxter open before her, and her thoughts wandering far from the text.

There were some sad thoughts mingled with her full contentment in a union which had seemed to her royal and triumphant as Esther's bridal with Ahasuerus. She had been quick to perceive the consternation her appearance had occasioned on that first evening; and she was conscious that beneath Judith's cold civility and somewhat exaggerated politeness there lurked a disapproving spirit that was not to be conciliated. Let her be ever so assiduous to please her husband's sister, Judith would never love her; and, more than this, Judith had contrived to let her know, without any apparent unkindness or intention, that Joshua's marriage had lowered him in the esteem of his flock.

"We can't all be apostles and martyrs," said Judith; "but folks expected a great deal of my brother. 'He that is unmarried careth for the things that belong to the Lord, how he may please the Lord;' and he that's married, doesn't. St. Paul says that pretty plain, you see; there's no getting away from the right meaning of his words. And people will naturally cast that up at my brother — marrying a second time, and a girl younger than his daughter. I don't blame you, my dear. I dare say if you'd thought of these things you'd have said no, especially as your own inclination would have led you to prefer a younger man."

"I could never have loved or honored any one as I love and honor my husband," protested Cynthia, flushing with anger at the suggestion.

"Ah!" sighed Judith, with a world of significance; "of course, it was a great thing for you to come to such a home as this, and a husband as comfortably off as my brother. It isn't many young women in service that get as well provided for."

"I hope you don't think — " cried Cynthia, eagerly.

"I trust I'm too much of a Christian to think evil of any one," replied Aunt Judith, with dignity. "I'm thinking what other people will say. You can't stop their tongues. If they choose to say that my brother Joshua has fell away from his own principles and the First of Corinthians by a pretty face, and that you married him for the sake of a home, there's no law in the land to hinder 'em from having their say."

Thus, for the first time in her life, Cynthia heard of that invisible and irresponsible tribunal which is always sitting outside our doors; and was taught to feel that it was not to her Creator and her own conscience alone she had to answer, but that she ought also to shape her acts to meet the views of other people. Other people would measure her acts by their standard, sound the depths of her heart with their plummet; and, unheard, undefended, ignorant alike of her indictment and her sentence, she would be convicted and condemned.

This was a chilling revelation to one as innocent of life's complexities as Miranda or Perdita. One of the few lessons in the world's bitter school, which Cynthia had thoroughly learned, was to endure undeserved affliction patiently. She long bore Aunt Judith's sharp stings and quiet stabs as meekly as she had borne ill-usage from the tyrants of her childhood. But she felt her punishment none the less keenly; and already, ere she had been married a month, began to ask herself if Joshua had verily done wisely in marrying her, and whether it would not have been better for her to have gone on worshiping him at a distance all her life, spending her tranquil, industrious days in the little kitchen at Penmoyle, doing her duty, and being praised for faithful service, among people who were in nowise scandalized by her existence. It had been a very monotonous life, containing little for memory to dwell on, offering still less for hope to build upon; and the river of life, which youth would fain sail upon, is a bright and swiftly flowing current — not a tideless canal. But it had been a life full of peace, and already in this new life there had come a feeling which was not peace. Unhappily, Judith's Christian-like and candid remarks upon popular feeling at Combhollow were sustained by a foundation of truth. The minister's congregation did not contemplate his second marriage with entire approval. They were not prepared to take his youthful flaxen-haired wife to their hearths and bosoms with any warmth of affection. She would be invited out to tea, of course, and best tea-pots would be taken out of their chamois-leather enfoldings, and amber-hued cakes would be baked for her regalement; but there would be little heartiness in her reception: it would be ceremonial and civic only, like the welcome of a foreign princess when the nation feels their prince has made a foolish or insignificant choice.

There were so many things to be said against this marriage of Joshua Haggard's. In the first place, why marry at all? In the second, if he must needs marry, why not choose one of his own flock — a comfortable widow, for instance — and there were several comfortable widows among the Bethelites — whose antecedents would be patent to every body at Combhollow, whose life from the cradle upward would be as well known to the community as the pattern of her parlor carpet or the furniture in her best bedroom? Such a marriage, though unspiritual, and in somewise depoetizing the ideal pastor, would at least have recommended itself to the more practical members of the congregation as prudent and suitable.

Whatever disappointment such a marriage might have caused in those loftier minds which had elevated the preacher and teacher into the saint and apostle — minds to be found chiefly among the spinsters of Joshua's flock—it could hardly have occasioned scandal; but this unannounced, unexplained union with an unknown young woman from the far west of Cornwall—a girl who had worked in the mines, perhaps, and worn unlady attire, and toiled shoulder to shoulder with rough barbarians, speaking a strange tongue—this was enough to inspire unpleasant doubts in the minds of Joshua's congregation, to call all their prejudices to arms against the fair intruder.

Who was she — supposing that she had not worked in the mines? Who was she? whence came she? to whom belonged she? Questions to which no one could supply any categorical or satisfactory answer, though speculative answers and suggestions were to be had in abundance. Whence came this wandering rumor, traceable to no particular source, yet in every body's mouth; that Joshua had found his young wife by the wayside, a beggar, with bare feet, houseless, friendless, not even knowing the name of her kindred or the place of her birth, nor on what parish she might fasten her helplessness — the merest waif upon the stream of life? This notion could hardly have arisen from any imprudent communicativeness upon the part of Aunt Judith, for, when sounded by solicitous friends upon the subject of her brother's marriage, that lady had refrained from all expression of opinion save such dumb, inscrutable movements as shoulder-shrugs, elevation of the eyebrows, lips tightly drawn, and head shaken with a solemn significance. Whatever this dumb-show meant, Combhollow felt assured that it meant a great deal, and meant no good.

There was a general and growing conviction that Joshua had acted foolishly, if not wickedly, in marrying this strange young woman. "How are the mighty fallen!" cried the Bethelites; and in their lamentations over the degradation of their pastor, they indulged in a great deal of Scriptural language to his disadvantage. Perhaps the value of our Bible never comes so fully home to us as when we quote it against our erring neighbor. It was felt that Joshua held the same position in Combhollow that David must have occupied in Jerusalem after that lamentable episode in the princely life which brought greatness to the level of the sinful herd. The preacher read disapproval in the faces of his flock on the first Sabbath after his marriage. He discovered a coldness, an alteration in the tone of those customers at the shop who were of his congregation. His Church-of-England patrons, on the contrary, congratulated him heartily upon his marriage, and praised his wife's pretty face in the friendliest manner. But they had never canonized the pastor; they contemplated him solely in his aspect as a general dealer; and what more natural, what more distinctly human, than that a well-to-do grocer should beautify his autumn of life with the charms and graces of a young wife?

Joshua saw the change in his flock, and his heart rebelled against their hardness. Pride sustained him — a manly and honest pride, and a spiritual pride, which told him that he was better than the best of these who presumed to sit in judgment upon him. Who among them had toiled for the good cause as he had done? Who, among these professing Methodists, had trodden

in the footsteps of the great founder of Methodism as he had trodden, faithfully imitating that pious man's asceticism and self-denial? And were these people, whom he had served so faithfully, for whose spiritual welfare he had labored so hard, to turn the light that he had kindled against him—to distort the law he had taught them, in order to pass an iniquitous sentence upon their teacher? He felt these cold looks and altered greetings keenly as a deep injustice, and shut himself up in the armor of offended pride. God had given him this infinite blessing—the love of a pure and lovely woman; and was man's malice to poison his cup of bliss? No, he told himself. He could live without the world's regard. He had never served mankind for their own sake, and he could dispense with their affection. In his prayers and sermons at this time of estrangement, he raised himself so far above the level of daily life and earthly ills, that there was no taint of personal feeling to be perceived in any of his words, no murmur against man's injustice crept into his communion with God. Never had his teaching been clearer or more elevated; never were his prayers more fervent. Into that spiritual world of which he possessed the key, neither worldly malice nor worldly misconception could follow him.

Again, at the worst, were his flock never so ungrateful, he knew of one listener whose mute enthusiasm was in itself sufficient for inspiration. If he had not been able, of his own unassisted strength, to lift up his soul to the very gates of heaven, that look of Cynthia's, as she sat in the narrow little pew just under the square box of a pulpit, would have been the source of pure imaginings and holy thoughts. His Sabbaths were now such blessed days; for all the time he did not owe to duty he gave to his young wife. They walked together by that lovely sea which, in its jewel-like coloring, so often recalled the Oriental imagery of Holy Writ. They talked together of spiritual things with a fond familiarity which is natural to those whose only poetry, whose only knowledge of the beautiful, has been drawn from Scripture. Cynthia's greatest delight at this time was to hear her husband talk of his youthful career, his discouragements and successes, his alternate despair and triumph; those hysterical gusts of enthusiasm in the newly converted which had promised so much; those chilling disappointments, caused by backsliding in his brightest disciples, the sudden going-out of the sacred fire.

Perfectly blessed in such perfect love, Joshua was able to live his own life with supreme indifference as to the opinion of the outside world; and this independence of feeling speedily revealing itself to the flock, there was a general sense of disappointment at the discovery that Mr. Haggard had not been crushed by their disapproval, and then the cold looks began to give place to friendly smiles and salutations, as of old. The pastor was complimented on his last sermon; the more select of the community were pressing in their invitations to tea-parties of a ceremonious character.

Joshua, who had felt his affections outraged, was not so easily to be won back to the pleasant path of brotherly love. He rejected all invitations to tea, responded coldly to the warmest salutations, and heard men's praises of his eloquence unmoved. But in all pastoral duties he was faithful, as of old; ministered to the sick, taught in his school, gave three evenings a week to a class of young men belonging to the laboring community, who met in the loft over the chapel for serious reading and conversation by the light of two dip-candles, and joined in a hymn before they separated. It may be supposed, therefore, that, with the exception of those tranquil Sabbath hours between the services, there was not much time left for him to devote to his young wife, and that Cynthia had plenty of leisure in which to meditate upon things spiritual and temporal.

CHAPTER XV.

A FAMILY PICTURE.

THE year drew to its close, and society at Combhollow, which possessed something of that capacity for adapting itself to circumstances which is characteristic of society in wider circles, had got accustomed to the idea of Joshua Haggard's marriage; and, if not altogether reconciled to his union, had become, at any rate, resigned to the inevitable.

"It's a blessed mercy for Mr. Haggard that he's got a sister to look after his house and keep the furniture polished, and see that the bottoms of the loaves and broken pieces don't get thrown to the fowls," remarked careful housewives to each other, in the friendly loquacity of the tea-table, "or else things would go to wrack and ruin altogether, I should think, with a young wife like that."

"And so pretty, too," sighed a matron, gently shaking the stiffest of caps, as if prettiness were a crime.

"Pretty and useless, no doubt, poor thing. And he seems so foolishly fond of her. I'm sure, to see them out walking together, you'd think they were sweethearts that had only just begun to keep company," remarked Mrs. Pycroft, of The First and Last, whose conversations with her husband after marriage had been chiefly of a didactic or argumentative character.

Once, and once only, had Joshua, whose style of preaching was more personal and familiar than that which obtained at this time in the Established Church, where the chaff of abstruse doctrine was but sparsely qualified with the grain of moral teaching and Gospel truth—once only did Joshua approach indirectly the subject of his marriage.

He had been quoting Richard Baxter's "Call to the Unconverted," and, suddenly diverging from the theology of the preacher, enlarged upon the man and his life.

"It was in many ways a life of trial, yet in all ways a life full of blessing," he said; "nor do I count it the smallest of graces which Providence bestowed upon this great and good man that, at forty-seven years of age, he was blessed in the affection of a wife of three-and-twenty. He had come to that time of life without having ever known the sweetness of domestic happiness. But it pleased God that he should be the instrument of this dear girl's conversion, and that her heart should go forth to him who had brought her the message of salvation. There were some, perchance, in those evil days who were scandalized by this marriage; for it had been a part of Bax-

ter's creed that for ministers to marry was lawfully lawful. But Heaven smiled upon this wedded pair, who were verily married in the Lord; and Baxter has told us that he found in his wife a helpmeet, a comforter in all his sorrows, the sharer of his prison, and always the helper to his joy."

Before the year was ended Naomi had become completely reconciled to her father's marriage. She had suffered faint thrills of pain just at first, when she saw Cynthia draw her chair near Joshua's, and perhaps sit with her hand in his, while he read the evening Scriptures. She had felt it just a little hard to see her father's eyes rest with such ineffable love upon the face of the stranger; but she had schooled her heart to submit to this loss—if loss it could be called—since her father was more affectionate to his children than he had been before his marriage. She had subdued all human jealousy, and had taught herself to be glad that her father had won so fair and faithful a companion. There was something indescribably touching in the young wife's childlike affection for her husband, her intense belief in him, her unbounded admiration for his talents and powers as preacher and teacher, her implicit faith in his judgment. If flattery be a pleasant poison, Joshua was in a fair way to be poisoned by the sweetest of all flatteries—the exaggerated estimate which springs from womanly love. Love with a woman of this temper is but another name for worship; and Cynthia's love had begun in a spiritual idolatry which had set Joshua but a little way below the saints and apostles he had taught her to reverence. In a man so truthful as Joshua, closer communion revealed no flaw, familiarity was not followed by disillusion. After two months of married life, the husband still occupied the pedestal upon which Cynthia had elevated the teacher; but, although she had suffered no disappointment in the man himself, her vivid and romantic mind began to find something wanting in her surroundings. The atmosphere of her daily life was depressing; the young, eager spirit yearned for work of some kind, and was flung back upon the dull blank of idleness. She sighed for keener air, a wider horizon, yet scarcely knew what she desired. She had secret aspirations for her husband, and rebelled against that commonplace trade which occupied one half of his life—that buying and selling and getting gain, which seemed to her enthusiastic mind a practical denial of the Gospel which the teacher preached on Sundays, the lesson which he taught his flock on weekdays. These divided duties, this solicitous service to a worldly master, struck her as out of joint with her husband's sacred character. To her, who had known no other church than this Dissenting community, and who hardly knew that they were Dissenters, Joshua was as holy as if episcopal hands had been laid upon him, and she was troubled by the incongruity between the trader and the priest. Yet, seeing that Joshua saw no harm in his calling, that he held honest trade as an honorable office, she dared not lift up her voice in remonstrance, and accepted the shop as one of those things which, like Aunt Judith, were an inevitable element in her life.

Christmas brought cheerful thoughts and friendly relations between the minister and his flock. Presents rained upon Joshua at this season, and those stiff-necked members of his congregation who had lifted the nose at his marriage atoned for their unfriendly feeling by the fattest of turkeys and youngest of geese. *Noel* was a season of much eating and drinking at Comblehow; and even Methodism forgot to be ascetic, and gorged itself with beef and pudding, with a riotous delight in the good things of this mortal life that would have made William Law's hair stand on end. The Established Church woke up from its comfortable doze, and sung carols on Christmas-eve; the ecclesiastical feeling for color displayed itself in sprigs of holly, stuck here and there in convenient places by the hands of beadle and pew-opener; and a dole of bread, provided by the bequest of the virtuous dame Margery Hawker, of this parish, was meted out to five-and-twenty poor women on Christmas morning. New bonnets, modeled upon the coal-scuttle of the period, were to be seen above the high oaken pews of St. Mary Magdalene, and enlivened the crowded congregation at Little Bethel. It was altogether a season of pleasant thoughts and general contentment—a season which seemed very sweet to Naomi, as she walked in the leafless woods with the lover who was so soon to be her husband. Early in March, before the birds had pecked the crocuses to death, before the daffodils had begun their fairy dances in the windy afternoons, Naomi and Oswald were to be married at the gray old parish church. It was a wonderful thing to think of. Naomi was to be a great lady, and live at the Grange, and have that pretty morning-room, with its dainty book-cases, and neat duodecimo edition of the old poets, bound in white vellum, for her very own. She was to belong to the old squire and his son; the gardens and the park, where the cattle browsed, and the beautiful, mysterious wood, with its glades and dells, and lopsided old trees, and knolls and thickets, which one could never quite know by heart, were to be hers—a part of her life, inseparable from all her future years.

"You will let me go to chapel, Oswald?" she asked, earnestly; "you will never try to keep me away from Little Bethel?"

"My dearest, I would rather go there with you than hinder your going. You shall be free, my dear. These things are more to you than they are to me. It would be hard if I were to oppose my prejudices to your deep-rooted faith. And who shall say whether John Wesley's creed is right or wrong? It is a comfortable doctrine, most assuredly, that sin brings us closer to Christ, and that the deeper we sink in the mire the nearer we are to the stars."

"Oh, Oswald, you don't understand. It is our consciousness of sin that brings us to the Fount of grace, not the sin."

They were very happy at this Christmas-tide. It was one of those green Yules to which popular prejudice accredits the filling of church-yards, although the *Times* obituary goes far to prove the good old-fashioned Christmas, with his icicle diadem and his mantle of snow, Death's sterner coadjutor. Blackbirds were merry in the woods at even-song, and mistaken dog-violets struggled into untimely bloom under the shelter of tall hedges. Oswald dined with his father upon the great festival, and, as soon as he decently could do so, stole away from the fire-lit dining-room, leaving the old squire asleep in his big arm-chair, where he would, in all likelihood, slumber peace-

fully until bed-time, when he would awake with wonderful briskness to go his round of the lower chambers, and see that every bolt was duly drawn against thieves and burglars; for although half a dozen spoons and forks, and a pair of salt-cellars with corpulent bodies and attenuated legs comprised the utmost display of silver that ever decorated the squire's table, there was a goodly store of old tankards, venison-dishes, soup-tureens, and smaller plate stowed away in the great oak closet in old Mr. Pentreath's bedroom.

Oswald walked straight to the minister's house —but not quite so fast as he had been accustomed to walk in the same direction. The air was wondrously mild; the western sky a pale primrose; the wooded horizon-line bluer than it is wont to be. It was a winter twilight that might tempt a man to linger, and Oswald was full of thought. Early in March—so soon—for him as for Naomi, that approaching marriage was an event to be contemplated with wonder, almost with disbelief. His apprenticeship, which at the beginning had seemed to him as long as Jacob's, was nearly ended. His patience and truth and constancy were to have their reward.

"Dear girl!" he said to himself, thinking of his betrothed. "She is the best and noblest of women; where could I find so perfect a wife? I do not believe there is a flaw in her goodness. I always feel myself a better man when I am with her. Yes, that is what a wife ought to be."

And then, in his low, legato tones he repeated that familiar line of Wordsworth's,

"A perfect woman, nobly planned,"

from a poem which seems to concentrate in thirty lines all that can ever be said or sung in praise of womankind.

He could see the ruddy fire-light shining in the minister's best parlor as he came round the bend of the road. It was tea-time, and they were all assembled there, no doubt: Aunt Judith in her best gown, which was such an excellent fit across the chest as to be faintly suggestive of a straight waistcoat; Naomi sitting in her favorite corner, with the red light flickering upon her glossy hair, and those deep, dark eyes of hers full of grave thoughts; and on the other side of the hearth that child-like face and figure, the very type of innocent and guileless maidenhood, his idea of Goethe's Gretchen, nestling close to Joshua's side, looking up at him now and then with worshiping eyes.

Oswald saw the family scene from afar off, as if it had been a mirage picture. He turned the handle of the door and went in. The passage was dimly lighted by an oil-lamp. He knocked at the parlor door, by way of ceremony, and the minister's deep voice bid him enter. Yes, the scene was just as his imagination had shown it to him; Aunt Judith seated at the tea-board, the old brown Bible at Joshua's right hand, Cynthia's fair hair looking like palest gold in the uncertain light, Naomi's dark head drooping thoughtfully, Jim screwed as close as possible to the fire, stooping to roast chestnuts between the bars—a peaceful home-picture. They all looked up and gave him welcome, but Naomi's gratified smile was worth all the rest.

"I did not think you would be able to come," she exclaimed.

"Luckily for me, my father indulged in a

heavier dinner than usual, and fell asleep immediately after it. But I should have contrived to come under any circumstances. I hope I am in time for a cup of your excellent tea, Miss Haggard. It is not every one can make such tea as yours."

"Every one hasn't been making tea in the same pot for five-and-twenty years," replied Aunt Judith, obviously mollified by this compliment. "You want to know your pot, and to know your tea, if it's to be worth drinking."

Miss Haggard dispensed the beverage with an abnormal stiffness peculiar to festive occasions and best gowns. Social gatherings of a cheerful nature did not induce Aunt Judith to unbend. On occasions of this kind she assumed a spinal inflexibility which, in her mind, was the surest indication of a virtuous bringing-up and a polite education. And this backboard politeness was accepted at Combhollow, where Miss Haggard was considered "quite the lady."

"I don't know what's coming to the women in this place," said Aunt Judith, presently, when there was a pause in the conversation, "but I think they must have set their hearts on spending money one against the other. I counted four new bonnets in chapel this morning, without counting Mrs. Spradgers's that had been fresh trimmed; and she only had it in October, for I sold her the ribbon for it—a lovely maroon with an orange spot."

"I hope you had something better to do in chapel than count the new bonnets and think badly of your neighbors, Judith," remonstrated Joshua.

"I've got eyes in chapel as well as out of chapel," answered Judith, "and there's times when the most serious-minded Christian can use 'em—while the hymn's being given out, for instance: our time's our own then, I should think. All I can say is, that if milliners' made-up bonnets—drawn silk trumpery that one heavy shower will spoil—don't bring Combhollow to ruin, nothing else will. There's Mrs. Flitton, that I've sold many a serviceable straw to in days gone by, decked out in a velvet cottage with a bird of paradise from Barnstaple. It was luxury of this kind that led to the French king losing his head when we were young folks, Joshua. I've heard you say as much many a time, so don't deny it."

"If you thought less of your neighbors' shortcomings, Judith—"

"I can't help thinking of them when I've got fourteen straw bonnets, best quality, left out of last summer's stock. The shape will be old next year, I dare say. Fashions change so quick nowadays. I shall have to sell 'em to the servant-girls half-price."

"How you do worry about a few shillings, aunt!" cried Jim, in a disgusted tone. "We make more on our side of the shop in a day than you can lose on your side in a week."

"Thank you, Mr. Pert. When your father loses money by *my* department, I hope he'll tell me so. I haven't heard of it yet."

"Then why do you make such a fuss about half a dozen straw bonnets? You *said* you were going to lose by 'em."

"If I lose by my bonnets, I shall come home upon my ribbons, you may be sure, Mr. James; and when you know the grocery business as well as I know the drapery, you may take me to task, not sooner."

"We won't talk any more about the shop this evening, Judith," said Joshua. "We may be too assiduous in business."

"The Bible tells us not to be slothful," replied the aggrieved Judith, "but I dare say it vexes Mrs. Haggard to hear such talk. She'd have liked to have married a bishop, with his carriage and pair."

This was a hit at Cynthia's dislike to the shop, which the girl had revealed involuntarily upon one or two occasions.

"I should be glad if my husband had nothing to distract his thoughts from his chapel and his schools," answered Cynthia. "Any man can keep a shop. It seems a hard thing that his time should be taken up with selling grocery."

"Does it seem a hard thing that he's got a comfortable home and money in the bank, and a fortune to give his daughter?" demanded Aunt Judith. "He wouldn't have got those out of Little Bethel."

Cynthia sighed. It seemed to her that it would have been a far happier life to have wandered with her husband from village to village, tending him and comforting him in his pilgrimage, than to lead this prosperous life in a settled home, where there was so much to draw his mind away from his great work. And was it for the sake of a substantial house and daily food, for money heaped up in bank, that the teacher consented so to limit his sphere of usefulness, nay, in a manner to hide his light under a bushel? Naomi had talked to Cynthia of that missionary life which seemed so glorious to her, and the younger girl had caught the enthusiasm of the elder. She felt as if her husband's true vocation lay far away beyond the wide, strange seas, among the races that had never heard of the Christian's God.

Happily for household peace upon this festive occasion, the clearing away of the tea-things, and the retirement of Judith to wash them, put an end to a discussion that had tended toward unpleasantness.

Naomi and Oswald were able to enjoy their quiet talk on one side of the hearth, while Joshua read one of his favorite Puritan divines on the other, Cynthia sitting by him in meek silence, full of sweet thoughts, and dreamy aspirations after an unknown good. James went on roasting his chestnuts, which ever and anon exploded with a fizz and a splutter, to his own delight and the consternation of the assembly.

"How pretty she is!" whispered Oswald to Naomi, contemplating Cynthia's thoughtful face during a pause in his talk. He watched her with the same pleasure and interest he might have felt in the contemplation of a pretty child: something soft and sweet and helpless, which he looked down upon from the altitude of his mature years.

"Yes, she is very pretty, and very good. My father is quite happy in his marriage."

"Why does she never come with us in our walks? I must be dull for her of an afternoon when your father is out."

"She goes for a walk with Jim sometimes."

"But why not with us?"

"I don't know. She's very shy. I rather think she's afraid of you."

"Afraid of me! Oh, that's too ridiculous,"

"She thinks you a very fine gentleman."

"That's delightful! You know how much of a fine gentleman there is about me, Naomi. I am afraid she must be rather silly."

"Oh no, indeed. She is wonderfully bright and quick in every thing."

"Is she? I should hardly have thought her so. We are talking of you, Mrs. Haggard," pursued Oswald, abandoning his confidential, half-whispering tone; "I have been asking Naomi why you never join us in our afternoon rambles. Perhaps you don't care for woods and hills."

"Yes, I do," answered Cynthia; "I am very fond of this beautiful place. It is prettier than any thing I ever saw before."

"I should think so," said Aunt Judith, sharply. "It's bare enough in the mining country where you come from, I've always heard say."

"You should come with us sometimes, Mrs. Haggard," said Oswald.

"Yes," said Joshua, looking up from his book. "It would be better for you to go out-of-doors oftener, Cynthia. I find you sitting reading, or working, in the parlor every afternoon when I come home to tea."

"There's nothing so bad as poring over a book for a young woman's spine," said Aunt Judith. "Mrs. Haggard will be round-shouldered before she's thirty if she doesn't take care."

Judith's backbone was her tower of strength. Years might creep on, the insidious approach of age might show itself in a sprinkling of gray hairs among the dark ones, by crow's feet at the corners of the eyes; but Judith's spine defied the assailant Time. It straightened itself against the enemy, and at eight-and-forty Miss Haggard was more erect than she had been at eighteen.

"Yes, my love, you must really have more air and exercise," said Joshua.

Cynthia gave a faint sigh. She was very happy, on such an evening as this, in her husband's company, sitting next him, stealing her hand into his now and then, or leaning against his shoulder to read a page or so of the book he was reading; but there were times in her life when she felt as if she belonged to no one. Thus it was that she had taken to pore over books, or to sit long at some laborious piece of plain needle-work. There was so little for her to do: she was never happier than when Joshua allowed her to go and sit in some stuffy cottage, beside the bed of sickness or decrepitude, and read the Book she loved. She felt then that she, too, had her mission in the world, and that she was in somewise worthy of the husband who had chosen her.

Not a festive Christmas evening this for those who have been wont to associate the occasion with cheery family circles, merry children, old-fashioned games, cards, forfeits, and snapdragon—the good old traditional Christmas immortalized by Washington Irving and Charles Dickens. A pack of cards had never been seen in Mr. Haggard's house, and forfeits and snapdragon he would have accounted childish folly. His children had never been gratified with such empty delights. In the day when he took up John Wesley as his guide and model, he put away from him all small pleasures, all sensual gratifications. At heart he was an ascetic, and it grated a little upon his sense of right to see the board loaded with cold turkey and chine and plum-pudding upon this particular evening. He would have been happier

eating his dry bread and hard cheese, and feeling that he was denying himself while all the rest of the world were feasting and reveling. There was a touch of the Pharisee's spiritual pride here, perhaps, but the pride had its source in that idea of calling and special grace which was implanted in the preacher's heart. Had he not been chosen and elected in the days of his youth, when he first felt himself called to do God's work? He could name the day and hour. It was no slow awakening to solemn truths, no gradual leavening of the human mind with spiritual grace, but a sudden and absolute conversion—an instantaneous call to righteousness. Yesterday a child of wrath; to-day the heir of salvation, a citizen of heaven, an inhabitant of eternity. Wondrous, mysterious had been this pentecostal season; he looked back at it with love and pride. How pitiful a price had he paid for so great a treasure, in surrendering the transient pleasures of this world.

And now Heaven had rewarded him with the sweetest of all earthly blessings—the blessed joys of home.

He looked at his daughter, happy by her lover's side; at his son, healthy, intelligent, active, dutiful; at his useful sister, rough and bitter, like medicinal herbs, but a faithful servant; at his wife, dearest of all; and thanked God for these manifold blessings.

CHAPTER XVI.

CYNTHIA TRIES TO BE USEFUL.

MARCH had come. The anemones were white in the woods; the gummy chestnut-buds were bursting in sheltered corners of the land; there was a perfume of violets in the lanes; and primroses began to peep out like pale earth-stars, amidst tender green tufts fringed with the ragged disorder of last year's leaves. The gaudy daffodils were flaunting everywhere. March was growing old, but Naomi Haggard's wedding had not yet come to pass. The date had been fixed, and all things had gone prosperously till within a week of the appointed day, when the squire, returning on horseback from Barnstaple, where he had been to take counsel with his lawyer as to the ejectment of a troublesome tenant, had been overtaken by a heavy fall of rain, which lasted with a cruel persistency throughout his homeward journey. Instead of immediately resorting to a hot bath and dry clothes as a cure, Mr. Pentreath had sat by the dining-room fire, while he soaked himself with a tumbler of hot brandy-and-water before changing his raiment. The consequences of the wet ride and of his imprudence showed themselves next morning in a sharp attack of bronchitis, which speedily degenerated into inflammation of the lungs. Before the week was out the squire's life was in danger, and Naomi's wedding was deferred to an indefinite period.

Oswald was in much distress about his father's state. They had not loved each other tenderly, but the son was soft-hearted, and felt a curious, aching pity for the lonely old man lying on his death-bed, more friendless than the lowliest hind on his estate. The family surgeon and sole doctor of Combhollow, who attended all the families round about, and killed or cured by the pharmacopœia without let or hinderance from any opposing practitioner, declared that the squire's only chance of recovering lay, not in medicine, or blood-letting, or blistering, but in good nursing. And who was to nurse this peevish, cantankerous old man, who, while groaning in the agonies of mortal disease, would grudge the nurse her feed and feel an extra pang at every meal she eat? The professional nurses of Combhollow were ancient females of the sibyl or witch type, women one might expect to meet on solitary moors, or in fever-haunted swamps, gathering simples under a stormy moon, and whose ignorance was only matched in degree by their cunning and cruelty. The house-maid at the Grange, who had such a conscientious regard for the oak panelling that she would begin beeswaxing at six o'clock in the morning, was not so deeply attached to her old master. When Oswald appealed to her for aid, she told him she had never been where there was sickness, and did not know much about invalids' ways, and that she should scream if any one asked her to handle a leech. The housekeeper was old and purblind, and cooked her dinners by the aid of habit and memory, rather than by any existing sense. Oswald could not trust his father's life to her.

In this difficulty, he naturally applied to Miss Haggard as a person likely to have all the resources of Combhollow at her fingers' ends.

"Do I know any woman that would go out sick-nursing?" she exclaimed, repeating Oswald's question. "If I know one such, I know twenty. There's nothing people won't undertake to do if you'll pay them for it. But if you ask me to recommend you a nurse for your father, Mr. Pentreath, that's quite another thing. There isn't a woman who goes out nursing in Combhollow that I'd trust with the life of a kitten, if I wanted the kitten to grow up to a cat."

"That's conclusive," said Oswald, despondently. "Yet I suppose people in Combhollow get nursed somehow when they're ill."

"Somehow; yes, that's about it. Sometimes they die, and sometimes Providence is extra kind to them, and pulls them through their troubles, nursing and all."

This was depressing. Oswald sat looking at the fire gloomily, wondering what he ought to do. It was tea-time. Aunt Judith was in her accustomed place before the tea-tray. Naomi stood by the mantel-piece looking at her lover, too much disturbed by his despondency to obey that rigorous code of etiquette which her aunt had imposed upon the household, and in which sitting down to meals the instant they were ready was a stringent article. Cynthia had taken her place, and was cutting bread-and-butter for Jim with a calm, matronly air which became the fair young face. She was always pleased to be useful, were it in the smallest detail.

"I wish I could nurse your father, Oswald," said Naomi, earnestly.

"But you can't," exclaimed Judith, with prompt severity. "A pretty thing, indeed, for you to go and live in the squire's house before you've any right. A nice scandal there'd be in Combhollow. You, a minister's daughter too! You ought to have more sense than to talk of such a thing."

"I can't see that it would be wrong," cried Oswald, with some show of heat. "Who has a better right to be at home in my father's house than my future wife?"

"If young men like you were able to draw a line between right and wrong, right and wrong wouldn't get mixed up so often as they do," replied Judith, sententiously. "As to Naomi making herself at home at the Grange till she's Mrs. Pentreath, it's out of the question, and she ought to have known it. Besides which, she knows about as much of sick-nursing as a babe in its cradle."

"God would teach me," said Naomi, "and my love for Oswald would make me strong to help his father."

"I believe that, Naomi," exclaimed Oswald, with a grateful look.

"Let me nurse the squire," said Cynthia, with a subdued eagerness. "I have so little to do at home. I should hardly be missed. And I do know something about sickness. I nursed Miss Webling, a lady who had the quinsy very badly—the doctor thought she would die; and I put on leeches and blisters, and sat up with her fifteen nights; and I have nursed the poor people here, haven't I, Joshua?" she asked, looking up at her husband, who had this moment entered the room.

"Yes, love, you have been a ministering angel by many sick-beds, and you would have done more if I had suffered you. But what is all this talk about nursing?"

"If some of you will sit down," remonstrated Judith, "I'll pour out the tea. But I don't feel as if any body wanted it while you're standing about higgledy-piggledy."

Thus reproved, Naomi took her seat meekly; and Oswald, feeling that the reproof applied with double force to him as a visitor, seated himself in a desponding attitude at a corner of the table.

"I want to nurse old Mr. Pentreath, Joshua," said Cynthia. "Miss Haggard says there is no nurse to be trusted in Combhollow, and the doctor says the old gentleman must have good nursing. Will you let me go to the Grange for a little while and sit up with him, as I did with Miss Webling?"

Joshua watched her earnest face with a tender smile.

"Why, my love, how anxious you are! And do you think you know enough about sickness—that you would have strength for such a task?"

"It would be a good work, and I should do it with all my heart. God would give me strength and knowledge. I have no fear. I feel often that my life here is of very little use. I am never happier than when you let me visit the sick people. Let me go to the Grange, Joshua, and nurse poor Mr. Pentreath."

"You are too good to offer such a thing," cried Oswald, wondering at the ardor of this delicate, flower-like creature. "It would be a troublesome task. You have no notion how cross my poor old father is. He abuses the doctor in a most ferocious style—accuses him of picking his pocket. Our house-maid will scarcely go near him. There is a scrub of a girl who works about the house under every one else, a stupid, good-natured thing, too much accustomed to hard words to mind them, and she is the only creature I can get to stay in my father's room; but she is clumsy and sleepy."

"Do you really wish to go, Cynthia?" asked Joshua, seriously. To his mind there was nothing unnatural in this desire of his young wife's

He belonged to a community in which to minister to the sick was a paramount duty, in which affliction was a period of closer brotherhood, a drawing-together of those links which bound the little flock to one another at all times. True that the squire was an ungodly person, outside that circle; but he had been in a manner united to Joshua's household by his own choice of Naomi. Here was a sick man to be snatched from the jaws of death; here was something higher and nobler, a soul to be saved from the clutch of Satan. That the squire's body must perish was, in all probability, inevitable—an event not to be staved off by leechings and blisterings—or all the resources of medicine; but there was a great battle to be fought for that immortal part of him, that impalpable, indestructible spark, destined for an eternal future of good or evil.

What had the Church of England—of those slumberous days—done for the squire? Well, it had taken tithe of his substance, and thereby secured to itself his antipathy; it had preached diluted Tillotson, South, and Barrow over his head while he dozed in the noontide sun; it had christened and married him, and held itself in readiness to bury him; and for the rest it had civilly and obligingly let him alone.

It seemed to Joshua Haggard that if his wife succored the squire in his fight with disease and death, he too could be by the bedside to defend the sinner against the onslaughts of his invisible foe; for Joshua's positive theology had never been troubled by any doubt of the reality and personality of man's first tempter and perpetual adversary.

"If you really feel that you have a call for this good work, Cynthia, I should be sorry to forbid your obeying it," he said, after a thoughtful pause.

"It seems too bold to say that I am called to do it," answered his wife, humbly; "but indeed, Joshua, my heart is drawn toward the poor, lonely old man in his sickness and pain."

"Then you shall go, my dear," said Joshua, decisively.

Cynthia rose as if to depart that moment.

"God bless you for that permission!" cried Oswald.

"You may as well wait till tea's finished," exclaimed Judith, tartly; "other people want their teas, if you don't. We didn't use to have tea in such a fashion."

Whereupon Cynthia resumed her seat meekly, and begged pardon of the authorities for this breach of the household law.

"I don't know how to thank you both," said Oswald. "You for your generous offer, Mrs. Haggard, or your husband for his goodness in letting you obey your benevolent inclination; but I am more grateful than I can say. I will take care that you are not overfatigued by your task. Phœbe—that's the girl I spoke of just now—will do any thing you want. She'd work till she dropped, I believe, poor girl, and only requires to be taught. My poor father was delirious last night. That won't frighten you, I hope—if his mind wanders?"

"No," said Cynthia, "I was sitting with a poor woman yesterday who was light-headed. She talked of all kinds of strange things. Yet every now and then she spoke quite clearly, and followed the sense when I read to her. I shall not be frightened."

After tea, when the bondage of etiquette was loosened a little, Naomi stole to her young stepmother's side and kissed her tenderly.

"I am so grateful to you, Cynthia," she said. "Dear Naomi, there's no reason for gratitude or praise. I am only doing my duty. I am sorry you were not permitted to perform this task, dear, as I know it would have seemed sweet to you, for Oswald's sake."

———

CHAPTER XVII.

"E'EN AT TURNING O' THE TIDE."

CYNTHIA took her place at the squire's bedside, and assumed the care of the sick-room with as much calmness and self-possession as if she had been trained in a city hospital. That intense faith which made the two Wesleys so strong to resist all earthly opposition, is the staff and anchor of all true followers in that wide school which they and Whitefield founded. Joshua's young wife had no fear that her strength would fail her in this ordeal. Whatever strength she needed would be given to her.

It was not a pleasing or an easy task either, this attendance upon an irritable old man who had served no apprenticeship to sickness, and to whom acute bodily pain was almost a new thing.

"Mrs. Haggard has been so good as to come to nurse you, father," said Oswald, when he brought Cynthia to the bedside.

The squire looked at the small gray figure—"a shadow like an angel with bright hair"—doubtfully.

"I don't know that girl," he said. "Your mother was never so pretty."

"Will you let her nurse you, father?" inquired Oswald.

"I don't want nursing; I only want to be let alone. Give me something to drink," said the squire, with some inconsistency.

Cynthia examined the table by the bed, upon which empty medicine-bottles, discarded poultices, rags, and dirty tumblers were crowded in unseemly confusion. There was an uncorked bottle containing half a tumbler of claret.

"Does your father drink that wine?" asked Cynthia, as she washed a tumbler swiftly, while the squire expressed a general sense of discomfort by feeble moanings.

"Yes; the doctor says he may have claret, but no other wine."

Cynthia put the tumbler into the wasted hand, which clutched it with a tremulous eagerness, and supported the old man while he drank. She seemed to have a natural capacity and handiness which made these offices of charity easy to her.

"Phœbe will get you any thing you want," said Oswald, looking on helplessly.

Phœbe was standing on the other side of the bed, breathing hard and staring at Mrs. Haggard, open mouthed and open-eyed, as at a supernatural appearance.

But on being thus referred to, she made a courtesy, and said she should be pleased to wait upon the lady.

"And do you really think you shall be able to get on?" asked Oswald.

"I shall get on very nicely. You need not be

anxious, Mr. Pentreath. It will be best for your father to be kept very quiet."

"Yes, I dare say. I'll go to my own room. It's on this floor, and I shall be at hand if my father should ask for me. You'll send for me if he does, won't you?"

"Yes; Phœbe shall come for you."

Oswald lingered by the bed-side before going away, and bent over his father with that helpless feeling which robust youth has in the presence of suffering age. It can pity, but can hardly sympathize. If it could share the burden in any way, take half the pain, or all, it would do so; but it can not measure or understand that agony.

"How are you feeling now, father?" asked the son.

"I feel as if a wolf were gnawing me, that's all," gasped the old man. "Go away. You only keep the air from me."

Cynthia took a loose blanket from an arm-chair and spread it over the squire's chest and shoulders, and then went quietly to the nearest window and opened it. The sweet, cool night air blew in like a rush of refreshing waters upon a thirsty land.

"That's better," cried the old man.

"You didn't oughter open the windows," said Phœbe; "the doctor said we was to keep 'm warm?"

Cynthia found a screen in one corner of the room, and this she placed as a guard against the keen edge of the draught. She had a conviction that the sufferer needed air, but she was not going to do any thing rash or reckless.

"Tell me what the doctor said about the leeches, and the poultices, and every thing that is to be done, Phœbe," she said.

At midnight Oswald looked into the room again. His father was sleeping the fitful, painful slumber of disease. Phœbe was snoring by the fire. Cynthia was seated by the bedside, reading her pocket Bible by the dim candle-light. What a graceful figure it was in the neatly fitting gray stuff gown, the Puritan muslin kerchief crossed over the delicately molded bust, the little white cap giving a matronly air to the bright young face!

The room seemed changed somehow since Cynthia's coming. The accumulated litter of the past week had been carried off. Every thing was in its place, snowy linen on the bed, the hearth neatly swept, a small, bright fire in the shining grate, a cheerful, home-like air in the room which a few hours ago had looked so desolate. And all had been done quietly, with the least possible inconvenience to the invalid.

"Has he been long asleep?" asked Oswald.

"About half an hour. I read to him a little before he went off."

"Out of your Bible?"

"Yes."

"Did he like your doing that?"

"I think it soothed him."

Oswald could hardly realize the idea of his father being instructed in the Scriptures by a Methodist preacher's wife. It seemed a general upheaving of things.

This went on for many days and nights. The squire's life seemed to these patient watchers to tremble in the balance, though the doctor had made up his mind which way the balance was to turn at last. For many days and nights, without weariness or murmuring, Cynthia performed the painful tasks of the sick-room, and was full of love and care for this grim old man, who, in his weakness, seemed like a baby in her arms, and was fain to submit to be ministered to as a baby might have done. While caring for this poor mortal body of his, she was full of tender anxiety for his imperishable soul; and this disciple of Tom Paine was fain to listen to that ineffable story which even the most hardened unbeliever must hear with some touch of love and awe. Cynthia had not been taught to be doubtful of death-bed conversions; in her direct and positive creed, this sinner—who perhaps, in all his life, had never done a good action or sacrificed a selfish desire—was as near the gates of heaven as the man of spotless life and active benevolence, could he but be brought to acknowledge his unworthiness, to believe in the all-atoning Sacrifice which had been made for him, to accept in implicit faith the pardon that God was forever holding out to sinners. A shibboleth, perhaps, this parrot cry of instantaneous conversion, but this shibboleth was to Cynthia a great reality.

Curious it must have seemed to the ear of the listener—had there been any one by—to hear this child fighting Satan beside that dying bed; arguing with the unbelieving mind, sharpened and hardened by fifty years' mature worldliness; pleading, praying, repeating divinest messages of compassion and love. The squire heard her patiently, which was much. One night she sung one of Wesley's hymns, in a low, sweet voice. The sound pleased and soothed the sick man, and after this he often bid her sing to him. Oswald paced the corridor softly sometimes of an evening, listening to those clear and pure tones, which had a soothing influence for him as well as for his father.

"I wish you would let my husband come and read to you, Mr. Pentreath," Cynthia ventured to say one afternoon when the squire seemed a little better than usual, and quite free from pain.

"Your husband! Who is he?"

"Joshua Haggard."

"What, the Ranter? No; I'll have none of his preaching. He's a decent fellow, in his way, and has made money. My son is going to marry his daughter; but I'll have no ranting. I won't have fire and brimstone pelted at me on my death-bed. You may read what you like; it does no harm."

"I don't think you know what kind of man my husband is," remonstrated Cynthia, gently.

"Don't I! I know what field-preachers are. You may hear 'em a mile off, raving about Sodom and Gomorrah, and the worm that never dies. Haggard preached in the fields before he built that chapel of his. I'll have none of his howling."

This was discouraging; but the Established Church, which, represented by a port-winy vicar of the good old school, had called politely, during the squire's illness, to offer its ministrations, had also been kept at arm's-length by Mr. Pentreath, who swore that no tithe-pig parson should cross the threshold of his chamber while he had sense enough to forbid him.

Oswald showed considerable anxiety about Cynthia's comfort during this weary time of watching, and Joshua came to the Grange at least once a day to see for himself that his wife was not injuring her health by this work of charity. The acute attack of bronchitis had been conquered, chiefly by Cynthia's nursing, as the doctor frankly acknowledged; but the foe left the citadel in so dilapidated a state, that the cessation of active disease was by no means a warrant for the patient's recovery. The lamp flickered in the socket, and might at any moment be suddenly extinguished. The worn-out frame was not easily to be patched up by high feeding and stimulants, quinine or iron.

Once in every day Joshua Haggard came up to the long gallery, where the family portraits faced the searching north-west light, which showed every crack in the surface, for a brief interview with his young wife.

"I'm afraid you are not getting enough rest, dearest," he said, turning the small, pale face toward the spring sunshine, and looking at it with anxious scrutiny.

"Yes, indeed, Joshua. I have some hours' sleep every day, while Phœbe watches for me. I let her sleep at night, poor girl; for it seems so painful to her to keep her eyes open after the clock has struck ten."

"I am pleased for you to do this good work, my love—I am proud of you; but, remember that you have my happiness in charge. You must not sacrifice health even to duty—for my sake."

He advanced this plea with a consciousness of its weakness, its selfishness.

"I walk in the garden every day when it is fine," said Cynthia, anxious to re-assure him as to her well-being. "Naomi and Oswald take me for a little walk every afternoon. It is such a happiness to me to see her, dear girl!"

"Yes, she has told me about your walks together. I am pleased to think of your being so united; I feared there was a want of sympathy on Naomi's part."

"No, Joshua. She has always been good to me; but I think we have been more drawn together since the squire's illness. How glad I shall be when he gets well, and we can have the wedding! I want to see Naomi in that lovely gray silk. Does Dr. Harrow say that he will soon be well?"

"Dr. Harrow does not seem very hopeful; he thinks his patient in a sadly weak state."

"But that racking cough is almost gone, and we shall soon make him strong."

"I hope so, dear; but there is a disease called old age. The squire has lived a hard life. He did not spare himself in his youth, when he gave himself up to what the world calls pleasure, and he has not spared himself of late years, while he has been a slave to Mammon. The thread of life is worn very thin, my love."

This was a disappointment to Cynthia, who had begun to hope for the squire's recovery. He was not an agreeable old man, but she had nursed him and cared for him, and she had grown in somewise attached to him. Oswald looked on wonderingly while she bent over the bed, soothing her charge with pretty, tender speeches, supporting the grizzled head, holding the feverish hand, feeding the grim old sufferer as lovingly as if he had been a pet bird.

"How good you are!" he exclaimed one day. "Is it in the nature of all women to be so tender? I can just remember my mother nursing me in some small illness, and she was like you; but then I was her favorite son, the creature she loved best on earth, as they tell me. You come here to nurse a stranger, and yet your tenderness for him seems inexhaustible."

"I am so sorry for your poor father that I can not help loving him," Cynthia answered, simply.

"Ah! I see; that is what the old saw means: 'Pity is akin to love.'"

These walks with Naomi and her lover were a delight to Cynthia at this time; so keen a delight, that it sometimes occurred to her this pleasure might be sinful, a snare and a temptation which she ought in somewise to resist; for Joshua's teaching dwelt much upon snares, and the liability of weak human nature to be led astray by inclination.

After close confinement in the sick-room, the very air of heaven was a source of rapture. The bright spring afternoon, the windy sky, with patches of deepest blue shining through white fleecy clouds, and just one dark cloud overhead, holding the promise of an April shower; the daffodils waving with every gust; the yellow chestnut buds just unfolding; the tender young ferns peeping up through the mossy ground in sheltered places, snake fern and adder fern—what could be more beautiful than the neglected old manor at such a season! Even the dark-red cattle had a friendly air, Cynthia thought, and looked at her with grave kindliness.

Never had Naomi been so kind or so loving to the poor little step-mother; and Oswald, who had seemed quite a remote, unsympathetic personage a little while ago, came now so near as to be almost brotherly in his kindness—he was so grateful for Cynthia's devotion to his sick father.

For the space of an hour by Oswald's watch, these three perambulated the path on the skirts of the wood, making fresh discoveries of nature's progress every day, and admiring the wonder of this gradual yet swift awakening of old Mother Earth after the dreary winter sleep. How quickly the flower-buds opened, and the little curled-up leaflets widened into leaves. Here, under last year's dead branches, are the ferns of next summer; the willows are yellow-green already; the mossy ground is enameled with primroses and bluest violets.

"Please God the poor old father picks up strength, we shall be married before the hawthorns are in flower," said Oswald to his betrothed.

Naomi's only answer was a sigh; for her father had told her how little hope the doctor entertained of his patient's recovery.

There was an appearance of improvement, however, at this time which deceived Oswald and Cynthia and the good-hearted drudge, Phœbe. The squire's cough was almost gone, though his breathing was still troublesome, and his wits somewhat given to wander in the pauses of wakefulness between his brief slumbers; he was able to be moved from his bed to the great easy-chair, in which spacious piece of furniture he looked like a living mummy, propped up with pillows. This seemed a great advance upon his condition of ten days ago; and Oswald fancied him on the high-road to recovery—an opinion shared by the patient himself, though in querulous moments he declared that he shouldn't trouble any body long, and that Oswald would soon have the handling of the estate.

"And a nice mess he will make of it, for he knows no more of business than a baby," grumbled the squire.

Seeing her charge so far restored, and believing his recovery an assured thing, despite her husband's despondent view of the case, Cynthia was now anxious to return to her home duties. Those duties were not manifold, certainly, since Judith Haggard was the main-spring of the household machine; but Cynthia was at least her husband's companion, and she knew that she was sorely missed by him. She had carefully instructed Phœbe in all the offices of the sick-room, and felt that she might now leave the squire to that damsel's care, with just a little supervision and assistance from Oswald, who was a light sleeper, and might look in upon the invalid now and then of a night to give him his lemonade or his medicine.

When, however, Mrs. Haggard ventured to hint at departure, the squire's distress was piteous to behold. Could she be so cruel as to talk of leaving him when but for her he should be in his grave? If she left him, he should die. Phœbe nurse him, indeed! Phœbe would murder him, with her big, rough hands and her clumsy ways. He might die in his bed at any hour, with not a soul to help him, while Phœbe was snoring like a pig by the fireside. That girl thought of nothing but sleeping and eating; she was a lump of selfishness, like all the rest of his servants.

The old man shed tears; and the tears of feeble age are sad to see. What could Cynthia do? The tender heart, in which love and pity were the ruling instincts, was moved to deepest compassion. She told her husband of the squire's distress, and he said stay.

"Stay, my love, if you can bear the trial of witnessing the end. It will not be long."

"Does the doctor really think he will die?"

"Yes, dear; the doctor is quite hopeless. Nothing less than a miracle could save him, he says, and God has ceased to work miracles for our worthless mortal bodies. His supernatural dealings are with our souls."

"Then I would not leave him on any account."

"You have never seen death, Cynthia. You are not afraid to face the end?"

"No," she answered, bravely; "I fear nothing since you have taught me where to put my trust."

So Cynthia staid and ministered to the departing sinner, and made these last days of his life sweeter to him than all the arid years of his widowhood, in which human affection had been as dead in him as if he had been one of those comical stones which antiquity chose for its gods. He had grown really attached to his fair young nurse, and submitted to her with a senile docility.

"If I had had a daughter like you, my dear, I should have been a better man," he said.

"You have a good son, dear Mr. Pentreath."

"Yes, Oswald has never given me any trouble; but there's not much in him—a young man to be drawn any way. I'm afraid he'll spend my money like water. It's a hard thing to know one must lie in one's grave, not able to move a finger, while one's property is being made ducks and drakes of. That's the sting of death."

"No, no, dear friend; the sting of death is sin."

"And isn't it sinful to fool away a fine estate?" cried the squire, testily.

Wheeled close up to the glowing hearth, in his big arm-chair, with a tumbler of warm negus, weak and harmless, but soothing to the spirits, on the little table at his elbow, the squire listened with great complacency to Cynthia's Scripture reading. If the Bible had been something less than it is, the keen old man would hardly have tolerated it, for he started with a strong prejudice in its disfavor. But the mighty Book compelled his attention, and seemed to appeal to him individually with a force his mortal weakness could not withstand.

Oswald now began to spend his afternoons in the sick-room, save that one hour which he spent out-of-doors with Cynthia and Naomi. The squire liked to have him there, and was fond of calling his attention to certain passages of Scripture which, in the father's mind, bore upon his son's deficiencies. Oswald was the most patient listener to that pious reading, to those touching Wesleyan hymns which Cynthia used to sing in the gathering twilight. Joshua, while following that sect of Primitive Methodists and field preachers, which the Rev. Hugh Bourne had founded early in the century, had adopted the Wesleyan hymn-book, and differed from the modern Wesleyans chiefly in his closer adherence to the principles of their pious founder.

Sad, yet not unpleasing, days gliding gently by in that quiet chamber; a spacious bedroom, oak-paneled, with three deep-set windows, a carved mantel-piece, six feet high, and a curious old basket grate set round with blue-and-white Dutch tiles, Scriptural illustrations, to which the squire referred now and then when Cynthia was reading.

"David! Ah! there he is, slaying Goliath—the third from the top. I remember when I was a boy I used to take him for Jack the Giant-killer. And David was a sinner, was he, though the Lord loved him? Ah! the Lord had need to be fond of me, for I've been a great sinner. I wonder if John Wilkes is in heaven?"

Sweet, slow days, which hardly left a trace behind them, one being so like another, save a vague memory of a pleasing sadness. It seemed to Oswald, by-and-by, as if all his life were shut in this grave old room, and the outside world were something in which he had no part. Naomi noticed that his manner was dreamy and absent-minded at this time, a change which she ascribed to natural anxiety about his father.

It was about half-way between midnight and morning, just when the night is coldest, most silent, most dismal, that the squire called Cynthia to his bed-side. He had been a little more restless than usual, and had wandered more between his snatches of broken sleep; had talked of his wild youth, naming old friends, old loves, long dead and half forgotten.

"What was the name of that fellow who supped with us at The Blue Posts?" he asked, eagerly. "You know, don't you? a man with big whiskers and a belcher handkerchief—a fighting-man."

Cynthia knelt down by the bed and took his cold hand, and chafed it gently. There was a sharp ring in his voice which she had never heard before.

CYNTHIA'S SCRIPTURE READING.

"That's a good girl, Polly; yes, my hand's very cold. You always had a good heart, Polly; but too fond of spending money. Yes, Polly, better marry the cheese-monger. He means well."

Then the dull eyes turned suddenly on Cynthia, with slowly returning consciousness.

"Is it you, child? And you say God loves sinners?"

"God loves all things that he has made," answered Cynthia, earnestly; "and Christ died to save sinners. If you repent of all your sins, dear Mr. Pentreath, and believe in that atoning sacrifice."

"I'm sorry I didn't live a better life, and that I hadn't a daughter like you," said the squire, faintly; and, letting his head sink softly upon Cynthia's breast, he quietly loosened his feeble hold upon this mortal life, and passed into the unknown land beyond it.

Not at first did Cynthia know that this was death; and when the truth dawned upon her, she uttered no cry, gave way to neither terror nor agitation, but gently laid the lifeless head upon the pillow, and went quietly to tell Oswald Pentreath that he was fatherless.

She was surprised, even in this awful moment, to see that his door was ajar, and a light burning in his room. She knocked, and he answered at once, "Come in."

"Why has he been sitting up?" she wondered.

He was sitting at a table with an open book before him, the candles burned down to the sockets of the old plated candlesticks, his hair and dress disordered as if he had been lying down, his eyes hollow and weary-looking. He started at sight of Cynthia, but did not move from his seat or change his dejected attitude, his elbows on the table, his head leaning on his hands.

"What is the matter?" he asked. "Is my father worse?"

"All his pain is over, dear Oswald. God has taken him to his rest."

"And you were with him at the last—alone—he died in your arms?"

"Yes."

"You are a saint—an angel!" cried Oswald, passionately, brushing the tears from his eyes. "You came into this house an angel of mercy—you brought life to my poor old father's darkened mind. You made his last days the sweetest he had ever known. How can I ever forget your goodness?"

"There is nothing for you to remember. I have only done my duty. How pale you look, Mr. Pentreath! This sudden loss has shocked you. He died so peacefully, and his last words were good. Is not that comforting?"

"How could his thoughts be evil with an angel at his side? Poor old man! And he is gone! Yes, it is very sudden."

"Why were you sitting up all night? Had you a presentiment that the end was so near?"

"No," with a bitter laugh. "I sat up because I have lost the knack of sleeping. My thoughts are too active, and I try to quiet them with philosophy; but I can no more read than I can sleep. My ideas travel in a circle, and always come back to the same point."

"You have been too anxious about your father," said Cynthia, with a look that was half pity, half wonder.

"Yes; I am too devoted a son—that is my strong point."

"Will you go and see him?"

"Yes. And there will be people to send for, I suppose, as soon as it is light."

He opened a shutter. The stars were pale, in a cold gray sky; day-break was at hand; and in that chilly half-light Oswald Pentreath's haggard face looked like a ghost's.

He followed Cynthia to the squire's room. Phoebe had roused the small household. The house-keeper was there already, and had begun the last dismal offices which life can render to death.

"I laid out your sweet mother, Mr. Pentreath," faltered the crone. "She looked lovely in her coffin."

The old butler had gone to the village to awaken the sexton, in order that the passing-bell might speedily inform Combhollow that its seigneur had departed. Phoebe stood at the bottom of the great four-post bed, with her apron over her face, weeping as in duty bound—not that she had loved Squire Pentreath, but because it was proper to cry at a death or a funeral. To weep for her deceased master was an obligation which, although not expressly set forth in the Catechism, was implied in the general idea of doing her duty in that state of life to which it had pleased God to call her. And if the squire, although a hard man, should have happened to do the right thing in the way of legacies and mourning, it would be a comfort to remember having honored him with these disinterested tears.

Oswald went round and kissed the cold brow of the dead, and then stood by the bedside looking down at that unconscious clay, with a curious blank look in his own face, as if he knew not whether there were any further duty required of him. "He looked clean daft," the house-keeper said afterward, when she and the old man-servant discussed the dismal scene over a substantial breakfast.

The shutters had been opened, and the candles burned with a yellow glare in the cold gray light. Cynthia looked at her neat silver watch, Joshua's gift upon her wedding morning.

"Half-past five o'clock," she said. "I think I had better go home now, Mr. Pentreath. If Joshua should hear the passing-bell, he would be coming to fetch me."

"Why not wait till he comes?" asked Oswald.

"I would rather save him the trouble. I can do no more good here."

"No, you can do no more good."

She took her black mantle from a drawer, and put on her bonnet, and then went up to Oswald, who was still standing by the bed, with that helpless, absent look in his face.

"Good-bye, Mr. Pentreath. I hope you will take comfort to your heart in this loss."

"I am coming with you. You can not go home alone at this hour."

"Do you think I am afraid of the birds or the opening flowers?" Cynthia asked.

"You must not go alone."

"Come with me, if you like. Joshua will be glad to see you. You can stop to breakfast with us and see Naomi."

Cynthia thought it a work of charity to take him away from that death-chamber. Joshua could comfort and advise him.

7

The morning air blew in coolly when Oswald softly opened the great hall door. That clear, cool light of dawn had a soothing influence; the solemn stillness of park and wood, the hollow murmur of yonder steel-gray sea, flecked with whitest foam, awed and yet comforted the heart, or so it seemed to Cynthia, as she walked beside her silent companion. The bell began to toll as they came from the park into the wooded lane that led down to the bay and the open space at the beginning of the High Street. Each slow and dismal stroke made Cynthia shiver, as if each repetition were a surprise.

She made no attempt to console her companion during this lonely walk, which might be supposed a fitting opportunity for the expression of sympathy. If he needed human consolation, Joshua's wisdom could better measure and administer to his necessity, she thought; and, next to Joshua, Naomi would be the best, the most natural consoler.

But to Cynthia's surprise, when they came to the little green gate. Oswald refused to go in. The parlor shutters had been opened, and the household was evidently astir. She urged him to stay to breakfast, or at least to see Joshua.

"No," he said, "it is very kind of you to wish it; but I am too much upset. I would rather go back. I shall have many things to arrange. I may be wanted."

"Joshua shall come to you, then," replied Cynthia. "Good-bye."

She gave him her hand. He held it in both his own for a moment or two, looking at her with an expression full of sadness, half piteous, half pleading. He bent his head over the cold, gloveless hand, and kissed it. There were tears upon it when he let it go, and, with a scarcely audible blessing, he left Cynthia Haggard standing at the gate, and walked quickly back toward the Grange.

CHAPTER XVIII.

THE SORROWS OF WERTHER.

OSWALD PENTREATH, having set his father's papers in order, and reduced the dusty chaos of the old squire's private study into form, found himself, comparatively speaking, a rich man. Those long years of retirement at which Squire Pentreath had held himself aloof from all social intercourse had not been spent in vain. They left their fruit behind them in the shape of stock and shares and bonds, which all meant money; for Mr. Pentreath had not speculated his savings in wild ventures, but had cleaved to safe investments, and had been content with a reasonable percentage. Not even for the chance of doubling his capital would he have risked it. His was not the genius of the stock-jobber, but rather the plodding temper of the village miser, who puts coin to coin, and finds an all-sufficient joy in the growth of his hoard.

The estate was in excellent order—every mortgage paid off—and the rental was close to three thousand a year. The squire's investments were worth another thousand, and brought Oswald's income to an amount which, to a young man who had seldom enjoyed the unfettered use of a five-pound note, seemed inordinate wealth.

The squire had made a will, dated the year of his son Arnold's flight, bequeathing twenty pounds a year to each of his old servants, and all the rest of his property, real and personal, to Oswald. There was no mention of the younger son. In the letter which informed Arnold of his father's death, Oswald affectionately urged his brother to give up a sea-faring life and return to Combhollow, where he should have one of the farms and a thousand a year. "My father's will was evidently made in a fit of anger against you," wrote Oswald; "you must not think that I could be so unjust as to take advantage of my father's injustice and keep all for myself. No, Arnold; I am sure you know me better than to suppose me capable of such iniquity. I shall be a rich man, in any case. You must have had enough of the sea by this time. Come back, my dear brother, for the sake of the good old days when we were boys together. I want you more than I can say. I love you as dearly as I did when we were children, and I was the big brother. Do you remember that summer day when we lost ourselves in Matcherly Wood, and you were so tired I was obliged to carry you home? When we had got about half-way, you wanted to carry me, though I was twice your size. I never pass that corner of the wood without remembering what you said, and your clinging arms round my neck, and your warm cheek next mine."

The squire being laid with his forefathers, and honored with a handsome funeral, which was attended by many people who had detested him living, but reverenced him as a parochial institution dead, life at the Grange fell back into its old quiet round, save that the door was more frequently assailed by importunate tenants, who boldly asked favors of the new lord which they would not have dared to hint at to the old one. The old servants felt that the spirit of parsimony was gone from the household, and kept a better table; but they had been so long and severely trained in economy, that extravagance was an impossibility for them, and Oswald had nothing to apprehend upon that score. For his own part, the new master had a curious feeling of freedom as he paced the dull, old rooms, and rattled the money in his pockets absently, wondering how it had come there.

He looked very handsome and melancholy in his sable suit, and the young ladies who came to the parish church, where he worshiped alone in his big pew on Sunday mornings, thought it a hard thing that he should have engaged himself to a Methodist parson's daughter.

He attended Little Bethel of an evening, they were informed, which seemed an unusally dallying with two creeds—to say nothing of chapel being so much less genteel than church, and a mode of salvation peculiarly adapted for the shop-keeping class, who did not mind perspiring together in a limited space, and inhaling one another's breath.

Naomi's wedding seemed a long way off in these days, when the squire's funeral was still the newest topic in Combhollow, and when people had not yet left off disputing in a friendly way as to the number of the mourning-coaches, or inveighing bitterly against those tenants who ought to have attended the funeral and had not done so. Shadowy and remote—the merest speck in a cloudy future—seemed that marriage-day which had once been so near, the fair to-morrow of life. Oswald was quite broken down by his father's death—more grieved than even Naomi, who best knew the softness of his nature, had expected him to be. It was not likely that he could talk of marriage at such a time, and Naomi was neither surprised nor offended at his silence about the wedding that was to have been, and the far-off wedding which was to be.

She put away her wedding-dress on the day of the squire's funeral, while the sepulchral bell, which had rung out its solemn note for the passing of his soul, tolled again in the windy April weather, while, through changing lights and shadows, by fluttering young leaves, and under the blue sky where the lark was singing above the dark-brown earth, newly pierced by the green corn-spears—came the black funeral train—sable plumes, horses' manes, mourners' scarfs tossing in the fresh April breeze—slowly winding down the hilly road into Combhollow.

The funeral bell was in Naomi's ears as she folded the pretty pearl-gray silk—the first silk dress she had ever possessed—shedding some quiet tears as she smoothed the folds, and laid the garment in a drawer, wrapped in fresh, white linen, with a sprinkling of dried lavender, as beseemed so precious a fabric. There was the serviceable brown cloth pelisse, too, which she was to have worn on her journey to Cheltenham, where she and Oswald were to have spent their honey-moon. That also must be put away for the days to come. Naomi's wear for the next six months was to be sombre black. She had put on mourning for her betrothed's father, as in duty bound. Cynthia also wore black, and Aunt Judith had produced a suit of ancient sable, rusty but whole—not sorry to have this opportunity of wearing out the surplus stock left from her mourning for her sister-in-law, when Joshua, in his character of grief-stricken widower, had been naturally liberal, and had allowed her to lay in large supplies of bombazine and crape.

Oswald said little about the postponed wedding, but he came to Mr. Haggard's as often as before his father's death; and even Judith, who was lying in wait for a deterioration in his character now that he had come into his fortune, could not yet put her finger on a flaw. He was changed, nevertheless; but the change was sweet and commendable in his nature, as it was in Hamlet, when that young prince gave way to moodiness and despondency after the loss of a parent. He was melancholy and often absent-minded, his cheek paler than of old, his eye heavier.

Never had Naomi loved him so tenderly as now, when, for the first time since their betrothal, he needed sympathy and consolation. To her who so deeply loved her father, this grief for a parent seemed in nowise strained or unnatural. True that the squire had not been one's ideal of a father—not a gracious and dignified figure like that dead Hamlet who revisited the glimpses of the moon; but death has a sanctifying influence—nay, even a fantastical power, which lends new attributes to the image of the departed—and Oswald, whose youth had been made a time of restraint and deprivation by his father's meanness, was soft-hearted enough to regret his tyrant.

Never did a man seem less inclined to take advantage of a loosened rein, and run into riot and extravagance. Day after day Oswald led the same calm, orderly life—riding or reading in the mornings, according to the weather, devoting his afternoons and evenings to his betrothed. He had thoughts of buying, or building, a yacht, but deferred even this indulgence in the hope of Arnold's return.

"We'll build our yacht here, in Combhollow," he said, "and Arnold shall superintend the work, and be skipper."

Oswald looked forward to his brother's coming with an almost feverish impatience. It seemed as if there were some innate weakness in his character which made him incapable of enjoying the privilege of independence. Now that his father was gone, he wanted his brother for a guide and adviser. Or it might be only the affection of the elder brother for the younger, made a barren love by long years of separation, which now yearned for the unforgotten companion of boyhood. Whatever feeling it was that made him anxious, Oswald's anxiety was very evident; and Naomi sympathized with him in this longing, and loved to hear him talk of his brother.

"How fond I shall be of him!" she said, one evening, when they were sitting on the old stone bench in the wilderness talking of Arnold. "He is like you, Oswald; I have heard my father say so. He remembers you both as boys."

"Yes, we were always considered very much alike. But Arnold is stouter and stronger-built than I—a man of tougher fibre altogether. It seemed the most natural thing in the world for him to run away to sea. You might have prophesied of him when he was two years old. Such a hardy, bold, uncompromising little vagabond, but brimming over with affection."

"And fond of you, Oswald?"

"Fond of me! Bless his loving little heart! He used to run after me like an affectionate puppy when he first began to toddle; such a round, fat little thing in those baby days, always ready for fisticuffs in my defence, though I was twice his size. There was a time when he would not go to sleep of a night unless I sat on the edge of his bed and told him stories. Yes, I have good reason to love him, dear fellow; and the strongest claim he has upon my love is my latest memory of my mother, when I saw the sweet, pale face lying on the pillow, and Arnold's baby eyes looking up at it."

The tears came to his eyes as he spoke of that sad memory, almost dream-like in its remoteness. Naomi put her hand in his without a word. Only by that gentle touch did she remind him that it was her mission to share all his griefs, even the old unforgotten sorrows of his earliest days.

It was a mild May evening—an evening on the edge of summer, with a perfect calmness in the atmosphere and sky—an evening on which the soul broods on sad, sweet thoughts. The lovers had been sitting alone for an hour or more, talking by fits and starts, with lengthening intervals of silence.

"My father has been dead five weeks, hasn't he, Naomi?" Oswald asked, after a long pause, during which Naomi's needle had been methodically traveling along a fine linen wristband, leaving a line of pearly stitches behind it. The manufacture of a shirt for her father was a work of high art with Naomi.

"Yes, dear; five weeks yesterday."

"Then in seven weeks more we must be married, Naomi," said Oswald, as seriously as he had spoken of his mother's death.

This was his first word about the postponed marriage, and it startled Naomi as if it had been the most unlikely subject for a lover's discourse.

"So soon, dear?"

"Three months, Naomi—surely that is long enough to wait out of respect to the dead. It is not as if we meant to have a grand wedding. We will just walk quietly into the old parish church some morning, with your father and his wife, and Aunt Judith and Jim, and there shall be a post-chaise at the lich-gate, ready to drive us to Cheltenham. Let me see, this is the twenty-fourth of May. We might be married early in July. Why should we wait any longer?"

"Dear Oswald, you must know I have hardly a wish that is not yours," Naomi began, earnestly.

"I know you are all goodness."

"But—"

"But what, love?"

"I have fancied—it may be nothing more than fancy perhaps, but you must not be angry with me for speaking of it—I have fancied lately that there was some change in your feeling for me; it is not that you have been less kind or affectionate, yet I have felt the change. You remember how my father wished that we should be very sure of each other's sincerity. That is why he wanted us to wait two years before we were even engaged. The two years are not gone yet; and if—if the change has come—the change he thought likely, he who knows the human heart and its weakness—let us loosen the bond, dear Oswald. There shall be no word of complaint from me—I should neither blame you nor think ill of you, dear love—I should honor you for being frank and truthful with me—and keep the memory of our happy days as the most sacred part of my life—and be your affectionate friend to my death."

"Best, noblest, dearest, you are only too good for me!" cried Oswald, clasping his betrothed to his breast, moved to a rapture of reverence and regard by her generous kindness. "No, I have never changed to you—no, I could never change in my esteem, my admiration for all that is highest in woman. Do you remember those verses of Waller's, dear:

"'Amoret! as sweet and good
As the most delicious food,
Which, but tasted, does impart
Life and gladness to the heart.'

You are my Amoret, dearest. What do I want with Sacharissa's beauty, 'which to madness doth incline?'"

"But you ought to go to London, now that you are free and rich; you ought to see the world, Oswald, and in London you may meet your Sacharissa," suggested Naomi, radiant with happiness.

She had said what had long been in her mind to say. She had made her offer of self-sacrifice, in all good faith, and it had been rejected. She had no further fear or hesitation.

"I don't care about London, love. It is nothing but a den of thieves, according to my poor father's description. When I see it we will see it together, and go to the Tower, and St. Paul's,

and the wax-works, and Westminster Abbey, like regular country cousins. Come, Naomi, let us be serious, and talk about the future. There is the old house to be brightened and smartened a little before I take my wife home to it. I should have had much ado to coax a new carpet and a coat of whitewash out of my father; but I am master now, and I can pull down the Grange and build an Italian villa after Palladio, if you like."

"Dear Oswald, you must know that I would not have you disturb a stone of the old house."

"In good faith, dear, I shouldn't care to do it. It is the house my mother lived and died in, the first house my eyes saw, the house where my brother was born, the only house that has ever been home to me, though, Heaven knows, it has been but a cheerless home at times. No, we won't alter, Naomi; we will only beautify. I have been too idle all this time. I'll send to Exeter for an architect, and put the business in hand at once."

The architect arrived on the scene about a week later, and made a somewhat supercilious inspection of the good old house, which had seemed to its occupiers solid enough to last for another three hundred years, but which, according to the architect, was in a very perilous condition. He tapped the oak panels contemptuously, pronounced the flooring of the upper stories too worm-eaten for any thing save entire reinstatement, feared that the whole fabric required under-pinning, and took an altogether despondent view of the matter.

"You want the thing done thoroughly, I suppose, Mr. Pentreath," he said.

"I should like the drawing-room painted, and the sitting-room upstairs; and if you could build a greenhouse anywhere—"

"Of course, of course—you must have a conservatory opening out of the drawing-room. If we were to glaze that western end, now, and throw out a rotunda at the end for tropical plants—palms and so on, you know. I did the same thing for Sir Brydges Baldry's place on the other side of Exeter, and it had a charming effect. I'll make you a sketch if you like."

"You are very good," said Oswald, dubiously; "but I don't think my father would have liked—"

He had conscientious scruples about spending so much money—squandering hundreds of pounds upon fanciful improvements—not that he set undue value upon the money himself, but from the thought of what an agony of indignation such an outlay would have caused his father. Rotundas, forsooth! Could that lean old miser lie quiet in his grave while his beloved guineas were being wasted on such trumpery?

"Really, now, Mr. Pentreath," said the architect, with the easy assurance of a professional man employed by the best families, "I should imagine the question was not so much what your father would have liked, were he living to enjoy his opinion, but what will please your wife when you bring her home here. Rather a dismal house for a young lady, I should think. A circular conservatory, now, at the end of this drawing-room, would have an enlivening effect. As it is, there is a meanness about the room; long and narrow, no variety, no relief. But you must please yourself. Shall we go to the boudoir?"

The room which the architect insisted on calling a boudoir was the pretty parlor on the first-floor which Mrs. Pentreath had used. Here the professional adviser suggested so many improvements—a marble mantel-piece and a more civilized stove, French windows and a balcony, an alcove built out at the end for a statue, with a painted glass window behind it—that Oswald felt as if the Grange were going to be improved off the face of the earth unless he made a bold stand against the improver.

"This was my mother's room," he said. "I wouldn't alter it for the world."

The architect shrugged his shoulders and felt inclined to ask, "Then what do you want me for, sir, if you have made up your mind to keep your money in your pockets?" But there were certain things about which the architect was arbitrary—flooring which must be taken up, warped and shrunken oaken panels which must be replaced by new ones, passages and servants' offices which must be altered and improved, to adapt them to the requirements of a more civilized form of life.

"Think of the change which has taken place in our habits," exclaimed the architect, conclusively.

Oswald submitted, and a voluminous specification was the result of this interview. This in due course was submitted to a builder of Barnstaple and a builder of Exeter; whereupon the Exeter builder, as the man of more advanced views and larger capital, or credit, won the day, and about a fortnight afterward sent a small army of white-jacketed men to Pentreath Grange, who took the place in hand, and made haste to render it utterly odious and uninhabitable. Oswald contrived to sleep in the old house, shifting his quarters as the men followed him from room to room, now taking out his windows, anon cutting a rotten patch out of his ceiling, and descending upon him, like Jove, in a shower of plaster.

Having no home of his own at this period of disruption, he spent his days in the house of his betrothed, sharing the minister's homely fare, hearing all Aunt Judith's complaints against the general incapacity of her subordinates, and spending long and quiet hours talking or reading aloud in the neat parlor where Naomi and her stepmother sat at work.

"What women you are for plain needle-work!" he exclaimed one warm afternoon, in a sudden burst of impatience, wearied by the rhythmical movement of the two needles methodically stitching on, no matter how passionate the subject of his reading—whether Rebecca was standing on the verge of the castle parapet, or Constance de Beverly left to perish in her living grave. "I never saw any thing like your perpetual industry. One would suppose it were a kind of feminine treadmill, by which you do penance for your sins."

"We have nothing else to do," said Cynthia, with a faint sigh. "Naomi is teaching me to make her father's shirts; if I could but do that, I could do nothing for him. But I'm afraid my stitching will never be so good as Naomi's."

Oswald looked out of the window listlessly across the row of stocks and carnations in red flower-pots. It was a midsummer afternoon, warm to oppressiveness. There was a perfume of newly cut hay from the meadows behind the First and Last, a faint breath from distant bean-fields in flower, the warm air heavy as with the incense Earth offers to her goddess Summer. The brick-layers were hard at work up at the Grange; and there was a run upon that thin and sour cider which had been the old squire's household beverage, and which nothing less than very warm weather and honest toil could render acceptable to the human palate.

Oswald had an air of being tired of life this afternoon, as he threw himself back in his chair, and sighed, and stifled a yawn, and looked far away across the hay-cocks yonder. Naomi glanced up at him now and then from her work with grave, observant eyes. It seemed to her that there was a jarring chord somewhere. He was not happy. And how was it, and why was it? Not grief for his father's death, surely; that cloud had passed. Impatience for his brother Arnold's return, perhaps. That seemed more likely.

There was no idea now of the marriage being early, or late, in July. The improvements and reparations at the Grange would not be finished till October at the earliest, and Oswald must have his house ready before he could take to himself a wife. Naomi felt that the wedding was still far off.

"I shall bring you a new book to-morrow afternoon," said Oswald, rousing himself from his reverie.

"By the author of 'Waverley?'"

"No; you can not have a new novel by the author of 'Waverley' every day, though he writes two, and sometimes three, a year. This is quite a different kind of book—a study of the human heart—a man's great sorrow described by himself. He was coward enough to let the sorrow make an end of him, instead of making an end of his sorrow—strangling it as Hercules strangled the snakes in his cradle—as a brave man would have done, no doubt," with a short laugh, half scorn, half bitterness.

"Is it a book that a Christian may read?" asked Naomi. "But I am sure you would not bring us any book in which there were evil thoughts."

"There are no evil thoughts in this—only an irresistible fate governing a weak soul. There is no sin in the book—only foolishness and an overmastering sorrow."

"What is it called?"

"The 'Sorrows of Werther,' a translation from the German of Goethe, a book that set Germany in a blaze many years ago, but which I never saw till the other day. I bought the volume at a book-stall in Exeter, when I went over to settle with the builders."

The reading of "Werther" began on the following afternoon, in the wilderness. Naomi and her lover were alone, Cynthia having gone to sit with an old woman of the flock, whose frame was a kind of museum for the exhibition of interesting varieties in the rheumatic line. Oswald looked disappointed at losing one of his auditors.

"I thought Mrs. Haggard would have liked 'Werther,'" he said.

"She always reads to old Mrs. Pincote on Wednesday afternoons. She said you were to begin the book all the same—she would enjoy hearing any part of it. But if you would rather not begin to-day—"

"My unselfish Naomi! No, dear, I shall read

to you. It is of your pleasure I think at all times, you know, Naomi."

"You are too good to me."

Oswald began rather lazily, and dawdled so much over the pages—stopping to talk now and then, and stopping to yawn very often—that he got no farther than the threshold of the story when five o'clock struck from the old gray tower, and it was time to go back to the house for tea.

"I'm afraid you don't find it very interesting so far," said Oswald.

"It is not like 'Ivanhoe' or the 'Antiquary,'" replied Naomi; "but it is very pretty. The young man seems kind and amiable—fond of children—warmly attached to his friend—fond of picturesque scenery."

"Yes, he is all that. It is a picture painted in delicate half-tints at the beginning—the strong coloring comes afterward."

They went into the woods next day for their afternoon ramble, Cynthia accompanying them, and Oswald carrying "Werther" in his pocket. They peeped in at the Grange on their way. It looked a chaos of raw plaster and new deal, and did not invite a long inspection. Oswald had consented to the rotunda for tropical plants, and one end of the long drawing-room was opened to the daylight.

"You are going to be mistress of quite a handsome mansion, Naomi, and will have to play the great lady," said Oswald, laughing at the look of consternation with which his betrothed contemplated the improvements.

"That I shall never be able to do, Oswald."

"There I can't agree with you. Nature intended you for a person of importance. There are only a few details to be learned—how to issue invitations, the precedence of your guests, to drive a pair of ponies, to play the Lady Bountiful with discretion, and so on. I have more to learn as country squire than you as the squire's wife."

"I wish Providence had not made you so rich, Oswald. It seems ungrateful to repine at blessings, but if you had been my equal in birth and fortune I should have been the happiest of women."

"It will be very ungrateful of you if you are not the happiest of women with that rotunda," said Oswald, gayly; and then they went across the park—it was to be really a park in future, and Oswald was eager to introduce a herd of deer—and from the park into the tangle of greenery, amidst the ever-shifting lights and shadows of the wood.

Here they found a ferny bank, more luxurious than any sofa, on which the two girls sat down to work, while Oswald lay on the grass at their feet, and resumed the story of Werther. He read long, and read well, losing his own identity in that of the melancholy hero. He came to the pretty house on the skirts of the forest, and the picture of Charlotte cutting lunches of black bread for the eager little brothers and sisters before setting out for the ball. That innocent image of youth and beauty was something new to the listeners. Not even in the pages of Scott had they met with so pure and perfect a picture of womanhood.

Then came the rustic dance, and the thrill of rapture that moved Werther's breast when his hand touched the maiden's for the first time, and floated in the waltz with her, and felt a lightness he had never known before, as if he no more belonged to groveling humanity; the consciousness of sorrow and loss when he heard that she was pledged to another—the thunder-storm—the simple, childish games by which Charlotte beguiled the terrors of her companions—the whole description as artless as Goldsmith's pictures of the Primrose family, but with a ground-swell of passion below the placid surface which Goldsmith knew not.

"And since that time sun, moon, and stars may go their ways; I know not day from night; the world around me has vanished."

Cynthia's work dropped on her lap. She sat with her large blue eyes fixed on the reader, her lips slightly parted; all her soul in that listening look. For the first time she heard the story of a love that was fatal—not like Rebecca's unrequited passion, elevating and strengthening the soul by the ordeal of a silent sorrow—but an over-mastering love taking possession of a weak nature, and holding it as the seven devils held their fated prey.

And this was what love meant sometimes in the world; not a reverential affection, not gratitude, esteem, respect, such as she had given to Joshua, and which had made marriage with him seem the highest honor that Providence could bestow—but blind, unreasoning passion—a fire kindled in a moment, and consuming the soul. She knew that Werther would never be happy again. She longed intensely to follow that devious path of his: to know if he struggled and conquered, or yielded and fell. She found herself wishing some evil fate—at least a convenient fever or merciful consumption—for Charlotte's excellent betrothed.

"No, I do not deceive myself! I read in her eyes a deep interest in me and my fate. Yes, I feel, and in this I will trust my own heart, that she—oh! dare I, can I, breathe the heaven in those words? I feel that she loves me!"

At these words Oswald closed the book suddenly, with a sigh.

"Will you read to us again after tea?" she asked, eagerly, when the inexorable church clock warned them that they had but just time to be punctual in their attendance at the tea-table.

"I thought you would like the book," said Oswald.

"It is beautiful," she sighed.

He looked up at her, and their eyes met. Dangerous for such eyes so to meet, such thoughts in the minds of each, such disquiet in either heart. Cynthia's delicate color had faded to ivory pale before that lingering look had ended. Fatal book, which told them what was amiss in their lives!

They walked home for the most part in silence, though Oswald tried to be merry about the rotunda, and the tremendous things that the Exeter architect was doing with the Grange, half against its owner's will. His gayety had a forced sound, and Naomi looked at him wonderingly. Why was it that since his father's death he had been so unlike his old self—so fitful and variable?

After tea they went to the wilderness, and sat there while the soft summer light faded gently into gray evening, and the bats skimmed to and fro above their heads, and distant nightingales called to each other in the woods. Oswald read into the heart of the book—read until Werther's passion had grown from dawn to midday—from a rose-colored dream of innocence and beauty, pure as morning, to the lurid gloom of a thunder-charged sky.

The earliest stars were up, silver pale, when he shut the book without a word. Joshua Haggard came through the little orchard and looked at the group with a grave smile.

"Reading all this time, Oswald!" he exclaimed; "and some foolish fiction, I'll be bound. How much of your life you waste upon fancies!"

"Fancy is sometimes sweeter than reality," answered Oswald, "and real life has given me very little to do."

"A pity," said the minister.

"We can not all have our mission. One man is born a preacher, like you; another a soldier, like Wellington; or a lawyer and defender of the oppressed, like Brougham. I was born nothing; born to enjoy the hunting in winter, and the sunshine in summer; to lie in Pentreath woods and read Byron; to do no harm, I hope, and any good that I can."

The minister sighed.

"The blessings Providence gives us are charges," he said. "We shall have to account for them."

They went back to the house together, and Oswald took his place at the usual assembling of the household for evening prayer. To-night the preacher chose the parable of the Talents for his reading and exposition. Oswald felt that the moral drawn therefrom was intended for his admonition. His house, his gardens, park, farms, woods, shares, and stocks, were the ten talents for which he was at present in nowise able to give a satisfactory account. So far he had done nothing to improve the condition of the laborer upon his land; to let in the light of Gospel truth or the free air of heaven to those stone cabins, in which the hind and his family pigged in the company of their pigs. He had thought of improving his own house, but not of draining those stifling dens. He had been too easy a landlord, ready to grant any favor his tenants asked; but had taken no trouble to discover the state of the toil-bowed tiller of the soil and his half-starved wife and children—the husbandman who was compelled to receive two shillings of the nine that made his weekly wage, in the shape of sour cider.

The time had been when Oswald Pentreath's mind was full of plans for doing good to his fellow-men, and when he had looked upon the day of his independence as the dawning of a new era for the laborers on his land; but since his father's death he had been the victim of a distraction which had put all philanthropic intentions out of his mind.

"When Arnold comes back, I shall be able to set things going in a good way. Arnold has more energy than I have," he thought, expecting every good thing as a consequence of his brother's return.

————

CHAPTER XIX.

"TWO SOULS MAY SLEEP AND WAKE UP ONE."

It was about a week after Mr. Pentreath had begun 'Werther,' and he was now approaching the end of the story, when he came to the minister's house at his usual hour, and found Cynthia sitting alone in the parlor. Naomi had a headache, and had gone upstairs to lie down. It was not often that Joshua Haggard's daughter gave way to any such feminine ailment, and it was a surprise to Oswald to find her absent. He had been riding among his farms all the morning, looking at ancient tiled roofs that had a tendency to subside in the middle; at barns and cart-sheds, with moldering thatches and worm-eaten timbers; at inclosures of meadow-land, where primroses, cowslips, and wild hyacinths grew abundantly, but where the grass was sour for lack of draining.

"I wanted her to rest on the sofa here," said Cynthia, "but she fancied she would be better in a darkened room. She has been looking ill for the last few days. I am sometimes afraid"—timidly, and with hesitation—"that she is not quite happy."

"I am afraid we are none of us quite happy," answered Oswald, with an undisguised sigh.

Cynthia's needle traveled to and fro with the usual rhythm. It seemed to Oswald as if it were some weary time to which he was forced to listen.

"Shall I go on with 'Werther?'" he asked presently, after he had looked at the stocks and carnations, and over them at the sleepy old inn, where the landlord stood in his porch and contemplated his neighbors, like an image of immutability. People who could remember Combhollow twenty years ago remembered just the same figure in the porch. It had grown a trifle more obese in the twenty years, that was all.

"I would rather you waited till Naomi was well enough to hear the end," said Cynthia.

"But are not you anxious to know what becomes of that unhappy wretch? Have you no pity for him?" asked Oswald, almost angrily.

"I pity him for being so wretched," answered Cynthia; "but I think if he had been good and wise and brave, he would have gone far away, where he would have never seen Charlotte any more. Instead of writing unhappy letters to his friend, he would have prayed to God to help him, and fled from temptation."

"You will see that in the end he did go away—very far from Charlotte and temptation. But you have seen him in the heat of the battle; you will see him by-and-by a conqueror—or conquered—whichever you like to call it."

"Will you let me read the end for myself? You can read it aloud to us both when Naomi is better."

"No; you shall hear the end, as you have heard the rest—from my lips."

"But Naomi—" expostulated Cynthia.

"I will read it again to Naomi. Why should I not read it to you this afternoon? You have been more interested in the story than Naomi."

Cynthia made no further objection, but went on with her work silently. Oswald took his favorite seat by the open window, in the shadow of the chintz curtain, with the spicy odors of stocks and carnations floating in upon the sultry air. They had the room almost entirely to themselves. Aunt Judith came in and out two or three times in the afternoon on some small errand, and looked at the two with a curious expression in her sharp, black eyes—a look which might have set Oswald thinking, had he been observant enough to notice it. But he was deep in the sorrows of Werther, who was fast approaching his final agony, and Cynthia was listening as she had listened that other day in the wood, with her hands lying idle in her lap, and the glossy white linen she had been working upon crumpled in a heap under those idle hands.

"Very nicely Joshua's new shirts will get on at that rate, and she so eager to set about them!" mused Judith, as she went back to the shop, with close-locked lips. "To think that novel-reading and such abominations should flourish in my brother's house! But what else could be expected of such a marriage? Lucky for Joshua if nothing worse comes of it."

Oswald read on, in nowise disturbed by Miss Haggard's entrance to look for an account-book in the bureau, or to get her thimble from the chimney-piece. He had come to that scene of abject passion—of self-abandonment and despair—when Werther, having resolved to put an end to his misery, comes in the winter evening to see his idol for the last time. Forgetful of herself for the moment, Charlotte reproaches him for coming. She shrinks from the idea of being alone with him, and recovers her self-possession with an effort. She seats herself at her harpsichord, and begins a minuet; then asks Werther to read to her his own translation of a part of Ossian, which he brought her a few days ago. Perhaps no scene in the wide range of sentimental fiction surpasses this in restrained power, in suppressed passion. Not a whisper, not a thought of impurity sullies the picture from the first line to the last; there is only a fatal, irresistible love.

"She tore herself from him, and in hopeless bewilderment, trembling between love and anger, she cried, 'This is the last time, Werther! You must see me no more.' And, casting a look full of love upon the wretched one, she fled into the adjoining room and shut the door behind her. Werther stretched out his arms after her, but dared not detain her. He lay upon the ground, his head on the sofa, and remained in this position for half an hour, until a sudden noise recalled him to himself. It was the servant, who came to lay the table. He walked up and down the room, and when he found himself alone again, went to Charlotte's door, and called in a low voice, 'Lotte, Lotte! only one word—one farewell.' There was no answer. He waited and knocked, and waited again—then tore himself away, crying, 'Farewell, Lotte! Farewell forever!'"

Cynthia sat listening with dilated eyes and hands tightly clasped, as if the whole scene were reality—as if she could see Werther there, at her feet, groveling on the ground. There stood the open harpsichord at which Charlotte had been playing. The vivid picture shaped itself before her eyes; the winter evening, and home-like, fire-lit room; the hopeless sinner lying there unpitied and alone, the suicide's dark resolve in his mind. And Charlotte knew not his fatal intention. She refused him the poor comfort of a last farewell. No hand was stretched out to save him. It was too awful a picture.

Cynthia clasped her hands before her face and burst into tears. In the next moment Oswald was on his knees beside her, trying to unclasp those small, nervous hands.

"You pity him," he cried, passionately; "pity me, then, for I suffer as he suffered; I love as he loved, and yet have courage to live, and to go on fighting with an invincible passion—though I feel the struggle is vain—and to try to be happy with another—yes, to hold firmly to the tie which once promised happiness, and which now means only bondage. Pity me, Cynthia, pity me—not that poor shadow in the book, who lived and suffered, and is dead and at rest—for there was such a man. Pity me, Cynthia, for I have loved you, and have been fighting against that love ever since that sweet time before my father's death, when you came to his sick-bed as an angel of mercy, and brought woe unutterable to me."

He had poured forth his confession in a torrent of words not to be arrested by Cynthia's choked sobs or look of horror, or the pleading gesture of her tremulous hands.

"Oswald, how can you be so cruel?"

"Cruel! Is it cruel to suffer, to be miserable, to know myself the worst and weakest of men, and to hate myself—as I do, Cynthia, from my soul? Do you think I have not struggled? Yes, and conquered myself, after a fashion. I am going to marry Naomi, and we are to be a happy couple, as married couples go nowadays—happier than nine out of ten, perhaps, for at least I can admire and respect my wife, and I once believed I loved her, before I knew you and the hidden depths of my own heart, and the meaning of that word 'love.' Yes, we are going to be vastly happy. The builders are doing wonders for our house, and we shall be thought much of, and looked up to by the neighborhood. I may keep a pack of hounds, very likely, by-and-by, and teach my wife to ride across country. I am not going to shoot myself as Werther did."

"Why did you read that book to me?" asked Cynthia, with a piteous accent that thrilled him. It sounded like an admission of weakness—a faint cry of despair.

"Why?" he cried, trying to take her hands in both his own. "Can't you understand why? Because it is my own story; because it was my only way of telling you my love; and I burned to tell you. It was an irresistible longing. I could not keep silence any longer; somehow—in some language, if not in plainest speech—I must tell you. And now bid me die, my Charlotte, and I will slay myself like Werther. Only say to me, Life would be easier for all of us if thou wert dead, and I will not live another day to disturb your placid existence. I am your slave, dearest—your abject, obedient slave."

"If you are," said Cynthia, trembling violently, and paler than the wood anemones she had gathered to deck the old squire's sick-room—"if you are, you will obey me. Never speak to me again as you have spoken to-day. Forget that you have ever been so wicked. Ask your Saviour to give you a better heart, and respect my dear husband and his daughter."

Before Oswald could answer, honest Sally entered with the big mahogany tea-tray, knowing no more of the thunder-cloud of passion in the atmosphere than the maid who laid the supper in the story of Werther. Mr. Pentreath had risen

"IT IS MY OWN STORY."

from his knees to pace the room after that last speech of his, and there was no extraordinary picture offered to the eye of the handmaiden. Cynthia folded her work even more carefully than usual, but with hands that trembled sorely. She smoothed the white-linen garment which had progressed so slightly toward completion this afternoon, and laid it in its allotted place, and took her stand by the window, watching for her husband's return. She tried to seem at her ease, but not the faintest tinge of color relieved the absolute pallor of her face. Strangely was that face changed from the radiant countenance that had welcomed Joshua Haggard at Penmoyle, one little year ago.

Oswald walked up and down the parlor while Sally set out the homely feast—a big loaf in an iron tray, a brown butter-pot of Wedgwood ware, a dish of lettuce and overgrown radishes. Anon appeared Miss Haggard; and had either Oswald or Cynthia been in an observant mood, they might have remarked that the industrious Judith had not paid as much attention as usual to her afternoon toilet. The corkscrew curls were somewhat roughened, the large mosaic brooch, which she was wont to put on by way of evening dress, was missing.

"I think I'll go and have a look at the builders," said Oswald, taking up his hat. "I'll come round again in the evening, perhaps, and see how Naomi is."

No one attempted to hinder his going; so, after a brief adieu to the two ladies, he departed, leaving "Werther" lying on the little round table by the window. Cynthia took up the volume, and turned eagerly to the page at which he had left off reading.

"Ah!" sighed Miss Haggard, "that's the worst of novel-reading. It grows upon people,"

Cynthia neither heeded nor heard. Her thoughts were with the suicide who was roaming bareheaded in the winter night, outside the gates of the little town, not knowing whither or how long he wandered.

Joshua came in while his wife was standing with the open book in her hand, absorbed, unconscious of his entrance.

"Why, little one, how pale you are!" he said, in that gentler tone which his voice assumed unwittingly whenever he spoke to his wife. "I missed your welcoming look as I came across the street."

"There's too much novel-reading in this family," snapped Judith. "You mustn't expect things to go on as they ought, if you let the young squire bring bad books into your house."

"This is not a bad book," cried Cynthia, indignantly. "It is a beautiful book,"

"I say that it is a bad book," answered Judith, fiercely. "And I've good reason to know it—a book that puts bad thoughts into people's heads. Gainsay me if you dare, Mrs. Haggard,"

Cynthia's white face turned from her doubly. What did she guess? What had she overheard? Something, assuredly. Deepest shame took possession of Joshua's wife. She felt the burden of unspeakable guilt—she who was only the passive object of an unauthorized passion.

"Why, Judith! Cynthia! what is this? Who would dare to bring a wicked book into my house; my son that soon is to be, above all?

And if he were capable of doing such a shameful thing, would my wife read the book?"

"It is not wicked," said Cynthia, handing him the offending "Werther." "It is a story of sorrow—not wickedness. If stories are to be written at all, they must tell of sorrow—and human weakness and sinfulness. Even the Bible tells us that life is made up of these,"

"Very much so," remarked Judith. "There's nothing the Bible says about human nature's wickedness that human nature doesn't faithfully carry out."

Joshua took the book and glanced at it helplessly. He was not able to take a bird's-eye view of plot and style, swoop upon a catch-word here and there, and straightway make up his mind that the book was altogether vile, after the manner of certain modern critics. He turned the leaves thoughtfully, saw a story told in a series of letters, much talk of the beauties of nature, a little philosophy, some mention of a country pastor, and children—their innocent gambols in rustic gardens, their affection for a kind elder sister, bread-and-butter, village life, a pastoral air altogether: not a bad book assuredly, decided Joshua,

"I do not think, my dear Judith, that you are a very acute judge of literature," he said, mildly.

"Perhaps not," assented Miss Haggard, with a faint moan. "But I hope I am a tolerable judge of human nature."

"I can trust my future son's honor for not bringing any ill-chosen book into my house; and I can trust my wife's purity well enough to know that it would revolt against any thing evil,"

"Nothing like trustfulness in this life," remarked Judith, sententiously, as she took up the tea-pot.

Now, a general proposition—indisputable in its nature though vague in its drift—flung out in this way, has a tendency to instill disquiet into the most tranquil mind. There was not much in the words, but the tone meant a great deal; most of all, a kind of scornful pity. It was like that remark of Iago's anent Michael Cassio's honesty: the plainest, most straightforward observation, yet dropping the poison-seed of doubt into the heart of the listener.

Joshua Haggard looked at his sister's pursed-up lips wonderingly, and then at his wife's pale face, in which there was an expression that was new to him.

Great heavens! what did it mean? Not guilt: not the lightest taint of evil? No; he could never believe the faintest shadow of evil his beloved—not even the most venial deceit, the smallest double-dealing. She was the purest of the pure: pure as the saintly damsels of old—the women who ministered to the apostles in the sweet early dawn of Christianity. He could admit her to be no less pure than these—as white a soul—unsullied by human frailty. He had preached the sinfulness of the human heart—it was the very key-stone of his creed—a sinful humanity in need of being called and regenerated, chosen and purified, redeemed by a vicarious sacrifice. But here he was false to his own theology: he would not admit of original sin in this one pure soul. Love had issued his imperious edict, like a papal bull, and this one woman was to be without sin.

"My love, you are trembling," said Joshua, taking his wife's cold hand, after a long and earnest scrutiny of the pale, sad face. "There must be something amiss in the book, if it has agitated you so."

"It is a very sorrowful story," she faltered; "I could not help crying—at the end."

"Oswald must bring you no more books to make you unhappy. I heard you all laughing pleasantly one afternoon when he was reading some Scotch book, about an old gentleman and a dog. He must bring you only pleasant books. In a world where there is so much real sorrow, it is foolish, and even wrong, to waste our tears upon story-books. That is one reason why I have always tried to keep such books out of my house."

"I will never read such stories again," said Cynthia, earnestly. "Only tell me how to please you, and I will be obedient in all things."

Judith sighed audibly. It was a way she had at times, and always exercised a depressing influence upon her family circle.

"Is there any thing wrong, Judith?" inquired the minister.

"No, brother; it's only my chest."

This was her invariable answer; but as medical science had never yet discovered any thing amiss in this region—not so much as a brief attack of indigestion—the reply was generally accepted as a sort of formula, and her sighing was taken to mean something which Miss Haggard did not choose to communicate.

"My dearest, you have always been obedient," said Joshua, pressing his wife's little hand. "I have never been dissatisfied with you. But I do not like to see you low-spirited about a foolish book, written by some weak-minded German," said Joshua, with a sublime ignorance as to the pretensions of the great Wolfgang.

"Try me with some hard thing," exclaimed Cynthia, with increasing earnestness; "put my gratitude and affection to the proof. Do I forget what you have done for me—how you saved me from heathen ignorance—how I owe you all that I am and all that I hope to be? Could I be ungrateful to you, my benefactor and my deliverer?"

Had Judith Haggard been a student of Shakspeare, she would have here quoted Ophelia's remark upon the player-queen, inwardly or audibly,

"Methinks the lady doth protest too much!"

But as her sole notion of the poet was that he had been rather a low and loose-lived person who wrote plays, and glorified much drinking of sack and canary as a cardinal virtue, she relieved her feelings with another sigh, deeper than the last.

"Don't mind me, brother," she said; "it's only my chest."

Joshua neither heard the sigh nor the excuse; his eyes were fixed upon his wife's white face, down which the gathering tears rolled slowly.

"Ungrateful, my love!" he cried; "have I ever claimed gratitude from you? My part has been to thank God for having given me so dear a companion. Only be happy, my darling; that is the sole obedience I ask from you. Let no foolish fancies out of books disturb your peace of mind. God has given us real happiness, dear; let us be thankful for it, and value it, lest the cloud should come upon us because we have made light of the sunshine."

He drew her to him and kissed her tenderly; and in that hour, at least, there was no shadow of distrust in his mind.

CHAPTER XX.

"AND ALL IS DROSS THAT IS NOT HELENA."

It was some time before Oswald saw his betrothed, after that last reading of "Werther," and the book remained a broken story for Naomi, who knew not the issue of Werther's fatal love. Cynthia carried the volume up to her own room and read it, and wept over it in secret, and then hid it under the little stock of ribbons and collars and feminine prettinesses—all of the simplest, most puritanical kind—which she had acquired since she had been Joshua Haggard's wife. She put the book away out of sight, as if it were a guilty thing, feeling that it had brought her face to face with a guilty secret. But for the book, those wicked words of Oswald's might never have been spoken. The sad—the awful, inexpiable guilt would have existed, all the same, in the depths of two erring hearts, but it might never have found a voice. "Werther" had given form and language to that mysterious and sinful passion—bitterest proof of poor humanity's ingrained iniquity.

"Not by ourselves can we escape sin," she cried, on her knees, in abject self-abasement. "We are nothing of ourselves: not even faithful to the most sacred ties—not even true to our own affections—not even pure or constant. Only by thee, O Redeemer!—only by thee can we escape the snares our erring hearts set for us; only through thee can we break loose from the bondage of original sin. Oh, pity him, spotless Saviour—pity this helpless sinner; pity me, for I love him." She was not afraid to carry this secret sorrow, sinful as it was, to the foot of the cross. Her husband's theology had taught her that Calvary was the sinner's altar—his temple of expiation; the threshold of heaven, on which all guilty hearts could lay their burdens down, and pass, purified from earthly stain, and liberated from earthly chains, through the golden gate beyond it. The deeper the guilt, the surer welcome for the penitent.

Cynthia's guilt was but a thought—a fond, weak yielding to a dream of impossible happiness—a sinful regret for the things that might have been. She had not stood firmly against the insidious approach of the tempter; she had suffered him to steal upon her footsteps unawares; she had not shut her eyes and refused to see the dangerous, dazzling vision. Passion was an unknown element in this purely sentimental and poetic nature. Love, for Cynthia, could never mean storm and fever, guilt and ruin; but it might mean corroding remorse, a slow and silent despair.

When had she first discovered that something amiss in her placid life—that little rift in the lute which made life's music dumb? Closest self-examination would have scarcely enabled her to answer that question. It might be, perhaps, that on the morning when Oswald parted from her at her husband's door—in the blank sorrow of his face, with its look of mute appeal, in the tears he shed upon her hand as he clasped it in his own—she had faintly understood a secret which was to become plainer to her by-and-by. The thought, vague though it was at first, had brought sorrow. She had felt a restraint in the presence of Naomi's lover, and had striven to avoid him. But the days in which she did not see him seemed desolate and empty; and then, not weighing the consequences or meaning of her acts, she weakly yielded to the desire to be in his company, and allowed herself to be the companion of Naomi's walks, the sharer of her lover's attentions. This was the sin she now looked back upon as the black spot in her life—this was when she had suffered the tempter to overtake her steps, to walk by her side.

O happy fatal afternoons in wood or wilderness—on the hills—by the malachite and purple sea! She could see the bright face looking up at her; she could hear the low, thrilling voice reading sweet, sad verse that seemed to speak straight to her heart—to have been written and meant only for her; she could see and hear the earthly tempter even now, in this hour of penitence and grief.

"Oh! if I had never seen you, if I had never known you, I should have been innocent and true all the days of my life; worthy of Joshua's noble heart."

She could pray no more. She sat upon the ground, lost in foolish memories, recalling her first days at Combhollow, and all the peaceful time, before she had given up her soul to this guilty dream. She remembered that autumn afternoon, the first time she saw Oswald—she standing by the hearth, with her bonnet in her hand, he coming in at the door.

"And he was nothing to me," she thought, wonderingly. "If he had died that night, I should only have been sorry for Naomi's sake."

She had thought him handsome—different in every way from all other men she had ever seen—a new creature. He was like a picture that Joshua had shown her in an old country-house they went to see in their brief honey-moon—the portrait of a young man in dark-green velvet clothes of a curious fashion, with fair hair falling on his shoulders, and a melancholy look in his eyes. How often she had seen that melancholy look in Oswald's eyes, after the squire's death, and had known only too well that it was not grief for his father that made him sad!

How gradually it had crept into her heart, this weak, wicked love! Had it come like a bold assailant, she could have repulsed it; but sweetly, slowly, gently, like the tender dawn of a summer morning, this new light had overspread the sky of life. How should she bear her life without it!

"Duty, duty!" she cried, wresting herself from this web of foolish memories. "Oh, let me remember all I owe my husband; let me remember how I worshiped him one little year ago; what a grace and honor I counted it to be chosen by him! I loved him because he was the best and wisest of men. He *is* best and wisest—kindest, truest. Whom have I ever known equal to him?"

When Naomi went down to the parlor, a little later than usual, on the morning after that last reading of "Werther"—languid still from yesterday's headache—she found a letter from Oswald on the chimney-piece. Cynthia was sitting at work by the window—just where *he* had sat yesterday. Judith was washing the breakfast cups and saucers in a little crockery pan which she was accustomed to bring into the parlor for that purpose.

"Dearest,—I have made up my mind quite suddenly to go to London and inquire about Arnold's ship. It seems such a strange thing that I have had no answer to my letters, and I am getting really uneasy. I shall go to Lloyd's—or whatever the right place may be to obtain information about a ship in the merchant-service. Forgive me for going away so suddenly and without waiting to say good-bye. An irresistible impulse took hold of me. I shall only stay long enough to make all needful inquiries, and to take a hasty look at the city; and I shall write to tell you how I get on. God bless you, dear, and good-bye. Your always affectionate
                                        "Oswald."

Naomi read the letter twice over, surprised at this sudden impulse in Oswald, who was not subject to impulses, or at least not subject to carrying out their promptings when they prompted immediate action. He was rather of a dreamy temperament, never doing any thing to-day which he could possibly put off till to-morrow.

She read the letter a third time aloud to Cynthia.

"Did he say any thing about this yesterday?" she asked. "Had he any idea of going to London?"

"I think not," answered Cynthia, working steadily. Oh, blessed mechanical click-click of the needle, which went on with its measured paces, while the pulses of the heart throbbed so stormily! Naomi gave a little sigh as she folded the letter. It was hard to lose him for an indefinite time, were it ever so short. And her wedding-day seemed so far off now. The neglected old Grange no longer awaited her with its sober old-world look—the look it had worn since her infancy. Confusion had fallen upon the old house, and Naomi felt as if she could have no part in the new house which was to arise from this chaos. Money was being spent recklessly to make the grave old mansion fit for a fine lady, and Naomi knew that it was not in her to become a fine lady. All the money in the world would never make her like Mrs. Carew of the Knoll, who wore rouge, and drove a curricle; or like Miss Donnisthorpe, the daughter of the master of the hounds, who hunted the innocent red deer in a short green habit, with a gold band round her velvet hunting-cap.

"If he would only keep to the old simple ways," she thought, looking back at the departed squire's miserly plainness of living with a touch of regret, "I am sure we should be much happier; he would spend his money in doing good."

She knew, by the experience of one who had succored and cared for the poor, all the sad details of that dark picture which lies behind the fair outside of country life. That lovely landscape, rich in its variety of color as the queen's regalia, is the theatre in which many a drama of sin and suffering, guiltless poverty and unmerited woe, has to be acted. Yonder cottage, whose thatched roof makes so pretty a feature in the view, shelters starvation: a mother toiling to feed her children, while their father lies in jail for—a rabbit. Pinched faces, untimely wrinkles, meet the traveler in those delightful lanes where the wild apple and the clustering elder suggest to the poetic mind a land of milk and honey and pomegranates—faces marked with the brand of premature care, defiled by the cunning that is engendered of childish struggles with tyrants and task-masters, and a hard, inexorable fate. Not in fetid alleys and festering London back-slums only is man's fight with difficulty a bitter and crushing battle; but here even, where earth is a paradise, and the untainted sky an Italian blue, man starves and perishes, and learns to curse the unequal destiny that gives his master all, and him nothing.

Naomi knew what poverty meant in a rural district; and she longed for the power to help and improve, and to use the knowledge which experience had given her. She had talked to Oswald of the laborers' homes on his estate—hovels rather than houses—and had gently urged the need for improvement. He had put her off lightly, in his pleasant, yielding way; so full of grace and beauty in her sight, that she forgot the weakness it indicated.

"It shall be done, dear; 'The sooner, sweet, for you,' as Othello says. We will do wonders for the poor things. The Exeter architect shall make a plan—after we are married. You must let me finish the Grange first, and then I will do any thing you like; but I can't take the builder off that till his work is done." As if there were no other builder in the world!

Oswald was in London, trying to find his Lethe in the somewhat prosaic distractions of that capital; not the London of to-day, with its Viaduct and Embankment, and houses as tall as those of old Edinburgh and Paris; its innumerable railway-stations, and theatres, and restaurants, and music-halls, but a city of narrower streets and more jovial manners. He knew no one, and put up at the busy commercial hotel at which the Western coach deposited him, taking no trouble to seek a more refined habitation. He made his inquiries about his brother's ship, and, after some trouble, found out the last port she had touched at in the China seas. Yet this was not much; for Arnold might have exchanged to another ship, for any thing Oswald knew to the contrary. But to gain intelligence about his absent brother had not been Mr. Pentreath's only business in London, or even his chief reason for going there. He went thither in quest of forgetfulness—to cure himself, were it curable, of a passion that threatened to be fatal at once to peace of mind and honor. He had torn himself away from Penmoyle with a wrench, thinking that to turn his back upon Cynthia might be to forget her; but, alas for youth's constancy to a forbidden dream! the sweet face followed him to the crowded city, and harassed him by day, and held him awake at night; the soft blue eyes betrayed love's sad secret; the tremulous lips seemed to him to murmur, "Yes, dearest, I love and pity you; though it can never be—though we are parted in life and eternity—I love, I pity, I deplore."

Not quite in vain had he loved her if she but loved him in return; though all hopes, dreams, delights that love could give, were it ever so erring, must be here laid down; a solemn sacrifice to duty and honor. Yes, there was much comfort—nay, more than comfort, a rapture that thrilled him—in knowing that he was loved. And he did most assuredly know it, though no admission had fallen from Cynthia's lips. Their spirits had touched, as flame touches flame, but a moment—swift as the quivering arrows of fire that flash and fade in the instant; yet the touch was a revelation. He did not doubt that she loved him.

He had never meant to speak of his love. This he repeated to himself deprecatingly in his hours of remorse. Passion had forced his secret from him, and he despised himself for the confession that had dishonored him. He had meant to speak only through "Werther," finding a morbid delight in dwelling upon the record of sufferings so like his own, half assured that Cynthia understood and recognized his passion veiled in the words of another; and then impulse and emotion had been too strong for him, and he had given loose to the desire of his heart, and disgraced himself forever in his own eyes, and in the sight of the woman he loved.

"She could not look upon me without loathing, after that wretched scene," he told himself. Yet the vision of Cynthia which he carried with him everywhere did not regard him with loathing, but with a tender pity, a sad, immeasurable love.

He tried to steep himself in London dissipations, knowing about as much of them as a baby. If he could have fallen in with the mohawks of the day—the gentlemen who went to Epsom races in a hearse, and wrenched off harmless citizens' knockers, or plucked out their bell-wires; who drank porter with hackney-coachmen and their watermen, and made bosom friends of prizefighters—he would perchance have enrolled himself in that band of choice spirits, and tried to discover a new Lethe in the porter-pot, wherein the Corinthian Tom of the period was generally so fortunate as speedily to find that oblivion which goes by the name of Death. But Oswald Pentreath had no introduction to this patrician set, and was fain to seek for distraction in such simple pleasures as Vauxhall and the theatres, where he found something at every turn which reminded him of himself and of Cynthia.

Sometimes a face that had been sweet and fair flashed past him, under the colored lamps in the Vauxhall groves, bright with artificial hues, in its venal smile dimly recalling Cynthia's innocent beauty; sometimes a face upon the stage reminded him of hers, or a tone of voice in some young actress thrilled him like hers. Forget her! Every thing in life was associated with her. He could not even remember what life had been like before he loved her.

He saw all that London could show him—parks, streets, theatres, gambling-houses, race-courses, folly, extravagance, vanity—but found no forgetfulness. Nay, his passion grew and strengthened in absence. The aching void in his heart went with him everywhere. At the play, when the house was roaring at "Tom and Jerry," and the Charlies were being carried off bodily in their rickety old watch-boxes, Oswald sat staring blankly. His thoughts were in the parlor at Combhollow, acting that foolish scene over again —living again in the light of Cynthia's eyes— draining deep delight from every look—however sad, however reproachful—which told him he was beloved.

He did not yield himself up to despair without a struggle—which was a manly struggle for one whom Nature had made of no heroic mold. He wrestled with himself, and tried to make a stand against the tempter, and had it in his mind to thrust Joshua's wife out of his heart, and to be faithful to Joshua's daughter. He would go back to Combhollow in a month or so, regenerated, and would hurry on his marriage, and begin a new life as a useful and worthy member of society.

"Arnold may be home by that time," he thought; "and the delight of seeing him again will make me forget every thing."

In the mean while he wrote twice a week to Naomi decorous and amiable letters, describing all he saw, and telling nothing of his feelings or impressions—hardly one word of himself from beginning to end. Poor Naomi read and reread the letters, and puzzled herself sorely about them. He seemed to be enjoying himself, for he was always going to theatres and operas and races; and he was staying in London longer than he had intended, which proved that he was pleased with what he saw. Naomi was contented to bear the pain of severance, for the sake of his pleasure; but to be parted from him was a sharper pain than she could have thought possible before he went. Life was so empty without him! She had her father, always the first in her esteem, she had told herself; she had all her old home duties and home ties; but Oswald's absence took the sunshine and color out of every thing.

CHAPTER XXI.

"IT WAS THY LOVE PROVED FALSE AND FRAIL."

A CLOUD had fallen upon that quiet household at Combhollow. A sharper pain than Naomi's sense of loss had crept into the breast of Naomi's father, and gnawed at it in secret, while the strong man kept silence, ashamed of his suffering—nay, angry at the human weakness which made it possible for him so to suffer.

That little scene with Cynthia—that unexplained mystery about the book called "Werther" —had not been without its influence upon Joshua Haggard's mind. He might have forgotten it, and gone on trusting implicitly—as it was his nature to trust where he confided at all—had he been true to his own instincts; but this privilege —the melancholy privilege of being happy and deceived—had not been allowed him. Judith had hinted, and whispered, and looked, and insinuated, and, without committing herself to any direct statement, had contrived to poison her brother's mind with a shapeless suspicion of his wife's purity.

Cynthia had drooped somewhat after that evening on which she sobbed out her despair upon her husband's breast. The pale cheek had not regained its wild-rose bloom; the sweet, blue eyes had grown dull and languid. The young wife looked like one who sickened under the burden of some secret sorrow. She was not strong enough to suppress the outward signs of a heart ill at ease.

Joshua saw the change; at first wondered at it, and then, enlightened by Judith's hints, began to suspect.

Cynthia was not happy. It was no bodily sickness which oppressed her, but a secret grief. Was it that she regretted her marriage with him—that she had chosen him hastily, mistaking religious fervor for love? This seemed likely enough.

"How should she love me," he asked himself; "a man more than twice her age; grave—full of cares for serious things? Is it natural that she should find happiness in my society, or in the life she leads here? Naomi is different; she has been brought up to this quiet life—to see all things in the same sober light. Cynthia was a wanderer, used to motion and variety—to crowds and noise. How can she help it if the longing for the old gypsy life comes back to her? How can I blame her if she wearies of my dull home?"

This is how he would have explained the change to himself; but Judith's oracular sentences hinted at something darker.

"What is it that you mean, Judith?" he asked one day, with a burst of anger; "you and my wife speak fairly enough to each other's face, and seem to live peacefully together; but there is something lurking in your mind—there is something underneath all this smoothness. Is it Christian-like to deal in hints and dark looks?"

"I should think it was Christian-like to stand by my brother," answered Judith, with her injured air, "and to consider him before every body."

"Is it a sign of consideration for me to speak unkindly of my wife?"

"What have I said that is unkind? Perhaps it might be kindness to say more. There's things that can't go on without bringing misery to more than you, brother; but it isn't my business to talk about 'em if you've no eyes to see 'em for yourself."

"What do you mean, woman?"

"Yes: things must have come to a pretty pass when my only brother, that I've toiled for and served faithfully all my life, calls me names. A minister, too, who preaches against bad language. But I knew what it would be when that young woman crossed this threshold. Good-bye, family affection! The man who is led away by a pretty face turns his back upon blood-relations. He's bound to follow where his new fancy leads him."

With these random arrows of speech did Miss Haggard harass her victim and relieve her own feelings.

"Judith, do you want to drive me mad?" he cried, with exasperation, "or to make me think that you are fit for a mad-house yourself? How has my wife offended you? What evil have you ever seen in her?"

He stood with his back against the parlor-door, facing his sister, with a resolute look in his dark eyes—resolute even to fierceness, which told her that a crisis had come. She would be obliged to speak out; and to speak out was the very last thing she desired. Never before had she seen that sombre fire in Joshua's dark eyes. She quailed before the unknown demon she had raised.

"What is amiss?" he demanded, savagely; "how has my wife sinned against purity, or against me?"

"I am not accusing her of sin," faltered Judith. "You shouldn't be so hot-tempered, brother; it isn't becoming in a Christian minister. I do not accuse her of sin; but there's foolishness which brings young women to the threshold of sin; and, once there, it is easy to cross over to fire and brimstone. I say that a girl of nineteen is no wife for a man of your age; that Providence must have meant her for a trial of your patience; that's what I've always thought and shall always say, as willingly before her face as behind her back."

"Is that all you have to say? You might have said as much the night I brought my wife home. Is this the upshot of all your dark looks and insinuations? You have kept me on thorns for the last three weeks; and, driven into a corner, you can only beat about the bush like this."

His scornful tone stung her. To be ridiculed—to be made of no account in her brother's household—was more than Judith Haggard could bear. Whatever wealth of affection there was in her nature had been given to Joshua. He was the one man she believed in and honored, even when least respectful in her attitude toward him. She could not tamely see him wronged; and her jealousy of Cynthia was quick to suspect and imagine wrong. She had seen and heard enough to give force and meaning to her suspicions; and her bosom had been laboring with the weight of that secret knowledge. She wanted to tell Joshua—she wanted not to tell him. The secret gave her a sense of power. It was as if she held a thunder-bolt which she might launch at any moment on the heads of the household; but the bolt once launched, and the domestic sky darkened, her power would be gone. Pity for Joshua she had none, although she loved him. He had wronged her love too deeply in marrying a nameless girl. It would do her good to see him suffer through his wife. She would stand by him afterward—stand by him and console him, comfort him with her love, instead of Cynthia's. But Providence—and Judith as an instrument of Providence—meant him to suffer this ordeal.

"You've no call to make light of me," she said; "I'm not one to speak without authority. I can hold my tongue as I've held it for the last twelvemonth. Do you want me to speak plainly? Do you want me to say all I know?"

"All—to the last word," said Joshua, white with rage.

"Don't turn round upon me afterward and say it would have been better if I'd kept my counsel."

"Say your say, woman, and make an end of it."

"Well, brother, I've seen a change in Mr. Pentreath ever since his father's death; absent looks—and smothered sighs—and restlessness—and no pleasure in life. Grief for his father, you'll say, perhaps; but is it likely he'd give way like that for an old man that kept him short of money and hadn't any body's good word? It isn't in nature."

"Who made you a judge of nature? But go on."

"Well, brother, I had my own ideas, and I kept 'em to myself, and should have so kept 'em as long as I lived, if I'd had no stronger cause for suspicion. But when I see a young man on his knees at a young woman's feet, and hear him asking her to pity him because he's miserable for love of her, and threatening to shoot himself, and the young woman sobbing as if her heart would break all the time—and that young woman my brother's wife—when things come to such a pass as this, I think it's my duty to speak."

"Lies! lies!" gasped Joshua. "You see my happiness, and envy me! You hate my wife because she is lovely, as you never were; passionately loved, as you never were."

Judith laughed hysterically.

"I don't know about beauty," she said; "but I had a high color, and jet-black hair with a natural curl, when I was a young woman; and that used to be thought good looks enough for any girl in my time; and I might have married a hundred and fifty acres of land and a flour-mill. But I'm sorry to see you so beside yourself with passion, Joshua, because I speak plainly for your own good."

"Is it for my good to tell me lies? My wife listening to Oswald Pentreath's wicked love! No—I'll never believe it."

"Turn it over in your own mind a little more before you call your only sister a liar. Have you forgotten the last afternoon Mr. Pentreath was here—when Naomi was lying down with a sick headache, and those two—Mrs. Haggard and the young squire—were alone together from dinner till tea; and you came home and found your wife all in a flutter, and as white as a sheet of paper; and I accused her to her face of reading a wicked book; and you turned against me to take her part; and she burst into tears in the middle of tea, and told you she was grateful to you, and would do her duty by you? What was that but a guilty conscience? Why, a mole could have seen through it! But a man of your age, who marries a young woman for the sake of her pretty face, is blinder than the blindest mole. He has no eyes to see any thing but the prettiness."

Joshua wiped the sweat-drops from his forehead with a broad muscular hand that shook like a leaf. Never had his manhood been so shaken—never in all the trials of his early life, when to hold fast by his thorny path had cost him many a struggle, had he felt the hot blood surging in his brain as it surged to-day. There was a fiery cloud before his eyes. He could scarcely see his sister's face, looking at him full of angry eagerness, intent to prove her own case, to assert her own dignity—and with but little consideration for his anguish.

"Judith," he said, falteringly—and that strong voice of his so rarely faltered that its weakness had a touch of deepest pathos—"you are my own and only sister. I can not think you would tell me lies on purpose to make me miserable. Forgive me for what I said just now. No; I can not believe my sister a liar. I will not believe my wife unfaithful to me by so much as a thought. But this young man is a weak vessel. Tell me—plainly—all you saw and heard."

"That's easily told. He had been reading that book to her—what's his name?—Werther. I went in and out to fetch my thimble, and such-like; and whenever I went in it was the same story; 'Didst thou but know how I love thee,' and 'Charlotte, it is decided—I must die,' and such rubbish; and there sat your wife, with her work crumpled up in her lap, staring straight at him with tears in her eyes. It was close upon tea-time, and I was going in again when I heard something that stopped me. The door stood a little way ajar—it's an old box-lock, and the catch is always giving way, as you know, Joshua—and I waited outside just to find out what it all meant, for I felt that I was bound to do that much by my duty to you. I could just see into the room. He was on his knees, holding her hands, and she sobbing as if her heart would break. He told her how he loved her, and asked her to pity him; and she never said him nay, only went on crying, and presently told him he was cruel; and oh, why did he read such a book to her? Because it was his own story, he said, and the only way he could find of telling her his love."

"And she did not cry out against such iniquity?" cried Joshua; "she did not reprove him for such wickedness—rise up before him in her dignity as an offended woman, and my true and loyal wife?"

"I heard myself called in the shop just at that moment, and I was obliged to go," answered Judith. "When I came back to the parlor, Sally was laying the tea-things."

"I will answer for my wife's truth and honor," said Joshua, firmly. "I will pledge myself that she repulsed and upbraided this guilty young man as he deserved—that she looks upon his wicked passion with abhorrence. That was why she looked so pale—shocked to the heart, my gentle one! That was why she clung to me so piteously, seeking sanctuary in my affection. My lily, no villain shall sully thy purity while I am near to shield thee! My dearest! has the tempter assailed thee so soon—sin's poisoned breath so soon tarnished thy soul's whiteness? I will love thee all the more—guard thee more closely, honor thee more deeply—because thou hast been in danger."

Judith stared at her brother in dumb amazement. Against such infatuation as this the voice of reason was powerless. It almost tempted her to believe in witchcraft—a superstition by no means extinct in this Western world. Judith had put the thought behind her hitherto, as a delusion of the dark ages unworthy of a strong-minded woman. But here, surely, was a case of demoniac possession—an example of something more foolish than mortal folly.

"But as for him," continued Joshua, with clenched fist, "for the tempter—the would-be seducer—he shall never cross this threshold again; and let him beware how he crosses my path, lest I should slay him in my righteous rage, as Moses slew the Egyptian."

"And Naomi's engagement?" suggested Judith, timidly. There was a power in her brother's look which awed her.

"Naomi's engagement is canceled from this hour. My daughter shall marry no double-dealer—swearing to be true to her at God's altar with lips that are defiled by the avowal of love for another man's wife. My daughter shall go unmarried to her grave rather than be the wife of such a man, were his place the highest in the land."

"It was a very grand match for her," said Judith, with a propitiating air; "but, for my part,

I never saw happiness come from an unequal marriage, and I've seen many such in my time. But I'm afraid Naomi will take it to heart."

"Poor child!" sighed the father. "Is it my sin that I have brought this sorrow upon her? How could I know that her lover would prove so base? Poor child! She must bear her burden, she must carry her cross."

He was deadly pale; and, now that the angry light had gone out of his eyes, his face had a faded look, as if the anguish of many years had aged him within the last half-hour.

"I can't but remember what Jabez Long said the day the *Dolphin* went down: 'No good ever came of saving a drowning man; he's bound to do you wrong afterward.' It's come true, you see," said Judith.

"Do you think I believe that heathen superstition any more because Oswald Pentreath has proved a villain? I thought you had more sense, Judith."

"Well, I don't say I believe it; but, to say the least, it's curious. However, I never did think much of young Mr. Pentreath, or of the stock he comes from. But it seems hard upon Naomi. Shall you tell her the reason?"

"Tell her that a villain has insulted my wife! No, Judith. My daughter will obey me, though I bid her sacrifice her heart's desire; as Jephthah's daughter obeyed when she laid down her life in fulfilment of her father's promise."

"Ah," sighed Judith, with suppressed gusto, "it's a world of trouble."

She felt more in her element, now that things were going wrong, and that she was at the helm once more, in a manner. Her little world had been given over to two girls, and she had felt herself, in her own language, a cipher.

It was hardly in Joshua's nature to be slow to act, however painful the business which duty imposed upon him. On that very evening he found Naomi alone in the wilderness, on her knees before a craggy bank, planting some wild flowers which she had discovered in her afternoon rambles.

She looked up from her clustering ferns and humble way-side blossoms with a smile, as her father approached; but the troubled expression of his face alarmed her, and she rose quickly and came to him.

"Dear father, is any thing wrong?"

She had not seen him since his interview with Judith, and that aged and altered look in his face, which had struck the sister, alarmed the daughter.

"Yes, my dear, there is something very wrong. Providence bids me inflict pain upon one I fondly love—upon you, my Naomi."

He drew her toward him, looking down at her with tender pity. It seemed very hard that she should suffer—that this young life was so soon to be clouded.

"Dear father, what has happened?" cried Naomi, tremulous in her agitation. "It is about Oswald. The evening post has just come—you have had a letter—is he ill? Yes, yes, I can see that it is about him."

"He is well enough, my love; I have heard nothing to the contrary. I am very sorry that he is so dear to you."

"Why, dear father?"

"Because I have learned lately that he is unworthy of your affection; and I must desire you, as you are my true and obedient daughter, to give up all thought of marrying him."

The girl's face blanched, her eyelids closed for a moment, and the slender figure swayed against Joshua's arm as if it would have fallen. But only for a moment; Naomi was not made of feeble stuff, nor prone to fainting. She lifted her eyelids and looked at her father steadily, holding his arm with fingers that tightened upon it almost convulsively in that moment of pain.

"What have you heard against him, father, and from whom?" she asked, resolutely. "You are bound to tell me that, in common justice. It is my duty to obey you, but not blindly. I am not a child—I can bear to know the worst. What has he done, my love, my dearest—too gentle to hurt a worm—what evil thing has he done, that you should turn against him?"

"That I can not tell you, Naomi; and in this matter you must obey me blindly as a child. He has sinned; and his sin proves him alike false and feeble—a broken reed—a man not to be relied on—unworthy of a woman's trust. Naomi, believe me, your father, who never deceived you, that if I inflict pain upon you to-day, in forbidding this marriage, I spare you ten thousand fold of misery in days to come. It is not possible that you could be happy as Oswald's wife."

"Let me be the judge of that. It is my venture—it is my happiness that is at stake. Let me be the judge. What is his sin?"

"Again I say I can not tell you. You must trust me and obey me, Naomi, or you cease to be my daughter. Oswald Pentreath will never cross my threshold again with my sanction. I shall never more speak to him in friendship?"

"Father, is this Christian-like?"

"It is my duty to myself as a man."

"How has he offended you?"

"By his sin."

"But he has not sinned against me," said Naomi, piteously. "Why am I to renounce him?"

"He has sinned against you and against God."

"If he has sinned, he has so much the more need of my love. Am I to forsake him in his sorrow—I, who would die for him?"

"He does not need your love, Naomi, or desire it. It is for the happiness of both that you should be parted."

"For his happiness?" faltered Naomi, with a look of acute pain.

It was as if all her vague doubts of the past few months were suddenly condensed into a horrible certainty.

"Do you mean that Oswald has ceased to love me?"

"Yes, Naomi. At the beginning I was doubtful of his stability. I feared that his was a character in which impressions are quick to come and go. I stipulated for delay, in order that your lover's constancy might be tested. The event has proved my doubts but too well grounded."

"I offered to release him only a little while ago," said Naomi, "and he would not be set free. He assured me of his unchanging love."

"He was a liar!" cried Joshua, fiercely, and his daughter recoiled before the fury in that dark face. Never had she seen such anger there till to-day—never had she believed him capable of such passion. The revelation shocked her; the father whom she so tenderly loved was degraded in her eyes by this unchristian-like resentment.

"Why are you so angry, father?" she asked, pleadingly.

"Because I hate falsehood, treachery, double-dealing—a fair face and a foul heart. I can say no more, Naomi. I have said enough to warn you; it is for you to accept or reject my warning. Marry Oswald Pentreath if you choose; but remember that, from the hour of your marriage, you cease to be my daughter. I will never acknowledge that man as my son. I will never acknowledge that man's wife as my flesh and blood. It is for you to choose between us."

"Father, you know I have no choice; you know that you are first—have always held the first place in my heart. There is no one else whose love I could weigh against yours—not even Oswald, though I love him dearly, must love him to the end, love him all the more for his weakness—for his sorrow. I am your true and loyal daughter, dearest; and I give you up, my heart, as I would give up my life—yes, dear father, freely, gladly, for your sake."

"That's my own brave Naomi. It is for your own welfare, believe me, dearest, however hard the trial may be to bear just now. The man is not true; there could be no happiness for you with him."

"Do not say any thing more against him, father," pleaded Naomi, gently. "I give him up; but let me honor him as much as I can—let him hold a high place in my thoughts. It is easier to bear the pain of parting from him if I can keep his image in my heart undefiled."

"I will say no more, Naomi. You will write to him, and tell him your engagement is ended, at my desire. A few decided words will say all that is needful. His own heart will tell him the reason. I do not think that he will question or plead against your decision."

"I will write, father."

Joshua folded her in his arms, and kissed the pale, sad brow, drawn with pain.

"May God bless and comfort you, dearest, and give you joy in this sacrifice!" he said, solemnly. "On my honor, as your father and your pastor, it is for the best."

And so he left her, standing in her desolated wilderness, from which the beauty had gone forth forever. Her ferns and hedge-row blossoms smiled at her in the rosy evening light—feathery mosses, trailing periwinkle, opalescent dog-roses, steeped in golden glory; purple fox-gloves towering from a sea of fern—all the sweet wild things she had gathered together looked at her, and gave her no comfort in this hour of bitter agony. She cast herself, face downward, on the grassy path, and gave herself up, body and soul, to despair.

Yes, she had known it long ago; he loved her no more. She had tried to put away the thought. She had made her direct appeal to him, and been reassured by his loving reply. But the aching pain had lingered at the bottom of her heart. She had not been happy.

Better so—better, as her father said, to renounce him altogether—to give him back his freedom—than to let him chain himself in a loveless wedlock. Better any thing than the humiliation of an unloved wife.

But this sin which her father spoke of with

such deep resentment — this offense which had kindled such unseemly anger in a Christian's breast — what was this deadly and desperate error? Herein lay the bitterest trial of all — to be kept in the dark, not to be able to comfort or succor the sinner.

CHAPTER XXII.

"THE DEEP OF NIGHT IS CREPT UPON OUR TALK."

JOSHUA proved a true prophet in so far as related to Oswald Pentreath's line of conduct on receipt of his betrothed's letter. To Naomi's sad epistle, renouncing all claim upon him at her father's desire, he answered briefly:

"Your letter has taken me by surprise, dearest; but harsh and sudden as your decision seems, I acquiesce. I know not how your father may have arrived at his estimate of my character, or what has influenced him to desire that our engagement shall be canceled; but I am willing to abide his sentence. He may be right, perhaps. I am by nature unstable. I am not worthy of so noble a heart as yours. Yet be assured, Naomi, that, although unworthy, I am at least capable of appreciating and admiring your character as well as a better man. To the end of my life I shall honor and esteem you. To the end of my life I shall deem you the purest and noblest of women, and think those days of my life happiest in which I loved you best, and when there was no shadow of mistrust between us.

"God bless you, dearest, and farewell! It may be long before I revisit Combhollow, and this may be a life-long farewell.

"Your friend, your servant, always,
"OSWALD PENTREATH."

"He is grateful to me for letting him go," thought Naomi, with a touch of bitterness. She could read gratitude for his release between the lines of this letter. It confirmed all her sad doubts.

"He might have spared me much pain if he had been more candid," she told herself — " if he had confessed the truth that day I told him of the change I had seen in him."

She opened the drawer where her wedding-dress lay on the day she received this final letter — the last she could ever expect from Oswald Pentreath. She looked at the pale, silken gown with such sorrowful eyes as look upon a corpse. Was it not the dead corpse of her lost happiness which lay there, with sprigs of rosemary among the folds of its shroud?

"Poor wedding-gown!" she said to herself; "I shall give it to Lucy Simmonds. Why should it lie and fade in a drawer, when it would make her happy? Would it be any comfort to me to look at it in years to come, and remember that I was once young, and very happy, fancying myself beloved?"

Lucy Simmonds had been Naomi's favorite pupil in the Sunday-school of Little Bethel — an intelligent Biblical student, who knew "Kings" and "Chronicles" as well as a bishop, and had never been known to confound the miracles of

Elijah and Elisha. She had blossomed into womanhood, and was about to unite her fate with that of a promising young butcher — a staunch member of Joshua's congregation.

Naomi folded the dress carefully, and packed it in a large sheet of white paper. The skirts of those days were scanty, and the silk dress did not make a large parcel. She wrote a loving letter to her old pupil, and sent the parcel to the widow Simmonds's house that afternoon. The dress might be too good for Lucy's present station, but not for her future position as the wife of an aspiring butcher. The young matron would wear that pretty gray silk at friendly tea-parties and Christmas gatherings for years to come, and would think affectionately of the donor. It seemed a small thing, this giving-away of her wedding-gown, but to Naomi it meant the total surrender of hope. There was nothing left for her in life but duty, and her love for her father.

She bore her cross meekly. None could have told how withering a sorrow had passed over her young life. There was a curious compound of pride and humbleness in her nature. She accepted her lot humbly, as a trial which was but her portion of humanity's common burden; but she was too proud to let others see how deeply she had been wounded. She put on a brave front, and her father gave her credit for stoicism, in no wise suspecting that the weight of her secret grief was almost intolerable.

Very little was said in the small household about this change in Naomi's fortunes. The cancelment of her engagement was accepted as an act of Joshua's. He had forbidden the marriage for some good reason of his own. No one dared ask him why — his wife least of all. She could not have spoken Oswald's name to him. Her heart was full of fear, sorrow, and deepest pity for Naomi. Yet she dared not offer her sympathy. There was a look in Naomi's face that forbade all approach — every offer of love. Cynthia felt that there was a gulf between them. Naomi tacitly avoided her. She was not unkind, but she shrank from all companionship with her father's wife; and henceforward Cynthia's life became very lonely. Her husband's hours were closely occupied, and spent for the most part away from her. Naomi lived her own life as much as possible apart from her step-mother, and Judith was harsh and unfriendly. Jim was always Cynthia's friend and champion, but his busy life did not admit of much companionship. The small household met at meals at the same hours, with the same regulations and ceremonies, but these family assemblies were silent and gloomy.

"Our dinner-time is getting uncommonly like a Quaker's meeting," observed the audacious Jim at one of these dreary gatherings: "I wish the spirit would move some of us to be lively."

"When you've as much trouble on your mind as your father has, you won't be quite so active with your tongue," retorted Aunt Judith.

The works at the Grange had undergone a sudden check. Oswald had written peremptory orders to his architect. The contract was to be carried out only so far as concerned the substantial repairs of the house. There was to be no rotunda, and the end of the drawing-room was to be walled up again.

"I am going abroad," he wrote; "make as

good a job as you can of the place, and write to me at the subjoined address for checks as you want them."

The subjoined address was that of a London solicitor, a man who had done business for the old squire occasionally.

The architect wondered and talked; and before many days every body in Combhollow knew that Mr. Pentreath's engagement to Joshua Haggard's daughter was broken off. There was a great deal of talk, and much discussion and disputation about details, but a wonderful unanimity of opinion. The match would have been most unsuitable. Naomi Haggard was much too serious for a squire's lady. The Grange could never have held up its head properly under such a mistress, and a glass rotunda would have been absurdly out of keeping. "He ought to marry Mr. Pinkley's only daughter," said Combhollow, deciding for him off-hand. "There's only an accommodation road between Pinkley's land and his."

The builders finished their work; the end of the long drawing-room was walled up again; and there was no more talk of palms, or fountains, or an Italian garden. The Grange resumed its air of gloom and emptiness, and looked almost as dismal as in the life-time of the old squire.

So the summer ripened and grew more glorious, bringing no delight of heart to the minister's small household. The colors of the sea took a more vivid lustre from the fullness of the sun, like jewels in an Indian temple shining in the glare of many torches. There came over the land the sultry hush of the days before harvest. Very little doing in those rich fields, where the corn was gently stirred by the hot south wind, like the waves of a golden sea; very little doing in the big farm-yards, where the cattle stood knee-deep in the tawny gorse-litter, and contemplated the outer world listlessly, with dreamy, brown eyes, and a general air of benevolence—stillness and repose on all things. Cynthia Haggard looked at this lovely external universe languidly, with eyes that saw its beauty dimly, as in a dream in which one absorbing sense of overwhelming trouble makes all things faint and blurred. Her husband had spoken no unkind word to her since that scene with Oswald, yet she felt that he was estranged. He read more; he shut himself up in his own thoughts, gave himself up more completely to his contemplative and subjective religion, and that religion seemed to take a more gloomy and inexorable character. In his sermons he dwelt less on the divine love and charity, and harped on a harsher string—the doom of sinners destined to perdition—wretches on whom the divine light had never shone, for whom that all-saving faith, which could lift the sinner out of the mire by one upward impulse of an awakened soul, was a dead letter.

Cynthia shuddered as she listened. Was Oswald Pentreath one of these lost spirits?

She could see that her husband was unhappy, yet had no power to comfort him. That weighed upon her heavily. She dared not complain to him of this disunion, lest she should be drawn into a confession of her sinful weakness, and constrained to admit her guilty love for the sinner. She could not have stood up before that righteous man and spoken falsely.

He never questioned her about Oswald Pentreath; yet she felt that there must be some strong suspicion of evil in his mind and at the root of his arbitrary conduct in canceling his daughter's engagement. It never occurred to her that Oswald's wild talk that afternoon had been overheard, and told to Joshua. She looked upon his knowledge rather as the result of some occult power of his own. His wisdom had penetrated the guilty secret.

One night, a little while after Naomi had given up her lover, Joshua came up to his bed-chamber somewhat later than usual. He had staid in the parlor after supper, writing or reading. Cynthia was lying awake, full of sad thoughts, vague forebodings of evil, aching pity for that weak sinner wandering she knew not where. Joshua walked up and down the room in silence for some minutes, and then stopped suddenly beside the bed, and looked down at the small, pale face on the pillow, the sad, blue eyes glancing up at him timidly, deprecating blame.

"I am glad you are not asleep," he said; "I want that book—'The Sorrows of Werther.' I have been thinking of what my sister said about it. I want to judge for myself. I looked at it too hurriedly last time. I want to see what kind of book it was that made you unhappy."

"You can't read it to-night, Joshua, surely? It's so late, and you must be tired."

"I am tired, but not able to sleep. I would rather read than lie awake. My thoughts have been a burden to me of late. There was a time when my wakeful hours were full of sweetness, when I could lose myself in communion with my Redeemer. That time is past. Human trouble has made a wall between this poor clay and the spirit-world."

This was a reproach which smote the erring wife to the heart.

"Joshua, it is my fault," she faltered. "You were happier before you married me."

"Happier!" he cried, bitterly; "I never knew the extremes of human joy or human pain till I knew you. Well, the pain has been immeasurable as the joy. If I erred, I have paid the penalty. Give me that book, Cynthia."

Cynthia rose without another word, went to the drawer where she had hidden that fatal romance of real life, and brought the book to her husband with a meek obedience that moved him deeply. Even in his doubt and distrust of her—for he did doubt her, despite his brave words to Judith—there was an abiding love for her in his soul—a yearning to take her to his heart and forgive her, and comfort her, and offer her deeper love than was ever given to woman—the wide, strong love of a heart that had only awakened to passion in the maturity of its force and power. Could the love of youth, in all its glow of romance and poetry, be in any wise equal to this?

Cynthia put the book into his hand, and then remonstrated gently against the folly of midnight studies. "Read it to-morrow, dear Joshua. You look tired and ill. Hark! it is striking eleven."

"Go to bed and sleep," he said, sternly; "I can not. I want to read the book that melted you—and Oswald Pentreath. I wonder whether it will move me to tears."

He set the candle on the old mahogany escritoire at which he wrote sometimes, and seated himself in the wide horse-hair-covered arm-chair, edged with brass nails, like an old-fashioned coftin. He opened the book with a resolute air, as a man who meant to plod through it, whatever stuff it might be. He read, and read on with an intent face, turning leaf after leaf at measured intervals, Cynthia lying with her face turned toward that gloomy figure, watching him as if he were reading in the book of doom. To her mind that book held the confession of Oswald's weakness and of hers. Joshua would know all when he had read that. Had it been an acknowledgment of sin written with her own hand, signed and attested, she could not have thought it more complete or final.

He read on deep into the night, Cynthia dozing a little now and then, but for the most part watching him. The small hours struck, one after another, on the solemn old church bell; a faint chilliness crept into the summer air: then slowly, softly, mysteriously, like a dream, came the gray dawn; first with a glimmer at the window, then with a broad, cold light that filled the room, and made the flame of the candle pale and ghost-like: then with gleams of saffron and rose, and dim morning sunbeams, like an infant's vague, sweet smile. Still Joshua sat reading, in the same fixed attitude; reading on with indomitable resolve, bent on knowing the utmost and the worst. For him, too, the book was a confession and a revelation. Werther was Oswald Pentreath; Charlotte was Cynthia; and they loved each other; their young hearts yearned to each other, overflowing with tenderest sympathies, with unspeakable affection; and fate, duty, religion, and honor stood between them in the person of the unloved husband, separating them forever.

The room was flooded with sunlight when he closed the book, with one long sigh. He could not refuse the sinner that one expression of pity—so lost, so given over to an unconquerable passion, and yet with so much in him that was gentle and true and worthy.

Cynthia had fallen asleep at last. Joshua looked down at the sweet face on the pillow, full of compassion, pitying her, pitying himself. "Those two lived happily together when Werther was dead," he said to himself, thinking of Albert and Charlotte; "but then Albert did not know that his wife's heart had gone from him."

He washed and dressed himself, and went down to his daily round of labor, and said no word to Cynthia about the fatal book.

CHAPTER XXIII.

"A STORM WAS COMING, BUT THE WINDS WERE STILL."

No life could have been more self-contained than Naomi's in this fair summer-time. She claimed sympathy from no one, but bore the anguish of her widowed heart in a resolute silence. From Cynthia she shrunk, with a feeling that was more nearly akin to aversion than she would have liked to confess to herself. Womanly instinct had fathomed the mystery of Oswald's desertion. She had looked back, and remembered, and weighed looks and tones of his, which had but faintly impressed her at the time, but which now, considered by the light of his subsequent conduct, had fullest significance. His heart had gone astray, and it was to Cynthia,

her father's wife, that truant heart had wandered —not with deliberate sinfulness; she could not believe him deliberately wicked. The tempter had set this snare for him, and he had weakly yielded. Cynthia's childish beauty, Cynthia's innocently simple ways, had allured him from the straight path of righteous dealing. He had struggled, poor sinner, fought and striven with the Evil One, and, finding the powers of darkness too strong for him, had turned and fled. It was wisest, it was best so.

Naomi loved him with so fondly indulgent an affection—a passion so unselfish—that she could find it in her heart to forgive him for having fallen away from her. She could pardon and pity him, though he had taken the light and glory out of her life, and left her world empty as an exhausted crater. But she could not so easily forgive Cynthia. Her father's wife should have been above suspicion, unassailable by temptation. And if Cynthia had not shown some tokens of weakness, Oswald would surely have been stronger. Cynthia, the wandering waif, cherished and garnered by the most generous of men, should have loved her husband with a love strong enough to shield her from the possibility of temptation; and yet in this false wife's pallid face, in the heavy eyes and sad, set lips, Naomi read the secret of a guilty sorrow. She, Cynthia, grieved for the absent one—she shared Naomi's sacred grief, she intruded upon that privileged domain of fond regret. The knowledge of this silent distress made Naomi angry and unforgiving.

One evening in the beginning of August, soon after Joshua's reading of "Werther," Naomi walked alone in Pentreath Wood. Such lonely evening rambles were her melancholy comfort, and this wood her favorite resort. Her wild garden had been neglected of late. It was too narrow for her grief. Jim, or Aunt Judith, or Cynthia might intrude upon her at any moment. But here, in this wide, shadowy wood, she was really alone—no one to spy out her tears or offer humiliating pity—no companions but the stars high up yonder, shining through over-arching beech and oak—the unknown life in brambles and under-wood, dry fern, and last year's leaves, which were stirred now and then mysteriously by those unfamiliar creatures that make merry at nightfall, or the distant hoot of some ancient owl, sounding ghost like in the dimness, or the red-brown cattle lying in the grassy hollows and sheltered corners, restful but unsleeping.

Here Naomi could nurse her grief as she pleased. She could bring forth her sorrow from its hiding-place, and cherish and caress it as if it had been a fondly loved child. Here she recalled Oswald's looks and tones, when she had believed him true, and lived over again the happy days in which he had been all her own; the time before Cynthia came and brought sorrow and shameful thoughts into Joshua Haggard's peaceful home. Every turn and wind of the dear old wood, every veteran oak, ferny bank, and knoll and hollow, was associated with that lost lover, and aided fancy to conjure up his image. Here he had read "Ivanhoe," here "Marmion." Here, in a lazy mood, he had lain stretched at full length, and told her the story of Caleb Williams, and how he had once seen Kean play the part of Sir Edward Mortimer, in "The Iron Chest," at the little theatre in Exeter. Here, leaning against the silvery bark of this giant beech, he had recited Byron's "Isles of Greece"—thrilled with a fervor which was almost inspiration. Oh, happy, irredeemable hours—the dead, departed delights of life!

Here, on this August evening, Naomi walked and meditated. It was a dim and hazy twilight, with a pale new moon shining faintly behind the tree-tops in a sky of translucent gray. The young trees, and the under-wood beneath them, had a ghostly look in this half-light. It might have been a scene made up of shadows.

Bitter, beyond all measure of common bitterness, to remember the days—but a little while ago—when Naomi and her lover had roamed in this very wood, when there was but the red-brown glow of coming foliage on the leafless beech boughs, and the chestnut fans were still unfolded, and the anemones whitened the hollows, and the blue dog-violets smiled up at the blue April sky. Cynthia had been with them always —the fair young sick-nurse in her neat gray gown and little Quaker cap. She had been with them sharing all their talk; and Naomi had nothing suspected, nothing doubted. It was only now that she understood the drama in which her own part had been so sad a one—only now that she could fathom the meaning of that low, subdued voice, those pauses of silence, and lapses into dreamy thoughtfulness, which had marked Oswald's manner during this time.

"It was then he began to care for her," she told herself. "God help and pardon them both! I do not believe that either entered deliberately upon this path of sin. But if Cynthia saw that he was so weak, so wicked, she ought to have left the Grange at once; she ought never to have seen him again. It was her duty."

Easy enough to say this, but a moment's reflection showed Naomi that it would have been no easy thing to do. To avoid temptation thus would have been to create a scandal. And Oswald had made no confession of his weakness. Those subtle differences in his tones and looks may have been meaningless for Cynthia.

"No," thought Naomi, with a burst of very human passion, "she must have understood them; his words and looks must have been clear to her, for she loves him."

Pondering thus—as she had pondered on many an evening since her lover's desertion, traveling over and over again the same sad pathway of thought—Naomi came to the skirt of the wood, and from the wood into the park, where the trees stood far apart, and the smooth sward rose and fell in gentle undulations. She could see the house from this point. How lonely it looked, how deserted—a gloomy dwelling that might have been so bright!

"I was to have been a fine lady, with a drawing-room, and a conservatory," Naomi said to herself, full of bitterness; "and coaches were to come rolling over that gravel drive, where the weeds grow so thickly. And there were to be lights in all those windows; and music sounding in the night—a life like fairy-land. Poor Oswald! How he used to talk of our future! And he was true then—he meant all he said. Oh, my dearest, my dearest!" she murmured, with clasped hands; "I wanted no lights or music; I wanted no grand visitors—no bliss other than

this common world can give, while I had you. My life would have been all happiness, had Providence made you the poorest of God's poor, and our home a hovel, and our days full of toil, if we had only spent them together—if you had only been true to me!"

She stopped, with tears rolling down her cheeks —tears that gushed forth unawares at the sweet, sad thought of what life might have been. She stood looking straight before her with those tear-dimmed eyes, looking at the dull old house.

Not a gleam of light? Yes, the heavy hall door opens slowly, and she sees the dim lamp within. A figure comes out of the dusky porch, and walks at a leisurely pace along the broad gravel terrace at the side of the house.

Naomi gave a faint, awe-stricken cry, as if she had seen a ghost—a cry so faint that it could not reach the ears of yonder solitary muser, pacing the gravel path with bent head. She turned and hurried back to the wood, and was quickly lost in the darkness of that green mystery of oak and beech; and then, secure from observation, walked slowly home, meditating upon what she had seen.

He had come back; he who had said his path of life was to lie in other lands; he, the self-banished exile, the new Childe Harold. Why had he come? and was it for long? How was it that the village had not been aware of his coming, and made his return common talk—an inevitable consequence of such knowledge? Had he any purpose in returning secretly—in hiding himself from his little world? Naomi was perplexed and troubled by these unanswerable questions.

It was late when she entered the little parlor at home. Prayers were over, and the family were seated in the usual formal array round the temperately furnished board. The huge junk of single Gloucester, about the size and shape of one of those granite slabs which bestrew the path of the adventurous tourist who tempts the perils of the Loggan Rock, stood up in the centre of the table, like a family idol, round which the family had assembled for evening worship. The brown beer-jug—simulating a portly figure in a three-cornered hat—occupied its accustomed corner. Everything was precisely as Naomi remembered it in her earliest childhood. The quiet monotony of life had never been disturbed by new crockery, or a change of form and color in the vulgar details of existence. The Druids could hardly have lived more simply than this Methodist household.

And now that the mainspring of life was broken, this sordid sameness seemed odious, nay, almost unbearable. Naomi looked at the familiar home picture with a shudder. Affection gave it no beauty in her eyes to-night. A fair enough picture of domestic peace from the outside, if there had been any one in the street to contemplate that candle-lit circle through the window; some vagabond, perchance, homeless, and deeming that there must be bliss in a home. Yet, save honest Jim, who sat munching his bread-and-cheese with a countenance of equable discontent, there was no member of that family circle whose bosom was not racked by anguish or passion.

"Half-past nine, Naomi!" exclaimed Joshua, looking up reproachfully, as his daughter came into the room. "The first time I've read prayers without you since I can remember—except when you've been ill. What has kept you so long?"

"I've been frightened," answered Naomi, looking not at her father, but at Cynthia. "I was in Pentreath Park, and I thought I saw a ghost."

"A ghost, Naomi? I thought you were too good a Christian to believe in such folly."

"Saul saw a ghost," interjected Jim, with his mouth full of lettuce, "and you wouldn't say that was folly."

"Saul lived in days when God taught his children by miracles."

"And if Providence chose to send a ghost to Combhollow, who's to hinder it?" cried Jim, with unconscious irreverence. "I'm sure ghosts are wanted—people are wicked enough. I dare say the Cork Lane ghost would have done a deal of good if a pack of busy-bodies hadn't made her out an impostor. And there are the ghosts that worried the Wesley family. You can't fly in their faces."

"Sit down to your supper, Naomi," said Joshua, rebuking Jim's flippancy by a grave disregard which was more crushing than remonstrance; "you ought not to be wandering about so late of nights. It is not respectable."

Naomi sighed, and made no answer. Those weary ghosts in Dante's nether world, wandering in their circles of despair, might have felt very much as she did, had any accuser charged them with levity or unseemly conduct. She looked at her father with eyes full of a wondering reproachfulness, as if she would have said, "Can you, who know my burden, upbraid me?"

"What about the ghost?" asked Aunt Judith, sweeping her crumbs into a neat little heap with the back of her knife. "Don't tell me it was Mr. Trimmer. Sally had the impudence to hint at his walking, only last Sunday night; but I think I stopped her tongue."

Mr. Trimmer was a retired miller who had died of dropsy "up street," and who was supposed to be not quite comfortable in his mind about the division of the property which he had left behind him, about which there had been some squabbling among his nephews and nieces. This disagreement of the miller's heirs had given rise to the report of ghostly visitations—of an erratic and inconsecutive character—on the part of the miller.

"I won't swear to his having walked," cried Jim, eagerly, "but there have been groans heard down at the red mill. That I can vouch for, because Joe Davis's father heard it coming home from his work last Saturday night."

"Why, Trimmer hadn't worked the mill for ten good years," exclaimed Aunt Judith. "What could he want down there?"

"To look after the money he'd buried," replied Jim, with conviction. "You may depend that what he's left behind him above ground isn't half what he's left beneath."

"Was it Trimmer?" asked Judith, letting her natural love of the marvelous get the better of common sense.

"No," answered Naomi: "it was nothing but fancy, I dare say. The mists were rising—white clouds of vapor that looked like the shadows of the dead."

"Let there be no more said upon the subject," said Joshua, sternly. "It is sinful to dwell upon such folly. Eat your supper, Naomi, and let there be none of these evening wanderings."

It is not easy to eat when one is bid. The home-made bread, sweet as it was, seemed bitter to Naomi's parched mouth. She drank a long draught of water and held her peace, and there was silence till the end of the meal. Naomi lifted her downcast eyelids once or twice, and looked at Cynthia with thoughtful scrutiny. There was nothing in the young wife's countenance to betray any knowledge of Oswald's return to the Grange. There was only that settled sadness which had become a part of the sweet face lately.

"She will know very soon, I dare say," thought Naomi, bitterly. "It is not to see me that he has come back."

Her heart burned with indignation, as if Cynthia had by some unholy witchcraft, some subtle silent exercise of womanly artifice, lured the false lover back to her net. She could not give her credit for innocence, or even for helpless, unconscious yielding to a guilty love. No, it was her fault that Oswald had gone astray. Had she been strong in purity of heart, Oswald would never have been so weak.

When the time came for bidding good-night, and Cynthia approached with her pretty, pleading look and rose-bud mouth ready to kiss, Naomi turned away from her step-mother with a stony face and left the room in silence. Cynthia looked after her wonderingly, but said not a word. She knew but too well what it meant. Oswald's treachery had made a lasting breach between them. Her only hope was that Joshua had not seen that cruel repulse. But he had seen it, and formed his own conclusions thereupon.

CHAPTER XXIV.

FULL OF SCORPIONS.

"WILL he come—will he come to see me?"

This was the question which Naomi asked herself when she rose next morning, to see another peerless summer day smiling at her, but to feel none of the joy of harvest; only a heart as dull and desolate as if she had awakened to find herself amidst some dwindled hope-forsaken land hemmed round by cruel arctic seas. What was summer to her, or harvest, or all the common joys of life—joys that gladden hearts which are not broken?

All through the feverish, wakeful night the same doubt had agitated Naomi's mind. Might not her lover have repented and returned to her? So blessed a thing was just possible. He had loved her dearly once: surely that old love could not die. He had often told her that love was deathless. Fancy had gone astray, perhaps, and love had been true all the time. Absence had taught him that she was still dear. Oh, how tenderly she would have welcomed the returning prodigal, could she but be sure of his repentance, sure that her love could even yet make him happy! Thus argued hope; but despair took the other side. He had come back in secret, for some evil purpose. He had come back to see Cynthia.

This day would show if he meant well or ill.

If well, he would not fear to show himself at Mr. Haggard's house. He would come, and make peace with his betrothed. Oh, long hours of waiting, between morning prayer and noontide —hours in which the simple household tasks were performed while the girl's heart was given to alternate hope and despair! Would he come? Would he prove true and good, despite of all that had gone before?

Noon came, and dinner, and afternoon, and he did not appear. Hope died in Naomi's breast. She went about the house listlessly, yet was too restless to sit long at her work. It happened to be a busy afternoon in the drapery department, and Aunt Judith was too well employed behind the counter to observe her niece's idle moving to and fro, or else there would have been the small bitterness of that maiden lady's lectures superadded to the great bitterness of Naomi's despair.

Cynthia and Jim were in the garden. Those two were very friendly just now. The poor little step-mother clung to the honest, outspoken lad, in this time of cloud and brooding storm. Naomi's coldness cut her to the heart. She felt that there was a great gulf between her and her husband. Of Judith's dislike and distrust she was inwardly assured.

But Jim seemed fond of her, and he was of her husband's flesh and blood. The poor little timid soul went out to him in its loneliness.

"Do you really like me, James?" she asked to-day, as they were tying up the carnations in the long garden border, Cynthia's small face shaded by a big dimity sun-bonnet.

"Liking isn't the word, Cynthia," answered the boy. "I'm uncommonly fond of you; and if you'd only summon up a little spirit and make Aunt Judith give up the housekeeping, I should have a still better opinion of you. Why should she stint us to one or two puddens a week, and those as hard as brickbats? and a fruit-pasty once in a blue moon, when the garden's running over with gooseberries and may-dukes? It isn't her place to order the puddens: it's yours. It was all very well to be trodden under her foot when we were orphans, but you're our mother now, and you ought to stand by us. Why don't we have bacon and fried potatoes for breakfast, like Christians? She'd let a whole side go rusty before she'd give us the benefit of it. And my father sits at the table and starves himself, and quotes William Law to show that starvation is a Christian duty. I've no patience! I'm sure I wonder I've grown up the fine young man I am, upon such short commons."

Jim came into the house half an hour later, and found Naomi in the parlor. She was standing by the window, idle, her work in her hands, staring absently at the bend in the road yonder, by which Oswald used to come on Herne, the hunter. Poor old faithful Herne! the tears came into her eyes when she thought of him. He had been turned out to grass, and she had seen him looking over gaps in the hedge, a haggard, unkempt beast. She had called him, and coaxed him, and held out her hand to invite his approach, and he had come with a shy, sidelong gait close up to her, and then shot off like a sky-rocket before she could caress his honest gray nose.

Jim burst into the parlor like a whirlwind.

"I thought you was fond of those hart's-tongues I got for you?" he exclaimed, breathless with indignation.

"So I am, Jim, very fond of them."

"Then you'd better get a bit of black stuff out of the shop and make yourself a mourning-gown."

"Are they dead?"

"They're as near it as any thing in the fern line can be—as yellow as the inside of a poached egg, and as dry as chips. How long is it since you've been in the wilderness?"

"I don't know; a few days—a week, perhaps."

"You're a nice young woman for an industrious brother to toil for! The place is as dry as an ash-pit. What's the use of my getting you fine specimens, if this is the way you treat 'em? There's the parsley fern crinkled up like a bit of whity-brown paper. Cynthia and I have been giving the things a good dousing, but they've been shamefully neglected. I should have thought you could have found time to look after them. You're not in the business," concluded Jim, with a superior air.

"Don't be cross, Jim," faltered Naomi, gently. "It was wrong of me to neglect the ferns that you've taken such trouble to set for me, but I have not done any gardening lately; I have not been feeling well enough—"

And here Naomi burst into tears—Naomi with whom tears were so rare.

Jim had his arms round her in a moment, and was hugging her like an affectionate brute.

"There, there, there!" he cried; "don't fret. I oughtn't to have been so cross. You've had your troubles lately—father going and breaking off your marriage without rhyme or reason. Nobody ever heard of such tyranny. I'll be sworn I dare say William Law, the father of Methodism, is at the bottom of it. Suffering is good for us. It's blessed to deny ourselves. And my poor little sister mustn't marry the man she loves! Cheer up, Naomi; it will all come right in the end, I dare say, though things are going crooked now. Don't worry about the wilderness. Cynthia and I are making things tidy —weeding and watering, and training the creepers over the rock-work. You can come down and look at us, if you like. It will cheer you up a bit!"

"I'll come presently, Jim, dear," answered Naomi, drying her tears.

"Be sure you do," said Jim; and then he hurried back to his work.

Naomi sat in the parlor for a quarter of an hour or so. She shed no more tears, but sat with dry eyes looking straight before her.

Why had he come back? Not for her—oh, not for her!

The day was nearly done. She would hear the rattling of tea-cups in the pantry. Sally was getting her tray ready. That meant half-past four o'clock. Naomi rose, with a long, heavy sigh, and went out into the garden. It was to please her brother she went. There was no pleasure or interest for her in earth or sky.

She walked slowly down the long straight garden path, where the clove carnations and double stocks were in their glory, and through the little orchard to the wilderness. Jim was hard at work—the perspiration running down his forehead, his coat off, and his shirt-sleeves rolled up to the elbow—dividing great tufts of primroses and overgrown hart's tongue. Cynthia was on her knees weeding, a pretty picture of youth and fairness in the yellow sunlight.

Naomi stood and looked at her. What was the charm in her which had lured that false lover? Could the eye of another woman see the bait that had won weak and fickle man—the enchantment which had wrought alike upon the strong man in his meridian of knowledge and wisdom, and the youth in his folly?

Yes, the charm revealed itself even to the cold eye of a resentful rival. It was not so much absolute beauty which allured in this nameless waif, as a soft and gracious innocence, a flower-like loveliness, that stole upon mind and heart unawares.

She charmed the senses, as roses and lilies do in the early morning, while the dew is still on them. She appealed to the eye, and held it, like some picture which, in a long gallery, stands out from all other images, and transfixes the spectator. She stole upon the soul like music.

Nor was it this outward charm of perfect fairness and grace only which attracted. The soft lovableness of her disposition accorded with the tender grace of her beauty. She had the clinging affectionateness of a soft and yielding nature; a humility of spirit which made her ready to reverence the strong; a tenderness of heart which inclined her to pity the weak. In one word, she was lovable—a woman created to be adored.

Naomi stood and looked at her, full of bitter thoughts. For the first time in her life she envied the gifts of another. She felt all the good things that Providence had given her of no account when weighed against the bewitchment of fair looks and winning ways.

"How wicked I am growing!" she thought, shocked at her own bitterness.

"There!" exclaimed Jim, pulling down his shirt-sleeves; "I think I've done a tidy afternoon's work. You'll have oceans of primroses next year, sis."

"If they don't all die," said Naomi, not hopefully. "Do you think it's quite the right time for moving them?"

"Primroses!" cried Jim. "As if you could hurt a primrose! I know what I'm about, sister. They wouldn't take any harm by my moving if they were the delicatest flowers in a hothouse."

He pulled on his coat, put away trowel and rake, and came out of the wild garden into the orchard. Cynthia rose too, with an absent-minded sigh, and followed him.

"Now look here, little step-mother," he said, in his patronizing way, "you'd better go in and make yourself tidy for tea, while I show Naomi what I've done to her primroses."

Cynthia obeyed without a word, and left them. Jim tucked his sister's arm under his own, and began to perambulate the orchard.

"What's the matter, Jim?"

"Cheer up, old woman! I've got some good news for you. I won't see you trampled upon, not if I can help it. I won't have your early affections blighted, and young Pentreath sent to the right about, if I can prevent it. Don't be afraid, sis. I'll stand by you."

"Jim, what do you mean!" cried Naomi, piteously.

"I've got a letter for you."

Naomi's heart leaped with sudden overwhelming joy. He had written. Thank God, thank God! She was not utterly forgotten.

"A letter, Jim?" clasping his arm rapturously. "How did it come?"

"How should it come? He brought it himself, of course."

"And gave it to you? You saw him? Dear, dear Jim, tell me all about it. How is he looking—ill or well?"

"White and fagged; as if he'd been going to the—well, you know—all the time he's been in London. I only just caught a glimpse of him above the wall."

"And he gave you the letter—"

"No; that's the fun of it. He didn't see me. It was just as I came back to the wilderness after I left you in the parlor. Cynthia was sitting reading on the bench yonder. Just as I came to the gate, I saw a pale face look over the wall, and then a white hand went up and threw something over. It fell among the ferns, not a yard from step-mother. But she never saw it; that was the lark. Her nose was in her book—poetry or some such trash. I gave a whistle, and off went my gentleman like a shot—scared away."

"And what became of the letter?"

"Why, I picked it up unbeknown to Cynthia when her back was turned. It's wrapped round a stone. There's no address on it—too artful for that—but I knew the party it was meant for."

"Are you sure it's for me?" asked Naomi, trembling a little. That exceeding great joy fainted in her heart. A letter unaddressed, and thrown at Cynthia's feet!

"Of course it's for you. Step-mother sat with her back to the wall, and her head and shoulders smothered in that great sun-bonnet of hers. He might easy take her for you."

"Give me the letter, dear," said Naomi, with suppressed eagerness.

He handed her a little parcel—a goodish-sized pebble packed neatly in a sheet of letter-paper, and carefully sealed with the well-known coat of arms which had hung a year ago from the squire's fob.

"Ain't you going to read it?" demanded Jim, as his sister stood looking at the packet.

"Not just yet, dear. I had rather read it when I'm quite alone."

"Oh my!" ejaculated Jim. "For fear some of the love should run over, like clouted cream that hasn't set properly. What it is to be in love! Well, sis, I'll leave you to the enjoyment of your love-letter while I go and clean myself."

He ran off, leaving Naomi alone in the orchard. Fear held her hand for a moment, though hope whispered that this little packet was full of comfort and sweetness. It had fallen at Cynthia's feet, said fear. Was it not possible that it had been meant for Cynthia?

She broke the seal and carefully unfolded the sheet of Bath post—the fair, wide paper which our forefathers used when letters were worth having.

It was a letter of three pages, written by a hand which betrayed its owner's emotion. Naomi's eyes shone with an angry light as they hurried over the lines. There was a name written here and there—a hateful name that told her the letter was not for her. "My Cynthia. My

Cynthia—mine by that mutual love which is our mutual sorrow."

"Villain and traitor!" cried Naomi, with a burst of passion which transformed her.

Had he stood before her in that moment, and she armed, she could have stabbed him. This Naomi, who could have laid down her life to accomplish some good and great thing, was—for this one instant—capable of murder.

Such cruel perfidy, such heartless treachery, such shameless iniquity, outraged her sense of justice. It seemed to her as if Heaven had created a monster.

She had not yet read the letter, but Cynthia's name stood out from the tremulous lines as if it had been written in fire. Slowly, with her hand pressed against her burning forehead in the effort to keep brain and understanding clear, she addressed herself to the hateful task.

She would know the lowest deep of man's infamy: a lover who could forsake his sworn love; a man, calling himself gentleman, who could try to seduce a good man's wife.

The letter was incoherent, passionate—despair's foolish appeal against fate:

"I must see you once again—yes, dearest, at whatever hazard to you or me—at whatever cost. I have made up my mind to live and die far away from the dear place that holds you. The wide, bleak, barren sea shall roll between me and my beloved. I am going to America: that is far enough, surely! Death could part us no wider than the Atlantic. I shall look at that great sea and think how the green waves roll up the golden sands of home and kiss your feet; how the white spray blows into your hair and caresses you like a cloud; and I am no Jove to be in that cloud, love. I shall be severed from you forever. But before I sail for the other side of the sea, I must see you once more: yes, Cynthia—my Cynthia—mine by that mutual love which is our mutual sorrow—I must see you once more, clasp your hand, and say farewell! bless you, and be blessed by you. Trust me, trust me, my beloved, with but one meeting. There shall no evil word be spoken: you shall not even hear me complain against fate. I will only take your hand in mine and say good-bye. Vain blessing, you will say; but, dearest love, the memory of that moment will comfort me in weary days and nights to come. I would but know that you pity, and forgive, and pray for me; and that, if Fate had willed it so, you might have loved me. It will be like a parting between two friends when one is doomed to die. I shall think the executioner is waiting at the door, and the death-bell ready to toll. Oh, dear love, by thy tender and pitying heart, I adjure thee, grant me this last prayer! Thy Werther, despairing unto death, pleads to thee!

"I have come back to Devonshire for this only—to see thee once more. I have taken my passage for New York. All is settled; nothing can alter my decision. I am not weak enough, or guilty enough, to remain within reach of thee. I thought that in London I might forget, but your image followed me everywhere I went; in crowds or in solitude you were always near; nothing but a life-long exile can cure my wound or expiate my guilt.

"Let me see you, beloved one. I shall contrive to convey this letter to you by some means in the course of to-day. Meet me to-morrow afternoon, and to-morrow night, by the coach which starts from The First and Last at eight o'clock, I will leave Combhollow forever. Your afternoons are always free: I shall wait for you, from two to four o'clock, on the common beyond Matcherly Wood, near the old shaft. It is rather far for you to come, but I think it is the safest place for our meeting. No one ever comes there but a stray cow-boy in quest of his cattle.

"Come, dearest; it is the only boon you can bestow upon one whose heart you have broken unawares. Yours till death, Oswald."

This was the letter. Naomi read it slowly to the end, then folded it neatly and put it in her pocket.

A shrill shriek from the house door roused her from abstraction.

"Naomi, are you coming?" at the top of Aunt Judith's high pitched voice.

"We never do have our teas like Christians, nowadays!" complained Miss Haggard as Naomi came into the parlor breathless. "Have you seen another ghost, girl?" she asked, staring at her niece. "You look as white as a yard of calico. Here's your father not home to his tea again; that makes the third time this week."

"He is attending to his duty, no doubt, aunt."

"Who says he isn't? But I wish he could contrive to combine duty with punctuality at meals. I hate a disorderly table."

Joshua came in just as they had finished their meal. His large cup of tea had been put on one side for him, covered with a saucer. He sat down in his arm-chair and drank his tea in silence. He was looking exhausted and weary.

"I am afraid you have had a hard afternoon's work, Joshua," Cynthia said, sitting down beside him thoughtfully.

"I have been in the house of death, my dear; that is always trying to weak humanity. And I have walked a long way in the sun."

Naomi sat by the window darning Jim's stockings. Aunt Judith washed her tea things, and then retired to the drapery department. Joshua leaned back in his chair with closed eyes. Cynthia took up a book; it was Milton's "Paradise Lost," one of the few imaginative works of which Mr. Haggard did not disapprove.

They sat thus for some time, in a silence only broken by the lowing of distant cattle and the gentle lapping of summer waves upon the pebbly beach. Then Jim looked in at the door and called Cynthia. She rose quickly and went out to him, and Naomi was alone with her father.

This was the opportunity she had been waiting for. After reading Oswald's letter, she had come to a desperate resolve. These lofty natures have a touch of hardness in their composition sometimes. A sense of immunity from sin and weakness makes them stony-hearted judges of erring humanity. Oswald's wrong-doing had awakened that latent element of hardness in Naomi's nature. She thought she was only doing her duty in taking desperate measures. Or was it jealousy which put on a mask and called itself justice? She took the letter out of her pocket and looked at her father. He was not asleep, only resting with closed eyes.

"Father," said Naomi, in a low voice, "here

is a letter which has come to me by accident, and which I think you ought to see. It is from Oswald to your wife."

She put the letter into his hand and left him: she dared not await the issue of her act.

CHAPTER XXV.

"FAREWELL, CONTENT."

JOSHUA read the letter slowly, every word going to his heart like the thrust of a knife. He had been told that a man had addressed a confession of guilty love to his wife, and the knowledge that this thing had been had preyed upon him like a corroding poison. But, even in all he had suffered since Judith's revelation, he had never realized the greatness of the wrong as he did now with the betrayer's letter in his hand, the audacious confession deliberately set down in black and white.

"He dared to write this!" he muttered. "He dared—to my wife! O God! how low she must have fallen in his esteem before he wrote this letter!"

Here was the cruelest sting. Could Oswald have penned this passionate appeal had he not been sure of a hearing? Did not this letter imply that he knew himself beloved? Ay, there were the abhorrent words burning the paper, "Our mutual love, which is our mutual sorrow!" This villain made very sure that he was loved. Must he not have been so assured before he dared to ask an honest woman to grant him a secret meeting?

Joshua Haggard sat with the letter in his hand, and a look in those dark eyes of his—a lurid fire under black, lowering brows—which would have struck terror to the hearts of his admiring flock could they have seen their shepherd in his lonely agony. What was he to do—how find revenge great enough for this gigantic wrong? Revenge was not the thought in his mind; retribution, justice, rather, was what he demanded. He felt himself like Orestes, privileged—nay, appointed—to slay. The Furies might come afterward, but in this present hour it seemed to him that he might claim this man's blood.

That gentleman-like institution, the duel, was in full force in Joshua's day. Had he been a man of the world, nothing would have been clearer or more easy than his course. But for the shepherd of souls, the preacher of peace, to take up the sword! Would it not be the renunciation of those principles for which he had lived? How often from his pulpit had he anathematized the slayer of his brother's blood, hurled his thunders against that corrupt society in which murder could be deemed honorable!

He sat with the letter in his hand, and all was dark before him. Could he ever trust his wife again—believe in her purity, cherish with a fond and almost fatherly pride that sweet and girlish innocence, that utter ignorance of evil, the freshness and beauty of life's morning, which had first won his love? Never more: never more! His Eve had gathered the fatal fruit: the serpent had lifted his venomous crest from among the flowers: the glory of life's paradise had faded. Never more could he love or worship or trust.

Henceforth he must hold her loathly. If this letter had reached her, how would she have received it? Would she have listened to the tempter's pleading? Would she have stolen in secret to meet him, to hear his poisonous vows, to pity his weak, unmanly lamentings?

"I should like to know that," he said to himself. "I should like to know how she would have answered this letter."

And then it occurred to him that he might easily put her to the test. The seal had been broken, but the paper round it was untorn. It would be easy to reseal the letter, making the second seal just a little larger than the first. And Cynthia would not examine the outside of the letter too closely.

He lighted a candle and resealed the violated letter, then paused for a moment or so, wondering how he should get it conveyed to his wife. "She shall find it somewhere," he thought. "Her guilty conscience will tell her it is from her lover. He may have written to her before, perhaps. God only knows the greatness of her sin—God, who made us, and knows the blackness of our unregenerate hearts. And I thought that there could be one exempt—one free from humanity's universal taint. Fool, fool, fool!"

He went slowly upstairs to the bed-chamber, the airy, orderly room, with its substantial, old-fashioned furniture, and look of homely comfort—the room that had once been his father's. There hung the old grocer's turnip-shaped silver watch on the mahogany stand upon the mantel-piece, ticking with as lusty a beat as when its sturdy proprietor carried it in his ample drab-cloth fob. There were the samplers which testified to the industry and skill of Joshua's mother and Joshua's wife—the pyramidal apple-trees innocent of leaves—the angular figures of Adam and Eve in the garden, with a curly serpent standing on tiptail between them. The evening sun shone into the room, and glorified the gaudy sunflowers on the chintz bed furniture, and glittered on the brazen handles of Joshua's escritoire. A bowl of freshly gathered roses and carnations on the table perfumed all the room. Joshua knew whose busy hand had plucked the flowers, and the sight of them smote him with an aching pain. Oh, wounded heart, for which every new thought was a new torture!

The escritoire stood open, and there was "The Sorrows of Werther," lying where he had placed it after his long night of waking. There had been no need for Cynthia to hide the book any more. It had told its story.

Joshua's sombre glance lighted on the volume. "Accursed book that taught them to sin!" he exclaimed: "they might never have fathomed the wickedness of their own hearts but for thee."

This was hard upon the innocent and noble Charlotte, the misguided but generous Werther.

A thought full of bitterness and anger came into Joshua's mind as he looked at "Werther." He would put Oswald's letter between the leaves of that detested book. She would find it there, be felt assured: the book was her own love-story, it talked to her of her lover. He could fancy her hanging over the pages—sucking poisonous sweetness from every line. Werther and Oswald were, in Joshua's mind, one.

He put the letter in the book, and was going slowly down-stairs, when he stopped, with his hand upon the banisters, and pondered for a minute or so.

The thought came over him that he could not pray with his household, or teach, or exhort them to-night. It was as if an evil spirit were at his shoulder forbidding him that holy and familiar exercise. He felt that it would have been a kind of profanation to lay his hand upon the Bible, that anchor of his life, which had never before seemed insufficient mooring for his wind-driven bark.

"Not to-night," he muttered to himself—"not to-night."

He called over the stairs to his daughter, who had just come in from the garden.

"Tell your aunt to read a chapter and a psalm, Naomi," he said; "I am too ill to come down-stairs again to-night."

Naomi hurried to him, full of apprehension.

"Dearest father, what is the matter? Can I do any thing? can I get you any thing?"

Conscience smote her. Why had she afflicted him by the sight of that wicked letter? It would have been better to have taken it to Cynthia and spoken words of Christian reproof and warning. Why had she made him, her dearest upon earth, to suffer?

"No, my dear, you can do nothing. It is the mind that is ill at ease, not the body. My soul is too dark to hold communion with her God. The blow has been heavy."

"Dear father, it was so wicked of me to show you the letter—an evil, revengeful act. And, after all, the sin may not be so deep as it seems to us. They are but children—weak, foolish, easily led astray. Let us pity and forgive them."

"I may come—some day when I am old and doting—to pity her. I can never forgive him." He put his daughter aside, went into his bed-room, and shut the door. Naomi dared not follow him. She went slowly down-stairs greatly troubled.

It is one thing to launch the thunder-bolt, and another to survey the ruin the bolt has made.

Joshua Haggard turned his face to the wall and gave himself up to darkest thoughts. He rose soon after day-break, and his first look was directed to "Werther." The letter was gone. Yes; there was nothing now between the pages but a few faded rose-leaves and withered fern tendrils which marked a favorite passage here and there.

He looked from the book to his wife, lying with her face turned from the light, and one round white arm, dimpled like a young child's, thrown above her head. Was she sleeping placidly with that guilty secret in her breast, or only pretending to sleep? He could not tell.

"She is all dissimulation," he thought, "fairest seeming, sweetest show—bitter as ashes within."

<hr />

CHAPTER XXVI.

"WE TWO STOOD THERE, WITH NEVER A THIRD."

In the sultry August afternoon—earth glorious in the full power of the sunshine—Oswald Pentreath went up to Matcherly Common. It was a long walk and a hot one; but in this land of beauty there were many welcome spots of shade—cool lanes shadowed by tangled greenery, natural arcades of oak and hawthorn, wild apple and elder-berry, from which he could look out on the glittering sea, almost intolerable in its sunlit splendor. There was the wood to cross; a deep and cool retreat, where interwoven boughs made summer days seem a perpetual even-song. Only here and there stole a shaft of vivid light through the beechen branches, while here and there the ruddy fur of a squirrel flashed like a flying gleam of color through the gloom.

Oswald walked slowly, his hands clasped behind his back, giving himself up to the soft influence of the scene and hour, and thinking of Cynthia.

Would she grant his prayer? Would she meet him? Love and hope said yes—and the thought of the meeting was rapture, though despair lay beyond it. He was to die to-night—or at least all of him that made life worth having—but he was to be happy first; happy for the briefest flash of time in which he could hold her in his arms and press one kiss upon her innocent brow, and bless her and leave her.

The thought that his letter might reach the wrong hands had not occurred to him. He had seen Cynthia sitting in the wilderness, and had thrown his letter almost at her feet. Jim's approach had made him retreat rather suddenly, but it had never struck him that Cynthia might not see the letter and that Jim might.

The common was on high ground rising above the wood—a broad tract of undulating land clothed with furze, and with a pool of water here and there, just like that stretch of heath far away, where Joshua Haggard had found his second wife. The mines, whose deserted shafts disfigured this billowy expanse of golden bloom, had never been worked within the memory of man. They had yielded well enough in their day, had made some men rich and ruined others; and there stood the tall shafts, wide apart across the common, like sentinel towers on the coast of a golden sea.

Cynthia was there. Oswald found her sitting on a yellow bank, the base of the abandoned shaft, sitting with a book open in her lap trying to read. She started up, as he came toward her, with a frightened look, as if his coming had been a surprise to her, and stood before him very pale and with clasped hands.

"Dearest, best, how shall I thank you?" he cried, taking her hands and kissing them, in a rapture of gratitude.

"Do not thank me at all, Oswald—indeed, I am afraid I have done very wrong in coming. You ought not to have asked me; you ought never to have come back to Combhollow, unless it was in your heart to be true to Naomi. Oh, Oswald, why can you not love her as she deserves to be loved, as you did once love her? She is so good, so noble, like my dear husband in all high thoughts. Why can not your heart come back to her? Why should we all be miserable because you are inconstant?"

The poor little soul had come here to say this. She had come with a clear and honest purpose in her mind—come to bring the wanderer back to the path of duty.

"Can a man help his fate?" said Oswald, gloomily. "It is my fate to love you. I shall

CYNTHIA WAS THERE.

love you till I die. But don't be frightened, Cynthia; I will be the cause of misery to none of you. I am going to America; my mind is quite made up on that point."

"And you will break Naomi's heart. If you could see the change in her since you left us, you could not help being sorry."

"I am sorry. My soul is sick with its burden of sorrow. But my heart can not go back to Naomi. It never was hers. I never knew what love meant till I loved you. I made the fatal error of mistaking affection for love. I am sorry for her; sorry that I have wronged so noble a creature; sorry for the loss of that peaceful life which I once thought to share with her. But I can not go back. You might as well ask me to be a child again. The star of my manhood shone upon me when I saw you."

"I wish I were wiser," said Cynthia, sadly; "I wish I could speak as I feel I ought to speak; I might convince you then, perhaps."

"Not if you had the eloquence of Brougham and the wisdom of Bacon. Naomi and I are parted forever, dearest, and at her own desire. It is best that it should be so. Providence has been good to me in loosening a bond that would have made two lives miserable."

And then he said no more about Naomi, but began to talk of himself, and love, and fate, and parting, and despair. Foolish words that have been said so often—empty breath, for the most part, bearing no result upon this earth save idle sorrow and wasted tears, yet which mean so much for the speaker and the one who listens. Cynthia had come there to hear no such passionate complaints and protestations. She had come, intent upon delivering her pious lecture—talking to him of grace and redemption, and the sacred stream which washes away all sin—and winning him back to duty and Naomi. Yet she lingered and heard him. It was the last time; they were parted forever. Who should blame them for this one half-hour, which would stand hereafter like a chasm in the life of each, parting youth and passion from sober age and duty? It could matter to no one that they had met thus, and thus parted.

"You will try to lead a good life?" pleaded Cynthia, when Oswald had told his pitiful story—told how he had honestly striven to forget her, and had failed; "you will cling to the cross? Oh, let me think, when you are far away across that wide, cruel sea, that your soul is safe—that you are one of the elect—that I shall meet you where the seas are jasper, and the glory of the Lamb lights the shining streets. You will try to be good, Oswald? Promise me that!"

"I would wear raiment of camel's hair and a hempen girdle for thy sake, dearest."

"You will go to chapel—church is so cold and dull. It has no awakening power, it does not call the lost home. You will seek out some stirring preacher like Joshua, and let him lead you to the sheltering rock, and you will drink the living water and be saved."

Oswald looked down at the fair young face, lifted to his with such utter earnestness; not one thought of earth in the pleading soul—only thorough and implicit belief in something higher and better than earth, a prize to be struggled for and won. In the Greek race called the *lampadrome*, in which the runners carried lighted lamps

in their hands, they were the winners who reached the goal with their lamps still burning. So in the Christian race, the light once quenched, there is but little hope for the runner. It might be safely said of Cynthia, as she looked up at her lover with truthful, innocent eyes, charging him to be thoughtful for eternity, that her lamp still burned with purest light.

Oswald looked down at her through a mist of tears.

"Yes," he said, "for your sake I will try to go to heaven. I have been careless of these things. I meant to let Naomi make me a Christian, but she was to have had all the trouble. But for your sake, to meet you hereafter in a fairer world, to see this dear face again shining amidst the angel faces, I will struggle, I will strive, to make my life worthier and better!"

"God bless and comfort you, and establish you in well doing!" said Cynthia; "and now goodbye. I must not stay a moment longer. I have been too long already."

She looked at her watch. Four o'clock, and she had three miles to walk before five. There would be much astonishment and questioning if she was not punctual in her appearance at the tea-table.

"You will let me walk through the wood with you?"

"No; what would be the use? I have said all I had to say. It would only make us more unhappy."

"It would give us one more hour together," said Oswald—"an hour in paradise."

"The Christian's paradise is to be reached by thornier paths than those through Matchely Wood," answered Cynthia, with a reproving air. "Good-bye, Oswald."

Her earnestness dominated him, weak and childish as she looked, with the fair hair clustering in tiny baby curls under the shady cottage bonnet. Very soft and gentle, but very firm at the same time she seemed, in her simple straightforwardness of purpose; and Oswald obeyed her.

"Since it must be so, then, good-bye," he said, gloomily. "I promised that I would be content with a brief farewell, such as condemned criminals have. You have given me a little sermon into the bargain. I ought to be more than satisfied. Farewell, my best beloved; the seas will roll between us soon, and there will be nothing left for me but the picture and memory of today—nothing but the dreams that haunt my pillow —the sweet unreal presence of her I love."

He took her to his breast; she having no more force to resist those circling arms than a lily to recoil from the hand that gathers it; took her, gently and solemnly, to his heart, and pressed his lips on the white forehead. It was a long and fervent kiss; but if there was passion in it, that passion was no low or sensual feeling, only the passion of a great love and a deep despair.

"Bless you, my darling!" he cried. "God bless you, and guard you, and make all days and paths pleasant and peaceful for you when I am far away!"

And so they parted—forever. Unhappily, there was one who saw the lingering meeting, the fond embrace, the fervent kiss, but could not hear the words that went with them.

—— ◆ ——

CHAPTER XXVII.

"IT IS A BASDISH INTO MINE EYE."

Tranquil and monotonous days hung like a cloud upon the little household of Combhollow. The daily round of labor, of eating and drinking in a spare and Spartan fashion, of praying and preaching, went on with pitiless regularity; but of household joys there were none, of family love but little. A gloomy change had come over Joshua Haggard. He was still the enthusiastic apostle of Primitive Methodism—a man ready to go out and preach the Gospel in wild and barbarous places, to be the bearer of glad tidings to those who despised and rejected such messengers, to be hooted by a brutal rabble, if need were, and driven from village to village at peril of his life, and to escape from his persecutors by the skin of his teeth, as John Wesley did, more than once, in his long and difficult career. He was ready to endure all things. Day by day his discourses grew more fervid, but, alas! more darkly fraught with a message which was not glad tidings—the message of an offended and an avenging God. Christ, the Saviour, was almost excluded from the preacher's exhortations. When he talked of man's Redeemer, it was as of one who turned his face from a sinful world, in which there were very few to be saved. If he had lived in that awful time before the Deluge, when all the earth was peopled with reprobates, he could hardly have been more despairing of humanity's ultimate destiny.

His flock were in no wise offended by this gloomy view of their spiritual condition, although it implied so mean an opinion of their personal merits and conduct. The more vehemently threatening Joshua Haggard's sermons became, the more eagerly the sinners crowded to hear him. It was as if they liked to hear themselves upbraided and denounced. Perhaps every body saw the barbed shaft fly straight to the goal of a neighbor's heart, and did not feel it rankling in his own. When Joshua talked of the frivolity and extravagance of an unregenerate race, Mrs. Pinter thought of Mrs. Mivers's last new bonnet, which was clearly a superfluous and culpable outlay; such bonnet not being due to Mrs. Mivers, from an economic point of view, until Advent Sunday, whereas the lady had flaunted it before the disapproving eyes of the flock early in October. If Joshua denounced sensuality and the vile indulgence of earthly desires, Mrs. Pentelow's thoughts flew at once to the Poldhele family, who were known to have hot suppers—squab pies, and other savory meats—every night in the week. You could see the grease oozing out of their complexions on warm Sunday afternoons, as if digestion as well as respiration were a function of the skin.

From the day when he gave up humanity for lost, and plainly told them so, Joshua's popularity increased in a marked degree. The darker his doctrine grew, the better his congregation liked to hear him. It was not milk for babes which they wanted, but strong meat for men of iron thews and sinews, and women with vigorous constitutions and masculine strength of mind. They liked to hear that the devil was among them, at their shoulders, prompting them to evil, fighting for the mastery of their souls.

"I can see him, I can feel his presence," cried Joshua, in a passion of despairing ecstasy. "He is among us; his sulphurous breath burns me with a foretaste of eternal fire; his whisper hisses in my ear as the serpent's hiss stole into the ear of Eve. He will not loose his hold. He is fighting for the possession of my soul; he is striving to drag me down into the pit. What shall I do to be saved? How shall I win the fight against so omnipotent an adversary—omnipotent to destroy—omnipotent to inthrall and enchain souls? He wants to people hell, my brethren. He is not content with his victory over willing sinners; the profligates and harlots are too pitiful a prey for him! He wants to have the virtuous man in his net. He would have liked to get John Wesley, or George Whitefield, or William Law. He tried for them as he is trying for us. He is a fallen angel himself, and it pleases him to entrap men of high estate —to take the Christian in his toils—to make the white scarlet, and the wool like unto blood."

Naomi heard, and shuddered. Was this her father, who had preached infinite faith in God's mercy, in Christ's redeeming grace? He talked now as if mankind were abandoned as a prey to the Evil One, with no guardian and champion to protect and save—no all-merciful Judge to adjust the balance; as if humanity, forgotten by God, were left to struggle single-handed against the devices of the Great Enemy. Of our ever-interceding Redeemer, of guardian angels, and ministering spirits, and saints who had fought and conquered, Joshua now rarely spoke. He described a world given over to the Prince of Darkness.

Nor was this the only change which Naomi beheld with remorseful grief, believing herself in somewise to blame for this gloomy transformation. In his home as well as in his pulpit, the minister was a new man. It was not in his nature to become a domestic tyrant. He interfered with no one's liberty or comfort, but he sat in his domestic circle like a statue; he banished all cheerfulness by his silent presence; he breathed an atmosphere of gloom.

Even Judith regretted this alteration in her brother's temper, though she had been apt in happier days to think him far too easy and indulgent a father. She, like Naomi, had her moments of remorse, thinking the change her work. Better, perhaps, if she had held her tongue about that foolish young man, and let time and Providence cure him of his folly. Naomi's marriage would have been a feather in the family cap; and although Miss Haggard had been disposed to begrudge her niece this exaltation, it was a trial to receive the condolences of friends whose affected sympathy thinly disguised their inward satisfaction. Yes, taking all things into consideration, Judith was sorry she had not held her peace. She had acted for the best, of course. When had she ever done otherwise? But the worst had come of it, instead of the best.

Cynthia bore her cross and made no murmur, and had neither kindness nor pity from any one except James Haggard, who thought it a hard thing that his pretty young step-mother should lead so dreary a life. She had not even the business and the delightful consciousness of increasing profits to console her, nor the power to restore exhausted nature with a surreptitious handful of figs or pudding-raisins when the dinner had been more than usually Spartan. James was sorry for the "poor little woman," as he called her, and was kind to her always, for which grace she rewarded him with heart-felt affection.

But her husband — the teacher, master, and friend — whom she had loved so dearly, reverenced so deeply, and to whom, even when weak enough to pity and return Oswald's romantic passion, she had always rendered homage and affection, he had withdrawn his favor from her; he loved her no longer; he was doubtless sorry that he had linked himself to so weak and useless a creature.

"What am I in his life?" she asked herself, in deepest despondency. "I can not even keep his house for him; others do that. I sit by his fireside a useless intruder. He will not let me share in his higher life. If I ask him about the books he reads, or talk to him about our religion, I can see a cold and disdainful sneer upon his lip. Sometimes I think that he is getting to hate me."

This thought was poison. Cynthia searched her life to see in what article of it she had offended her husband, and could discover no cause for his anger. That she had erred in letting Oswald love her, in letting her heart go out to him, she knew, and had repented of her sin with many tears; and having bid the sinner an eternal farewell, deemed that error a thing of the past, repented of, and in some wise atoned. She did not believe that jealousy was the cause of her husband's estrangement. Jealousy was allied to love, and her great fear was that Joshua hated her. She did not know that there is a kind of jealousy, and that which has its root in the deepest love, which puts on the garb of hate, and has not seldom culminated in murder—such jealousy as made Othello strike Desdemona before the Venetian emissaries, the passion of strong natures.

She endured her husband's unkindness with a sweet submission which might have softened a sterner temper than Joshua's, and would assuredly have melted him but for the corroding influence of a sleepless jealousy—jealousy of the past—jealousy of a ghost—for the departed Oswald was nothing more than a shade.

Joshua had said no word to his daughter about Oswald's letter. All through that day on which Cynthia went to Matcherly Common, Naomi had been full of anxiety and fear. How would her father act? Would his anger against Oswald take any violent shape? That was assuredly a contingency to be dreaded, an evil she had not foreseen when she gave Joshua the letter. But passion is fatally blind. The harm being done, she could see the possible danger plainly enough.

All through the long summer day she was restless and watchful, fearing she knew not what, or, rather, not daring to tell herself what she feared. The morning wore by very quietly; Cynthia sitting in the parlor sewing. Naomi busy about her usual household labors. She went in and out of the parlor a good many times, and always found Cynthia in the same attitude, working assiduously at that fine stitching which would have tried older eyes.

Had Joshua spoken to his wife about the letter?

Yes. Naomi thought he had. There was one bright spot of color on Cynthia's pale cheek that told of agitation studiously suppressed. Once when Naomi spoke to her she answered absently. She must know something about the letter, Naomi thought.

After dinner, Cynthia went up to her bedroom, and came down again five minutes afterward with her bonnet on. It was a busy afternoon in the shop. Aunt Judith and Jim had returned to their duties, and Joshua had gone out. There was only Naomi in the parlor when Cynthia came down ready for her walk.

"I am going for a long walk, Naomi," she said. "I shall be home by tea-time."

There was no fear of Naomi offering to accompany her step-mother. They had not walked together since Oswald Penreath's departure. Day by day the gulf had been widening.

This walk of Cynthia's set Naomi wondering. Could she be gone to meet Oswald? That seemed of all things most unlikely. Joshua had the letter; it was Joshua who would keep the appointment. And then, O God! who could tell what might be the issue of the meeting!

Naomi went about the house and the garden like a wandering spirit for the next hour, and then it seemed to her that this suspense was beyond endurance. She must follow her father to the old shaft; she made very sure that he had gone there; she must be on the spot or near it, whatever harm was to come. Oh, why had she given him that shameful letter? Blind and wicked rage which prompted so wild an act!

"Did I want to make my father's life miserable, or to bring evil upon Oswald?" she cried. "Yes, I was wicked enough for any thing yesterday; I was mad with anger and jealousy." She put on her bonnet, and went out, unseen even by Sally, who was washing in the cool, brick-floored back kitchen. The sun was blazing upon the neat little town. The white houses were of a dazzling brightness, the sweet-williams and red roses shone like spots of fire, the ruddy glow of the forge looked pale against the sun-glory. Naomi took no heed of the heat; she walked rapidly to the end of the lane that led to Matcherly, and then ran along the shaded narrow way till she came to the edge of the wood. Here she paused for a little, breathless and exhausted. They would be coming homeward by this time, she thought — Cynthia and Oswald, and he who had gone, perhaps, to watch their meeting, or to disturb it. She might come face to face with her false lover. Her heart beat wildly at the thought.

There was one central path through the wood, a clearly defined cattle-track, which she felt assured, would be taken by any one going in the direction of the old shaft. It was easy to skirt this broad, grassy track by a narrow footway that wound through the under-wood, and among the smooth, silvery beech-boles and the rugged, greenish-gray oak trunks. The path ran like a thread through the bracken. By this narrow way Naomi went swiftly till she came to the rising ground that sloped upward to Matcherly Common. Here she chose her post of espial behind a sturdy old oak, bearded with gray lichen, and half strangled with ivy — a Methuselah of trees, from which time had lopped limb after limb, but which still held numerous arms aloft, like a woodland Briareus, and seemed to threaten or denounce surrounding nature. So one might fancy some prophetic Druid transformed into a tree, dumbly prophesying evil to come upon the earth.

Sheltered by this broad trunk, which stood waist-high in hawthorn and bracken, Naomi waited to see her father and Oswald pass by, and to be assured that all was well with them. They would hardly fail to return by the cattle-track. It was the only direct path to Combhollow, and on either side the under-wood was too thick and wild for the perambulation of any thing but the furred and feathered inhabitants of the forest.

She waited for what seemed a long and weary time; then, a little after four o'clock, she saw Cynthia go by, walking slowly. She was very pale, and the white, wan cheeks bore the trace of tears; but she had a resigned look as of one whose soul is not lost to peace.

"She has been to meet him," thought Naomi. "And yet she does not look like a shameless sinner." Then Naomi began to pray that Joshua might not have seen that clandestine, unholy meeting—that he might have been spared the temptation to any evil act.

The time she had to wait for her father's coming hung heavily, so great had become that burden of nameless dread. Yet it was but half an hour after Cynthia had gone by that her husband came slowly along the forest glade, and passed within a yard of the tree behind which his daughter was watching.

She rose as he approached, and stood leaning against the bulky old trunk, gazing at her father's face as she had never looked before at any thing under God's heaven. Never had any other spectacle so thrilled, so frozen her being, as this one view of a familiar countenance. To have looked in the face of the dead would have been less awful.

White to the lips, and with big drops of sweat upon brow and cheek, the mouth rigid, the dark eyes almost hidden under the lowering brows, Joshua, the Christian preacher, the man sure of election and grace, passed under the flickering lights and shadows—like some horrible vision of sin and vengeance passed—and was gone. Naomi leaned against the tree, her hands clasped, her eyes gazing at the empty air, the shaft of afternoon sunlight upon which a million atoms, each a life, danced and sparkled; yet still seeing that blanched and awful face—the face of a man who had come straight from some hideous death-scene—the face of a man burdened with the secret of a crime.

"O God!" cried Naomi, with an overmastering despair, "why didst thou create us, predestined sinners, judged, doomed before we were born? The best of us, the most earnest, the truest, the noblest, given over a prey to the Evil One! My father, even my father, lowest, blackest of sinners!"

She stood in the same attitude, supported by the mossy trunk; stood as in a trance, and saw the sunlight dip lower behind the black branches, and change from gold to rose, from rose to crimson, from deepest red to tenderest purple. She watched these changes in a kind of semi-consciousness and a strange feeling of uncertainty as to her own identity; this Naomi Haggard, leaning against a tree, seeming to her—the actual entity—to be a forlorn and stricken creature

sorely to be pitied. She pitied herself, and was sorry for herself with a half-scornful compassion. And so she waited, in a dreamy watchfulness, till nature gave way, and she sank, worn out, into a heap at the foot of the tree.

Here, faint and exhausted, but not unconscious, she still watched till thick night came down upon the wood, and she heard the owls hooting, and saw the rabbits running within a few feet of her resting-place. Only when the darkness closed round her did she rise and go home, too familiar with the wood to lose her way even in the deep shadow of a woodland night-scene. She went homeward slowly, caring little who might question or wonder at her absence.

And in all the time of her watch she had not seen Oswald Pentreath go by. He might have taken some other path easily enough, doubtless; though the way by which she had taken up her stand was the one direct way. He might have had some motive for taking a circuitous path after he parted from Cynthia—from Cynthia, the temptress—the germ of all this evil that had ingulfed Naomi's little world.

"But would to God that I had seen him!" thought Naomi—"that I had seen him once more in this weary life."

CHAPTER XXVIII.

"AND YET I FEEL I FEAR."

UNDER that quiet surface which life wore in Joshua Haggard's household there were troubled waters.

Naomi had never forgotten the awful look in her father's face that afternoon in the wood. It haunted her in all places and at all seasons. The impression it had made upon her mind would not pass away. What it meant she knew not—dared not shape the thought in her mind—but she was very sure that it meant evil of some kind, evil to her father's soul, wrong to Oswald.

If she could have known for certain that Oswald had carried out the intention set forth in his fatal letter to Cynthia, she would have been, comparatively speaking, at ease and happy. But of this she knew nothing. Whether he had really gone to America, how and when he had left Combhollow, of these things she was ignorant. Cynthia might know, perhaps; but not even to set these anxious fears at rest could Naomi stoop so low as to seek for any information about her lover from the woman for whose sake she had been abandoned. No; if Cynthia knew any thing for certain, the knowledge must remain locked in her breast. Save in the merest outward and ceremonial form, a bare civility in every-day intercourse, there could be no contact between Naomi and her step-mother. The gulf that sundered these two was impassable.

Oswald's letter had stated that he meant to leave Combhollow by the night-coach. He had not gone by that coach, for James Haggard, who was fond of an evening stroll when the shutters were up, and who took a lively interest in other people's business, had watched the departure of the coach on that particular evening, and entertained his family at the silent supper-table with a detailed account of that exciting event in the every-day life of his town.

"There was only one inside, and that was old Mrs. Skevinow, who is going to Exeter to see her married daughter," said Jim: "she had three bandboxes, two umbrellas, a pair of pattens, and a pair of the new-fashioned clogs—she bought 'em of Aunt Judith the day before yesterday—a hamper of pease, a green goose, a basket of eggs, a tin of clouted cream, a red cotton handkerchief full of bullaces, two pasties done up in brown paper, and a pig's cheek. Won't her friends be glad to see her?"

"Who were the outsides?" asked Judith.

Jim ran over the names, checking them off on his fingers.

"Was there no one else in the coach?" asked Naomi, looking at her father, who sat in his usual place with bent brows, neither eating nor drinking.

"No one."

He had not gone by that coach, then, thought Naomi. But presently it occurred to her that Mr. Pentreath's return to Combhollow having been a secret and underhand proceeding, he would hardly care to leave the place under the broad glare of his town's-people's eye. The departure of the coach from The First and Last inn was a public event. To leave by that vehicle, at that point of departure, and not be seen, came hardly within the limits of possibility, unless a man had got himself hidden away in the boot before the spectators assembled. No; if Oswald had made up his mind to travel by that coach, he had doubtless walked on to some quiet spot, to be taken up as the mail passed.

This reflection quieted Naomi's fears in some measure, yet did not set her heart at ease. Her father's face haunted her like some unholy image sent by Satan to suggest evil. What had passed between Joshua and that weak sinner—what violence of upbraiding had the minister used against his wife's lover? That there had been an angry meeting of some kind, Naomi did not doubt. Only a wild indulgence of evil passion, only an utter abandonment of himself to man's omnipresent tempter, could have conjured up such a look in Joshua Haggard's face. The dark mind of the spirit of evil was there reflected. The lurid gleam in those darkly brooding eyes was the red glare caught from the open doors of hell.

There had been hard words spoken, words of hatred and fury, perchance even some open act of violence, a blow struck by that strong hand of Joshua's, who might have spurned the sinner as if he had been the tempter himself, in his base form of serpent. But it was over, and Joshua had doubtless begun to repent of his violence, and Oswald was on his way to a distant world, to begin a new and wiser life.

"God keep him and guard him, and lead him aright," thought Naomi, "and make him a good and great man. I could bear the pang of parting with him, could I feel secure about his happy future here and in the better world."

O empty life from which he had vanished forever! O dreary days which hung upon this young spirit like a burden, and weighed her down to the dust! Yes, verily, to the dust; so that, in her utter weariness, she felt as if it would be a good and pleasant end of all things to lie down in some lonely corner of the land—lie face downward among the fern and wild flowers, and wait for death. Surely the dark angel would take pity upon her, joyless fate, and come and fold her in his sheltering wings, and comfort and cure her.

"There is no other comfort, no other cure," she said, forgetting all the old pious lessons in her despair, forgetting even to do good to others in the sharpness of her pain.

She sought for consolation from no one—not even from honest Jim—who was distressed at seeing such blank, hopeless faces in his home, and was eager, after his rough-and-ready fashion, to administer comfort.

"Come, Naomi, cheer up and be bright, like a sensible girl," he would say. "There's as good fish in the sea as ever came out of it; and though you've missed landing a fine salmon through father's foolishness, you'll have your net full by-and-by, I'll warrant. A good-looking, straight-built lass like you will never want a sweetheart."

"Jim, if you talk to me like that, I shall hate you," cried Naomi. "I shall go single to my grave, and you know it; or if you can think otherwise of me, you're not worthy to be my brother."

"Hoity toity!" cried Jim, "what fine notions run in our family! Here's father refusing the lord of the manor for his son-in-law, and you talking of dying an old maid because your last affections have been blighted. Why, if my first love takes a wrong direction, I shall turn my heart into the right road as easily as I guide gray Dobbin down a lane where he doesn't want to go. Just a shake of the reins or a touch of the whip, and off we start."

Crushed by this weariness of life, Naomi strove, notwithstanding, to do her duty. Even Aunt Judith found no room for complaint with Naomi or Cynthia, unless haggard eyes and pale faces, and low voices with no joyous ring in them, were sufficient ground for upbraiding. The household work was faithfully performed. The starching and ironing, the dusting and beeswaxing, the sewing and darning, were duly done. Cynthia had finished her dozen of shirts, without a gusset set awry, a seam puckered, or one deviation from a right line in the pearl-like stitching of collars and wristbands; and now she had taken to knitting Joshua's gray woolen stockings, which was a pleasantly dreamy occupation, calling for very little exercise of the intellectual faculties till one came to the heel. She used to sit in the garden or the wilderness in the calm September afternoons, with a grave, quiet face bent over her flashing needles—a face that told of an abiding sorrow. The Miss Weblings would scarcely have recognized their cheerful, sunny-faced little maid in the serious young matron, with a complexion almost as white as her cap. Joshua rarely saw that patient figure sitting in his place on the grass-plot, for he had been growing more and more indefatigable in his visits to among the scattered members of his flock, walking great distances to lonely homesteads or laborers' cottages, or, when not thus occupied, spending his afternoons in solitary wanderings by the wild sea-shore, holding commune with his troubled soul.

Save at family prayer and at meals, he was now seldom seen in his own house, while he had

9

almost wholly deserted the shop. Aunt Judith bewailed this falling-away from the good old habits which had made Haggard's the leading commercial institution in Combhollow. The salvation of one's soul was a vital transaction, doubtless; but a man secure of his calling and election in eternity could well afford to attend to his temporal business, instead of wandering about in desolate places like John the Baptist, without having any one to baptize.

"He might as well live on the top of a pillar like St. Simon What's-his-name, and have his meals sent up to him by a ladder," said Judith, contemptuously, "if his mind is never in his business. We're always running out of things now, for want of proper attention to the stock."

To Naomi it was a small thing that her father should be indifferent to loss and gain, and turn his back upon the business by which his father and grandfather had maintained their importance and respectability in the little town. The change she saw in him was more alarming than this neglect of daily duties—a change which she associated involuntarily with that bitter day on which she had seen his gloomy murderer's face pass by her in the woodland dimness.

In the autumn evenings, when she could escape from the joyless house, Naomi felt herself drawn, as by a magnet, to Pentreath Wood. It was not that she found peace there, or consolation. She loved the shadowy scene as a place in which she could feed her grief, and haunted it as an inconsolable mourner haunts the burial-ground where lies her dead. How desolate the place seemed in the season of earth's decay, all the winding ways deeply strewed with the red-brown leaves, soft and sodden in the hollows where the autumn rains lay longest; frogs creaking in the marshy places, and a dead snake lying here and there among the brambles!

It was not often that Naomi went within sight of the deserted house, where the old servants lived on in a lazy seclusion, waiting their master's bidding; almost as slumberous a household as that which slept for a hundred years in the old fairy story, only that here there was no lovely princess shining like a jewel in the innermost chamber of the castle. Here were only empty rooms, and dust and loneliness.

One evening early in October, Naomi roamed a little farther than she had intended, and found that, to reach home in decent time, she must take the nearest way, which was across the park, and out into the road by the park gate. This would take her very near the house.

It was a fine, bright evening. The sun had set redly behind the trees before she had entered the wood, and now the moon had risen, and was shining over the great sea yonder—a lovely evening, mild and peaceful. She was loath to go back to the lighted room at home, and her father's evening lecture, now always of so gloomy a character as to minister to her despair rather than to lift up her soul from its depth of sorrow.

The hall-door stood open, and a light burned dimly within. Old Nicholas, the butler, was sitting in the porch. He recognized Naomi as she skirted the outer garden, and got up quickly and came after her.

"I beg your pardon, Miss Haggard, but, seeing you go by just now, I made bold to follow you. Have you heard any news of the young squire? I've wanted to ask sometimes, when I've been up at the shop to get my bit of tea and sugar; but your father wasn't about, and I don't like to ask your aunt—she's apt to be snappy."

"No, Nicholas, we have had no news. You would be more likely to hear of your master than we."

"Deary, now! I knew there was something wrong when he came down here so sudden and told me I was to say nothing about it, and he was going off to Ameriky, and I was to keep the place in order agen Mr. Arnold came home, and then he was to be the master here. A power of changes to happen in such a short time, ain't it, miss? I feel as if the world was topsy-turvy, somehow. The poor old master gone! He was dreadful near, to be sure: but I'd got used to him, and I misses his fidgety, pinching ways, looking after every candle-end, and such a nose of his own if he suspected we was frying a bit of bacon for supper. Well, he's gone where scraping and saving won't help him, poor gentleman. There's no candle-ends in the heavenly Jerusalem."

Nicholas sighed despondently, as if he doubted whether an immortal home, in which cheese-paring could not be practiced, would satisfy his departed master.

"And you haven't heard nothing, miss?"

"Nothing," answered Naomi. "But there is hardly time for any one to have had a letter yet—is there, Nicholas?"

"I can't say, miss. Perhaps not. It were the beginning of August when he went away, warn't it? And here we are in October. I suppose there wouldn't be time; and yet I begin to feel oneasy in my mind about him. There was something queer about his going away, you see."

"How do you mean?" asked Naomi, looking at him intently.

"Well, you see, he says to me, 'Nicholas, you get they two big trunks down to the coach this evening, and that there bag.' The trunks was what he'd packed his clothes and books in, and such-like, that morning, purpose to take them with him to Ameriky. 'I shall walk on ahead, and let the coach pick me up this side of Henbury turnpike,' he says. 'But you get they trunks safe in the boot,' says he. So the gardener and I puts 'em in a barrer and wheels 'em down, and gets 'em safe packed into the boot afore seven o'clock."

"Well, what then?" asked Naomi, with suppressed eagerness.

"What then, Miss Haggard? Why, they trunks and that there bag is in the young squire's room now—come back, like a bad penny!"

"Come back?"

"Yes. The coach never picked him up this side of Henbury turnpike. The coachman never set eyes upon him all along the road. When he got to Exeter, there was no one to take to they trunks, no directions left about 'em, so he just brought 'em back; and if the young squire be gone to Ameriky, he be gone without his luggage. Lord, miss, how you do trimble! I hope there's nothing wrong, but it comes over me sometimes that things ain't altogether right."

"He may have changed his mind at the last," said Naomi, falteringly. "He may not have gone to America."

"AND YOU HAVEN'T HEARD NOTHING, MISS?"

"Perhaps not, miss; but wherever he's gone, he's gone without his luggage—even the carpet-bag, with his razors and night-clothes."

"He may have had other luggage in London."

"He had a black portmanteau at the inn where he'd been stopping in London, but it wasn't a big one. It wouldn't have been luggage enough for America, or anywhere else in foreign parts. And then the books and things that he was so fond of, and his writing-desk, and most of his clothes—all in they big boxes. It's odd he didn't send for 'em."

"He may not want them."

"But it's queer for him not to want 'em all this time. And if that there coach didn't pick him up—and we know it didn't—how did he get away? Nobody saw him leave, nobody heard of him. Lord-a-mercy, miss, how white you be! I didn't ought to say such-like things, but it weighs so heavy on my mind. It's a comfort to talk about it. The London lawyer he sends me down my wages monthly, and board-wages for me and the others indoors. We might live on the fat of the land if we chose, only our constitutions have got used to pinching, and we likes it. We couldn't have a better place, only they two trunks weighs upon my mind, and I sha'n't feel easy till I've had a letter from my master."

What comfort could Naomi give him—she whose thoughts were full of fear? She went home, and found the family circle waiting for her. It was past the customary prayer-time by ten minutes or so.

"Rambling again, Naomi!" said her father, severely, and then opened his Bible and began to read a chapter of Jeremiah, which he afterward expounded, dwelling darkly on all that was darkest in the text. The prayer that followed was rather a cry of self-abasement and desolation than a supplicatory address, curiously different from that simple and single-minded appeal which the Divine Teacher dictated to his disciples. Joshua asked for no common wants of common life; he pleaded not to be forgiven as freely as he forgave; but he groveled in the dust before an angry God, and heaped ashes upon his head, and abased himself with humility which touched the confines of fanaticism.

"What kept you out so long, sis?" asked James, when they were seated at supper.

"Nicholas, the butler at the Grange, stopped me to ask about his master. He is very anxious about him."

"Why?" asked her father, sharply.

"Because he has been away so long, and has not written."

Cynthia lifted her languid eyes, large with sudden terror.

"How could any one get a letter? He has not been gone three months. And even if there were time enough, why should he write to Nicholas?" said Joshua.

"Nicholas is anxious about him, anyhow," answered Naomi.

She said nothing about the luggage left behind, which was the chief cause of the old servant's uneasiness.

"Well, all I can say is, that a young man with such a property as that was a fool to go to America," remarked Jim, conclusively.

It was a generally accepted fact by this time that the young squire had gone to America, and there were various versions of his motive for this exile. The male gossips inclined to the idea that he and Naomi had quarreled, and that this lovers' quarrel had been the cause of his departure; the female portion of the community pinned their faith upon the young man's fickleness. He had repented of his engagement to the grocer's daughter, and had gone away to avoid its fulfillment.

"It was all very fine while his father was living, and likely to live to a hundred, and he hadn't a five-pound note," said Mrs. Spradgers. "He knew that Mr. Haggard was a warm man, and he might do worse than marry Naomi; but it was quite another thing when the old gentleman went off, and the property turned out better than young Mr. Pentreath had ever expected. It's only natural he should look higher. Circumstances alter cases."

The year wore to its close, and yet there came no tidings of the young squire. There was, perhaps, no reason why he should trouble himself to write to any one at Combhollow, argued Naomi, trying to shake off that burden of unquiet thoughts which oppressed her. He could hardly be expected to write to his old servants; he had provided for their comfort through his London solicitor. His rents were collected by a local agent and paid to the same man of business. There was no one at Combhollow who had any right to expect letters from him. He had broken away from all his old moorings, and began a new life in a new country. He was happy, perhaps, amused and interested by the novelty of his surroundings—occupied—adventurous, a light-hearted traveler, while her thoughts of him were so full of gloom.

"Why can not I banish him from my mind altogether?" she asked herself. "It is a sin to dwell thus persistently upon an earthly loss. 'If thy right hand offend thee, cut it off.' He came between me and heaven—for I loved him too well. Even now that he is far away, the thought of him binds me down to earth. Why can not I forget him?"

There was another question in her mind which hardly shaped itself in direct words: "Why can not I forget my father's face that day in the wood?"

The new year began, and there was no change in the quiet household, save a change in Cynthia, which had been so gently wrought that it was invisible to the eyes that saw her daily. The minister's young wife had faded and drooped since that troubled summer-time of the year just gone. The slender figure had lost its graceful curves, the white arm was no longer round and full, the oval of the cheek had fallen, and the blue veined lids drooped languidly over the gentle eyes, in which there was a look that seemed to plead for pity or forgiveness.

Joshua's popularity was at its height this winter. Those stirring sermons—those eloquent theological fulminations—acted on his hearers as a stimulant and a tonic. People flocked to hear him from distant villages. He was proud of his popularity, lifted up and exalted by the idea that he was bringing sinners home to God, fighting hand to hand with the devil and all his angels. He lived apart from his own household, a stranger among them, though sitting by the same fireside. It was as if they were people of old time giving shelter to a prophet. They scarcely dared speak to him, but approached him with an awful respect. It was an understood thing that he had no more to do with the business which had in years past occupied half his time and some portion of his care. James now took the helm in the commercial vessel, and felt that he was of the stuff that makes great captains. Joshua seemed hardly aware of the change that had come over his life. He was a dreamer, and lived in a world of dreams.

So the year began, and it was early spring again, and Naomi felt that her youth was gone, and that the years could bring her nothing but age and death. They would come and go, and make no difference in her life. They held no promise, they knew no hope.

CHAPTER XXIX.

THE WANDERER'S RETURN.

It was March—just a year since the old squire had been stricken with his fatal illness. The daffodils were blooming in sunny places. There was a faint tinge of green upon the hedge-rows.

Naomi was sitting alone in the twilight parlor in the calm gray evening. She had done all her daily duties, and could afford to rest from her toil. She looked at the familiar scene—the glimpse of sea, the curve of the road winding up the hill toward Pentreath Grange—with sad, hopeless eyes. No bright harbinger of joy would ever come to her by yonder road, down which she had seen the squire's funeral train slowly descending, with wind-tossed plumes and scarfs, less than a year ago.

"I had such a strange sense of loss that day," she thought, remembering the dismal procession, and her own feelings as she watched its approach. "I seemed to know that the end of my happiness had come; that change, or sorrow, or death was near."

Twilight deepened, and the scene took a shadowy look. Who was this walking down the hill at a leisurely pace, with a careless, easy gait which seemed familiar? Nay, it was familiar, for it set Naomi's heart beating vehemently; it made her cold and faint. This was no peasant returning from his work. She knew how the Combhollow population carried themselves. This tall, slim figure, so straight, and yet so easy of motion, was no son of the soil, no hard-handed agricultural laborer, no fisherman smelling of tar and sea-weed, with wet raiment all glistening and scaly.

She stood up, and opened the window—stood with the chill March breeze blowing upon her pale, terror-stricken face. This time she felt verily as if she were seeing a ghost.

"He has come back," she thought. "He is not dead. Oh, foolish fear! Oh, wretched doubt of the best and truest upon earth! He is safe; and has come back again. I shall see him once again—living and happy. My God, I thank thee!"

The figure came nearer. Yes, it was Oswald Pentreath. She saw the well-remembered face in the dim light. How well he looked—how strong—how brave! Travel and strange countries had improved him. His chest had expanded—he walked with a firmer step—held his head higher. And he was coming to her father's house—boldly; with no stealthy approach. He came as a man who had done no evil, and had no cause for fear.

"He is cured of his folly; he is my true and noble lover once again. O God, thou art full of mercy; thy love aboundeth."

The familiar figure was close at hand. There was nothing but the narrow front garden between him and Naomi; yet now there was a strangeness—her heart grew lead. The young man looked up at the house inquiringly, like a stranger who reconnoitres an unfamiliar place. He glanced up and down the street—quite empty of humanity at this moment, the solitary young woman with a basket, who had constituted its traffic a minute ago, having just gone in-doors—then looked again at the house, and became conscious of Naomi's pale face at the window.

"I beg your pardon," he began, courteously. "Is this Mr. Haggard's?"

Life-long sorrows are not so keen as a sudden stab like this—an arrow that pierces the heart and kills its hope forever. It was not Oswald's voice. There was a likeness in the tone; that family resemblance so often to be found in the tones of kindred; but these tones were more decided—rougher. They lacked the poetic languor—the gentle sweetness—of Oswald's utterance. This speaker was one who had commanded men on the high seas; not the musing idler who had wasted half his life lying listlessly in summer woods, or wandering with his rod beside autumn's swollen streams.

It was not Oswald. For the space of half a minute the surging blood in Naomi's brain almost blinded her. For an instant or so reason faltered, and she was on the verge of unconsciousness. Then the strong young soul resumed her power, and she comprehended that this was no shade from Avernus, but her lost lover's sailor-brother, the squire's runaway son.

"Yes," she answered, with a steady voice, "this is Mr. Haggard's house. Do you want to see my father?"

"Ah, then you are Naomi," cried the stranger, eagerly. "I think I would rather talk to you than to your father. You can tell me more. I have only just come home, and I am very unhappy about my brother. May I come in, please?"

How friendly, how dear his voice sounded in its resemblance to the voice of Oswald! The familiar tones comforted Naomi, somehow, after that bitter disappointment just now. Her heart was lifted up from its despair. Arnold had come home—Arnold would find out all about his beloved brother.

At that thought a sudden dread came upon her, like a vision of doom.

If there were any guilty mystery in Oswald's fate, would not his brother bring the deed to light? Her shapeless fears rose up like Gorgons, and confronted her.

She opened the door for Arnold, and stood dumbly as he came in and held out his hand to her.

"How deadly cold your hand is," he exclaimed. "I'm afraid I startled you, coming so suddenly. People say I am very like my brother; and I dare say you are anxious about Oswald."

He had gone into the parlor with her, and seated himself with a familiar friendliness close to the chair into which Naomi had sunk, scarcely able to stand.

"Yes; I have been very anxious," she said, faintly.

"I can see that. Please God, there is no real cause for fears though old Nicholas has frightened me a little by his raven-like talk. The last letter I had from my brother was written in London on the 11th of July. He urged me to come home, and told me he had some thoughts of going to America; and that, if he went, I was to take care of the estate in his absence, and to consider myself master, and so on, in his generous, reckless way—as ready to give up all his privileges as Esau was to swap his birthright against a dish of lobscouse. This letter has been following me from port to port, and I only got it nine or ten weeks ago at Shanghai, where my ship was waiting for a cargo. I went straight to Oswald's London agent when I left the docks; but he could tell me nothing, except that my brother had made all arrangements for a long absence from England. He was to have sailed for New York on the 14th of August. But a thing that puzzled this lawyer fellow a little was that Oswald should have drawn no money since he left home. 'He may have taken plenty with him,' said I—for, you see, Oswald was brought up to make a little money go a long way, or to do without it altogether mostly. 'So he may,' said the lawyer; 'but I find that young men generally do draw a good deal of money when they've got any sources to draw upon—and even, sometimes, when they have not. It's a way they have.' This made me rather uneasy, and I came down here as fast as three blundering coaches, which hardly do five knots an hour, could bring me. And the old house looked so lonely and dismal without Oswald, that the mere sight of it made me miserable; and then old Nicholas's raven croakings made me worse—so I came straight off to you for comfort."

"I can tell you nothing," answered Naomi, with a sigh.

"Nicholas told me you had received no letter. That's strange, certainly. He would have written to you before any one, I should think."

"No, I had no right to expect any letter from him. I expected none."

"What—not as his betrothed wife?"

"Our engagement was broken off some time before he went. Did you not know?"

"Not a word. His last mention of you was full of affection—not in his latest letter, by-the-way, but in the one which told me of my father's death. I was to come home, and he very fond of you, and we were all to be happy together."

"Yes, I know," said Naomi, with a pang of bitterest remembrance. How often had Oswald talked to her of union and love and happiness—sweet domestic joys which Arnold was to share!

"But why was your engagement broken off?" asked the sailor, bluntly. "Did you quarrel?"

"Quarrel? No."

"He must have behaved very ill, then."

"No, no. It was my father's wish. I obeyed my father in setting Oswald free. And he accepted his liberty—he was grateful for his release. Love does not always last a life-time;

there is a difference, you see. I think that he once loved me, but—"

Here the tears rained down upon her trembling hands. Arnold drew nearer to her, and gently pressed one of those cold hands with a brotherly kindness.

"My poor girl—my sister that was to have been! He behaved badly, I'm afraid. There was something wild and queer in his last letter; and, then, that sudden resolve to go to America! I ought to have seen that things had gone wrong with him. Poor Oswald! And I expected to see him so happy with you."

"Providence willed it otherwise. I was too happy with him, I think—too much absorbed in the joys of this world."

"Why should we not be happy in this world? God would never have made so fair a world for a scene of suffering. You can't imagine—you stay-at-home people—how beautiful this earth is. The birds, and animals, and reptiles, and insects are happy. All free creation enjoys itself, from its birth till its death. Why should man be wretched, or the source of misery in others? Why should Providence be offended because you and my brother loved each other and were happy?"

Naomi could not answer. It was an article of her religion that Heaven disapproved of too much earthly bliss.

"But you must have known where he was going—he told you his plans, surely?" asked Arnold.

"No, I knew nothing of his intentions—directly," answered Naomi, a faint blush dyeing her pallid cheek.

"Did you not see him when he came back to the Grange in the beginning of August? He came to bid you good bye, I suppose?"

"No, I did not see him."

"Then, why did he come back to Coolhollow at all? I can hear of nothing that he did in the way of business, except to pack those trunks, which he left behind him, after all his trouble. What was the motive of his return?"

"Indeed, I can not tell you," faltered Naomi, sorely distressed.

Arnold looked troubled. He got up and walked up and down the narrow parlor as he had walked his quarter-deck in many an hour of doubt and difficulty.

"I can't understand it," he said. "It is the strangest business altogether. Why did he come back and pack his trunks, and have them taken to the coach, and why did he not appear to claim them? If he did not leave by the coach, how did he get away?"

"There are vessels that sail between Rockmouth and Bristol, are there not?" suggested Naomi. "He may have gone that way."

"A slow, roundabout way for him to choose, after making up his mind to go by the coach. I begin to feel as anxious as Nicholas. Oh, my dearest Oswald, where are you, and why this mystery? God grant that he is safe and happy somewhere! God grant there has been no foul play!"

At these words, Naomi's face took a death-like hue. But the room was too dark for Arnold to see the change.

"If harm of any kind has happened to him, Heaven help the wrong-doers, for they shall have no mercy from me! I'll hunt them down. But no, I won't think it. I won't believe that he has come to an untimely end. The brother who carried me in his arms, and was so gentle and loving, and whom I loved, God knows, with all my heart, though I left him! How I have looked forward to our reunion, and counted upon it, and built upon it in all these years! And I come back to find him far away, and his fate a mystery!" He threw himself into a chair and sobbed aloud—honest, manly tears coming from a true and brave heart.

It was Naomi's turn to comfort now. She bent over him, and laid her hand lightly on his shoulder.

"Pray do not say that evil has befallen him," she said. "He may have changed his mind as to his way of traveling at the last; who can tell what trifling thing may have influenced him?"

"What did he do with himself all that day?" asked Arnold. "Nicholas tells me that he left the Grange before one o'clock, and the coach was not to pick him up till after eight in the evening. Where was he? With whom did he spend his time? He seems to have no friends in Combhollow but you and your family, and he was not with you?"

"No."

"Can not you help me to find out where he was?"

"No, I can not."

"That's a pity. If I could only find out the people who saw the last of him here, they might enlighten me as to his intentions. I must see what I can do elsewhere. I came to you, naturally, for help; but then I did not know your engagement was broken off."

Sally brought in the lighted candles, and started and stared at sight of the sea-captain.

"Don't be frightened, Sally," said Naomi; "this is Captain Pentreath, the squire's brother."

"Lor' sakes!" faltered the handmaiden, "I took he for the young squire's ghost."

"Is your father at home?" asked Arnold, presently; "I should like to see him."

"No, it is his class-night; he will not be home for nearly an hour. And I know he could tell you nothing more than I have told you," added Naomi.

"Perhaps not, but he might advise me; I have heard that he is a superior man. I should like to see him; I'll call to-morrow. Good-night, Naomi—I may call you Naomi, I hope, for my brother's sake? He told me to think of you as a sister."

"I should like you to think me so still, if you can," Naomi answered, gently. And then he pressed her hand, and was gone.

There was some kind of comfort in the sailor's friendliness—in this brave, strong, manly figure, suddenly introduced into the dull scene of a sorrow-shadowed life. He was so like Oswald, and yet so unlike. And he loved his brother so dearly, Oswald's fate would be no longer a mystery. All those unspoken fears, which had preyed upon her like a consuming disease, would be proved vain and foolish. He was safe, he was happy in some strange land. There needed only a little energy and cleverness to find out all about him, and Arnold would supply both.

Then there flashed upon her the memory of that awful moment in the wood, when she saw her father go by with a look upon his face that seemed to her like the brand of Cain, full of awful meaning.

CHAPTER XXX.

"WHERE IS THY BROTHER?"

"Father," said Naomi, at supper-time, "Captain Pentreath has come home, and wants to see you to-morrow."

"Captain Pentreath!" echoed Joshua, staring at her blankly; "who's he?"

"Oswald's brother."

"Oh, Arnold, the younger son; the boy who ran away to sea? He's come home, has he, to take possession of the estate? That's a good thing."

"Not to take possession, father; to take care of the old place, perhaps. He has no right to take possession in his brother's life-time."

"Not unless he had staid away seven years without being heard of," interjected Jim, the English mind having a firm grip upon this idea of seven years.

"Why should any one suppose him dead?" asked Naomi, with a look that was half indignant, half apprehensive. "He has only been away a little more than six months. His brother has come home to look for him; he is determined to find him."

"What's the use of looking for him at Combhollow, when every body knows he's gone to America?" cried Jim.

"I mean that Captain Pentreath is going to find out all about his brother—when and how he left England."

"Poor worm!" exclaimed Joshua, with lofty scorn. "His brother's fate is in the hands of God. As if he could make or mend it!"

"But he has a right to know, father, and it is natural he should be anxious."

"That shows he belongs to the unregenerate," said Jim, glad to have a fling at the creed which had been forced upon him before he was able to form his own estimate of its merits, like vaccination. "If he were sure of his own election, he needn't care a toss what became of his brother—"

"In time, perhaps not," said Joshua, with an awful look; "but how dreadful to know him lost in eternity! Better to remain forever ignorant of the fate of those we love than to be sure of their condemnation."

"Judge not, that ye be not judged," said Naomi, for the first time in her life daring to lift up her voice against her father. "Who can be sure of another's condemnation? It is blasphemy to say such a thing."

"What new Daniel is this?" exclaimed Joshua, scornfully. "Is my daughter going to be my teacher? I tell you, Naomi, there are some sins which can not be repented of. There is a guiltiness which seals the sinner's doom, and sends him, self-convicted, to receive his Maker's sentence."

"I have no fear that Oswald would be such a sinner," answered Naomi, meeting her father's dark look with defiant eyes. "Weak, erring, led astray by one more erring than himself—yes, he might be these, but not a deliberate offender, not obstinately guilty!"

What was this new feeling which made her talk to her father as if she were arguing with an adversary? She felt a thrill of horror at her own audacity. But she was not mistress of herself when her father spoke harsh words of Oswald Pentreath. Reason grew clouded, and the voice of passion cried aloud in defense of her lost lover. He was weak, and she would not let the strong man spurn him. He was absent, and she would not hear him condemned.

Cynthia sat silent, and heard them talk of the man who had loved her too well, whose only sin and sorrow was to have let his heart go out to her as a young bird flies from its nest into the glad new world. He had loved her, and that love had darkened his life. She could see him looking down at her, as on that last day, passion pale, bidding his eternal farewell. What a dream it had been—so fair, so sweet, so unreal! She had suffered herself to be beloved, and to love again, and in this dreaming, half-unconscious state had tasted an ineffable happiness. She did not regret this lost dream-world; she would not have recalled its vanished sweetness; she was honestly repentant of her sin against the husband she honored; but the past was ineffaceable—a part of her being.

> "I can not but remember such things were
> That were most precious to me."

Though full of anxious thoughts, Arnold Pentreath brought brightness and pleasant days to the old Grange and all who came within his influence. His candid, intelligent face, the frank heartiness of his manners, with just a dash of the seaman's bluntness, and that firm straightforwardness which comes from the habit of commanding others and restraining one's self—all these things gave him immediate mastery over the simple folks at Combhollow. The old servants worshiped him. He had been the most daring and mischievous of the two brothers in boyhood, and naturally the most popular. He had defied his old father, and had won golden opinions from the household by his juvenile mutinies. He came back a man, broad-shouldered and strongly built, bronzed and battered a little by all kinds of climates and hard weather, but all the handsomer, in the eyes of a sea-loving population, for his sunburned cheek and the stubborn crispness of his hair. He was fonder of his fellow-men than Oswald had been, and, instead of dreaming over "Childe Harold" in Pentreath Wood, was out and about all day, tramping along the lanes, making acquaintance with every hind who worked upon his land, tossing cottage children in his strong arms, with a kindly word for every one he met.

He had not been three days at the Grange before the fact of his return was known far and wide, and brought all manner of applicants to the old house to ask favors which no agent would grant. He heard all complaints with an equable good-nature, and lent his attention to the smallest detail. The slates blown off the homestead in "they high winds—now do'ee see what you can do for us, squire." The granary thatch which had "cotched fire" in such a mysterious way, after last midsummer's thunder-storm, that old Farmer Westall was firmly convinced it was the work of Nancy Dowden, the witch.

"For she be a witch, squire," said the farmer,

"that's well beknownst. And I do say as it ain't right a spiteful old woman like she should be allowed to meddle with forked lightning."

"Well, farmer, if it was witchcraft fired the barn, you can't expect me to pay for new-thatching it?" argued Arnold.

"But look'ee now, squire. It was the ould gentleman, your feyther, brought it on us. All they witches bore an evil eye toward him. He were so hard upon 'em, and that screwy, never a drop of milk or a fagot to give 'em."

"Wasn't it you, now, that refused old Nancy the fagots, Farmer Westall?" suggested Arnold.

"Well, now, you're a bit of a conjurer yourself, squire. There was one day as the ould ooman come for some wood to bile her kittle, and I wasn't in the best of tempers, for our ould sow had etten up seven pegs, and I thowt it was some o' Nancy's work; so I calls out, 'Now jist look yere, Nancy; you had a fagot yesterday, and another the day afore that, and I didn't make that stack o' wood o' purpose for you, old lady.' So she gives a sniff and a grunt, and off she goes, and it wasn't a week from that when the lightning caught the thatch o' my biggest barn. And I'm a man with a long fambly, squire, and I've had the roof covered up anyhow with some old boards and a bit of tarpaulin ever since, because Bill Stowell, the thatcher, asks a mort o' money before he'll make a good job of it."

"We'll see what can be done, farmer. Perhaps I might go halves in the expense, if the barn was roofed in to my satisfaction. I'm only a steward, you see—a kind of deputy for my brother."

Farmer Westall sighed and looked glum. Old Nicholas, the butler, had infected most of his acquaintance with his own dismal ideas about the absent lord of the manor. It was a general opinion that the vessel in which Oswald had sailed for America had gone to the bottom.

"There are some folks that'll never get no luck out o' the sea," said the voice of public opinion as represented by the fishermen of Combhollow. "Remember that storm, and the way the Dolphin went to pieces. The two sailors was saved easy enough, but the squire would have been drownded, or knocked to pieces on they rocks, but for Joshua Haggard. And what were the use of saving him? He never did no good to the Haggards; and here he is gone down to the bottom, as sure as fate. It was what were meant from the fust, and there's never no good in flying in the face of Providence. You may save a ship's cargo—that's man's business, and an honest way of providin' for a fambly; but they as is aboard the ship is in the care o' Providence, and it's clean blasphemy to risk your life in fishing of 'em out of the water!"

Captain Pentreath had exhausted his resources, and had found no clue to his brother's proceedings after that August noontide in which he had left the Grange, with the avowed intention of going to Exeter—on his way to London—by the evening coach. Arnold had gone back to London, and had seen the solicitor again, and had made his inquiries in every likely and unlikely direction, but he had learned nothing. The London lawyer did not know the name of the vessel in which Arnold had booked his passage to New

York. His client had told him nothing, except that he had made up his mind to go to America, and that he wanted his affairs administered in his absence. The household at the Grange was to suffer no alteration; and when Arnold came, he was to be master.

"Until your return?" the lawyer had said to him.

"My return is an event of the remote future," Oswald had replied; "I may never return."

Arnold went to Liverpool, and the result of his researches there convinced him that Oswald had not left that port in any vessel bound for America, unless he had sailed under an assumed name. From Liverpool he went to Cork—from Cork he went by water to Bristol—from Bristol westward to Plymouth; and the most searching inquiries at these places resulted as his inquiries had resulted at Liverpool. There was no trace of Oswald Pentreath's passage to America to be found in any shipping-office. He went back to the Grange sorely depressed, for his brother's fate was beginning to assume a hue of mystery which gave room for the darkest fears.

His conversation with Joshua Haggard had told him nothing more than he had already learned from Naomi. The minister had received him with a chilling reserve which held him at arms-length. The frank, outspoken sailor wondered that his brother could have written to him so warmly in praise of such a man.

He called on Joshua the day after his return from his round of inquiry.

"This is a bad business, Mr. Haggard," he began, plunging at once into the subject nearest his heart; "I have found out enough to feel very sure that my brother has not gone to America."

Joshua's grave countenance betrayed no surprise. "Why, the fellow is not a man, but a machine," Arnold thought, indignantly.

"You don't seem to understand what a serious question this is," said Arnold. "If my brother did not go to America last August, what has become of him?"

"That is a question that I can not be expected to answer, Captain Pentreath. We are all in God's hands. In life or in death, he deals with us as seemeth best to him. He may have appointed your brother for an evil end. You had best be content to leave all to him."

"Do you mean that if my brother has come to an evil end, I am to let his murderer go scotfree?" cried Arnold, indignantly. "Do you think that I shall fold my hands and wait for Providence to avenge my brother? Why, if I did, God would have the right to ask of me, as he did of Cain, 'Where is thy brother?' You do not know how dearly we two loved each other, Mr. Haggard."

"'Vengeance is mine, I will repay,'" quoted Joshua, solemnly; "be sure that if your brother has been murdered, an idea I do not for a moment entertain, his assassin has suffered, or will suffer, as heavy a punishment as any vengeance of yours could inflict."

"May God make conscience an undying worm to feed upon his soul!" said Arnold. "But it shall be my business to bring his body to the gallows."

Joshua heard him in silence. He sat with folded hands, and a countenance as mysterious in its solemn thoughtfulness as the head of Memnon.

"Come, Mr. Haggard, you must be able to give me some help in this matter, if you choose," urged Arnold, passionately; "my brother was your daughter's lover—her affianced husband, till you, for some motive of your own, forbade their marriage. There is a story underlying that act of yours—a story that might cast some light upon my poor brother's fate. You must have had strong reasons for such a step. A man of your principles would hardly be governed by caprice. Tell me honestly, as one who has a right to ask, what that reason was."

"I can give you no details upon that point," answered Joshua. "But I will tell you broadly that I had reason to disapprove of your brother's conduct in relation to another woman. I had reason to know that his heart had gone away from my daughter. He would have kept his promise, and married her, and would have believed that he was acting as a man of honor; but he would have lied at God's altar, and his marriage would have offended Heaven."

"You believe that my brother's heart had gone astray?"

"I know it."

"Then, for Heaven's sake, tell me all you know. This love affair may throw light upon his after-conduct—may give us the clue to his present whereabouts. There would be a false delicacy—an absolute cruelty—in hiding anything from me—from me, his brother, who am distracted by the most hideous apprehensions."

"I can tell you nothing more," answered Joshua, with a stern resoluteness which chilled Arnold to the heart. "I am withholding no knowledge which could help you in the smallest degree. Your brother sinned—and is gone. You must be content to know no more than that."

"I will not be content," cried the sailor, vehemently. "You are juggling with me—you, a preacher of God's Word, who ought to be truthful as the day. But I forgot—the prophets were dark of speech, and God taught his chosen people by dreams and allegories, and you seek to imitate those mysterious ways. Have you no human pity—as a man and a Christian—for a brother's grief for a lost brother? You could tell me something that would make this mystery clear, and you lock your lips, and abandon me to the agony of uncertainty. My brother respected, admired—nay, loved you, Mr. Haggard."

This wrung a sigh from a breast which Arnold had deemed marble.

"I tell you I am withholding nothing that could give you comfort," said Joshua, looking downward with fixed and gloomy brow. "I deplore your brother's fate, and the mystery which surrounds it. Yet for your sake—for the sake of my daughter who loved him—I say, May the veil never be lifted!"

"Why?"

"Because I fear he came to a bad end."

"You must have some reason for that fear. You know something," exclaimed Arnold, breathlessly.

"I am guided by my knowledge of his character—of his condition of mind last summer."

"You think he destroyed himself?"

"I do."

Arnold bowed his face upon his clasped hands; his strong frame was shaken by the agony of that moment. To have staid away from his brother all the days of his youth—to come home full of hope and pleasure—and to be told this! The cup was bitter.

When Arnold looked up, Joshua Haggard was gone.

He staid in the empty room, looking out into the windy March street—where one old woman was tightening a three-cornered shawl across her skinny shoulders—with eyes that saw not, and thinking over Joshua's words.

What did they mean? How much, or how little? Was this idea of Oswald's suicide a mere speculation on the minister's part, or had he sound evidence on which to found his conclusions?

"It is too bad of him to leave me in the dark," mused Arnold. "I have a right to know every thing that can be said or thought about my brother. He is a hard-hearted scoundrel. These overpious men are adamant. And yet he saved my brother's life at the risk of his own. Oswald told me the story, and the fishermen here are never tired of talking about it. Don't let me forget that. The man is better than his speech. And he tells me he is keeping nothing back. But to think that my brother took his own life—that he was wretched enough to find the coward's last release from difficulty! I will not believe it."

He rose to depart; but before he got to the door, Naomi came in, and they stood face to face, both startled, both agitated, by this sudden meeting, natural as it was.

"Oh, Naomi, I want you," cried the sailor, taking both her hands, and looking into the pale face with beseeching earnestness. "I want you to advise, to comfort, to enlighten me. I have been talking to your father, and he has almost broken my heart. Tell me, for pity's sake, the truth, dear, as sister to brother. Say that you do not believe Oswald killed himself."

"Killed himself?" she echoed, growing very white. "No. Who says so—who thinks so?"

"Your father."

"My father says that — my father believes that?"

"Yes, dear. He told me so five minutes ago. Only say that you don't believe it."

"I do not," she answered, with flashing eyes, "I know that he was unhappy, but I can not believe—I will not believe—that he could be so weak—so guilty. No, there was no such thought in his mind. He had made his plans for beginning a new life; he had taken his passage for America."

"You know that from himself?" cried Arnold, eagerly.

Naomi bowed her head in assent.

"God bless you, sister!" said the sailor. "You have comforted me more than I can say. You knew him—you loved him."

"With all my heart and soul — too much for duty, or peace, or righteousness."

"And you think he really did go to America?"

Naomi's troubled face took a still deeper shadow.

"I know he meant to go; he may not have gone, after all."

"Yet it was strange that he should not have left by the coach, after telling Nicholas that he meant to go that way. Very strange that he should leave those trunks behind him, after packing them."

"He may have changed his mind at the last. He was troubled in mind, and might be careless about things which people in an ordinary state of mind would consider important."

"True, my dear. How clearly you see every thing! Yes, that was so. And he sailed from some small port, perhaps—or from the other side of the Channel—Havre or Brest. The fact that I can not trace him is worth nothing. We will wait and hope, Naomi: hope for your husband and my brother's return."

"For our brother's return," answered Naomi, with a tender gravity. "He can never again be more to me than a brother; and to the end of my life I shall love him with a sister's love."

"Poor fellow!" said Arnold, dreamily; "he threw away a jewel above all price when he lost you."

———◆———

CHAPTER XXXI.

THE FACE IN OSWALD'S SKETCH-BOOK.

THAT idea of his brother's suicide took no strong hold upon Arnold, after his conversation with Naomi, but he could not put the possibility out of his mind altogether. That his brother had suffered some disappointment—that a cloud of some kind had darkened his life—he was ready to believe. Oswald's latest letter had betrayed a mind ill at ease: that sudden determination to leave his country, while independence was still a new thing for him, and with every advantage in life that could make a young man happy, argued the existence of some deep-rooted sorrow, a misery that made familiar scenes hateful, and exile a welcome means of escape from the haunting memories that follow a fatal passion.

But, having resolved upon exile, could Oswald have been so weak or so wicked as to seek the darker and more desperate Lethe of the suicide? Arnold argued that his brother was too good and brave a man to contemplate, much less to commit, such a crime. But, then, Arnold had not read "Werther," the apotheosis of suicide.

He went back to the Grange, after his interview with Naomi, more than ever at sea as to his brother's fate, more than ever resolved to unravel the mystery. His first act was to make an inquiry which had some bearing upon the suicide-question. Instead of entering the Grange by the hall-door, he went under the old stone archway that led into the quadrangle, from which the kitchens and stables alike opened, being tolerably certain of finding Nicholas, the butler, sunning himself on the solid old bench beside the kitchen-door.

There sat the old man, bare-headed, basking in the spring sunshine. It did not last very long, the sunshine of these April afternoons; but while it lasted, there was warmth, and a balmy sweetness in the air, and a yellow light that made all things lovely. The wall-flowers blended their rich red and gold with the cool grays and purples of the old stone archway, the dark-brown shadows on stable-doors and deep-set windows, the vermilion lights upon the tiled roofs. The stone-crop on the gables, the sage-green houseleeks nestling round the disused chimney-stacks, the fleecy clouds sailing high in a bright blue sky, were all beautiful to contemplate, but such familiar objects to the drowsy eye of old Nicholas, stretching out his feeble legs in the warmth, as he stretched them toward the kitchen hearth indoors, that he was scarcely conscious of their existence. If he had an idea at all about the old quadrangle, it was that all 'they' wall-flowers, and houseleek, and stone-crop, and rubbish ought to be swept away, and the whole place renovated with a coat of clean whitewash.

He was puffing slowly at his afternoon pipe when Arnold came up; but at the sight of his master he rose and did obeisance.

"Sit down, Nicholas, and go on with your pipe," said the sailor, in a friendly voice; "I want a little quiet talk with you."

The butler obeyed, and Arnold seated himself on the bench by his side, and took out a short German pipe, which he carried in his pocket, and began to smoke. It was in the days when a German pipe was a mark of a traveler, when for a gentleman to smoke a pipe of any kind implied a republican turn of mind.

Captain Pentreath looked round the quadrangle. There was no one within ear-shot. The stable-boy was throwing a pail of water at Herne's hind-legs at the farthest end of the yard—a liberty which the animal bore with the resignation engendered of custom; two fan-tail pigeons were pulling out their chests and spreading out their fans on the deep-red tiles yonder; and a most vagabond collection of poultry was disporting itself on a golden mountain of straw in a distant corner—a mountain which would have made the old squire wild with agony had he seen such a wasteful expenditure of litter; but Herne's bed nowadays was a Sybarite's couch, Arnold having taken his brother's horse under his own especial protection.

"You remember the day my brother went away the last time, Nicholas—the day you got his trunks taken down to the coach-office?"

"Yes, captain, as well as if it was yesterday."

"Did you see him just before he left the house?"

"Yes; he called me into the hall as he was going out to give me his last orders about their trunks."

"Do you know if he carried pistols? There was a pair used to hang over the mantel-piece in his bedroom. I've noticed the mark of them on the wall where the paneling has changed color. Do you know if he took them with him?"

"Yes, captain. I saw the butt-end of a pistol poking out of his breast-pocket. He wore a frock-coat buttoned up tight, and there was just the end of the pistol showing. They was pretty little pistols, as small as toys, and he was uncommon proud of 'em. They'd belonged to his great-uncle, the colonel, you see, and was furrin made. 'You beunt going to carry they pistols, be ye, squire?' said I, for I thought it was dangersome. But he said he wanted to take the pistols away with him, and he'd forgot to pack 'em in his box. 'And perhaps it's as well,' he says; 'for it beunt wise to go on a coach journey without fire-arms;' and I says, 'Lawks,

master Oswald,' for I forgets myself sometimes with 'un, and thinks he's still a boy, 'you ain't afeard o' highwaymen in these days, be ye, with the Reform Bill a-comin' to make things pleasant to every body?' But he on'y larfed, and shuk his head, and went out without another wurred."

"With a pair of pistols in his breast-pocket," thought Arnold, much disturbed by this information, for it seemed to jump with Joshua Haggard's idea of self-slaughter. He asked no further questions of old Nicholas, but went slowly to his own room—the large airy bed-chamber, with windows facing seaward, which had been Oswald's—and sat down at his brother's writing-table, to meditate upon the mystery that veiled the absentee's fate.

That there was a mystery of some kind, Oswald was fully assured. It was now high time that somebody in England should have heard from the wanderer. The brothers had corresponded more or less regularly in all the years of their separation, and Oswald had always been the best correspondent. The landsman had made excuses for the rover when Arnold's letters were in arrear, and had written by every mail; so that Captain Pentreath often found a packet of letters waiting for him, when his ship came into port, full of pleasant gossip about the old home which he dearly loved, although he loved the sea better. That Oswald should be away nearly a year, living, and in his right mind, and in all that time make no communication with his brother, seemed improbable to the verge of impossibility.

"Where did he go when he left the Grange that August day?" pondered Arnold. "Some one must have seen him; some one must know something about him. The woman he loved—for whose sake he jilted that noble girl—she could give me the clue to the mystery, perhaps, if I only knew where to find her."

Who was she? Who was the object of that fatal passion which had darkened Oswald's life just when it seemed happiest? Arnold wondered exceedingly. Some one his brother had known in London, perhaps; for it could hardly be any one at Combhollow without every one in the place knowing all about it; and the people who talked to Arnold about his brother were clearly quite in the dark as to the reason of his falling away from his allegiance to Naomi. No, it could be no one at home, or he would have heard of it at the street-corners; and yet it was evident to him that Joshua Haggard knew more about the circumstances of Oswald's sin or folly than he cared to tell. He had known enough to feel justified in breaking off his daughter's engagement—a strong measure, assuredly, where Naomi had so much to gain by the intended marriage. How had Oswald's conduct in London reached the Methodist minister's knowledge? That was puzzling. But even the remotest village has generally some channel of communication with the great city—some curious rustic, who has a brother or cousin living within sound of Bow Bells, and is occasionally gratified by his city friend with a dish of scandal. No latest rumor, or darkest insinuation about courts or princes, so interesting to Mr. Chawbacon as the news of his brother parishioner's doings "up in London."

There stood Oswald's two big trunks in the deep recess by the chimney, one on the top of the other, just as they had been placed when the coach brought them back from Exeter. Might not one of these hold the clue to their owner's intentions when he left his home? Arnold had his sea-going tool-chest close at hand. He had a good deal of mechanical skill, and had always rigged up his own cabin, with the book-shelves and three-cornered brackets, and small conveniences that give a comfortable and civilized air to an apartment which, to the landsman's eye, looks like an exaggerated rabbit-hutch.

Arnold had picked the lock of the topmost trunk before he had time to reason upon his idea. It was an old, leather-covered trunk of his father's, black with age, and iron-clamped at the corners, and so heavy in itself that it was a matter of comparative indifference to the person who carried it whether it was full or empty. Arnold lifted the lid with a curiously nervous feeling, as if some sudden and appalling revelation were lurking immediately beneath it.

This uppermost trunk contained Oswald's modest collection of books—the well-thumbed Shakspeare and Byron, the queer little duodecimo "Tom Jones," and "Joseph Andrews." Arnold took them up one by one, and looked at them tenderly. He, too, was a worshiper of that poetic star so lately set, and carried "Childe Harold" and "Don Juan" in his sea-chest, and had sat dreaming over their pages many a night, with no other light to read by than the broad, tropical moon; he, too, was a lover of Shakspeare and of Fielding. He turned over the leaves of that battered old Byron meditatively, and it seemed to him that the volume opened at the saddest passages, as if the reader had dwelt with morbid fondness upon the complainings of a kindred despair.

Below the books there was an old leather writing-desk, and below that nothing but clothes and boots, packed with a careless roughness, which indicated haste or preoccupation of mind on the part of the packer. In all the contents Arnold saw nothing that tended to his enlightenment, and he began to replace the things, putting them in carefully, with an orderly closeness of arrangement which reduced their bulk considerably.

He put in the books one by one, and had nearly finished his task, when his attention was caught by a shabby little volume without any title on the back, which had hitherto escaped his notice. It was bound in red morocco, and had grown dingy from much usage.

Arnold opened the book. It was a manuscript book, containing entries in Oswald's penmanship, alternated with pencil-sketches, and here and there a few verses, with much interlineation and alteration, to denote the throes of composition.

"This must tell me something," thought the sailor.

The pencil revealed the tastes of the owner of the little volume. The first pages were full of marine sketches, pencil dottings of familiar bits of coast. They brought back the memory of Arnold's boyhood—those old days when his chief delight was to get on board one of the fishermen's boats, and to be out at sea from dawn to sunset, or—better still—from sunset to sunrise. He had offended his father many a time by these unauthorized excursions, and his final offense had

been an absence of three days and nights at the beginning of the pilchard season. He had come home and begged pardon for his wrong-doing; but the squire, who had suffered some pangs of paternal anxiety for the first time in his life, resented this trifling with his finer feelings, and gave the truant a ferocious flogging. Whereupon the sea-loving acquaintance made up his bundle, and set out after dark to walk to Bristol.

It was fifteen years since he had seen these picturesque bits of coast, Clovelly and Hartland Point, and the remoter glories of Bude and Tintagel. Yes, every angle of cliff, every jagged rock, brought back the fervor and freshness of his boyhood—the days when his love of the sea was a worship, and not a merely professional arbor.

There was the *Dolphin*, pitching and rolling in heavy seas, or mirrored in summer lakes of sultry calm. There were a good many attempts at versification in this earlier part of the book, all savoring of Byron—addresses to "My Bark," invocations to storm and ocean, all unfinished.

Here, about midway in the volume, comes a woman's face—Naomi Haggard. Yes, although the likeness is by no means perfect, there is no mistaking the noble brow, the dark, deep eyes, with their look of thought; the masses of dark hair. This face was repeated many times: the heavy eyelids drooping, the full eyes lifted, in profile, three-quarter, full-front; and now the poetic effusions took a bolder flight, and it was no longer the sea, but his mistress, the lover apostrophized. "To N." the verses were sometimes headed, or "Midnight after leaving N." First love rang the changes in tenderest gushes of sentiment. All the old platitudes, the stock comparisons, were brought out, and the conventional Pegasus was duly exercised. He was not a winged horse, to soar over the topmost pinnacle of Parnassus, but a quiet cob rather, warranted easy to ride and drive, a steed that took his rider over familiar ground at a gentle trot, and never showed the slightest inclination to bolt with him.

The middle of the book was entirely filled with sketches of Naomi, and verses to Naomi, and here and there a faint murmur against Naomi's coldness jotted down in prose. Then came a change: Naomi disappeared altogether; there were no more poetic efforts, but page after page closely written—a journal, evidently, kept from day to day. The earliest date was in the March of the previous year.

And now appeared a face which was unknown to Arnold; a girlish face, in a Puritan cap, delicately traced—as if the lightest touch of the draughtsman's pencil had not been fine enough to mark the ethereal character of his subject. Sweet face—now grave, now pensive, now touched with a vague melancholy, now with deepest sadness in the tender uplifted eyes—eyes that seemed to pity and deplore.

"This is the woman he loved," thought Arnold. He turned to the diary, and read a page at random. It was dated April 12th, ten days before the squire's death.

"She is here still. It is a new life which I lead while she is near me. Nothing can come of it but sorrow and parting; yet the lightest sound of her footstep thrills me with joy: an accidental touch from her little hand sets all my pulses throbbing. I can not be unhappy in her presence; yet despair sweeps over my soul ever and anon, like a cloud across a sunlit landscape. My loved one, my dearest, why did we not meet sooner, or why meet at all? Two lives are sacrificed to a caprice of destiny—a cruel, hard, and inexplicable fatality, which rolls on like an iron wheel, and grinds men's hearts into the dust. I am almost an unbeliever when I think how Nature meant my sweet love for me, and me for her, and how Fate has come between and sundered us!"

"Poor Naomi! How true and good she is! How noble, single-minded, frank, unsuspecting! There shall be no more reviling of destiny. I will struggle with this wicked passion—struggle and conquer—or if I fail, end all!"

"Or if I fail, end all!" Arnold repeated, musingly.

"Yes, my Naomi, I will remember the days when you were all the world to me—when I had no sweeter hope than a placid life spent in your company, when that calm friendship and reverent admiration which I felt for you seemed to me all that is best and noblest in love. For the sake of those days I will conquer myself and be true to you; and if there can be no more happiness for me, there shall at least be peace and quiet days, and a conscience at ease. Perhaps, after all, those things constitute real happiness, and this fever-dream of passion is but a mock beatitude, like the wild, brief joys of delirium, the flashes of unreasoning delight that fire the maniac's brain for a moment, to leave him lost in deepest gloom. Oh no, I do *not* believe that passion means happiness, any more than storm or lightning means fine weather. Both are grand, both are beautiful; and they leave ruin and death behind them."

"When honor ceases to be my guide, let me perish."

"Death hovers near us, and our thoughts are full of sadness. A few days, a few hours may bring the inevitable end. Where she is, there is always sunshine. Her presence soothes me like tenderest music—like the songs my mother sang beside my cradle!

"God help me, for my heart is breaking!"

Arnold read on for an hour. The journal continued in the same strain, with much repetition of motive—going over the same ground very often, as the writer argued with himself, and made good resolves, which were evidently broken as soon as made. It was the old story of a fatal, unconquerable passion. Sometimes the sorrow deepened to despair, and Arnold read with a sinking of the heart, feeling that a man who could write thus might not be very far from the suicide's state of mind.

The name of the object of such an unhappy love was not once written, and there was a general vagueness in the journal which left Arnold considerably in the dark. He only knew that the woman his brother loved had been one who lived near him—with whom he was almost daily associated—some one belonging to Combhollow. Who could she be? Arnold was very sure that he had never seen the original of those delicate pencilings in his brother's book. Oswald's likenesses of Naomi were good enough to prove that there must be some degree of likeness in the other portraits—unless, indeed, these were not portraits, only the semblance of some airy nothing that lived but in the draughtsman's fancy.

No, the same face appeared too often not to be real. The face, and the confession of a fatal love, came too near each other in the book for Arnold to doubt that the sketches were faithful portraits.

"I have been to the parish church every Sunday since I came home, and I have seen no face that bears the faintest resemblance to this," thought Arnold, sorely perplexed.

Naomi could perchance have enlightened him. Naomi must have known to whom her lover's heart had gone forth when she lost him; but it would have been direst cruelty to ask Naomi such a question.

"And if I knew all, would it tell me my brother's fate?" Arnold wondered, sorrowfully; for since he had seen Oswald's diary it seemed to him that self-destruction was no improbable end for the writer.

"When a man once gets out of the right line, who can tell how far he may stray?" thought the sailor.

CHAPTER XXXII.

REPUDIATED.

CAPTAIN PENTREATH went back to London on business of his own. He had to wind up his affairs with the ship-owners who had employed him from the beginning of his career; and this was no easy matter, for the owners had rarely had so good a captain, and were disinclined to lose him. Arnold had made up his mind that his place was on shore for some time to come. His brother had left him the stewardship of his estate, and he meant to be faithful to that trust till Oswald came back to claim his own, if it pleased God to bring him safely back by-and-by—a result for which Arnold most fervently prayed. The neglect into which all things had fallen appealed strongly to the captain's love of order; there was a pleasure for him in making crooked things straight. He assumed the command at Combhollow with as much decision as if he had been on board ship, and people obeyed him as well as his sailors had done; and it is to be remarked that the most popular commander is the captain who is best obeyed.

Business kept him in London some time; but when he went back to Combhollow, he was a free man, and his career as land-steward lay before him—till Oswald's return. Hope had argued the question with fear, until Arnold had taught himself to believe that the idea of Oswald's suicide was a morbid delusion of Joshua Haggard's, and that, sooner or later, the welcome letter would come from some remote spot of earth to say that the young squire had forgotten his griefs, and was happy, and homeward-bound.

It was May when Captain Pentreath returned to the Grange in this more hopeful state of mind. The Exeter coach came in to Combhollow at five o'clock in the afternoon, and, after a hasty dinner, Arnold went straight to the minister's house.

He had made no friendships in his native place, and it seemed to him that Naomi Haggard was the nearest and dearest to him in his home. Had Oswald remained true, she would have been his sister. He felt all a brother's tenderness for her already.

"She shall be my sister," he told himself, "my friend and comforter. Both our lives have been made lonely."

Mr. Haggard's family had just finished tea when Arnold was ushered into the parlor. Sally had been carrying out the tea-board when she heard his knock, and had been so flurried by such an unusual circumstance as to be scarcely able to deposit her burden on the kitchen-table without loss or damage. When she opened the door and saw Captain Pentreath, she gave utterance to one of those suppressed screams with which she always greeted his likeness to his brother. "It was like seeing the young squire come back again, broader-chested, and nobler-looking," she told Jim, with whom she was on more confidential terms than with any other member of the household. Aunt Judith had gone back to the shop; Naomi sat reading by the open window; Joshua was in his arm chair, his head thrown back upon the cushion, his eyes half closed. He was resting himself after one of those pilgrimages over hill and dale which had of late sorely exhausted him. His whole life was much more exhausting than it had been; the candle was being burned more fiercely. Traces of fatigue showed plainly in the sharpened lines of his face, in the pallor of his skin, and the shadows about his eyes.

There was no one else in the room.

Joshua Haggard opened his eyes and started up. He looked at Arnold curiously for a moment or so, as if he scarcely knew him—like a man not quite released from the thralldom of a dream.

"I'm afraid I've disturbed you in a comfortable nap, Mr. Haggard," said Arnold.

"No, I was hardly asleep—only resting."

"You look as if you had much need of rest."

"Do I?" asked the minister, musingly. "Well, the scabbard must wear out in time, I suppose. It matters little if the sword is only bright till the last."

"You don't ask me if I have found out anything about my brother in London," said Arnold.

"Because I don't expect to hear that you have. I have told you my opinion," replied Joshua, gloomily.

"It is an opinion which I will never entertain until it is forced upon me by positive proof. My watch-word is, Hope—yes, Naomi, Hope," he added, turning to Joshua's daughter, who was looking at him gravely, with no answering ray of hope in her sad eyes.

He held out his hand to her, and they shook hands warmly, like brother and sister. Joshua sunk back into his chair, and took up an open volume from the table and resumed his reading, as if to indicate that he had no more to say to his visitor.

This reception was so cold as to be scarcely civil; but Arnold was not going to take offense easily. He wanted to know more of Naomi. In his mind she was the only person who could thoroughly sympathize with him in his longing for the absent, or in his grief for the lost. She alone in Combhollow had fondly loved his brother.

He began to talk of indifferent subjects, trying to infuse a little cheerfulness into the conversation; but there was a leaden gloom in the atmosphere of the minister's parlor which Arnold had no power to brighten. Naomi listened and replied with grave attention.

She was gentle and friendly, but he could not win a smile from her. She seemed weighed down by an inconquerable melancholy.

"Do they ever smile, I wonder?" thought Arnold. "Or has the household always this funereal air? Is it grief for my absent brother that makes her so sad? I should have given her credit for strength of mind to surmount such a grief, or at least to hide it. And the parson—well, I suppose that gloomy cast of countenance is simply professional."

Despite Naomi's lack of cheerfulness, Captain Pentreath was interested in her. That melancholy look lent a poetic air to her beauty. He felt that she was a woman of deepest feelings, one who would love but once and love forever. Even Oswald's inconstancy had not weakened her affection. He would have given much to be alone with her again for a little while, to have talked freely with her, heart to heart. He felt as if he could have spoken about his brother, and his brother's errors, without wounding her. But that figure of the minister sitting between him and the light oppressed him like a waking nightmare. There came an awkward silence presently, and Arnold felt he had no more to say, and must needs take his leave.

He had just risen to depart, when the door opened, and a girl with fair hair, pale face, and Puritan cap came into the room.

At sight of him she gave a faint cry and put her hand to her heart, and then, with a great effort of self-restraint, made him a grave courtesy, and crossed the room to an empty chair near Joshua.

"My God!" cried Arnold, turning very pale.

The sudden apparition wrung the exclamation from him before he had time to summon up his self-command. This was the face he had seen in his brother's journal. This was Joshua's young wife, of whose girlish beauty he had heard people talk, but whom he had never seen till this moment, for she had been ailing of late, and had kept much in her own room. And this was Oswald's fatal love—a love so wildly foolish, so deeply dishonorable, that it might well work the ruin of him who harbored it.

Joshua looked up as the door opened, and heard Cynthia's cry and Arnold's ejaculation, and saw the pale, startled look of one, the utter amazement of the other.

"He will be like his brother, perhaps," he thought, gloomily, and an angry shadow stole over his dark face. He looked at his wife as she seated herself quietly near him. She was very white, and her lips trembled. This sudden appearance of Oswald Pentreath's brother affected her as if she had seen a ghost.

Arnold took a hurried leave of the minister and his daughter, made a grave bow to Cynthia, and was gone. He could not have conversed calmly after the revelation which had surprised and shocked him. It was an awful thing to know that his brother had been guilty enough to fix his affections here.

Did Joshua know or suspect the truth? Yes, Arnold thought, he did suspect; and this suspicion was the cause of his coldness about Oswald, and that gloomy tone which suggested animosity.

Having discovered the fatal siren who had beguiled his brother from the paths of peace, Arnold's next desire was to be able to question her about his brother's fate. Who so likely to be in the secret of Oswald's intentions at the time he left Combhollow, as the woman he loved? Doubtless he had contrived to see her during his last brief residence at the Grange, and he had told her what he meant to do with his life.

The difficulty was for Arnold to obtain an interview with Joshua's wife without doing harm of some kind. Joshua was unfriendly and repellent in his manner, very ready to suspect evil, no doubt, of any one bearing the name of Pentreath. Arnold had also to consider Naomi's feelings. It was just possible that she was ignorant of her step-mother's part in the tragedy of her life.

Accident brought about a meeting which could have been only contrived with difficulty. Arnold had been out for a long, rambling ride on Herne on the third day after his return to the Grange, and, coming slowly homeward in the afternoon sunshine, he overtook Cynthia Haggard walking alone in one of the green lanes just outside Combhollow. She was walking very slowly, with bent head and listless step, like one whose thoughts are far away from the scenes that surround her.

The full western sunlight shone through the young oak leaves; the hawthorns were fleecy masses of white blossom, and filled the air with perfume; the sea glittered above the waving line of the hedge; and through the deep cleft in the rich red bank the little town of Combhollow showed its tiled roofs and many gables, its mellow thatches, and cool, gray slates, and shining ochre walls that seemed made of sunlight.

Arnold slipped quietly from his horse and put the bridle over his arm. Herne, having been as fiendish in behavior as in name during the first half of his day's work, was now in a calm and philosophic mood, and cropped the young ferns contentedly.

"Mrs. Haggard, may I have a few words with you?" Arnold asked, gently.

Cynthia had looked up, startled at the sound of the horse's hoofs. She dropped a courtesy, and answered nervously,

"If you please, sir."

"You wonder what I can have to say to you, perhaps?"

"Yes, sir."

"And yet you must know that my mind is full of anxiety about my brother."

Her cheek crimsoned, and then paled.

"I am—we are all anxious," she said. "It is so strange that he has not written to you. He was not likely to write to any one else—but to you, his brother, of whom he was so fond."

"You have heard him talk about me, then?" inquired Arnold.

"Very often. He looked forward so anxiously to your return."

"Would to God I had come sooner! I might

have kept him at home, perhaps. Come, Mrs. Haggard, be candid with me. This mystery about my brother is making me very wretched. Can not you help me? You may know something, perhaps, which no one else knows—something which might enlighten me as to his intentions when he left home. For Heaven's sake, be truthful with me! Do not be afraid to trust me. I know the trouble that made my brother leave his country. A diary of his fell into my hands a little while ago, with the story of his unhappy love written in it. I know that it was for your sake he became an exile. I implore you to tell me all you can that may help me to discover his fate."

Cynthia trembled, and grew deadly pale, yet looked at her questioner steadily. There was innocence in the look, Arnold thought. This was no guilty wife; but, not the less, a most unhappy woman.

"I know that he was going to America," answered Cynthia, "and I know no more than that."

"Did you see him on that last day?"

"I did. But pray do not tell Naomi or any one else. No one knows of our meeting. It was a secret. He wished to say good-bye to me before he went."

"Were you the last person who saw him?"

"I think so. When he left me, he was going to the coach."

"Are you sure he meant to go by the coach?"

"He told me so."

Arnold's countenance fell. This gave a darker aspect to the affair.

"What time in the day did you see him?"

"About four o'clock in the afternoon."

"And where did you meet?"

"Will you promise to tell no one?"

"Yes, I promise."

"On Matcherly Common, by the old shaft."

"I know the place. We played there many a time when we were children. Are you sure that no one knew of your meeting?"

"Quite sure."

"And that no one met you, or watched you, that afternoon?"

"I saw no one. I do not believe that any one saw me."

"My brother told you he meant to leave by the coach, yet he did not leave by it. You saw him at four o'clock that last afternoon, and I can not hear of any one who saw him after that hour. It is strange—alarming even—is it not?"

"Very strange. But I trust in God that he is safe, though we do not know where he is."

"That's an easy way of putting it," said Arnold, with a shade of bitterness.

"No one can be more sorry for him than I am," answered Cynthia, with a sudden sob. "It is my sin to be so sorry."

"Poor child! Forgive me for speaking harshly. I fancy sometimes that every one except myself is indifferent to my brother's fate. Your husband thinks he committed suicide; but I can't and won't believe that. You don't believe it, do you?" he asked, turning upon her quickly.

"Oh no, no, no!" she cried, with a startled look, full of pain, as if the idea were new to her. "He would never do that. He would never be so wild—so guilty—as to shoot himself, like Werther."

"Who is Werther?"

"A man in a book your brother read to us; but it was a real person, who was very unhappy, and who shot himself. He did not seem to know that suicide was a sin. But I can not believe that Oswald would be so rash. Oh no, no, God forbid that he should be tempted to such a dreadful deed. I can not think it. He was very calm when we bid each other good-bye. He blessed me, and promised to take more heed of serious things in days to come than he had done in days past."

"And there was no wildness in his manner? He did not talk like a desperate man?"

"No, indeed."

"I thank you for having been truthful and frank. It is a sad story. Would to God that he had been constant and faithful to that noble girl, your step-daughter!"

He could not spare her this implied reproach. His brother's fate seemed ever so much darker to him after what he had just heard; and for all this sorrow and uncertainty, the fair young creature standing by his side was in some measure to blame. Even that last secret meeting might have been in some wise the turning-point of his destiny.

"Had you been in the habit of meeting my brother secretly?" he asked, presently. "Had you met him often before that day?"

"Never in my life before," answered Cynthia, with an indignant look; "I should not have gone then, even though he made my going a last favor, if I had not had a purpose in seeing him. I thought I might win him back to Naomi. I knew he had once loved her dearly; and I thought perhaps it needed but a few words to awaken the old love in his heart."

"And do you think you were the best preacher to preach that sermon?" asked Arnold. "Well, you acted for the best, I dare say; and again I thank you for your candor. But I am no nearer the secret of my brother's fate than I was an hour ago. Good-bye!"

He raised his hat, and left her with a somewhat formal salutation, not offering her his hand. There was resentment in his heart against this fair-faced wife, who had spoiled Naomi's life and his own. He led Herne to the end of the lane, and there mounted him and trotted quickly home, the sagacious animal scenting the oats and clover in his now luxurious stable.

Cynthia walked slowly on, crying a little in a languid, helpless way, like one who was accustomed to solitude and tears. The sharp sound of Herne's hoofs died away in the distance. A lark was singing loud and shrill in the high, blue sky, and there was a drowsy bee among the hawthorns, but all the rest of nature was silent. Suddenly there broke upon that summer stillness a loud rustling of boughs, and a man sprang through a gap in the hedge, and confronted her.

She looked up full of sudden fear, expecting to see some unknown ruffian bent on robbery or murder; but the dark and angry face looking into hers was the face of her husband.

"Joshua! How you frightened me!"

"No doubt. Women who meet their lovers in secret are easily startled."

"My lover! Joshua! Are you mad? I have been talking to Captain Pentreath, who overtook me by chance a little while ago."

"By chance! Do you think I am going to believe that story? Woman, I know you too well. Satan set you in my path for my undoing—to the peril and loss of my soul; for my ruin and destruction here and hereafter. Fool, fool, fool!"—this with a cry of anguish, striking his forehead with his clenched fists. "I ought to have known it was a snare: the fair, strange face under the burning summer sky—the gypsy waif—homeless—nameless—a stranger to Christ and salvation—spawn of Beelzebub, why did I not recognize you?"

"Joshua, for pity's sake—I am your true wife—I have honored and obeyed you—"

"Honored! Was it to honor me you lured that young man to his doom? Was it for my honor you met him and kissed him? Yes—I saw him holding you in his arms under God's all-seeing eye, clasping you to his breast, as I held you that accursed night when I thought myself the happiest among men, because I had won you for my own. Won you! Oh, thou incarnate falsehood! fair as an angel to the eye, foul as sin to the heart that knows thee. And having tempted one brother to death and doom eternal, you are spreading your nets for the other. You would have him, too. You are like her that waiteth at the street corner, 'in the twilight, in the evening, in the black and dark night. Her house is the way to hell, going down to the chambers of death. Yea, verily, her feet go down to death; her steps take hold on hell.' Away with you, fair devil!"

His arm was raised to strike, but she fell on her knees, and thus by a happy chance escaped the degrading blow, and saved her husband that last shame.

"Joshua, what madness has seized you? I never wronged you willingly, as God knows. If I did do you wrong, it is because human nature is weak, and God does not always stand by us. He lets us stand alone a little while in order to show us how weak we are without him: how soon we stumble and fall when that heavenly hand is withdrawn. Yes, husband, I have been a sinner. God hid his face for a time. Oswald loved me, and I loved him, and forgot my wickedness in the sweetness of being beloved by him. It was like a dream. But when he spoke of his love my heart awakened, and I was your true wife. I have said no word to him—never, from first to last—that I dare not repeat to you, or that I am ashamed to remember. I am your true wife, and honor and revere you now as I did that first day when you took me to the only decent home I had ever known. Have I forgotten what I owe you, Joshua? Oh no, no, no. I am not so base, nor so ungrateful."

"Your speech is like your face," said Joshua, with set teeth; "passing fair—passing fair. But I know you, pretty one! Yes; look up, eyes blue as God's summer sky—look up in sad, innocent wonder. A lie—a lie; nothing but a lie, Satan has made you so. He painted your cheeks, and limned your smile, and every delicate feature, that you might lure good men to death and hell. Can he work without his instruments, do you think? He does not walk this earth in palpable shape, lest we should know him and avoid him. But he puts on such a pretty garb as yours, and counts his worshipers by the score. Every priestess such as you brings a crowd to his altar. But I have done with you. I have rent the net. I will have no further dealings with you. I will see your false face no more!"

"Joshua, have pity!"

"'Can a man take fire in his bosom and not be burned?'"

"Joshua!"

"'He that doeth it destroyeth his own soul. A wound and dishonor shall he get; and his reproach shall not be wiped away.'"

"Joshua, can you believe that there was any harm—any wrong against you—in my meeting with Captain Pentreath just now?" cried Cynthia, still at her husband's feet, looking up at him in an agony of supplication, trying to grasp those strong, cruel hands that thrust her from him.

"I know that you are false to the core. I know that Satan made you to lead me down to the pit. What do I know about you and Captain Pentreath? Very little. I was just in time for the fag-end of your interview. I came across the field, and saw you through a break in the hedge. You were standing in close converse with him just as you were with his brother—"

"Ah!" cried Cynthia, startled, "you were there that day—you saw us. You said so just now."

"The kisses were over, I dare say," continued Joshua, too much beside himself to heed this interruption. "The kisses were done with before I came. He heard my step, perhaps, and so left you with a stately salutation, as if you were strangers parting. Hypocrites, liars both—children of the accursed! But I have done with you. I turn my face away from Satan and his witchcraft, and I will make my peace with God before I die. Go back—go back to your tents—to the children of Baal. Go back to your juggleries and mummeries, and leave me to repent of my folly—to put on sackcloth and ashes—to go up alone among the hills, like Elijah in the mountains, to wait for the advent of my God."

"Joshua, for mercy's sake be calm—speak to me quietly, that I may know what you really mean. I have no wish but to obey you. If you say that I am to go away from you—to go back and be a servant, and work for my daily bread as I did before I was your wife—I shall go and make no complaint. But I am your true and obedient wife all the same. Do not doubt that. I will obey you when you are cruel, just as I obeyed you when you were kind, and I shall never murmur."

"Fair of speech, and fair of face," muttered Joshua. "Yes, Lucifer, her master, was beautiful as the morning-star."

"Do you mean to turn me out of doors, Joshua? Do you mean that your home is to be mine no longer?"

"I do. You have brought misery and shame into my house. You have poisoned my cup, turned my daily bread to ashes. I would fain be rid of you forever. I can not serve God while you are near me. Satan is too strong for me while he works in such a guise."

"And you wish us to part," she said, deliberately, "forever?"

"Yes. I love my imperishable soul better than that viler human heart which cleaves to you. In heaven there is neither marrying nor giving in marriage. In heaven I shall forget the anguish of an unsatisfied love."

"Joshua, I am your servant to obey you in this as in all things. You have but to say you wish me gone, and I shall go. When you cease to pity, God will forgive and take pity on me, because he does not make our burdens too heavy for us. Do you remember that night in the pine wood, Joshua, when you took me to your heart, and told me that I was precious in your sight? I said then that I was not good enough to be your wife, that it would be happiness for me to be your servant, and wait upon you, and work for you, and gather words of wisdom from your lips. But you would have it otherwise. I was wiser in this, you see, for now you are weary of me, and want to send me away. Let it be so, then; I will forget that I am your wife, and remember only that I am your servant, and bound to obey in all things. I am your servant, and you have dismissed me. I can go back to Penmoyle, and work for my living, far away, where I shall not disgrace you. Good-bye, sir."

She took his hand and kissed it, still on her knees. He shuddered at the contact of those rose-bud lips, but never looked at her. His eyes were fixed on the distant sea-line, wide-open eyes gazing blankly at the blue, bright light.

"Am I really to go, Joshua?" Cynthia asked, meekly, after a brief silence, in which the hum of insects, the sharp whirring sound of the grasshopper, filled the air.

He passed his hand across his brow wearily.

"Get thee behind me, Satan. Yes, go, go, go. I can never scale the walls of God's eternal city while this weight of earthly passion cleaves to me. Go far out of my reach, lest I should slay you, and think of your dead lover, and repent your sin."

"What! he is dead, then—and you know it?" she exclaimed, with a bitter cry.

"Yes," answered Joshua, flinging her away from him into the dust, "go and weep and howl for him. It was your sin that slew him!"

She lay for a little while where he had thrown her on the sun-baked grass of the bank, among the ferns and wild flowers, not quite unconscious, but with a brain in which strange and familiar images whirled wildly as in a demon dance. Then came a few moments in which all was blank, moments of blessed repose, and then she staggered to her feet and looked about her. The lane was empty. Joshua had said his last word, and was gone.

She stood looking round her in the westering sunshine, pondering what she ought to do. Not for an instant did she contemplate rebellion against her husband's decree. He had bid her to leave him, and she would go away, meekly, uncomplainingly, as Hagar went out into the wilderness.

"Ah me!" she said to herself, piteously, comparing herself with Hagar, "I have no Ishmael to be my comfort and hope."

It never occurred to her to go back to her husband's house and claim the place which was hers by right, and which no act of hers had forfeited. She did not even contemplate going back to claim her own—the clothes and books and small possessions, dear to womanhood, which she had acquired since her marriage. Empty-handed and penniless as when Joshua found her sitting by the water-pool on the distant Cornish waste, she left the scene of her

"I WILL SEE YOUR FALSE FACE NO MORE."

brief and hapless married life. She had neither purse nor scrip, not so much as a few shillings to help her on her way. But she turned her pale face steadily to the west, and set out to walk to Penmoyle. In all this wild world she had no other friends than the spinster sisters whom she could turn to for a refuge in her desolation, and even from them she could not feel quite sure of a kind reception. They had offered her their friendship, telling her, on the day she left them, to appeal to them in any hour of need. But how would they receive her when she told them that Joshua had cast her off—they who reverenced Joshua as a saint and prophet?

To them she must needs turn in her distress, having no other earthly haven. She had served them faithfully in the past, and had won their favor, and she was willing to serve them in the future for her daily bread and nightly shelter, and the privilege of worshiping her God in the faith Joshua had taught her. She thought of the white-haired old minister, with his gentle, old-world manners, and his ready kindness. She remembered how his praise had thrilled her at the thought that Joshua would hear of her well-doing and be glad. And now all was over. Joshua hated her. Joshua spurned her as a vile and guilty creature. No man's praise, no woman's favor, could ever lift her up in his esteem any more. She was degraded and cast off forever.

Well, she could be a servant again, and toil for her bread, and serve her God in patience so long as life's burden was laid upon her. It seemed to her that the road along which she had to carry her burden was not interminable. A little way off there came a region of mist and cloud, entering which, she would be at peace, and would lay down her load, and rest her weary head upon the sweetest pillow, and let her tired eyelids close amidst a divine sunshine, light as of the resurrection morning, when the glad sunbeams danced upon the hill-tops.

It was a long way from Combhollow to that little village high up among the rolling Cornish tors. Cynthia could not calculate the number of miles, but she had an idea that Penmoyle was very far away—many days' journey, at the rate at which she could walk, which was slow, for her cough and low fever had left her weak.

"Luckily, I know how to sleep under a haystack, and I am not ashamed to beg my bread when I see a kind face at a cottage-door," she said to herself.

She had her silver watch and chain, which she thought she might sell in one of the towns she had to pass through; and there was the gold keeper above her wedding-ring; this, too, she might dispose of, if hard pressed by want; but if people were kind, she could get on without money, so little would serve to keep body and soul together.

So she set out on her journey, a new Hagar, but with no sweet child-companion to make the desert blossom like the rose.

After his interview with Cynthia Haggard, Captain Pentreath reasoned himself into an easier state of mind about his missing brother. His sanguine nature leaned toward the brighter view of the question. Oswald had been calm and resigned when he parted with the object of his fatal love; he had gone away to begin a new life, had cast off the fetters of passion, and gone forth a free man.

"I shall hear from him in due time. All will be well," said Arnold.

Having made up his mind deliberately to go on hoping—and indeed entertaining the conviction that the riddle of his brother's destiny would be solved in time—Arnold Pentreath considered it his duty to inspire Naomi with the same hopeful view. It afflicted him to see her pale, sad face, to watch her slow, listless movements. It became his most ardent desire to cheer and console her.

With this end he went very often to the minister's house, and sat in the quiet old parlor where Oswald had spent so many hours of his life, and talked to Naomi while she sewed. There was no one to object to his visits. Aunt Judith was in the shop; Joshua was away, no one knew whither. It was his habit now to come home wearied at night-fall, save on those evenings when he had class-meetings, or Bible-meetings, or some kind of service in his chapel.

Cynthia was gone, and Joshua had accounted briefly for her absence by stating that she had gone to see her friends at Penmoyle.

"You had better send her trunk on by the coach," said Joshua to Naomi.

"But why did she go so suddenly, father?" Naomi asked, puzzled by this disruption of the household.

"Because it was her whim to go, and it was not my pleasure to say her nay."

"Has she gone by the coach?"

"I suppose so."

"And when is she to come back?"

"When I please to bid her come."

Naomi sighed, and obeyed her father's order. Alas for this change which made her father a person to be obeyed with fear and trembling, rather than with faith and love! Naomi had not forgiven Cynthia for all the misery she had wrought; but this sudden disappearance of her father's wife oppressed her with a sense of injustice and wrong done by Joshua. With what cruelty had he driven that meek and sorrowful offender away from him? His daughter had noted his conduct to his wife, and had seen his harshness, his coldness, his growing aversion—the chilling mask which passionate love puts on when jealousy gnaws the heart.

Cynthia was gone, and Naomi's life was now quite lonely. She was glad of Arnold's visit, and took some comfort from his hopeful talk about the absent master of the Grange.

"He will come back to his home and to you, Naomi," said the captain; "come back a new man, and an honest one, proud to redeem his faith."

"Were he to come back to-morrow, I should give him a sister's loving welcome," answered Naomi, "but never more than a sister's love.

He has broken my heart once — I won't let him break it again."

"But if he were honestly repentant and sincere, Naomi?"

"He might believe himself sincere. I could not trust him with my peace. Do not think that I am angry with him. I am only sorry that he should ever have been so mistaken as to believe in the reality of his love for me. He never knew what love meant till he gave his heart where it should not have been given."

"Well, Naomi, perhaps you are wise. The vessel that fails to answer to her helm in the hour of danger is hardly a ship to be trusted. Then we will think of Oswald as an absent brother only —and look forward hopefully to his return."

"God knows I try to hope for it," said Naomi, with a sigh.

"Why should he not be really your brother— brother in fact as well as in name?" pleaded Arnold, taking her unresisting hands. "Make him your brother, Naomi, by making me your husband. We have not known each other very long, but our mutual sorrow has brought us nearer together than years of common acquaintance could have done. I have looked into your heart, Naomi, and I know its worth. Let me take my brother's place, dear; I shall never wander; my love shall know no change. It is founded on a rock; for it was my esteem for your noble nature which first taught me to love you."

Naomi withdrew her hands from his, and stood up, looking at him seriously, with eyes full of tears.

"Never again let this be spoken of between us, Arnold," she said. "It can never be."

"Why not?"

"There is a reason which you must never know."

"But I am not to be satisfied like that, Naomi. There is no reason that I can recognize— unless you say you do not love me, can never teach yourself to love me."

"I will say that, then—I can never love you!"

"And your eyes are brimming with tears, and your lips tremble as you say the words. It is not true, Naomi; it is a lie, a lie against the might of love. You love me as I love you, and we were meant for each other, and for happiness. Why should you or I be miserable all our lives because a foolish young man has run away from felicity? Naomi, dearest love, make my life happy."

"You are good, and I honor you—like him, and my heart yearns toward you," answered the girl, falteringly; for it seemed to her at this moment as if the picture of a new life were suddenly unfolded before her eyes, and the vision was marvelously bright; "but I can never be more than your friend and sister."

"I see. You love the truant still. Did I not say so?"

"His memory is very dear to me."

Arnold said no more. Those eloquent eyes, those tremulous lips, had told him he was beloved, and yet this love was denied him. What was he to think? He was hardly inclined to despair, or to accept this answer of Naomi's as final. She had some mistaken notion of fidelity to a departed love, doubtless; she would sacrifice a lover in the present—a real and living love—for the sake of that inconstant lover in the past.

"Patience!" thought Arnold; "I shall be able to talk her out of her folly, sooner or later."

Meanwhile he was content to be accepted on the friendly and brotherly footing. He contrived to see Naomi very often. He found his way even into the wilderness, that burial-ground of dead joys and bitter memories. He met her in all her walks. It was difficult for her not to think that her lost lover had come back to her with a nobler mind and larger ideas. Here she found no languid indolence, no placid unconcern for the welfare of others, so long as summer skies were blue, and one could lie at ease under the beeches reading Byron. Arnold was full of care for the laborers on his patrimonial estate—full of sympathy and kindness for the struggling tenant farmers and their industrious wives, for the young men who desired a little more enlightenment and education than their fathers had deemed needful for the fullness of life's measure. With Arnold benevolent deeds were not castles in the air—Utopian schemes to be set on foot in some convenient hour of the future—but duties to be done at once, now, while it was yet day.

Arnold was glad of so intelligent a sympathizer with his cares as steward of his brother's fortune. Naomi was always ready to help him with counsel and experience. She had visited among the laboring poor, and knew their needs and short-comings—knew where disease found them weakest—how fever crept into their dwellings.

"I can't think what I should do without you," said Arnold; and it was a new happiness to Naomi to feel that she had been useful. Life at home was so empty and barren, her duties mechanically performed, her service unrecognized. The change in her father had made the very atmosphere of home gloomy and oppressive.

Cynthia had been away nearly a month, and there had been no tidings of her. This seemed strange to all the household; but as Joshua expressed neither wonder nor anxiety, it was supposed that his wife's absence was understood and approved by him.

"Poor, weak-minded mortal!" sighed Aunt Judith, after discussing the question with her niece at their lonely tea-table; "the first time I saw that pink-and-white piece of prettiness step across the threshold I knew what he was laying up for himself. A man of his years can't set his heart upon a wax doll without paying the penalty; above all, when it's a doll that has neither parents, nor a good stock of house linen, nor decent bringing-up. I knew what was coming." cried Aunt Judith, with a laugh of exultant irony; "and my only wonder is that things haven't turned out much worse."

"Poor thing!" sighed Naomi, thinking, with some touch of compunction, of the pale, sad face from which she had averted her eyes so coldly of late. "Do you think father sent her away?"

"If he did, he'd have done no more than was right," said Aunt Judith. "And if he'd done it when I first tried to open his eyes about her, he'd have shown himself a wiser man. But whether she got tired of her life here, and went off of her own free-will, or whether your father sent her away, matters very little to us. She's gone," concluded the spinster, decisively, "and I hope it's not unchristian like to wish she may never come back."

Having put the idea of his brother's suicide

out of his mind, Arnold had not attached any dark meaning to his interview with Cynthia. Her statement seemed to him natural and credible, and rather calculated to re-assure than to alarm. Oswald had been calm and resigned. He had stated his intention of going to a new world to begin a new life. What ground was there for supposing that a man in this frame of mind had been so false to manhood as to take his own life? Arnold sent to an Exeter bookseller for the "Sorrows of Werther," and read the story carefully; but not being of so sentimental a turn as his brother, and not being in love with another man's wife, he had found the reading rather a laborious business, and Werther a weak-minded youth, with a fatal habit of prosing about his own emotions.

"God forbid that my brother should ever follow the example of such a booby," said Arnold, when he had seen Werther laid in his unconsecrated grave, in the memorable blue coat and yellow waistcoat, with Charlotte's pink breastknot in his pocket; "I should have as much contempt for his want of sense as regret for his want of religion."

Arnold had not yet gone to look at the spot where Oswald had parted from Mrs. Haggard. He remembered the scene well enough in days gone by; the lonely common, with its hillocks and hollows and marshy spots, over which the swift-winged plover skimmed lightly, vanishing with a shrill cry into blue distance. The scene was so familiar to him that it had no special significance; it never struck him that just that one spot of all others, that little bit of sun-burned common by the abandoned mine, might be fatal; that here yawned a natural grave, ready for the end of a tragedy.

He went up to an old farm-house one afternoon to settle a question of roofing and thatching which had been for some time in discussion. It was the last house on the way to Matcherly Common — a house that stood on the edge of the wood, or almost in the wood. The latticed casements looked down a beechen glade. It was a place of silence and soft, cool shadows, a welcome retreat on a summer's day like this on which Arnold rode over to settle matters with Farmer Weston about his granary roofs.

Here had been made happy in a spacious stable where the good old white wagon-horses dozed over their hay and clover, and where the thud of a ponderous tail whisked round for the slaughter of a forest fly, and the slow munching of fodder, were the only sounds that broke the slumberous stillness. Captain Pentreath had made his inspection of the premises, and was drinking a glass of Mrs. Weston's famous perry before departing, when the farmer mentioned a subject which always found Arnold an attentive listener.

"You haven't heerd any thing of your brother, I suppose, captain?"

"Not a line. But I don't despair of getting news of him before long. He's not been gone a twelvemonth yet, you see, Mr. Weston, and a year is a short time when a man has to cross the sea. He may have changed his mind about America, and gone to New South Wales, and that's half a year's voyage, to begin with."

"That's where the convicks go, ain't it, captain? The young squire 'ud never go theer, surely."

"There's no knowing how far a man may go when he's once made up his mind to turn rover," said Arnold, cheerily.

"Ah!" sighed the farmer, "this here world of ours be a strange 'un; there's things in it that puzzles my poor old wits a'most as much as that theer thatch catchin' fire the identical day arter I refused Aunt Nancy her faggit."

There was a lurking significance in this remark that caught Arnold's attention.

"You have heard something about my brother!" he cried. "You can tell me something. For God's sake! keep nothing from me; it is a matter of life or death."

"The by's a truth-spoken by," said the farmer, "or I shouldn't ha' listened to 'un."

"What boy?"

"It isn't because a by earns his bit o' mate minding cows that he hasn't got a soul to be saved," continued the farmer, as deliberately as if pursuing a philosophical argument; "and I can't say as ever I found out this here lad in a lie."

"Will you tell me what you mean—how this bears upon my brother?" cried Arnold, breathless with impatience.

"My wife and me have sat under Mr. Haggard for the last ten years. He was the first to tell us our souls were in danger, and he's gone on warning of us ever since. 'Taint likely I'm going to speak agen him."

"Speak plainly, at any rate," exclaimed Arnold, "if you mean any thing. And from your manner it's clear you mean something. What has this boy of yours to do with my brother's fate?"

"It ain't what he has to do, but what he can tell. It was a hot summer day, you may remember, that day as the young squire was last seen at Combhellow—harvest-time, and regular harvest weather. This lad o' mine, Tim, was out in the forest mindin' cows. But perhaps you'd sooner hear it from the lad's own lips?" suggested the farmer.

"I don't care how I hear it, so long as I hear it quickly!"

"Well, I'll call the by; he's close handy, diggin' taties."

"Let's go to him," said Arnold, taking up his whip and gloves. The farmer wished to bring the boy to the parlor, as a mode of proceeding more consistent with the respect due to his landlord; but the captain was too eager to endure ceremony. He hurried to the straggling old kitchen-garden at the back of the house, where ancient espaliers, which had long outgrown their sustaining frame-work, spread wide their arms against the blue June sky.

Here, digging up the smooth, golden-skinned potatoes, they found the farmer's cow-boy, a frank-looking, blue-eyed lad, over whose sunburned forehead trickled the dew of toil.

"Now, lookye here, Tim," said the farmer; "I want 'ee to tell the captain what it was you saw and heerd that day in Matcherly Wood, when th' young squire passed 'ee by."

The boy wiped his forehead upon his shirtsleeve, shifted his spade from one hand to the other, and, after some moments of obvious embarrassment, found a voice.

"I were mindin' cattle in the forest, you see, sir, and theer were one cow wi' a white face;

she were a new 'un that master had boughten at Barnstaple last market-day, and she were strange, poor thing, and strayed away ever so far up toward the common; and I was goin' arter her, when who should I see but the minister on afore me, goin' right up to the common."

"Do you mean Mr. Haggard?"

"Surely. And he went on ahead o' me till he come right out o' the wood just wheer the old shaft be, and he looked about 'im a bit when he got clear o' the trees, and then went into the engine-house. I watched a bit, wonderin' what he were up to, and then I see 'im standin' just inside the door-way, where there's a lot o' fallen stones and rubbish, and tansy growin' as tall as young trees, and he stood there lookin' out, yet keeping of himself hidden like as if he were watchin' for somebody. And just then I cotch-ed sight o' the white-faced cow, ever so far across the common, and I ran after her."

"Strange, warn't it?" said the farmer; "but there's more to tell."

"I cotched the old cow, and I was taking of her back to the wood, when I comes right up agen the young squire. I was a bit scared at s'ein' he, for I'd heerd tell as he were away from Combhollow. He didn't take no notice o' me, but went on, swingin' his stick round, and singin' to hisself soft-like. Well, I thowt no more about 'im, and I was here and theer with they cows, and they would stray up toward the common; though there warn't much but tansy for they to eat up theer: and I were up close to the common about an hour afterward, when I heerd a shot fired, and then another, so close together they might 'a been one a'most."

A white blankness spread itself over Arnold's face—the vacant horror of despair. It was some moments before he could speak.

"You ran to see what those shots meant?" he cried.

"I couldn't tell wheer they come from, not for sartain: but I thowt it was somewheer near the old shaft, and I went up theer arter a bit, but theer was nowt to be seen, and no one about. I went into the engine-house, but the minister was gone."

"Why has this been kept from me?" asked Arnold. "Why, in Heaven's name, didn't you let me know this sooner, Mr. Weston? You know how anxious I have been about my brother."

"I only heerd of it t'other day, when I overheerd Timothy talkin' to our Prudence, the dairy-maid. He was tellin' her about the shot."

"Don't you think it was your duty to have told your master, boy?" asked Arnold.

"I didn't think it was any harm. It might ha' been some one firing at a rabbit or a gull. There's plenty o' say-gulls flies across Matcherly Common."

"You saw no more—you heard no more?"

"No, there was nowt arter that. It were milkin'-time, and I had to take the cows home."

"Now, look here, Weston," said Captain Pentreath, taking the farmer aside. "Those shots may mean nothing, or they may mean a great deal. I know my brother was up yonder, by the old shaft, that August day. I know he had an enemy, and was watched, and followed. I have no evidence that he was ever seen alive after that day. Till to-day I've hugged myself with

the hope that he is living in some distant country, and that I shall hear of him in due time. I begin to think that hope is a delusion, and that he never left this neighborhood. If he has been murdered, it is my business to bring his murderer to the gallows. But I must first find his murdered body. Will you help me? You've plenty of farm laborers in your service. Will you help me to search Matcherly Common, and the mine below it?"

<hr>

CHAPTER XXXIV.

AT HIS DOOR.

Naomi thought long and deeply of that last interview with Arnold Pentreath. She was in no wise inclined to admit to herself that the sea-captain could now, or in any time to come, take the place of his missing brother—that the heart which had been so freely and so entirely given to Oswald could ever belong to another. Yet, while looking upon this change of feeling as impossible, Naomi was conscious that Arnold had begun to exercise a powerful influence upon her mind, and that his most unexpected avowal of affection for her had moved her deeply.

He was like his brother, and he loved his brother. These two circumstances were alone sufficient to insure her regard. And now he had paid her the highest tribute that man can offer to woman. He had given her his loyal and kindly heart—that heart whose wide benevolence she had seen in many an inconsidered act of his life; he had tendered her his happiness, his future; and she had found only one cold answer to his prayer: "It can not be."

"If I loved him better than I ever loved Oswald, my answer must have been the same," she said to herself in those long hours of sorrowful meditation which made up the larger half of her joyless life. "While the dark cloud rests upon Oswald's fate I can have but one answer for any lover—you, Arnold, of all others. How do I know that I have the right to stand up with unbowed head among honest men and women, when my heart is tortured by the thought that my father—he who preaches the Gospel, and exhorts other men to repentance—may be the vilest sinner of all?"

This was the gist of Naomi's meditations. She had tried to put that awful fear away from her, but it was rooted in her heart. As weeks and months went by, and brought no news of Oswald, the fear grew stronger; and with the fear came remorse, a slow and consuming anguish. Had she been but patient, had she borne her own burden in silence and kept the secret of that cruel letter, this horror need never have been. She had put the scorpion into her father's hand—the scorpion which had stung that once noble nature to madness.

"Oh, my father, my lost and erring father," she cried, in an hour when her fear became almost conviction, "would to God that I could bear the burden of your sin! 'Twas I who tempted you; it was my vile jealousy that urged you to despair and guilt. Let the avenging rod fall heaviest on me. O God, pity and pardon him, thou who hast promised pardon and pity for the darkest sin!"

That there might be pardon even for this last and most hideous sin of blood-guiltiness, Naomi firmly believed; but could there be forgiveness for a sinner who added the sin of hypocrisy to his darker crime, and held his head high among men when it should have been bowed in the dust under the burden of his shame? Could there be pardon for a sinner who kept the secret of his guilt, and pretended to lead other men along the shining path to heaven? No, assuredly. That smooth-faced hypocrisy—the sin for which man's Teacher and Redeemer reserved his most scathing denunciations—must treble the infamy of the darker guilt it masked, and render pardon impossible. To the sinner who repenteth, pity and peace had been freely offered; but what mercy was ever promised to the Pharisee who, under the semblance of exceptional piety, concealed a deeper infamy than the worst act of the despised publican?

These thoughts were in Naomi's mind, as she sat in her narrow deal pew, in the soft June twilight, listening to her father's preaching. The chapel was full to suffocation, for this was one of those meetings which the people of Combhollow particularly affected; a service in which Joshua Haggard was expected to surpass himself, and in which Satan—so often and so directly appealed to as to seem an actual member of the congregation—was to be worsted and driven forth in confusion by the minister's eloquence. Some even went so far as to call these evening services "devil-hunts." The part which the congregation took in them was not altogether negative or quiescent. There were times when eager spirits assumed an active share in the proceedings—when from smothered sighs, and head-shakings, and hollow groans, as of inward and bodily disorder, the convulsed auditor was moved to speech, and poured forth his Satanic experiences before a hushed and awe-struck congregation. Joshua did not encourage or favor these lay utterances, and his powerful influence and vigorous eloquence did much to hold his flock in check; but he could not always dam the flood of inspiration.

"You're a powerful preacher, Master Haggard," observed a weather-beaten old fisherman, whose rambling discourse Joshua strove to arrest; "but when a ignorant man feels he's gotten the Holy Sperrit inside 'im, he ain't goin' to be cut short before he's had his say. Education goes for nothin' with the Sperrit. He don't mind grammar."

Upon this particular evening the flock had been content to express its feelings by means of groans and sighs, and brief ejaculations of a self-abasing character. Joshua stood in his square deal pulpit, with an open Bible on the green-baize cushion, and preached of erring humanity and man's darling sins. His sermons were always extempore, and had of late been obviously without plan or method—a change for the worse, which Naomi was conscious of, but which had scarcely been perceived by the flock, that congregation being satisfied with strong language and a flow of rugged eloquence, without looking too nicely for logical precision or directness. Joshua turned the leaves of his Bible, and seemed to draw new ideas from the page he glanced at.

He had been preaching longer than usual, though his sermons were apt to be long; and the twilight deepened as he stood in his pulpit, leaning forward with his elbow on the desk, and the other hand nervously turning the leaves of the Bible, which there was now scarcely light enough for him to see. He looked pale as ashes in that gray light; but his large, dark eyes gleamed with a sombre fire as they wandered round the upturned faces of his flock. Sometimes his eyes lingered wistfully on the pew where Naomi sat, and on Cynthia's empty place.

"Yes, my brethren," he cried; "yes, fellow-sinners, each has his darling sin. The world sees it not, knows it not. The world honors us—we bask in its smiles and favor. Men point to us as ensamples of godly life. Yet the darling sin is there, in our heart of hearts; we hug it close, we hide it from every human eye. But in the still night-watches it comes forth like a serpent out of his hole, and rears its venomous crest, and stings us with the horror of our guilt. We call ourselves soldiers and servants of God, yet know that our real master and captain is the devil. Yes, my brethren, the great recruiting sergeant has enlisted us. We have taken the devil's shilling; the image and superscription upon the coin are the image and superscription of Satan.

"Alas, my fellow-sinners! know you how swift a thing it is to fall? The fall of Lucifer himself was but the act and passage of a moment. There was no long deliberation—there was no broad gap of time between heaven and hell. In one hour an angel of light standing near the throne—in the next revolted, fallen, banished, the prince and leader of devils. So, too, with us the fall is swift, the fall is sudden. We are chosen and elected, called to grace—all our old sins forgiven. This regeneration is the work of a moment. We look back and remember the hour in which the light came down upon us, as at Pentecost. But we may extinguish this light in blackest darkness—we may lose this divine heritage, forfeit our citizenship in the eternal city; and this extinction, this loss, may be the work of a moment."

Groans both loud and deep, plaintive feminine sighs, disjointed ejaculations of "Alas!" and "Too true!" spoke the convictions of the assembled sinners.

"Oh, my brethren, wretched sinners, groveling in the dust and ashes of this little world, if at this moment the last trump should sound, and the heavens be rent asunder, and the great Judge appear shining in his unspeakable splendor, calling men to judgment, how many among us could answer to that awful summons without fear and trembling, and the knowledge that eternal death was our just doom? How many would be found in this crowded chapel fit to stand before him? how many of those blessed ones for whom judgment would mean reward everlasting? Would be find twenty, do you think, or ten, or five? Alas! my fellow-sinners, would he find one?"

He lifted his arms aloft at this solemn question, looking up as if he verily saw that appalling day—the great white throne, the compass of angels, the throng of saints and martyrs, the Divine Judge himself, in their dazzling glory.

"Oh, come not yet, awful Judge!" he cried; "we are not ready. Leave us a little more time to wrestle with Satan, to repent our iniquities, to loosen the bondage of this earthly tabernacle.

before we stand naked at thy throne. Who among all these is prepared to meet thy summons? Who does not tremble as I do at the thought of thine anger?'

"Ay, tremble, sinner; quail before the God you have blasphemed!" cried a resonant voice at the end of the chapel. "Tremble, hypocrite; for the sins of those whom you pretend to teach are white as snow beside the blackness of your guilt!"

There was a sudden commotion in the crowded chapel; every one turned toward the door at the end of the building, from which direction the voice came.

Naomi's heart sunk with an appalling dread. Too well she knew that voice, though she had never before heard it raised in those tones of withering denunciation.

"A worthy teacher!" cried Arnold Pentreath, facing the excited congregation, who were all standing up in their pews and staring at him, as he stood conspicuous among the crowd at the door; "a teacher to call sinners to repentance—a fit exponent of Gospel truth—a man whose soul is steeped in hypocrisy, whose hands are stained with blood?"

There rose a chorus of exclamations; and then one of the stanchest of Joshua's followers, a brawny farmer, opened the door of his pew and pushed his way out into the narrow aisle.

"Now look 'ee yere, Cap'n Pentreath," he said; "I ain't goin' to stand by and yere Mister Haggard abused. You'll just hold your tongue; and if you're gone mazed, you'll take your madness out o' this yere chapel."

On this there rose a general cry of reprobation at the captain's unseemly conduct, Joshua Haggard standing up in his pulpit all the while, looking down at his bewildered flock, firm as a rock, but pale to the lips.

"Come out, come out, all of you, and see the witness I bring against him. You think I accuse him without grounds for my accusation. I have my evidence close by—damning evidence. Let him confront it if he can. Do you know that this man—your teacher and guide—is a murderer, a secret assassin?"

"It's a lie!" roared the man who had last spoken; "it's a lie, and I'd ram your lying words down your throat if I could get at 'ee!"

"It's the truth, and he knows it. Look at him. He doesn't deny it, you see. Look at your teacher—he is dumb. His eloquence fails him for the first time in his life. He does not fear to insult his God by his lying oracles, but he shrinks from the face of the man he has injured. Come out, Joshua Haggard, and meet your accuser. He is at the door. He is waiting—oh, so patiently!—till you come and look him in the face."

Naomi could just distinguish the sailor's white face in the dim light. He stood above the crowd, raised on the step of the door, the entrance of Little Bethel being somewhat higher than the chapel itself.

All was over, then. The worst an avenging God could bring to pass had come. Her father was known to others as that which she had in so many an hour of agony suspected him to be. He was known as a murderer. By some means or other, the secret had been made known. God's ways are wonderful and mysterious. She had always thought that it would be so. Her lost lover's blood cried aloud for vengeance, and the great Avenger had heard the cry.

At last Joshua spoke, and that firm, full voice, in which he had so often swayed and moved his flock, silenced all ejaculations. Every eye was now turned toward the preacher, and all waited his indignant denial of the charge brought against him.

"I am accused of murder," said Joshua, calmly and deliberately, "and we are told the witness of my crime is at the door. Let us go forth and meet him. Those who know me best here know whether God ever meant me to be the shedder of my brother's blood. He maketh one vessel to honor, and another to dishonor. My position hitherto has been honor, and you who know me can say whether I have been deserving of any other lot."

"There is not a better man in the country," cried the farmer who had first taken upon himself to be Joshua's champion.

"Nor a more pious—nor a more charitable," clamored many voices.

"God, who knows all things," cried Joshua, lifting up his voice with a sudden burst of passion, "knows that whatever I have taught in this tabernacle of his, I have taught from my heart of hearts. I have travailed for this people, I have loved them, and striven for them. I have not cheated them with pleasant words, though my heart yearned toward them. Where others have chastised with whips, I have chastised with scorpions; but I have preached the Gospel with a single mind. I have had no thought save to teach and to save. O Lord, if I have been the vilest of sinners, at least in this thy house I have been a true and faithful servant!"

"Ay, and so ye have, Master Haggard," chimed in a chorus of women.

"And now let me go forth to meet my accuser," said Joshua, opening the door of his pulpit and slowly descending the stair.

Naomi had come out into the aisle. She threw herself in his way as he passed, and linked her arm through his; and, thus linked, they came along the narrow space together, the congregation falling back a little to let them pass.

Joshua did not repulse his daughter. He suffered her to hold his arm, seeming scarcely conscious of the contact. His dark deep-set eyes looked straight before him under bent brows; his firm lips were closely set. He looked a man who was ready to confront Satan himself in bodily form.

"Come," cried Arnold, beside himself with suppressed passion, "your accuser is not loud or clamorous. He will wait quietly till you go to him. It is I that am impatient to set you face to face."

Joshua and his daughter were at the door by this time. They came close to Arnold. Naomi almost touched him as the crowd swayed against her. She looked at him with an expression which he never forgot.

"Oh, Arnold, what have you done?" she said piteously, in a low voice.

"My duty to my brother."

They were outside the chapel in the next moment, in the clear summer evening. The stars were shining in the pale gray; the great green hills stood up against the cool night sky. All wore its accustomed look of rustic peace. And just in front of the chapel-door four men were standing with a litter, on which there lay a quiet figure covered with tarpaulin.

"Come and look at my witness," said Arnold, seizing Joshua by the arm and dragging him toward the litter, and bending over it to lift the edge of the covering which shrouded that motionless form.

"Stop," cried Joshua, with a shuddering movement, "you need not lift it: I can guess. It is death you would have me look on."

"Yes, death—the body of the man you murdered; my dead brother, whom you slandered in his unhallowed grave, telling me that he had died the death of the suicide. Hark ye, neighbors," cried Arnold, turning to the awe-stricken crowd; "it is my brother—Oswald Pentreath—who lies here, shot through the heart by yonder villain nearly a year ago. God only knows if there is evidence enough to bring him to the gallows; but God knows, and I know, that he did the deed. Before you all I accuse him—your preacher, your pastor, your example of righteousness—he is my brother's murderer. The corpse lies here, silent witness of the crime. He—your preacher yonder—was seen waiting for my brother close to the spot where that corpse was found, shots were heard by the witness who saw him, and my brother was never seen after those shots were fired—never seen; he was lying at the bottom of the old shaft, murdered, and flung there to rot forgotten and unknown. And the murderer looked me in the face, and told me my brother was a coward, and had slain himself. If earthly justice can not touch him, if human ingenuity can not bring this crime home to his door, may God's justice punish him as never man was punished by mortal avenger! May Heaven make his lot more bitter than the hardest doom man's inhumanity ever devised for his fellow-man's torture!"

"Take your corpse to the dead-house," cried Joshua, with a contemptuous calmness, as if those passionate threats of Arnold's passed him by like the wind, "and make your complaint to the coroner. It is his business to find out the cause of your brother's death. All here know that I saved Oswald Pentreath's life at the peril of my own. That is my answer to your charge."

"Ay, that we do!" cried ever so many voices, and the crowd turned angrily upon Joshua's accuser. "We all remember how he saved the young squire that stormy day four year ago—risked his life as if it weren't worth a groat, and brought him in alive off the rock when ne'er another would ha' done it. Doant 'ee be afraid, Mister Haggard. Let un try to lay a finger on 'ee!"

"Come home, father, come home," whispered Naomi, white as death, and trembling so that she could hardly stand, yet with firmness to make her careful for the father who had always been first in her love and reverence—who was first to-night even, when her lover's corpse lay there before her under its dark pall, awful, unsightly, a thing to be thought of with horror.

She held her father by the arm and led him away from that dreadful spot, scarcely able to walk herself, and yet supporting and sustaining him. The crowd followed, as if to protect their minister—followed and congregated round the garden-rails as Joshua went into his house; and Arnold was left alone with his dead and the little group of farm-laborers who had helped him in his hideous discovery.

CHAPTER XXXV.

AN OPEN VERDICT.

THE claims of the business had kept Judith Haggard away from the prayer-meeting at Little Bethel. She now came out to the door, surprised and alarmed by the appearance of the eager assembly at her brother's heels—still more alarmed by Naomi's pallid face, as the girl led her father into the dimly lighted passage.

"Why, what in mercy's name is the matter, girl?" cried Judith. "Has your father had a stroke, that you hold him like that, as if he couldn't stand without your help? and what brings all the town after him?"

Joshua's fixed eyes and rigid countenance—awfully calm, with a blankness of expression which was like death itself—might have justified the idea that he had lately been struck down by some mortal illness, and was but just emerged from a state of helpless unconsciousness.

"No, Judith," he answered, with something of his old firmness; "the visitation is not such as you think, and yet the hand of God is heavy upon me. A calamity has befallen me which you could never have foreseen, bringing shame upon my name and race, making all the days that I have lived here in honor of no avail. Arnold Pentreath has found his brother's body, and accuses me of being his murderer."

"You!" shrieked Judith, "you a murderer! —you murder the young squire, when you were all but drowned in the work of saving his worthless life! If Arnold Pentreath can bring that charge against you, he is a worse man than I should have thought him, knowing the badness of his blood as I do, and expecting as little as I do from any of his worthless race."

"He has so accused me."

"But why? On what grounds? Why suppose that his brother was murdered?"

"His body has been found—in the old shaft."

"His body has been found—but that doesn't prove that he was murdered. He may have fallen into the shaft."

"Spare us your arguments to-night," said Joshua, with a weary air. "We shall know more to-morrow. I am tired and sick at heart, and want rest. I am in God's hands, and he will deal with me as seemeth best to him. Yes, in the hands of God—not in the hands of men."

He left them without another word, and went slowly upstairs to his own room. The crowd had withdrawn quietly by this time, some hastening back to the spot where they had left Arnold and his ghastly burden—others dropping in at The First and Last to discuss the event that had convulsed their peaceful settlement. All were of one mind about Joshua Haggard, and agreed that the accusation brought against him was as wild and foolish as it was infamous.

"I allus said it 'nd be so," growled old Jabez Long, the fisherman, from his favorite seat in the chimney-corner, where he hung over the smoldering logs even at midsummer. "I allus said harm 'ad come of pullin' you puir chap out o' the say. There's never no good comes o' savin' a drowning man. Chuck un back into the water: that's wisdom—t'other's foolishness. Why, ye see this yere chap can't bide quiet in his grave till he's done Joshua Haggard a hinjury. He rises up agen his deliverer like the onclane sperits that come out o' the tombs."

There was an inquest held next day in the long, low-ceiled justice-room at The First and Last. The body of Oswald Pentreath lay at the Grange, and there awaited the visitation of coroner and jury. It lay in the long, white drawing-room—that stately saloon which, in its air of disuse and solitude, had always something of the look of death. Here to-day lay the master of the house—in the dress he had worn when he left it—a ghastly form, only recognizable by the garments that clothed it, and the color of the soft, golden-brown hair. A pocket-book stuffed with bank-notes, and the old squire's watch and seals, had been found upon the body—a proof that the assassin's motive had not been plunder.

Brief was the visitation of the jury to that awful chamber. They had heard the evidence of Arnold Pentreath, and the farm-laborers who had assisted in the finding of the body. The search had been long and careful. Guided by the statements of Farmer Westall's cow-boy, Arnold had gone straight to the old shaft. He had first searched the ground near the pit, and a few yards from the engine-house, under a furze-bush, he had found one of his brother's pistols discharged. The second pistol had been nowhere forthcoming. Then, by means of ropes and ladders, and with due precautions against the effect of noxious gases in the disused mine, Arnold and two of the men had gone down the shaft. Their quest was soon ended. Oswald Pentreath lay at the bottom of the shaft, with a bullet through his heart. To bring the body out of the mine was a labor of no small difficulty; but time, the men's sturdy willingness to help, and Arnold's inexhaustible energy, conquered all obstacles, and by the time the earliest star was shining in the calm evening sky, Captain Pentreath was alone in the engine-house, keeping guard over his unburied dead, while the men went to the farm-house to fetch a litter on which to carry the corpse to the Grange.

That dismal walk through wood and lane had taken a long time. The church-clock was striking ten as the procession entered the straggling village street. The windows of Little Bethel shone dimly, and Joshua's voice was raised in vehement exhortation.

It was the sound of that voice—the impulse of a moment—which led Arnold to enter the chapel, and denounce the man of whose guilt he had no shadow of doubt.

Old Nicholas, the butler, had been one of the witnesses called to identify the body of his late master. He remembered the clothes Oswald Pentreath wore that last day, and he had helped him to put on that coat, and he could swear to the pistol that had been found under the furze-bush. He insisted upon telling the whole story of his master's departure, and his own fears and wonderment when the trunks were brought back from Exeter. The Combhollow coroner was a patient gentleman, accustomed to a long-tongued

race, and listened quietly to the butler's statement. Here was a mystery to be unraveled, and there was no knowing whence the first gleam of light might come.

But when Arnold's evidence took the form of an accusation against Joshua Haggard, the coroner stopped him peremptorily.

"I can not listen to any such speculations, Mr. Pentreath, to the discredit of a man in Mr. Haggard's position."

"They are no speculations," answered Arnold, hotly; "they are convictions. Hear what the next witness has to say, and then you will see what reason I have for accusing Joshua Haggard of my brother's murder—though you can never know all the ground I have for certainty—the looks, the words by which that assassin has betrayed his guilt. Why, I ought to have known it the first time he talked to me of my brother; It was clear enough, if I had had eyes to see or a mind to understand."

The coroner protested against the irrelevance of such assertions; and then Timothy, the cowboy, was called, and told over again the story of that August afternoon on which he had seen Joshua Haggard go up to Matcherly Common.

That picture of the man standing by the door of the engine-house as if watching for some one impressed and puzzled the jury; but it could not shake them in their conviction that Joshua Haggard was a good man—a man who had taught and reproved them for many years, and who had always dealt honorably with them in temporal matters—a man whose weights were true as the sun-dial on the church-tower, and whose goods were of the best quality. That such a man could commit a base and cowardly crime savored of impossibility. Witchcraft alone could account for such a monstrous thing.

"He couldn't ha' done it unless he wur bewitched," said one of the deliberants when the jury took counsel together.

"Who knows if that young wife of his didn't bewitch him?" argued another. "There's many as marked a change in him from the time she came among us. His thoughts seemed to be roving like, half his time; and he stared at you, skeared like, if you spoke to him sudden, and he got careless about his business. You never found him behind his counter."

"Joshua Haggard is not the man to hurt a wurrum," said a third juryman. "He used to come and sit beside my puir old missus when she was down with her last illness, and read to her by the hour together, and she looked up to him as if he'd been a saint. I'll agree to no verdick that throws any blame on Master Haggard."

"Who wants to bring a verdick agen Master Haggard? But we mun come to some sort o' verdick, maunt we?"

"Make it accidental death, can't 'ee?"

"But he couldn't a got throwed down the shaft by accident."

"He might have fell in, mightn't he?"

"Ah! but who was it shot him?"

"He might ha' shot hisself fust, and just had strength enough left to throw hisself down th old shaft."

The discussion waxed warm after this, but the jurymen were finally agreed that Oswald Pentreath had been murdered by some person or persons unknown.

Arnold went to the coroner directly the inquest was over, and asked for a warrant to arrest Joshua Haggard.

"My dear sir, it is quite out of the question. There is no evidence upon which I can issue a warrant."

"Not the fact that the man was seen there, hiding in the engine-house, waiting for my unhappy brother. Is that no evidence?" cried Arnold, indignantly.

"There is no evidence that he was hiding; there is no evidence that he was waiting for your brother. The mere fact of his being seen at that place a short time before the firing of the shots amounts to nothing, even if we could be sure those shots the cow-boy heard were the shots that killed your poor brother. Joshua Haggard is a mystic, a fanatic; a man who spends half his life wandering in solitary places. I have often met him on the hills and commons. There is nothing strange in the fact of his being seen up yonder that day. Then, again, there is an absence of all motive."

"I beg your pardon," said Arnold, eagerly. "There was a motive, and a strong one; but there are reasons why I could not speak of this motive just now in open court. It involves error—though not actual guilt—on my brother's part."

He told the coroner the story of Oswald's attachment to Mrs. Haggard, and the meeting between them that afternoon.

"We have no evidence that Mr. Haggard knew of that meeting," said Mr. Penruddock, who was much disinclined to make himself odious to all chapel-going people by an unwise arrest of Joshua Haggard.

"We have the evidence of his presence at that spot—at that hour."

Arnold argued the matter, but in vain, and left Mr. Penruddock, of Wrinkles Close, with the idea that a rustic coroner was the most inept and useless of officials.

Once more Naomi heard the old church-bell tolling dismally in the afternoon sunlight. Again she saw the funeral train wind slowly round the curve of the hill, the same wind-tossed plumes—for even in this June weather the breeze blew fresh from the western sea—the same solemn figures and black horses, and poor pomps and vanities of earthly pride; and this time she turned from the shrouded window with the heart-sickness of despair, and cast herself upon the ground, and tried to shut out the light of day, and prayed for death as the one issue and release from her miseries.

They were carrying him to his father's grave—her murdered lover—slain by her father's cruel hand, and slain at her prompting. Had she never put that fatal letter in her father's hand, this thing would never have been. Oswald would have gone his way in peace to a new world and repentance, perchance, and quiet days, and Joshua Haggard would have known nothing of that stolen farewell.

"Half the guilt is mine," she cried; "let me bear all the punishment! God be merciful to my misguided father, maddened by jealousy and wounded love! O God, charge not against him his sin that day!"

She had not been alone with her father since that night in the chapel. They had sat at the same board, and she had looked in his face, which told no story of fear or agitation. He had gone about his business with quiet regularity; taught in his school, visited his sick, read and exhorted as of old—yes, even while the inquest was being held at The First and Last, and all his flock were in a state of wildest emotion on their pastor's behalf. There had been a crowd of Joshua's people about the door of the justice-room, a crowd that gave vent to its indignation in a half-smothered way as Arnold Pentreath went in and out of the court. The feeling that their pastor was being persecuted for his faith was strong among them. This accusation of Arnold's was too wild to be believed even by the accuser. It was a lying invention of Satan, designed to put this faithful flock to shame. This feeling pervaded the village, and wherever the minister went he received some new proof of his popularity. Women ran out of their cottage-doors as he passed by, and clasped him by the hand, and offered him their sympathy in this great trial. He shrank somewhat from these demonstrations of feeling. "Let me bear my own burden," he said. "It is not too heavy for me."

And then, when he was alone, he clasped his hands in prayer, and cried, "O Lord, reward these people for their affection and their trustfulness, for I can only bring shame upon them. I have built up a temple to thine honor, and pulled it down, and abased and ruined thy holy place with mine own hands. I have given thee half my heart, and sold the other half to the devil. Let these people, whom I have loved and taught, suffer no loss because of my iniquity. Let their faith endure steadfast to the end, though my life prove a lie."

Never had there been such a funeral as that of the young squire of Pentreath Grange. The old church-yard was filled with all the inhabitants of Combhollow, and a crowd of strangers from outlying hamlets among the hills and tiny fishing-villages along the rocky coast. This God's-acre lay on the side of a hill, and was a place of ups and downs, beautified by many a fuchsia-shaded tomb, and by myrtles that had grown into trees—a sheltered and pleasant spot, hidden from the sight of the sea, but not so remote that the murmur of the waves might not serve as a lullaby for quiet sleepers under the ferny turf.

Arnold Pentreath stood by the open vault, pale and haggard, and with a countenance which grief had made rigid as marble. He was quite alone in his place by the coffin—chief and only mourner. There was some sympathy felt with him, yet less than would have been given but for that accusation brought against Joshua Haggard. This the Little Bethelites could not pardon. False and monstrous as the charge was, it had inflicted disgrace upon their sect. It was a fact that would be remembered and recorded against them in days to come—a dark tradition, to be magnified and distorted by their enemies.

That last ceremonial completed—and oh, how brief and hasty a business it seems to the mourner who feels that this is the last!—the coffin placed in its stony niche, for worms to invade and toads to squat upon, and damp and mildew to disfigure—a place of decay and loathsomeness for evermore—Arnold walked slowly away from the church-yard, sick at heart, loathing the faces of his fellow-men. He would not go back to the lych-gate where the coach was waiting for him —would not be shut up again in the Barnstaple undertaker's musty chariot, to hide his grief behind a cambric handkerchief, and so be conveyed slowly along the straggling village street, the principal feature and object of interest for the assembled multitude. He left the church-yard by another gate that led up to the hills—the wild, lonely hills, where he could hug his sorrow, and be alone with his baffled vengeance and his passionate grief.

That was the sting—to know his brother's murderer, to have no shadow of doubt as to the assassin, and to be powerless to strike. Conscience had its scorpions, no doubt, and Heaven held in reserve its lash for the hypocrite and murderer; but this was not enough for the brother who had loved his brother. Human nature, in its weakness and narrowness of vision, yearned for personal vengeance. Arnold wanted to bring this man to the gallows—to be the instrument of his direct and immediate punishment. Nothing less could satisfy his wounded love. His brother's ashes cried to him for vengeance.

One consideration only came between him and this hunger for swift revenge. He remembered that appealing look of Naomi's. His Naomi— his most noble among women—the woman he had hoped to win in days to come—the woman he had pictured in the fair future sitting at his board, ruling his household, making life sweet and honorable for him.

Could he ever hope to win her now? In his own mind he dissociated her altogether from her father's guilt. She was no less pure in his eyes because her father's hands were stained with blood. He was, even in his direst anger, willing to believe that Joshua's crime had been an act of jealous madness, and not the deliberate guilt of a criminal nature.

He could understand now why Naomi had forbidden him to hope, while her looks and tones told him he was dear to her. She had known or suspected her father's guilt. This would account for that deep melancholy which no hopeful utterances of his could dispel.

And if he brought Joshua Haggard to the gallows, what then? Was it not to destroy utterly the woman he so reverenced, the woman he fondly loved? Could Naomi survive so deep a shame, so deadly an agony? or, surviving it, could she have any feeling but hatred for the man who had brought shame and suffering upon her? He remembered that agonized appeal in the chapel,

"Arnold, what are you doing?"

And he had answered her coldly; though that answer meant the destruction of those new hopes which had been so dear to him. He knew her well enough to be very sure that she would cling to her father till death; stand beside him on the gallows, were it possible, and be true to him after death. To hunt Joshua to his doom as he meant to hunt him must be to lose Naomi forever.

"Be it so," he cried. "What is my happiness, or her peace, that I should put it in the balance with my brother's blood? I have one duty to perform—clear, direct, inexorable. Let me do that, and then go back to the old rough life at sea, and forget that I ever dreamed of being happy on shore."

<hr />

CHAPTER XXXVI.

JOSHUA STOPS HIS WATCH.

LITTLE BETHEL was crammed to suffocation on the Sunday that followed the burial of Oswald Pentreath. Not only had the flock assembled in fullest force to hear their pastor improve the occasion, and enlarge upon the evil that had been wrought against him by the Philistine, but many who were not of Joshua's sect had been drawn to his tabernacle by curiosity. They wanted to see how the man would bear himself under circumstances so trying to manly fortitude.

The flock were not disappointed in the demeanor of their minister. Never had Joshua conducted his simple service with greater dignity. His prayers, those eloquent extemporary supplications, modeled upon the theology of William Law, yet with something of Jeremy Taylor's florid warmth in their coloring, carried his congregation along with him like rushing waters down which a fleet of frail boats are driven tumultuously, knowing not whither they drift. It was by his eloquence in prayer chiefly that Joshua had established his power over his flock. He elevated their souls by his own enthusiasm; they felt themselves raised to a spiritual height which of themselves alone they could never have obtained. They heard their cares and sorrows, their petty doubts and difficulties, their failures and shortcomings and evil acts, laid at the foot of the great throne, with such appeals for pardon and pity as their dull minds could never frame, their uneloquent lips never utter. Joshua took them up in his arms, as it were, and held them at the feet of their Saviour, and called down the eternal mercy for them. He used the Scriptures for their benefit, as a skilful barrister uses precedents for the extrication of his clients. He found bounteous promises that they had never dreamed of in those familiar words of Holy Writ, covenants and pledges of grace and mercy. He held a golden key, with which he opened the treasury of heaven, and brought forth promises and favors for his people.

To-day his prayers took a tone of deepest self-humiliation. He laid himself prostrate before offended Heaven, and there was none of the exultant pride which the flock expected to discover in his supplications, no thanksgiving for an unsullied conscience and a soul clear of offense, for rectitude which could laugh to scorn the revilings of the evil-minded. It was the publican, and not the Pharisee, who stood up to pray in that rural temple.

The hymn he chose was of a gloomy cast; but all his ministrations had of late been of a gloomy character. When he went up into the pulpit, and looked round at the upturned faces, and slowly opened his Bible, there was a hush of expectancy. It was thought that his text would have some bearing on the strange event of the past week, and that in his sermon he would take occasion publicly to declare the falsehood and iniquity of the charge that had been brought against him.

But when he had given out the text, with his usual deliberate distinctness, there was a general sense of disappointment: the verses he had chosen seemed to have so little bearing on the subject which filled the public mind.

"In those days they shall say no more. The fathers have eaten a sour grape, and the children's teeth are set on edge. But every one shall die for his own iniquity."

Only Naomi understood the meaning of those words of assurance. For each the burden of his own sin: the assassin's innocent children were to have no portion in the shame and agony of his guilt. Upon this text Joshua Haggard enlarged with more than his accustomed power. Very awful was the picture which he painted of the sinner's earthly doom, the slow agonies of conscience, the shameful shrinking from the face of his fellow-men, the caresses of his children stinging him like the sting of serpents, the reverence and obedience of his household a mockery and a reproach — the light of day intolerable, the sun a burden, the quiet night accursed. And when from this picture of the sinner's suffering on earth he turned to the contemplation of his punishment hereafter, the vision assumed a darker and more terrible aspect. Before the Titanic tortures of that land of shadows, earth's puny torments shrunk to the sting of buzzing summer flies, as measured against the venom of the cobra or the rattle-snake. Joshua conjured up those visions of horror with a strange, uncanny power, as if the fiend had lifted the corner of hell's curtain, and showed him the fiery gulf behind. He dwelt on those terrors with a gloomy relish, and spoke of hell and doom with a familiar knowledge, as if he had steeped his soul in the fires of Pandemonium.

"But for the sinner's children," he cried, at last, withdrawing his mind, as by an effort, from this contemplation of the nethermost pit, "they shall go free: Heaven will not lay upon them the burden of a father's sin. He shall perish, he shall go to his doom, but they shall remain seathless. On earth, perchance, their portion may be shame and suffering, for earth's judgments are lying judgments: but God is righteous, and will keep this promise, and will adjust the balance."

Coming out of chapel, amidst the crowd, Naomi found herself close to a stranger who was talking of her father.

"I can believe any thing of this man, now I've heard him preach," he said.

"Why?" inquired his companion.

"Because I am very sure he is a madman."

"I don't see that," said the other, startled by the assertion. "His sermon was violent and gloomy, but sane enough."

"No sane man ever preached as that man preaches, and you may take my word for it."

Here the crowd parted Naomi from the speaker; but what she had heard impressed her deeply. It was hardly a new thought which was thus abruptly presented to her. The change in her father had inspired her with fears, to which she had hardly dared to give their actual form. Who was to discriminate between perpetual gloom, moody silence, an unbroken reserve, and the tokens and indications of a mind distraught? That her father's whole character had undergone an alteration since the day of Oswald Pentreath's disappearance, she well knew. Was it not possible that, on that day, the clear light of reason was darkened forever? From that fatal hour he had broken loose from all old ties — from children and wife, and friends and business — he had been like an owl of the desert, a pelican in the wilderness.

But even with the horror of the thought there came a blessed sense of relief. If reason had left him in the hour of temptation, if the light was quenched before he did that fatal deed, her father was not accountable for his sin. It was not with his whole mind that he had broken the divine law. The clouded brain had not taken the measure of the act.

This offered a way out of her deepest sorrow. Dreadful as earthly penalties might be — shameful, intolerable, revolting — it was Heaven's anger she most dreaded for the father she so devotedly loved. Sure of God's pardon and pity for the sinner, she could see him perish on the scaffold with only earthly sorrow, with only sense of earthly suffering and loss; scenes of a fair hereafter, a glorious meeting in a land of rest and peacefulness, where the red robes of repentant sinners were to be washed whiter than snow.

Awful, then, as this thought of mental alienation was, there was comfort in it. She could cling closer to her afflicted father, pitying and pardoning him, full of remorse for her own share in his suffering, ascribing to herself half his guilt.

"If I had but spared him the knowledge of that letter, Heaven might have spared me this anguish," she thought.

Joshua was absent from the family board at the two-o'clock Sunday dinner — an uninteresting repast of cold provisions, which James Haggard regarded as one of the privations and trials of his career. Other people in Combhollow rioted in hot joints and savory potatoes, reeking with unctuous grease and gravy, followed by huge fruit pie or pasty, and, perchance, a bowl of cream.

"I don't call it honoring the Sabbath to sit down to a worse dinner than on a work-day," Jim remarked, argumentatively. "And all that Sally may sit in a corner of our pew and breathe hard all through the sermon."

"Eat your dinner, and be thankful," said Aunt Judith, severely; "or leave it, and hold your tongue. I wonder you can be so base-minded as to think of your meals at such a time, with such affliction come upon your house as we've had to bear."

"Do you mean Captain Pentreath bringing that charge against father?" asked Jim, contemptuously. "I'm not such a fool as to fret about that. Any lunatic might accuse us of murder, or arson, or high treason, or gunpowder plot. Poor Pentreath's head's been turned by finding his brother at the bottom of Matcherly Mine. I was over at The First and Last when the inquest was going on, and heard every body saying that it was worse than madness to lay such a crime at father's door. There's not a man in Combhollow would believe a word against father."

"It would be hard if they would," retorted Judith, "after the life your father has lived among 'em all these years, and no one able to bring a reproach against him, unless it was for foolishness in marrying a silly girl for the sake of her pretty face."

"I never saw any silliness in Cynthia," said Jim; "and for my part I wish she was home again. I miss her pretty face, though it was sad enough for the last twelve months goodness knows. I don't think we any of us made her too happy."

"She's a deal better away," replied Judith, with a sour look. "She turned your father's thoughts from his duties, and never brought any thing but trouble into this house. Let her stop with friends of her own station, if she has any."

"Ain't it rather like turning her out-of-doors to let her stop away so long?" asked Jim.

"I didn't know it was a son's place to find fault with his father's doings," said Judith. "Your father's the best judge of his duty to his wife, I should hope. It isn't for us to interfere. He didn't ask our leave when he brought her home, and it's not likely he'd want our leave to send her away."

"It's a pity things couldn't go smoother, anyhow," pursued Jim, persistently; "for she's a pretty little thing, and a good little thing, that would never do harm to any one."

"That's all you know, Mr. Clever. Perhaps you'll be kind enough to keep your opinion till you're asked for it. Why don't you eat your dinner, Naomi?" inquired Miss Haggard, sharply. "It's as good a bit of beef as ever was cooked, and I suppose you're not too dainty to eat cold meat on the Sabbath?"

"I'm not hungry, aunt," said Naomi.

She had been sitting with her plate before her, making no attempt to eat, hearing her aunt and brother talking, but in no wise understanding them. Her thoughts were with her father in his lonely room. He had pleaded a headache, and gone quietly up to his bed-chamber when he came in from chapel. How was he bearing his burden? Without consolation, without sympathy. Yes, verily without human sympathy; but for this believer, even in his depth of guilty despair, there still remained a pitying Ear that would listen to his groaning, and take account of his anguish. The Friend of sinners would not be deaf to his cry.

"I think I'll go upstairs and see how father is, and if he wants any thing," said Naomi, rising from her seat at the table.

"If I was you, I wouldn't go bothering and disturbing him," said Judith, with her accustomed tartness; "but of course you can do as you like about it."

This was an indirect order not to go; but, for once in her life, Naomi disobeyed, and went straight to Joshua's room.

She knocked, but there was no answer, and she went in quietly, hoping to find her father asleep.

He was sitting in front of the open escritoire, his arms folded, his eyes bent upon the ground. He did not stir, or look up at his daughter's entrance, nor even when she came close to him and laid her hand gently on his shoulder.

She stood for a few moments in silence, waiting for him to take some notice of her; but he sat like a statue, and never lifted his eyes from the ground.

"Dear father," she began, in a low and tender voice, as she would have spoken to him had he been lying ill at death's door, "I was obliged to come to you. I could not bear to think of you alone and unhappy. Dearest, it is a heavy affliction that has fallen upon us, but not heavier than we can bear. Father," sinking on her knees beside his chair, and putting her arms round him, "if your guilt is deep, I am guilty too. I sinned grievously when I gave you his letter. I suffered my evil passions to get the better of me. My heart was full of hatred and rancour. Let us repent, and seek for mercy together. We both have sinned."

"The letter," muttered Joshua, with a bitter laugh, "the letter was not so much. I saw him hold her in his arms and kiss her—saw her yield herself up to a love that was stronger than honor, or duty, or her love of God—saw her folded to his heart under Heaven's all-seeing eye."

"It was my fault, father. But for that letter you would never have known of that last meeting. It was but a stolen farewell, and they both meant to do their duty. They were so young, and had erred for want of thought."

"They were thoughtful enough to plan secret meetings — thoughtful enough to deceive me. And I believed her purest among women—free from all taint of sin. Do not speak of her—or of him. They sinned, and have reaped the fruit of sin. 'The wages of sin is death.'"

"Father, we have sinned grievously, you and I; and we can have no hope of mercy unless we repent," said Naomi, horrified at Joshua's hardness of tone, which implied an unconsciousness of the weight and measure of his crime.

"My life has been one long atonement. I have labored always in the work of salvation."

"But by one sinful act all might be undone — in one dark hour the labor of a lifetime might be lost," urged Naomi.

Her father made no answer.

"Dearest, will you not kneel and pray with me?" she pleaded. "Will you not help me to lift this burden from my soul? I am weary with the weight of my sin. I loved him, and yet betrayed him to you. Oh, it was the act of a Judas! He must have loved his Master. It was jealousy that made him a traitor. Father, if you can not be sorry for your sin, be sorry for mine."

In vain; the brooding eyes were never lifted from the ground. Naomi looked up into the rigid face. Yes, there was an expression there as of light quenched, at least a temporary aberration. He was not listening, he was not following her.

He sat for some time thus, Naomi still kneeling by him and watching him, but in silence. Then he stretched out his hand to the open Bible that lay upon his desk, and began to read.

"Leave me, my dear," he said; "I am better alone."

"I would so much rather stay with you, dear father. I will not disturb you."

"Go, dear; I wish to be alone. I have to command my thoughts. It will be time for chapel presently."

"I will go, then, dear father. But, while we are alone, let me say one thing."

"I am listening."

She put her arms round his neck, and rested her head on his shoulder.

"You know how I loved Oswald, father, to

"DEAR FATHER, I WAS OBLIGED TO COME TO YOU."

the last, even after his heart had gone away from me. But I told you then, as I tell you now, you were always first and dearest, always the object of my highest reverence and love. That could never change in me. No act of yours could lessen my love, no affliction Heaven could bring upon you could lower you in my esteem. Remember that always, father. Come what may, I am your loving daughter to the end!"

With this assurance she left him, a little more at peace with herself for having thus spoken.

The afternoon service was gone through very quietly. Joshua had a subdued and weary air, as if worn out by the effort of the morning. The congregation were less alert and exalted in their piety, as was natural in people who had dined heavily, and given way to fleshly snares in the shape of too substantial pastry. Even the hymns had a slumberous tone, and acted as lullabies upon some elder members of the flock whose feeble knees were an excuse for a sitting posture.

After service, Joshua taught for half an hour in his school, and said a few earnest words to the young men of his adult night-school, a class in which he had taken a special interest. They were very touching words, and well remembered afterward.

Joshua was absent from the tea-table, as he had been from the dinner-table. His headache was worse, he told his sister, and he was going to lie down. Naomi had an evening Scripture class to attend to after tea, a task that would occupy her for about an hour. She went to this duty at half-past six o'clock, while Judith enjoyed the one Sabbath luxury which she permitted herself, a half-hour's nap in the chintz-covered arm chair by the best-parlor window, screened from the gaze of passing pedestrians, going by at the rate of one in ten minutes, by the graceful droop of the well-starched curtain.

Joshua was alone, sitting by the escritoire, as he had sat when Naomi went to him in the afternoon. He had locked the door, determined to be free from all intrusion—free even from his daughter's pitying love. He wanted nothing between him and that awful solitude in which he had lived of late—the isolation which a mind unhinged makes for itself.

He sat thus till the twilight thickened and the pages of his open Bible grew dim. Even in the troubled state of his brain—a trouble which had been growing for months—that book was his rock of defense, his sheet-anchor. He looked into those pages for justification, for assurance of grace and redemption, and he seldom looked in vain. If he had sinned, had not David sinned also, and yet retained his exalted place in the love of God and men? Was he to humble himself more than David humbled himself? Had David ever ceased to be king and priest and teacher, chief and supreme among the people? If he had fallen, had not Peter also fallen, and yet received that divine commission which gave him charge of Christ's flock?

"I will preach the Gospel, and teach men while I have breath," protested Joshua, laying his hand upon the sacred book. "What have the burdens on my conscience to do with my teaching? What does it matter that I know myself a sinner, if I can expound the Word of God? He has given me a gift, and I will use it—to the uttermost and to the last. If this is to

be a hypocrite, my hypocrisy shall go with me to my grave."

This was the summing-up of his position in one of his calmer moods; but his mind was not always so clear, or his views so fixed and resolute. There were moments to-night, as he sat in the summer dusk while the shadows grew and deepened in the lonely, old-fashioned room, grotesque shadows of familiar things which he had known from childhood—there were intervals in which his brain grew clouded, and past and present were alike dim and distorted. His thoughts flashed far and wide, like the erratic gleams of a lantern—now alighting upon some picture of the past, now plunging into the dark gulf of the future. He saw himself as he had been at the outset of his laborious career—eager for self-sacrifice, careless of all worldly loss, sustained by an enthusiast's exaggerated hopes, and an enthusiast's indifference to suffering. He had labored, and had been plenteously rewarded. He had been a wandering light, shining in dark places and forgotten corners of the earth, and had brought many lost sheep home to the fold. Then his father had died, and he had been called back to his native place, to find that, after all, he had lost nothing of earthly gain by his constancy; for, despite the old man's threatenings, he had left all to his only son.

This day of inheritance Joshua felt to have been in some measure a time of temptation and falling away. He had turned aside from the desert and desolate places, to dwell in a land of fatness. He had been content to serve a few instead of serving many. He had sat down under his vine and fig-tree, and taught one little flock, instead of wandering from village to village seeking those whom the Church had forgotten, or cared for with a lukewarm love. True that he had labored hard for his flock, walked many miles, stretched his cure of souls to its utmost limits, taught the young, brought the light of education, both spiritual and secular, into many dark places; but he had from this time ceased to be a stranger and a pilgrim upon earth, a disciple who has given up all things for his Master.

Then came his prosperous first marriage, the birth of his children: new ties that bound him to the old home.

How strange and remote those early years seemed, as the fitful light of memory shone upon them!

The picture changed. Those peaceful, monotonous days were past. He was standing on the Cornish common in the pure sunshine, the great Atlantic glittering in the distance, the sandy knolls and hollows all ablaze with yellow furze, the subtle scent of that golden blossom in the air—standing on the threshold of a new life. Never, after that hour, was he to be the same man, independent of all human influence. Henceforth he was to be chained to humanity by mankind's most pitiful weakness — an unreasoning love for a weak fellow-creature.

"I verily believe I loved her from that first day," he thought. "Her image never left me. She was always before me, sitting in the sunlight, with her drooping hair like pale gold. Can I doubt that Satan set her there for my entanglement and ruin? 'His heart shall be heavy for her sake, he shall be so troubled that he shall grow dumb,' said the fiend. But I have cheated him of his prey. He has had my heart, and bruised and broken it; but he has not quenched my spirit, he has not silenced me. I have borne my burden, and continued to teach and exhort, and will so continue to the end. No snare of the arch-tempter hiding behind a fair face shall destroy me."

Then followed a moment of relenting.

"She seemed so innocent, so pure. She was so gentle and obedient, and owned so meekly that she had been tempted, and had sinned in hearkening for a little while to the tempter. O God, there could be no vileness in the soul that looked up at me from those gentle eyes! And I thrust her from me with violence and contumely, and sent her back to servitude and dependence. My wedded wife, the one creature I have loved most on earth!" He clasped his hands, and looked upward in exaltation of mind.

"Surely that was an atonement for my weakness. Surely that was a sacrifice which Heaven must approve. And yet I have known no peace of mind since that day. Heaven has given me no token of approval or forgiveness."

That intense egotism which is one of the characteristics of a mind off its balance had taken possession of him. He felt himself the centre of the universe. The Bible had been written for him. He stood face to face with his Creator, and felt himself worthy to be saved.

His daughter knocked at the door presently, and asked him if he would not have a light.

"No," he answered; "my soul can hold communion with God in the darkness. I am alone, as Elijah was upon the mountain, waiting for the voice of the Lord."

It was after midnight, when he laid himself upon his bed, wearied with meditations in which his brain had been hyperactive. Tired as he was with the long day and its double service, the long evening and its protracted thoughtfulness, he could not easily sleep; and when, at last, his weary eyelids closed, his slumber was more like a trance than a sleep.

He saw his wife's face looking up at him as she had looked that last day in the lane, pleadingly, piteously, full of grief and love. He saw it more vividly than faces are seen in dreams—saw it close to him as he lay upon his pillow, and was dimly conscious of lying there, and the hour of the night, and that this face was looking at him from afar off, though it seemed so near that he could have stretched out his hand and touched it.

Then came a voice that thrilled him:

"Joshua, Joshua, come to me!"

He was awake and on his feet in an instant. It seemed to him that his waking ears had heard that voice—that it was something more than a part of his dream. He stood listening for some moments, half expecting to hear the cry repeated, and his wife's hand upon his door.

He went to the door and opened it, and looked out upon the landing, faintly lighted by the stars.

No; the place was empty, the lower part of the house was dark and silent. Nothing had happened. It was only a dream.

"But it is a dream sent by Heaven," he said. "I will hearken to it, and go. Yes, my love, I forgive you: I am coming to you. I bring you pardon and love."

He struck a light from the old tinder-box, lighted his candle, and began to dress himself hurriedly. He had looked at his watch on first rising, wondering to find so little of the night was gone. It was twenty minutes past one o'clock.

Joshua took his watch from under his pillow, lifted the glass, and laid his finger on the hands and stopped them. Only once before in his life had he ever done this thing, and that occasion was the moment of his conversion, the instant in which the divine assurance of his election and calling had been breathed into his soul. At that blessed moment he had stopped his watch, that it might forever record that one hallowed hour. It was the watch he had used as a young man, and was still in his desk; he had never carried it afterward, and had endured no small inconvenience for the want of it till his father's fine old time-keeper had descended to him as a part of his inheritance.

It was a curious fancy which moved him to do the same thing to-night. He could have given no reason for the impulse; but he obeyed it blindly, and the loud ticking of the watch grew still at twenty minutes past one.

CHAPTER XXXVII.

JOSHUA'S CONFESSION.

ANOTHER bright June morning; newly blown roses looking in at the open windows, born, like the butterflies, for a day. Naomi was astir earlier than usual after a sleepless night, full of care for her father. Oh, if that sweet air of heaven, which is a joy in itself for the happy, could but blow away one's sense of abiding trouble, could but bring the promise of relief! This was what Naomi thought, as she stood at her open window, looking out at the calm hill-tops, from which the summer mists were rising, like a veil slowly unfolded by invisible hands.

She was at her father's door before six o'clock, knocking and waiting his reply with fast-throbbing heart, fearing she knew not what. There was no answer. She felt the floor reeling under her feet. Awful fears seized upon her. She knocked loudly, violently almost, and still no answer. She tried the door with shaking hands, expecting to find it locked, as it had been yesterday evening when she came to inquire about the light; but it yielded under her hand, and she went into her father's room.

It was empty. She looked round with wild, eager eyes, almost beside herself, in the agony of that great dread. The room was quite empty. The bed had been lain upon; the candle had been left burning, and had burned down to the brazen socket. There was a letter lying on the escritoire, which Naomi seized upon eagerly. It was addressed to herself.

She tore it open, still full of fear; for the letter might reveal some terrible determination. There was another letter inside, sealed, and addressed to Captain Pentreath.

"MY BELOVED DAUGHTER,—I am going to Penmoyle to seek my wife, and shall return to Combhollow no more. My duty there is done. I have taught my people to know the right path.

I can give them up into the hands of a new minister. I am going where the darkness has never been dispelled by Gospel light: I am going to find new duties in desolate places. But first I must see my wife. I would pardon and bless her before I go. Do not follow me. My lot is fixed.

"Do not fail to give the inclosed letter, with the seal unbroken, into Captain Pentreath's hands. Your affectionate father,

"JOSHUA HAGGARD."

Naomi lifted up her heart in thankfulness. He had gone to do no wicked and desperate act. He had gone to seek his wife, carrying with him pardon and love. The ice had melted. Who could tell what healing for mind and soul there might be in the change?

But this letter to be delivered to Arnold Pentreath? Here was a fearful thought. What if it were a confession of her father's guilt—a confession which would put his life in Arnold's power? And Arnold had already shown himself merciless. To withhold the letter would be to disobey her father's express command. To deliver it might be to endanger his life. What was she to do?

She sat by the escritoire with the letter in her hand, perplexed in the extreme. Then, finding thought useless to show her the way, she fell upon her knees and prayed for guidance, prayed long and earnestly.

She rose from this prayer resolved, whether for good or ill, she would obey her father's behest, and deliver the letter, trusting to God's mercy and her own influence with Arnold for the issue. He had pretended to love her—nay, had loved her—before this fearful discovery of his brother's fate. She must have some power over him still: her pleading must be of some avail. Yes, she would obey her father, and in so doing proclaim her trust in Providence.

"'Let me fall now into the hand of the Lord; for very great are his mercies,'" said Naomi. "Can I doubt that my father is in God's hands to-day, though men may seem to have the ordering of his fate?"

She lost no time in carrying out her determination, but went back to her room and put on her bonnet, and then ran down-stairs.

She was going out at the street-door, when it suddenly occurred to her that her father's absence most speedily be discovered, and would make a commotion in the house if it were in no manner accounted for. So she went to the kitchen, where her aunt was employed in her usual morning duty of giving out provisions for the day's consumption from a rigorously locked store-room.

To her Naomi quietly announced that her father had started early that morning, on his way to Penmoyle, to see his wife.

"Started early!" cried Judith, incredulously. "Why, the Truro coach doesn't go before half-past seven, and it's not a quarter-past yet. What do you mean by started early?"

"He may have set out to walk part of the journey, perhaps, aunt," answered Naomi. "You know how fond he is of walking. He was gone at six o'clock when I went to his room, and had left me a letter to say he was going to Penmoyle."

"I think he might have written to me," said Judith, with her offended air. "If he must needs go off at a moment's notice, throwing all the housekeeping into a muddle—you needn't roast the mutton to-day, Sally; the cold beef will be good enough for us—he might at least have had the civility to address his explanation to me. After keeping his house nearly thirty years, it's hard to have such a slight put on me."

"The beef, mum!" remonstrated Sally; "there's hardly any thing but bones."

"Nonsense, girl; there's plenty of picking between the bones. And if I've time, I'll make a treacle pudding."

Naomi vanished while the dinner was under discussion. Her heart was very heavy, as she went to the Grange. She had not entered the house since the days when she had been Oswald's plighted wife, and the future lay fair before her, full of the promise of happiness. And now there was a thought of horror in the very road by which she went. Twice had her murdered lover been carried along that road; and now he was lying quietly in his grave, and all earthly hopes lay buried with him.

The old house looked peaceful enough in the cheerful morning light. Gardens and shrubberies had been better kept since Arnold's return. The beds and borders were full of sweet-smelling flowers. The windows were all open, and a handsome red setter—a favorite of Arnold's—was lying in the porch.

Naomi rang the noisy old bell, which was answered, after a longish pause, by Nicholas the butler, who came across the hall, carrying his master's breakfast on one of those old silver trays which had been kept under lock and key during the squire's life-time, but which the less careful sailor had given out for daily use.

At sight of Naomi, the old man stopped short, with a startled look.

"Lord, miss, how you skeared me!" he exclaimed.

"Can I see your master, Nicholas?"

"To be sure 'ee can, miss. He's to his break'ast in the blue parlor—the room that was squire's study, you know; but the harkiteck had it all routed out and painted."

The butler opened the door of that small room on the left hand of the porch, and ushered Naomi into the presence of Captain Pentreath.

He started up with a cry, half surprise, half welcome, as if to see her only were in itself so glad a thing, that he forgot all the painful circumstances of their meeting. This oblivion lasted but for a moment. His face clouded, and he looked at her deprecatingly.

"Naomi, I have been longing for such a meeting as this. I want to tell you—to make you understand, if I can—that in what I have done I have been constrained by my duty to the dead. Had your father wronged me—that wrong the deepest one man could do another—I would have endured all for your sake; but my duty to the dead is sacred. At the hazard of breaking your heart, with the certainty of losing your regard, I was forced to do what I did."

"Hush!" she said; "do not speak of me or my feelings. You have brought great misery upon us—an irreparable shame. It may be in your power to work still greater misery for us. I can but do my duty to God and my father.

My first duty to both is obedience. I have brought you a letter."

"A letter?"

"From my father. But before I give it you, promise that you will make no evil use of it, that you will not make his own words the means of destroying him. I can not tell what he has written. I know that all yesterday his mind was sorely disturbed—that he has been oppressed and troubled in mind for a long time. How can I tell what he has written? Promise me that you will not use this letter against him."

"I promise," answered Arnold, with a touch of scorn. "It is not likely that a letter which your father writes to me of his own free-will can prove a weapon with which to strike him."

He opened the letter, prepared to find an artful and studied composition setting forth the minister's innocence of the crime charged against him, a plausible and subtle defense, such as the ingenuity of a clever and thoughtful man might elaborate at his leisure. The paper almost dropped from his hand as he read the first line.

"Arnold Pentreath, you accused me rightly. It was this hand slew your brother. But the deed was not so basely done as you think. We stood face to face, each with his weapon in his hand. It was what the sons of Belial call an honorable meeting, though my conscience tells me it was murder. He stole my young wife's heart—came between me and the most perfect happiness that Heaven ever vouchsafed to man. I met him with my wife's kiss still warm upon his lip. I had seen them part, mind you, as lovers whose hearts are cloven asunder in parting. I told him that he owed me his life, and he was willing to admit the debt. 'My life is of so little value that you are heartily welcome to it,' he said; 'I have often thought of taking it myself.' He had a pair of pistols about him, and proposed that we should fight on the spot; but withdrew his proposal the next moment, remembering that I had no practice in the use of fire-arms.

"I told him I was willing to set my want of skill against his bad cause. 'It is you that are the wrong-doer,' I cried; 'Heaven will be on my side.'

"We fought, and he fell. I was alone with his dead body, and all the horror of my position was suddenly revealed to me. According to my own creed, I was a murderer; and in the sight of the world I should stand revealed as a murderer if I were found with this dead man by my side.

"Satan, who had made me blind to the guilt of my act till it was accomplished, now tempted me to the baseness of concealment. I dragged the body to the edge of the shaft and threw it down, and went quickly home, and kept silence about your brother's fate till the day I spoke of him with you.

"I told you that in my opinion your brother had committed suicide. I say still that he flung his life recklessly away. Had he pleaded or argued with me, my blind passion might have been subjugated. He put the weapon which killed him into my hand.

"God rest his soul, and pardon my sin!

"I am going forth to a life as desolate as that of St. John in the desert. May God so appoint my punishment here that I may not lose my portion in glory hereafter!

"JOSHUA HAGGARD."

Naomi stood before Captain Pentreath with ashen lips, watching him as he read the letter, praying dumbly all the while, and with that sense of efficacy in her prayers, even in this moment of suspense, as only an implicit faith can experience.

"Thank God!" exclaimed Arnold, giving her the letter; "thank God it is not so bad as I believed! This confession has the stamp of truth; and—he is your father!"

No words can tell the depth of tenderness in that little speech, and the look that went with it. Both look and tone were lost on Naomi. Her eyes were rooted to the letter; triumph, gratitude, joy, illumined her face.

"It was not murder," she cried; "there was no treachery, no secrecy; they stood face to face—sinners both—blinded, maddened by passion. It was no murder. Father, how could I have wronged you by such base thoughts— I, who have known and loved you all these years? Guilty! yes, I will acknowledge your guilt; but not a treacherous assassin. My God, I thank thee!"

In days when the first gentlemen of the land asserted their sense of honor and superiority to the common herd by slaying one another in a formal manner, the idea of a duel was not so revolting as it is now. Even to Naomi, educated as she had been in a far different creed from the code of honor, the knowledge that her father had stood face to face with his foe, risking his own life against the life he took, was an infinite relief. In horrible nightmare dreams she had seen him, with the assassin's face, creeping stealthily toward his victim. The horrid image had haunted her sleeping and waking; and now that horror was laid at rest forever. Her belief in this confession of her father's was as implicit as her faith in God.

"Arnold," she pleaded, with deep humility, as one who asks an almost impossible boon, "can you ever bring yourself to forgive my erring father?"

"No!" he answered, stoutly; "but I no longer look upon him with loathing. There is one atonement left to him: he can stand face to face with me, as he stood with my brother, and let God judge between us."

Naomi flung herself at his feet, clasping his hands, as if he held the keys of life and death.

"No, no, no!" she cried; "you would not be so cruel, so wicked—you, who condemn the shedder of blood?"

"I want the life of the man who slew my brother. So much the better if I can have it in an honorable manner. Yes, Naomi, we will meet as men of honor should, and let the righteous cause win."

"Arnold," she cried, "I thought you loved me."

The pathos of that cry moved him. He bent over her as she knelt at his feet, resisting his effort to raise her, clinging to his knees in her agony, pleading as only women can plead for the love of their dearest.

"If I thought you loved me, and would give me love for love," he said, with a sudden change to passionate tenderness, "I would spare his life: yes, let him go unpunished to the grave; yes, forget that I ever had an only and beloved brother. It is a mean offer, a miserable bargain, proving me selfish, dastardly; but I am human, and I love you. My love, my only love, answer me."

"Can you forgive me for being my father's daughter?"

"When I believed the worst of him, I loved you, and held you unsullied by his guilt."

"You must forgive him, Arnold. You would forgive him, if you knew as much as I do. He was not in his right senses that awful day. I saw him go through the wood. Yes, I was there watching for him, fearing evil. His face has haunted me ever since. It was the face of a madman. It was my sin that caused all. Yes, Arnold, mine. You do not know how vile I am. I gave my father the letter your brother wrote to my step-mother! A lover's letter, full of despairing love. *That* maddened him, as it had maddened me. He was not in his right mind that day. He has never been the same man since—gloomy, austere, set against those he had loved before. You can not conceive how great a change there has been in him. We who have lived with him know and feel it. On my knees here, before God, I do not believe that my father was responsible for his acts that day."

Arnold raised her from her knees, and put her in the arm-chair by the open window. She was almost fainting, but the brave spirit struggled with bodily weakness.

Arnold paced the room for a little while, deep in thought.

"What am I to do, Naomi?" he asked, at last. "I love you—would lay down my life for you; but I owe a duty to my brother. That is a solemn charge. He loved me—was so good to me. I have his letter summoning me home, full of affection, overflowing with generosity. What am I to do, Naomi? Counsel me, if you can. You loved him?"

"Loved him? Yes; it was my love that made me mad with jealousy; it was my love that rose up against him and destroyed him. If you must have a life for his life, take mine. Yes, Arnold, take mine. I am most guilty. It was my jealousy that killed him."

"Naomi, we are all most miserable. I can do nothing; I feel myself tied and bound. Either way there are wrong and misery. I love you, and am miserable in loving you. I have my brother's death to avenge, yet can not bring myself to injure your father. Oh, my love, my love! your sad, accusing face has haunted me ever since that night when you turned and looked at me at the chapel-door. What can I do?"

"Forgive," said Naomi, solemnly; "that is what the Gospel teaches us—to forgive our enemies, even the enemies who have injured those we love. We can never err in being merciful. 'How often shall my brother sin against me, and I forgive him? Till seventy times seven.' That must mean pardon for wrongs man thinks unpardonable."

"You can teach me to believe any thing, Naomi. I am like a child in your hands."

"May God teach you to judge and act wisely! He will not inspire you with thoughts of vengeance. He has said, 'Vengeance is mine; I will repay.' My unhappy father has suffered for his sin, and will continue to suffer till death brings him peace; but I know in my heart that God will forgive him."

"And if God can forgive, erring man should not be obstinately unforgiving. That is what you would say, Naomi. We have an illimitable faith in God's capacity to pardon, yet find it so hard, sinners as we are, to forgive a fellow-sinner. It is a dark problem."

"Pray that you may understand God's will, Arnold. He will lead and uphold you."

"No; earthly passion will sway me. It is my love for you urges me to forgive your father."

"I would have you act from a higher light. I will leave you to seek a better guidance," Naomi answered, with gentle reproachfulness.

She felt that her father was secure from any violence of Arnold's after this interview. She left him full of faith that the right guidance would come, that the vengeful spirit which had threatened Joshua with ruin and death would be calmed and appeased. She knew that Arnold loved her; and though all thoughts of herself were vague and secondary, at such a crisis of her father's fate, she was glad of Arnold's love, for her father's sake.

CHAPTER XXXVIII.

CARRYING PEACE AND PARDON.

JOSHUA was far upon his road before Naomi had left the Grange. He had walked many miles in the dull gray of early morning before the shadowy clouds had parted, or the stars begun to pale in the saffron lights of sunrise. The energy that sustained him, the eager purpose that bore him on in that beginning of his journey, made him unconscious of time or distance. He had heard Cynthia calling; yes, his wife's cry, piteous and weak, as of one in distress, was still sounding in his ear as he hurried along the well-known road, which seemed just a little strange and dream-like, in the dim, gray dawn. He had heard her calling him, and he was going to answer her cry.

"Dearest, I am coming to you," he repeated inwardly. "I, who drove you away with undeserved reproaches, am coming to pray for pardon; I, who was cruel, unjust, savage, and inhuman, only because I loved too blindly—I am coming to ask for pity from the tender heart I wounded. Love, I was mad, and I have suffered for my madness—a long night of suffering. The morning has come, and peace and pardon. My eyes are opened; I see and understand."

It was only when a sudden faintness made him stagger dizzily, and stretch out his hands to save himself from falling, that he became aware of the hot sun beating down upon his head, and the fact that he had walked many miles.

He was nearly twenty miles from Combhollow. He had crossed the wild, craggy hills, and come back mechanically to the coach-road. He was at the top of a long hill, and saw the coach toiling slowly up the white, dusty road. He felt all at once that his strength was gone—gone utterly, as if it had left him forever—and thanked God for the coming of the coach. It seemed by a special providence that he had been brought across those wild hills back to the turnpike road in time for the passing of the coach.

"If I had missed it I should not have got to Pennoyle to-night; and my darling is waiting for me," he said to himself.

There was a vacant place on the seat behind the driver. Joshua hailed the coach, and scrambled into this place before the coachman had time to pull up his horses.

"You shouldn't ha' done that, Mr. Haggard," remonstrated the man; "it's dangerous."

Joshua took no notice. The man's voice sounded far off, as in a dream. The horses went downhill and uphill over the wild yet fertile country, by hills and woods that Joshua knew as well as he knew his Bible. They stopped to change horses in straggling little villages where he had preached in his young days; and people who remembered those days came out of their houses, and stood looking up at the coach and talked to him. He answered their inquiries and acknowledged their civil speeches mechanically, dimly conscious of their identity. He had a curious feeling of superiority to all these people, as if the universe had been planned for him, and they were only accidents in it, like the great black flies buzzing round the heads of the patient, blinkered coach-horses, to whom Providence had given no special mercy except mane and tail.

The time had been—and but a year or so ago—when he would have got down from the coach and peeped into those whitewashed cottages, and had his well-chosen word of greeting or counsel for each old acquaintance. To-day their faces looking up at him were blank and meaningless. The faces of the rabble round Stephen may have looked so to the saint and martyr in his death-agony.

Joshua's mind was going on before him. He fancied himself arriving at Pennoyle in the sunset. She would be standing at the gate, perhaps, watching for him, as he had found her on that unforgotten afternoon two years ago. He would see the sweet face, with the western light shining on it, the soft eyes kindling with love and happiness at sight of him. He had almost forgotten that bitter day of parting, the day when he had driven her into banishment, with more cruelty than Abraham had shown to ill-used Hagar; and it can hardly be said that the patriarch was a pattern to all future husbands in that transaction.

Oh, how sweet it was to dwell upon that picture of meeting and reconciliation! The burden on his conscience had been cast off since the agony of yesterday. It was verily as if he had laid down his load on the sinners' altar. He forgot all the silent pangs and tortures of the last year, and felt as if a new life of happiness were opening before him. He would carry the lamp of the Gospel into dark places; he would preach by the way-side, as in his youth; he would carry neither purse nor scrip, but wander from village to village, and from town to town, in that benighted north country he had read about in the lives of Wesley and Whitefield; or, if it were possible, still farther away, among the absolute heathen of the South Seas.

This was his vision of a glorious future. And she would be with him—his companion, helpmeet, and comforter. It was such a career as this to which she had aspired. Her spiritual nature had been revolted by the trader's petty life; she had sighed to see her husband doing the work of an apostle.

Such thoughts as these were in his mind all through the day. They rose and fell in his brain, wave upon wave, as regularly as the waves of the Atlantic were rising and falling upon the long, sandy shore beyond those brown Cornish hills. The day seemed very long to him, for his exaggerated activity of brain made minutes like unto hours. And yet he was ineffably happy. No fear of disappointment at the end of his journey clouded the radiance of his visions. He apprehended no further stroke from an angry fate. God had punished him with the undying worm called conscience, and had heard his prayers, and forgiven him. He feared nothing.

It was afternoon when the coach rumbled into the stony street of Truro. Joshua had to be reminded of his fare respectfully by the coachman. He was on the point of hurrying off without paying it.

"Your mind's full of better things, I know, Mr. Haggard," said the man; "but I thought you'd like me to remind you."

"Thank you, Norman," said Joshua, dreamily. "Yes, my mind was much occupied pleasantly, though, pleasantly, as one sure of God's bounteous mercy."

He gave the man a crown for himself. It was half as much as the fare—an astonishing donation.

"You may not be driving me again for some time to come," said the minister, kindly.

"Thank'ee, sir. It isn't many behaves as handsomely, and it's always a pride to drive such as you. But don't take it as a liberty if I give'ee one bit of advice. Don't try to get up to the outside of a coach before the horses are stopped. You're in the prime of life, sir, maybe; but you're a good many years too old to do that with safety."

"Yes, yes, Norman; I shall bear it in mind," said Joshua, walking away, without stopping at the comfortable inn for "bite or sup," as Norman remarked afterward.

"The fact is, the minister is wearing of hisself out," the coachman remarked to his cronies that night. "He's got oddish ways with him, and a look as if he didn't half know what's going on round about him."

CHAPTER XXXIX.

THE ODOR OF ROSEMARY.

It happened as Joshua had calculated. The sun was setting as he entered quiet Pennoyle. The walk from Truro had tired him more than he had supposed possible. He could hardly drag himself along the last mile or so of the dusty road, between hedges where the dog-roses and honeysuckle climbed high above his head, and where the fox-gloves were opening their purple bells. The salt sea-wind, sweeping over yonder swelling hills, seemed to have lost its refreshing power. He turned his eyes wearily toward the western point—the wild Land's End, with its rocks of many-hued granite, on which the seagulls and cormorants were perching in the rosy evening light. The scene was so familiar to him that he could see it all, in that clear vision of the mind, as he turned his gaze westward. Was there any thing on this vast earth more beautiful, he wondered, than that wild point of English soil, with the great Atlantic waves forever beating up against it—an impregnable natural fortress, the rocky seat of dead-and-gone giants, forever defying the assaults of ocean?

His thoughts wandered a good deal during these last miles, when his body was racked with the pains of exceeding fatigue. He thought of Nicholas Wild, his old pupil, and the little chapel among yonder hills. The young man had written him long letters, telling him of the rich reward that had crowned his labors, and how he had built a school for the children of his flock. Joshua had been too preoccupied to take any notice of the letters, and the memory of that neglect smote him now, as he came nearer his pupil's home.

"Poor Nicholas! he was always faithful and affectionate. We will go and see him, my wife and I," Joshua said to himself.

At last the old square tower of Penmoyle church rose, in its gray severity, above the avenue of limes that led to it. Then came the well-known street; the chestnut grove, where the children played at even-tide; the inn; the village pump; the cocks and hens, and a vagabond pig picking up unconsidered trifles in the middle of the road; the old yellow wagon, turned up on end after a day's usefulness. The sun was still visible—a shining crimson disk on the edge of the western hill.

It was a mere foolishness, no doubt, and Joshua chid himself for so weak a regret; but he felt strangely disappointed when he came in sight of the little green gate before Miss Webling's cottage, and did not see the graceful figure of his wife standing there, just as he had seen her that happy afternoon two years ago, when he had come full of benevolent intentions, and ignorant of his heart's mystery. He had counted on seeing her there. It would have been the natural fulfillment of his dream, it seemed to him, that she should be on the watch for his coming. She had called him, and, by some mystic power beyond the limits of flesh and blood, he had heard her summons. Why was she not watching for him, full of faith in his obedience? Was his sympathy with her stronger than hers with him?

He passed the chestnut grove. It seemed to him that the children were less noisy than of old. They were there under the spreading branches, the same boys and girls—the fustian jackets and lavender pinafores, the petticoated little ones, with chubby cheeks and great staring brown eyes. But there was a hush upon the scene. The elder children were congregated in little knots talking. Some of them suddenly perceived him, and there was a curious excitement among them immediately, and much whispering, and some pointing at him with eager fingers; and he could see that they all stopped their talk or games to watch him.

Joshua walked slowly toward the green gate, strangely disappointed and depressed. The windows of the Webling cottage face south-west, and it was only natural that the spotless blinds should be drawn to exclude such a blaze of sunset; but it gave the house a blank look not the less. The casements offered him no smile of welcome.

Here was a friendly welcome, however, from an unexpected direction. Before Joshua had opened the gate, Mr. Martin, the kind old minister, came hurrying across from his dwelling on the other side of the road, and clasped him by both hands, and looked at him with eyes brimming over with tears.

"God bless you! God sustain and comfort you, my beloved friend!" he cried. "I was watching for you. Oh, be composed, my friend, be composed! Such a blessed euthanasia! The precious soul of my Elizabeth was not more spotless or fitter for heaven. Dear friend, let us go in together."

Joshua turned and looked at him with wild, wondering eyes, then wrenched himself suddenly from the old man's friendly grasp, and moved toward the door.

"No, no," he muttered; "I don't want you. I am going alone—to see my wife. Cynthia!" he called, as he opened the door. "Cynthia!" in a louder and more urgent tone—"Cynthia, where are you?"

A fiery impatience had taken hold of him. He could not wait for formalities of any kind. The Miss Weblings would come, and there would be stately greetings, and cake and wine brought out of the wainscot cupboard, and all manner of ceremonies, before he could open his arms and clasp his ill-used wife to his heart, and weep over her and be forgiven.

Deborah came out of the kitchen and took his hands, just as old Mr. Martin had done, and looked at him in the same tearful way.

Were the people all mad here, or was he? Even the children had seemed to look at him strangely.

"Dearest friend," said Deborah, "this is a sore trial for all of us. Priscilla has been in hysterics all day; out of one fit into another. Quite dreadful! The feathers we've burned, and the vinegar, and all to no purpose. She has such a feeling heart."

It was Priscilla who was ill, then. That's what all this fuss meant.

"I want to see my wife," Joshua said, shortly.

"At once," faltered Deborah, looking at him timorously.

"Yes, at once; this instant. Have I not come all these weary miles to see her? This instant."

"Oh, dear sir, what need of impatience? Be calm, I beg you."

The doors of both parlors were open. Joshua had glanced in and seen that both rooms were empty.

"Where is she?" he asked. "Upstairs?"

"Yes, in our spare room," Deborah answered, huskily. "Let me show you the way."

"I know it," he said; and went upstairs before her.

The narrow corkscrew staircase was close and dark, like the winding stair in a church-tower. Midway Joshua started as if he had been shot, and came to a stand-still.

There was a pungent odor of freshly gathered herbs, a perfume he had not smelled thus, on the threshold of a bed chamber, since his mother's death.

"My God!" he cried. "Is it rosemary?"

"Yes," sobbed Deborah, "we always use it here. We've a bush in the garden on purpose. The neighbors come and beg a bunch of it when they've a death in the house."

Joshua staggered up the few steep stairs, lifted the jingling latch of the low wainscot door, and went into the room in which he had slept two years ago, when the new joys and pains of love began to grow in his heart.

That odor of rosemary had forewarned him what he was to see. No living wife, standing on the threshold to greet him, with warm arms ready to be wound about his neck; no sweet eyes lifted shyly to meet his own; no faltering words, or half-broken sobs; only a fair marble statue lying on a white flower-strewn bed, hands meekly folded, violet-veined eyelids closed over wearied eyes—a broken heart forever at rest.

He stood looking at her for a long time, as it seemed to the heart-stricken Deborah—looking at her with eyes that hung upon that silent beauty in a rapture of despair; then flung up his arms, with a sudden, gurgling cry, and fell upon the floor beside her bed like a stone.

He remained unconscious for many hours, breathing stertorously, and lying like a log upon the bed where his faithful attendants had laid him. The village doctor had bled him, and administered various orthodox remedies of a severe character, with but little result. Mr. Martin, the good old dissenting minister, staid with him all through the weary night, which might know no dawn in this world. The spinster sisters were indefatigable, Priscilla waiving her peculiar prerogative of hysterics, in her desire to be useful.

The sun had risen, and the birds were singing outside the open casements, when Joshua slowly lifted his heavy lids and looked about him with dim, blood-shot eyes.

For some minutes after he had struggled back to consciousness there was a dimness in his brain as well as in his eyes, and he looked at the anxious, watchful faces vaguely. Then memory came back with cruel distinctness.

"Tell me—every thing," he said.

"Dear friend," pleaded Mr. Martin, "let your mind be at rest for a little while. Repose, dear sir. You have been heavily afflicted, and you have had a stroke of illness which might have been fatal, had God refused to hear our earnest prayers."

"Tell me about my wife," urged Joshua, vehemently.

"She is at rest. She has gone to her heavenly home. I, who was with her at the last, have no doubt of her calling and election. She was one of God's chosen vessels, with a mind naturally attuned to heavenly things, like that pure spirit, my heavenly-minded Elizabeth, whose death-bed conversations it was my precious privilege to preserve for the edification of many. Yes, she came very near that sainted young woman in the holy simplicity of her nature."

"What was it that killed her?" asked Joshua, putting aside all these words with a motion of his strong hand. "Did she die of a broken heart? Was it my ill-usage that caused her death?"

"Your ill-usage, dear friend! Your senses must be wandering. She always talked of you as the best and most honored of husbands. Ill-usage, and from you! She loved you above all earthly things. Your name was on her lips with her last breath."

"Yes," cried Joshua, "she called me, and I heard her. Give me my watch," pointing to the chest of drawers where it lay; "see, I stopped the hands at the moment in which I heard her voice calling to me in a kind of dream—not a common dream, mark you—twice as vivid and life-like. It was after midnight on Sunday; see, twenty minutes past one."

"'This is the Lord's doing; it is marvelous in our eyes!'" exclaimed Mr. Martin, piously. "It was at that very hour her spirit took flight."

"Why was I not told that she was ill—dying?" asked Joshua.

"It was her wish that you should not be troubled. 'He will send for me, or come for me, when he wants me to go home again,' she said. 'He has higher things than me to think about.' She was so earnest in this wish that we did not like to override her."

"And nobody thought that she was dangerously ill," explained Deborah. "The doctor couldn't make her out. That was what he always said. It was one of the strangest cases he'd ever had to deal with. Some days she seemed so well and bright; and she was always industrious, anxious to be doing something for us; household work or needle-work, it was all the same—we couldn't give her enough to do."

"The journey here hurt her a great deal, I think," said Priscilla, "though she would never own to it. She walked a good bit of the way, I believe, and she was foot-sore and very weak when she came. I opened the door to her at dusk one evening, and I almost thought she was a ghost. 'I want to be your servant, dear Miss Priscilla,' she said, 'as I was in the old happy days.'—'Why, Mrs. Haggard,' said I, 'what would your honored husband think of such a notion?' But I'd hardly got out the words before she fell down in a faint at my feet; and for a week after that we had her laid up, and as low as could be."

"And you never wrote to me about her!" cried Joshua, with agonized reproach.

"Well, the truth was, we didn't like. We thought there was something wrong—a family quarrel, perhaps; second marriages often turn out so—and the poor thing seemed to have come to us for refuge, and clung to us so; and if ever we talked of writing to you, she seemed so distressed. And we had always been fond of her, and had missed her dreadfully after her marriage. She seemed like a daughter to us, now she had come back, and I'm sure we nursed her and took care of her in her illness as if she'd really been a daughter, as I know Mr. Martin will bear witness."

"You did," said the minister; "she could not have had better nursing or kinder treatment."

"It was only just at the last that there was any mention of danger," continued Deborah. "On Saturday morning the doctor found her very low, poor dear, and her mind was wandering a little. He seemed quite distressed as he came down-stairs with me, as if it was a shock to him to find her so. 'I don't at all like her looks this morning, Miss Webling,' he said; 'I begin to be afraid we shall lose her.' I never had such a turn in my life. Poor Priscilla and I were almost beside ourselves with grief, and it was as much as I could do to write you a letter, begging you to come at once. You don't seem to have received that letter."

"No; it must have been delivered after I left home. The post is so slow; you should have sent a messenger. Tell me, for God's sake—did she die happy, and did she love me at the last?"

"At the last, and always," answered Mr. Martin, earnestly. "She bared her heart to me. I know all its secrets, its waverings from the right, its weakness. She had always loved and revered you. She had been tempted, poor child, and her fancy had strayed to another for a little while—only a little while. Heart and mind were true to her duty. She was worthy of your fondest love; she was worthy of your deepest regret."

"And I cast her from me: I repudiated her; I spurned her as the vilest of sinners! Oh, friend, can her injured spirit look down upon me from Heaven, and pity? Can God ever pardon my sin? He gave me this sweet flower to wear in my bosom, and I cast it from me, and trampled it under-foot. I have steeped my soul in sin, I have dyed my hands with blood!"

The two spinsters and the minister looked at each other with an awful significance. These remorseful utterances seemed to them the tokens of a wandering mind. That this man, their model and pattern of uprightness, could deeply err, came hardly within the limits of belief.

CHAPTER XL.

"BETWEEN TWO WORLDS."

THE days wore on very slowly for Naomi, in her father's absence. Her heart was weighed down with anxiety on his account; but he had told her not to follow him, and, anxious though she was, she obeyed implicitly. A great burden had been taken from her mind by Joshua's confession. Bitter as it was to know that her lover had fallen by her father's hand, that the bright young life had been snapped short off, like a blossom from its stalk, in a burst of sinful passion, yet there was all the difference in the world between a fair fight and a dastardly assassination; and she was able now to think of her father as of other duelists she had heard and read about—red-handed sinners all, but not beyond the reach of human pity.

She was reconciled even to the idea of her father's prolonged absence, of a separation which might extend over years. It would be better, happier for him to go out into untrodden fields, and do difficult work, for his Master's sake. This pious labor would be his penance: in heathen lands he would find cities of atonement, from whose gates he might come forth loosed from the burden and stigma of his crime. She had longed herself to go into strange lands and teach heathen children the Gospel. What more natural than that her father, with his consciousness of a terrible sin to be expiated, should desire to brave dangers, and endure hardships and trials in the great cause?

"Let him come back to me ten years hence, old and bent and gray," said Naomi, "and I will praise God for his bounteous mercies. I will say that our lives have been full of blessings, even after all our sorrows."

This was her prayer—that he might go forth as a messenger of the Gospel and do his work of expiation, and come back to her purified and happy. It was the old heroic Greek idea of atonement, only in a Christian and better form.

A letter had come from Penmoyle for Joshua, and was laid aside, unopened, awaiting tidings from him. No one supposed that the letter was of any particular importance. What they all waited for anxiously was a letter from Joshua himself.

It was Thursday, and Oswald Pentreath had been lying in the family vault for many days and nights. It seemed a natural thing already to think of him resting there with his ancestors, and it was almost possible to forget that he had lain for nearly a year in the darkness of the deserted mine, none knowing his fate. Strange how soon poor human nature resigns itself to the inevitable. Arnold bore the annihilation of all his hopes about his brother better than he could have supposed it possible to bear so heavy a blow. That agonizing grief which he had felt when he supposed Oswald the victim of a treacherous assassin was lessened by Joshua's confession. At least, he had fallen face to face with death. The murderer had not crept behind him with uplifted knife, coming upon his victim in a ghostly silence. It had been a hard fate and a cruel one, but not so bad as this. And poor Naomi, the innocent sufferer from her lover's inconstancy and her father's sin—could he ever be sorry enough for her? Could he ever be sufficiently kind, or gentle, or thoughtful for her dear sake? Consideration for her pleaded eloquently against his desire for revenge. Joshua must go unscathed, so far as human vengeance went, and take his punishment from God. This was the result of many a weary hour of thought that followed upon Arnold's interview with Naomi.

Thursday morning brought another letter from Penmoyle, in the same handwriting as the last, but directed to Judith instead of to Joshua.

Miss Haggard broke the seal with a slight tremor, while Naomi waited full of anxiety. Why had her father not written?

"Chestnut Cottage, Penmoyle,
Cornwall, June 26th.

"DEAR MISS HAGGARD,—I hope you will pardon the above familiarity; but although we have not had the pleasure of meeting, you can be no stranger to one who loves and reveres your brother as I do.

"I deeply regret to inform you that Mr. Haggard now lies in a sadly precarious state. Indeed, our doctor and another gentleman, summoned at his advice from Penzance, entertain little hope of his recovery. The shock caused by his wife's death, which took place prior to his arrival, caused an apoplectic stroke. He recovered consciousness after several hours, but has never been quite right in his mind since the seizure.

"Feeling assured that you and the rest of his family would desire to be with him at such a time, I hasten to communicate the sad state of affairs, and beg you to make whatever use you please of our small abode. It is entirely at your disposal, and my elder sister and self will consider it a privilege to do all in our power to ameliorate your sorrow by such attentions as sympathetic hearts can offer. Our poor Cynthia's funeral takes place to-day. It is perhaps a blessing that in your suffering brother's state of mind he is scarcely conscious of passing events.

"Awaiting your speedy arrival, I remain, dear Miss Haggard, your obedient servant,

"PRISCILLA WEBLING."

Before she had read half this letter, Judith Haggard gave a shriek of horrified surprise, and her niece looked over her shoulder and read it with her. The two women stood side by side, devouring the lines with white, agonized faces, each in her own way feeling that this sorrow was the death-blow to all hope. James was in the shop, busy, happy, ignorant of this evil. He was whistling the last popular melody as he went about his work. How awful it seemed to hear him!

Naomi's grief found no outlet in tears or sobs or passionate speech. She stood with the letter in her hand, her lips trembling.

"The coach, aunt, the coach!" she gasped. "Is it too late?"

"Gone half an hour, child. We must have a post-shay. Jim!"

The shrill voice ran through house and shop, and Jim appeared with a scared face at the parlor door.

"What's the matter, aunt?"

"Your father's dying, and we're going to him. Get us a post-shay."

Jim looked from one to the other in awful wonder. Naomi tried to speak, and, failing, gave him Priscilla's letter.

"What!" he cried, hurriedly reading, "the poor little step-mother dead and buried! Has the world come to an end?"

"You unfeeling boy!" exclaimed Judith. "To think of any body else when your father's in such a state!"

"Father will come round again, please God; but poor little Cynthia — buried yesterday — so young and pretty! Isn't it dreadful?"

"Go for a chaise, Jim, for pity's sake!" cried Naomi. "Father may die while you stand wondering there. Oh, let me to go to him! let me go! let me keep him back from death!"

James ran across to The First and Last, the only place in Combhollow where post-horses were to be had. There was a burst of sympathy from the stout landlord when he heard Jim's news. The chaise should be ready in ten minutes—the best horses in his stable.

It was half an hour before the chaise was at the door, despite the landlord's promises. Naomi and her aunt had put on their bonnets and packed a few necessaries in a carpet-bag, and had been waiting in the parlor ever so long, as it seemed to them, before an ancient yellow-bodied chariot, like that which had brought Joshua's young bride to Combhollow, pulled up before the garden-gate.

"You'll stay at home, and mind the business till I can come back, Jim," said Judith.

"I'd rather go to poor father; but perhaps it's best so," answered Jim. "But if he should be very bad, if there's no chance of his getting over it, you'll send for me, aunt. I should like to see him before—"

A sob strangled the young man's speech, and he went back to the house, leaving them to get into the carriage unassisted. Some one was at Naomi's side before she could mount the steps. It was Captain Pentreath, breathless with running.

"Naomi, I have just heard of your sorrow," he said, gently. "One of our men told me as I came across the meadow. Dear sister, let me go with you. Let me go with you, Miss Haggard," he added, pleadingly, to Judith. "I should like to go—to be of service to you, if I can—to ask your brother's pardon for my violence the other night."

"You'd need be sorry for that, I think!" answered Judith. "What's the good of your coming? He'll want to see his blood-relations, poor dear—that's natural; but it can't give him much pleasure to see you."

"I may be of use to you on the journey. Let me come, Miss Haggard. Two unprotected women, anxious, agitated as you are, ought not to undertake such a journey. These post-boys are such ruffians. I shall be able to prevent loss of time, to insure you civil treatment."

Judith relented a little. Post-boys were an exacting and difficult race—greedy of gain, capable of abandoning their helpless fare upon a lonesome highway, or of colleaguing with highwaymen for a defenseless traveler's spoliation. Perhaps Judith, though strong-minded enough at home, where every one trembled at her voice, felt that she should be a weak vessel abroad. She had never traveled farther than Barnstaple in her life; and to go up alone into the wilds of bleak and barren Cornwall—the very stronghold of witchcraft—a place where half the people were savage miners, and the other half wreckers and smugglers; and to be benighted, perhaps, on a moor where the Druids sacrificed human beings before the days of King Arthur!

The terrors were too much for Judith. The proffered escort of a courageous young man, open-handed and ready to make use of his purse for the gratification of post-boys, was not to be despised. He had brought a false charge against Joshua in an hour of temporary madness; but he had repented, and this act of to-day was a confession of his past folly. All Combhollow would know of it, and see how baseless he now felt his idea of Joshua's guilt to have been. Judith gave way, but maintained her dignity even in the moment of concession.

"It matters very little to me whether you come or stay," she said. "My mind's too full of my poor brother to care about any thing else. But Naomi may be glad of your company on the dark roads—girls are so timid."

"Indeed, aunt, I am not frightened," exclaimed Naomi.

"I am coming with you," said Arnold, decisively.

There was a seat at the back of the vehicle, a kind of rumble, and into this he mounted, after dispatching a small boy to the Grange with a message for Nicholas, the butler, who was to send his master's valise on to Truro by the evening coach. Arnold would not ask so much as five minutes' delay, lest Judith should change her mind and decline his company. So the post-boy smacked his whip, and the chaise went rattling through the long village street, to the delight of the inhabitants, who flocked out of their dwellings to witness the unwonted spectacle.

A long journey at any time: a weary one for aching hearts. Naomi looked out of the carriage-window with dull eyes that roamed over hill and valley, wood and winding stream, and saw no comfort anywhere. Was the journey never to be over? she wondered, as the slow hours rolled on. Was there never to be an end of these green hedge-rows, and tangled honey-suckles, and clambering dog-roses, and dusty way-side ferns, and sudden hollows, and jutting walls of hill?—these perpetual hills, at the foot of which the travelers descended, to walk in mournful silence to the top, where all the glory of the valley below could not move Naomi's cold lips to a smile of gladness.

Arnold made no attempt at consolation. He entreated his companions to hope for the best, and after that made no further allusion to their grief. He talked to them very little, only showing himself anxious for their comfort and repose. He saved them all trouble about post-boys, or any of the details of their journey. They had nothing to do but be patient, and wait till darkness came, and the end. Even to eyes accustomed to the rustic seclusion of Combhollow, Penmoyle looked a curious out-of-the-world place, as the post-chaise drove into the wide village street after sunset on that June evening. Lights twinkled feebly in two or three casements, wide apart and rare, as if the majority had gone to roost at curfew. There was one light much brighter than the rest, which seemed to Naomi to shine like a star. Some instinct of her heart told her that it was the candle in her father's sick-room.

"There!" she cried, putting her head out of the window, and calling to the post-boy; "stop there!"

But Arnold had made his inquiries at the beginning of the village, and the boy was already pulling up his horses. That lighted casement belonged to Chestnut Cottage. The approach of the carriage had been heard within, and Deborah's stiff curls were waving at the door, as she came out to receive her guests.

"Oh, dear Miss Haggard! oh, dear Miss Naomi!" she gasped, "thank God you are come!"

"Not too late!" cried Naomi, going into the house; "not too late!"

"No, dear young lady, praised be Heaven! He has asked for you so often."

"Take me to him, please—at once."

"But you ought to be prepared for the change—"

"God will give me strength when his dear head is on my breast. Father, I am coming!" she cried, as if her voice would carry strength and new life to the sick man.

She went upstairs as quickly as if she had known the corkscrew staircase all her life. The door of her father's room was open; the window opened wide to the summer night. The old-fashioned tent-bedstead, with its dimity festooning and netted fringe, faced the door. Who was it lying there, still as a stone figure, with a white, strange face, and dark, cavernous eyes—a face Naomi had never seen before? For a moment her heart failed, and she shrunk away a step or two, as from something more awful than death. Was this her father?

Yes; the hollow eyes lighted up at sight of her, the livid lips moved tremulously, and then murmured, "Naomi!"

In the next instant she was on her knees beside his bed, clasping the heavy hands, crying over him, kissing him with those passionate, despairing kisses his gives to death.

"Dearest, I have come to nurse you, to bring you back to life. God will help me. I have been praying for you all through our long journey. Father, you will get well for my sake."

"I am dying, Naomi. The doctor and my old friend Martin have both told me so. Do not cry, dear; I am suffering so little. The passage is made very easy for me. And I have an infinite, inextinguishable faith in my Redeemer's love. I go to him without fear. He has loosed me from the burden of my sin. Yes, Naomi, it is no idle boast. I feel and know that I am forgiven. My punishment has been awarded here. My broken heart has reconciled me with my God."

"You shall not die!" said Naomi. "God can not be so cruel as to part us now, when there is no cloud between us any more, when I can love you and honour you as I did in my childhood. Father, you will live for my sake."

"No, dear, I have done with earthly life. God sent his stroke in mercy when I came into this house and found my darling dead. Oh, Naomi, my latter days have been full of sin! I have been the slave of passion. And yet I might have been so happy! I can see her still—sitting in the sunshine—hair like spun gold—so helpless and lovely, so ignorant of good and evil: like Eve when God gave her to Adam."

His mind wandered a little after this. All through the night he lay in the same attitude, a corpse-like figure, a soul hovering between life and death. Naomi never stirred from her seat beside his pillow, save to kneel and pray. Judith and Priscilla sat a little way aloof, watching the two, only coming nearer at intervals to moisten the sick man's lips with a feather dipped in brandy.

About an hour after day-break, Arnold, who had spent the night in the parlor below, came slowly up the stair, and stood on the threshold. Joshua had been lying for a long time with his eyes closed, breathing heavily, and his watchers had supposed him sleeping; but at the sound of Arnold's cautious footfall he opened his eyes, and those restless hands of his fastened with a nervous grasp upon the coverlet.

"Is that Captain Pentreath?" he asked his daughter.

"Yes, dear father."

"Let the others go away," looking dimly round at the two women; "I want to be alone with you and him."

Priscilla and Judith left the room, full of wonder.

"You got my letter?" he said.

"Yes, Mr. Haggard; and I am here to ask your forgiveness for the accusation I brought against you. When I found my poor brother in his secret grave, I believed him the victim of a murderer. I am willing now to believe that he was the victim of his own folly, and that he willingly staked his life against yours."

Joshua was silent. Some kind of struggle—whether bodily or mental, those who watched him could not tell—was racking him. His nether lip worked convulsively; the veins stood up darkly purple from the broad, strong brow.

"My letter told the truth," he said, after that painful pause, "but not all the truth. I am going to face an offended God—going to him confident in his illimitable mercy. Naomi, do not hate me when I am dead;" his hands wandered helplessly for a little, and then he clasped them round her neck, and let his head fall on her shoulder; "do not hate me, dear. Your lover was murdered. He was generous, and I was a dastard. We stood up, face to face, each with a pistol in his hand. I was to count three, he told me, and then take aim. But as I lifted my hand to aim at his heart I saw his arm flung up, his pistol pointed to the sky. It was but an instant, fleeter than a breath, before I fired straight at his breast. It was thirty years since I had pulled a trigger—not since I was an idle lad, and went rabbit-shooting with my father's old blunderbuss. Yet my aim was deadly. The bullet pierced his heart. He had fired in the air. I had just time enough to see and understand what he was doing before I killed him. This was the crime that weighed upon my soul and dragged me down to the pit. O God! I can see him now, with his face lifted up, the sun shining on it, his arm raised to fire in the air. It was but a flash, scarce time for thought, but when it was over I knew myself a murderer. O God! only an instant between everlasting glory and eternal condemnation, unless thine infinite sacrifice can blot out mine iniquity."

There was silence. Naomi's face was buried in the coverlet. Arnold walked across to the open window, and stood there looking out at the gray morning sky, deeply thoughtful.

"My God, my sin is heavy," ejaculated Joshua, after an interval; "thou only knowest my temptation. I, who had preached against dueling, became a duelist; I, who had taught men brotherly love, stained my hands with my brother's blood. Only in illimitable mercy can I find hope; and who shall tell the sinner his case is hopeless when God has given the promise of forgiveness?"

He lay for a long time after this in a state that was almost unconsciousness. The doctor came and felt his pulse, and told them that he was slowly sinking. It was only the vigor of his constitution which had held out so long against death. The nobly built frame had wrestled involuntarily with man's last enemy, while the spirit yearned to pass the mystic river, and rest in the fair Land beyond.

That day wore on, and the night which followed it, and another long summer day, which seemed to Naomi different even in the color of its sky from every other day in her life. The sunshine climbed the whitewashed wall, and touched with brighter gold the tarnished gilding of the old oval picture-frames, and glorified the old cups and saucers and quaint little pottery jars on the narrow chimney-piece; and still Joshua lay, awfully motionless, with his dull eyes turned to the light.

It was sunset when the dreaded change came. They were all on their knees, praying silently, when Joshua lifted himself up in the bed, and stretched out his arms toward that fading glory in the western sky.

"Cynthia—chosen—beloved," he cried; "innocent as a little child—ignorant of evil! Of such is the kingdom of heaven."

And so, with a long-drawn shivering sigh, he fell back upon the pillow; and, as the sun went down behind a dark range of moor-land, this little lamp of light went out with it, no less secure of resurrection.

EPILOGUE.

JOSHUA HAGGARD has been lying in his quiet grave among the Cornish hills just three years. It is midsummer-time again, and the long, straggling village of Combhollow is looking its gayest, beautified by nature, and not by art. There is an unaccustomed life and stir in the place—people dressed in their best clothes, new bonnet-ribbons as rife as butterflies, every one upon the tiptoe of expectancy—and Naomi Haggard standing by the open parlor window, very pale, in a gray Quaker-like silk—almost as pretty a gown as that wedding-dress she gave away four years ago; but it was not her father's hand this time which tested the quality of the silk, or her father's blessing which made the gift sweet.

Naomi has been an independent young woman for the last three years; for Joshua Haggard's will, made immediately after Oswald's dismissal, left his only daughter the five thousand pounds which had been intended as her marriage portion. She has suffered her aunt's domestic tyranny none the less meekly because of this independence. She has lived her quiet life in the old familiar home, so desolate without her father, and has taught her classes in the Sunday-school, and helped the new minister by many a quiet service, and held her place in the hearts of the Dissenters of Combhollow, who still honor Joshua's memory as that of a great and good man. This is Naomi's consolation. No shame or dishonor has ever been attached to her father's name in the public mind. The secret of Oswald's fate is known to none living save Arnold and herself.

To-day is a great day for Naomi—she has just she has known since her father's death; for the memorial chapel—the new Bethel, which she has built with a portion of her inheritance—is to be opened to-day. A fair, lofty building of gray stone—a little too much like a common chapel on a small scale, for the improved taste of a later part of the century, but in those days a temple of exceeding beauty. There are four tall, straight windows on each side, an oak pulpit and reading-desk, a commodious gallery, and a Doric portico; and in the eyes of Combhollow the new chapel is second only to Exeter Cathedral and Barnstaple Market.

To Naomi's mind the fairest thing in the brand-new chapel is a brazen tablet in front of the gallery, bearing this brief inscription:

" This Chapel was erected in affectionate remembrance of Joshua Haggard, Minister."

Naomi leaves the chapel after the opening service leaning on Arnold Pentreath's arm, tearful, but not altogether unhappy.   Friends gather round her and congratulate her, and are warm in their praises of the new Bethel ; but it is to be noticed that there is an unwonted reverence in the tone of these old acquaintances, and that Mrs. Spradgers, notorious for extravagance in millinery, drops a low courtesy to Miss Haggard, instead of extending her padgy hand in its black-lace glove.

Standing on the threshold of the new chapel, Naomi stands also on the threshold of a new life. Her lover—faithful and unchanging through his three years' apprenticeship—is by her side, and to-morrow is to be their wedding-day.

THE END.

ANTHONY TROLLOPE'S WORKS.

Anthony Trollope's position grows more secure with every new work which comes from his pen. He is one of the most prolific of writers, yet his stories improve with time instead of growing weaker, and each is as fresh and as forcible as though it were the sole production of the author. — *N. Y. Sun.*

Mr. Trollope's characters are drawn with an outline firm, bold, strong. His sketching is among the best which pass current in society are very keen.— *Congregationalist,* Boston

---

BROWN, JONES, AND ROBINSON. 8vo, Paper, 35 cents.

CAN YOU FORGIVE HER? Illustrations. 8vo, Cloth, $1 30 ; Paper, 80 cents.

CASTLE RICHMOND. 12mo, Cloth, $1 50.

DOCTOR THORNE. 12mo, Cloth, $1 50 ; 8vo, Paper, 50 cents.

FRAMLEY PARSONAGE. Illustrations. 12mo, Cloth, $1 75.

HARRY HEATHCOTE OF GANGOIL. Illustrations. 8vo, Paper, 20 cents.

HE KNEW HE WAS RIGHT. Illustrations. 8vo, Cloth, $1 30 ; Paper, 80 cents.

LADY ANNA. 8vo, Paper, 30 cents.

MISS MACKENZIE. 8vo, Paper, 35 cents.

NORTH AMERICA. 12mo, Cloth, $1 50.

ORLEY FARM. Illustrations. 8vo, Cloth, $1 30 ; Paper, 80 cents.

PHINEAS FINN, THE IRISH MEMBER. Illustrations. 8vo, Cloth, $1 25 ; Paper, 75 cents.

PHINEAS REDUX. Illustrations. 8vo, Cloth, $1 25 ; Paper, 75 cents.

RACHEL RAY. 8vo, Paper, 35 cents.

RALPH THE HEIR. Illustrations. 8vo, Cloth, $1 25 ; Paper, 75 cents.

SIR HARRY HOTSPUR OF HUMBLETHWAITE. Illustrations. 8vo, Paper, 35 cents.

THE AMERICAN SENATOR. 8vo, Paper, 50 cents.

THE BELTON ESTATE. 8vo, Paper, 35 cents.

THE BERTRAMS. 12mo, Cloth, $1 50.

THE CLAVERINGS. Illustrations. 8vo, Cloth, $1 00 ; Paper, 50 cents.

THE EUSTACE DIAMONDS. 8vo, Cloth, $1 30 ; Paper, 80 cents.

THE GOLDEN LION OF GRANPERE. Illustrations. 8vo, Cloth, 90 cents ; Paper, 40 cents.

THE LAST CHRONICLE OF BARSET. Illustrations. 8vo, Cloth, $1 40 ; Paper, 90 cents.

THE PRIME MINISTER. 8vo, Paper, 60 cents.

THE SMALL HOUSE AT ALLINGTON. Illustrations. 8vo, Cloth, $1 25 ; Paper, 75 cents.

THE THREE CLERKS. 12mo, Cloth, $1 50.

THE VICAR OF BULLHAMPTON. Illustrations. 8vo, Cloth, $1 30 ; Paper, 80 cents.

THE WARDEN AND BARCHESTER TOWERS. Complete in One Volume. 8vo, Paper, 60 cents.

THE WAY WE LIVE NOW. Ill's. 8vo, Cloth, $1 40 ; Paper, 90 cents.

THOMPSON HALL. 32mo, Paper, 20 cents.

WEST INDIES AND THE SPANISH MAIN. 12mo, Cloth, $1 50.

PUBLISHED BY HARPER & BROTHERS, NEW YORK.

☞ *Sent by mail, postage prepaid, to any part of the United States, on receipt of the price.*

We hardly know how to convey an adequate notion of the exuberant whim and drollery by which this writer is characterized. His works are a perpetual feast of gayety.—JOHN BULL.

"*This well-known humorous and sparkling writer, whose numerous laughter-provoking novels have so often convulsed the reader by their drollery and rollicking wit, seems to possess an endless fund of entertainment.*"

Lord Kilgobbin. Illustrated. 8vo, Paper, 50 cents; Cloth, $1 00.

The Bramleighs of Bishop's Folly. 8vo, Paper, 50 cents.

Sir Brook Fossbrooke. 8vo, Paper, 50 cents.

Tony Butler. 8vo, Paper, 60 cents; Cloth, $1 10.

Luttrell of Arran. 8vo, Paper, 60 cents; Cloth, $1 10.

One of Them. 8vo, Paper, 50 cents.

A Day's Ride. A Life's Romance. 8vo, Paper, 40 cents.

Gerald Fitzgerald, "The Chevalier." 8vo, Paper, 40 cents.

The Martins of Cro' Martin. 8vo, Paper, 60 cents.

That Boy of Norcott's. Illustrated. 8vo, Paper, 25 cents.

Maurice Tiernay, the Soldier of Fortune. 8vo, Paper, 50 cents.

The Dodd Family Abroad. 8vo, Paper, 60 cents.

Barrington. 8vo, Paper, 40 cents.

Sir Jasper Carew, Knt.: His Life and Adventures. With some Account of his Overreachings and Shortcomings, now first given to the World by Himself. 8vo, Paper, 50 cents.

Glencore and his Fortunes. 8vo, Paper, 50 cents.

The Daltons; or, The Three Roads in Life. 8vo, Paper, 75 cents.

Roland Cashel. With Illustrations by PHIZ. 8vo, Paper, 75 cents; Cloth, $1 25.

Published by HARPER & BROTHERS, New York.

W. M. THACKERAY'S WORKS.

Why have I alluded to this man? I have alluded to him, reader, because I think I see in him an intellect profounder and more unique than his contemporaries have yet recognized; because I regard him as the first social regenerator of the day—as the very master of that working corps who would restore to rectitude the warped system of things; because I think no commentator on his writings has yet found the comparison that suits him, the terms which rightly characterize his talent. They say he is like Fielding; they talk of his wit, humor, comic powers. He resembles Fielding as an eagle does a vulture; Fielding could stoop on carrion, but Thackeray never does. His wit is bright, his humor attractive, but both bear the same relation to his serious genius that the mere lambent sheet-lightning, playing under the edge of the summer cloud, does to the electric death-spark hid in its womb.—"CURRER BELL," Author of *Jane Eyre*, *Shirley*, *Villette*, and *The Professor.*

England in our day may regard it as some proof of her moral soundness, that her greatest living Wit (Thackeray) is in all his sentiments and sympathies the deadly enemy of hypocrisy, but the constant friend of virtue.—*Edinburgh Review.*

HARPER'S POPULAR EDITION.

8vo, Paper.

NOVELS: Denis Duval. Illustrations. 25 cents.—Henry Esmond and Lovel the Widower. Illustrations. 60 cents.—Pendennis. Illustrations. 75 cents.—The Adventures of Philip. Illustrations. 60 cents. — The Great Hoggarty Diamond. 20 cents.—The Newcomes. Illustrations. 90 cents.—The Virginians. Illustrations. 90 cents.—Vanity Fair. Illustrations. 80 cents.

HARPER'S HOUSEHOLD EDITION.

12mo, Cloth.

NOVELS: Vanity Fair.—Pendennis.—The Newcomes.—The Virginians.—Adventures of Philip.—Esmond, and Lovel the Widower. Illustrated. Six volumes, 12mo, Cloth, $1 50 per volume.

MISCELLANEOUS WRITINGS: Barry Lyndon, Hoggarty Diamond, &c.—Paris and Irish Sketch Books, &c.—Book of Snobs, Sketches, &c.—Four Georges, English Humorists, Roundabout Papers, &c.—Catharine, Christmas Books, &c. Five volumes, 12mo, Cloth, $1 50 per volume.

PUBLISHED BY HARPER & BROTHERS, NEW YORK.

☞ HARPER & BROTHERS *will send either of the above volumes by mail, postage prepaid, to any part of the United States or Canada, on receipt of the price.*

WILKIE COLLINS'S NOVELS.

Wilkie Collins has no living superior in the art of constructing a story. Others may equal if not surpass him in the delineation of character, or in the use of a story for the development of social theories, or for the redress of a wrong against humanity and civilization; but in his own domain he stands alone, without a rival. *** He holds that "the main element in the attraction of all stories is the interest of curiosity and the excitement of surprise." Other writers had discovered this before Collins; but recognizing the clumsiness of the contrivances in use by inferior authors, he essays, by artistic and conscientious use of the same materials and similar devices, to captivate his readers.—*N. Y. Evening Post.*

Of all the living writers of English fiction, no one better understands the art of story-telling than Wilkie Collins. He has a faculty of coloring the mystery of a plot, exciting terror, pity, curiosity, and other passions, such as belongs to few if any of his *confrères*, however much they may excel him in other respects. His style, too, is singularly appropriate—less forced and artificial than the average modern novelists.—*Boston Transcript.*

We can not call to mind any novelist or romancer of past times whose constructive powers fairly can be placed above his. He is a literary artist, and a great one too, and he always takes his readers with him.—*Boston Traveller.*

Mr. Collins is certainly the one master of his school of fiction, and the greatest constructionist living. His plots are marvels of ingenuity, and his incidents reach the height of the dramatic.—*N. Y. Evening Mail.*

HARPER'S POPULAR EDITION.
8vo, Paper.

ARMADALE. Illustrated.	60 cents.
ANTONINA.	40 "
MAN AND WIFE. Illustrated.	60 "
NO NAME. Illustrated.	60 "
POOR MISS FINCH. Illustrated.	60 "
THE LAW AND THE LADY. Illustrated.	50 "
THE MOONSTONE. Illustrated.	60 "
THE NEW MAGDALEN.	30 "
THE TWO DESTINIES. Illustrated.	35 "
THE WOMAN IN WHITE. Illustrated.	60 "

PERCY AND THE PROPHET. - - - - - - 32mo, Paper, 20 cents.

HARPER'S LIBRARY EDITION.
ILLUSTRATED. 12MO, CLOTH, $1 50 PER VOL.

AFTER DARK AND OTHER STORIES.	*NO NAME.*
ANTONINA.	*POOR MISS FINCH.*
ARMADALE.	*THE DEAD SECRET.*
BASIL.	*THE LAW AND THE LADY.*
HIDE-AND-SEEK.	*THE MOONSTONE.*
MAN AND WIFE.	*THE NEW MAGDALEN.*
MY MISCELLANIES.	*THE QUEEN OF HEARTS.*
	THE TWO DESTINIES.

THE WOMAN IN WHITE

PUBLISHED BY HARPER & BROTHERS, NEW YORK.